THE FROST EATER

BOOK 1 OF THE MAGIC EATERS TRILOGY

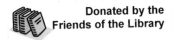

**Donated by the
Friends of the Library**

CAROL BETH ANDERSON

Eliana
—PRESS—

The Frost Eater by Carol Beth Anderson

Published by
Eliana Press
P.O. Box 2452
Cedar Park, TX 78630

www.carolbethanderson.com

Cover Design:
Mariah Sinclair (thecovervault.com)

Map: BMR Williams

Paperback ISBN: 978-1-949384-05-5

First Edition

To my husband, Jason, a guy who loves me, loves our kids, and loves sci-fi TV shows. How did this girl get so lucky?

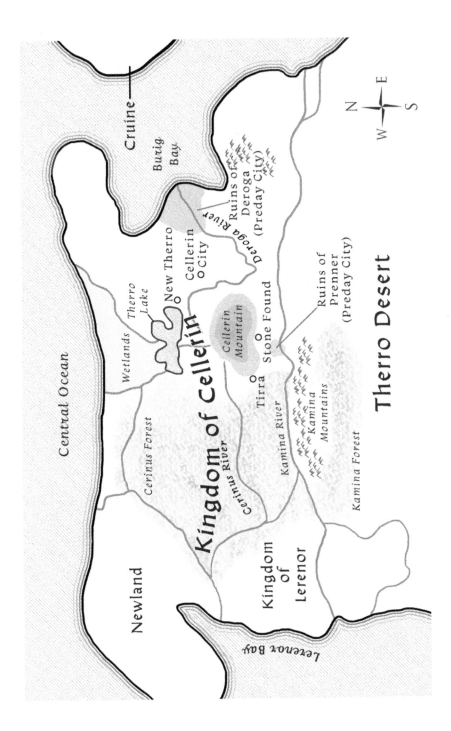

CHARACTERS AND PLACES

Characters

Nora Abrios (AH-bree-ose), Princess of Cellerin

Ulmin (ULL-min) Abrios, King of Cellerin

Mayor Ashler, Mayor of Tirra

Ovrun (OV-run), royal guard

Kreyven (KRAY-ven) West, goes by Krey

Minona (mih-NO-nuh), goes by Min, Krey's aunt

Evie, Krey's aunt

Zeisha (ZAY-shuh), Krey's girlfriend

Isla (EE-sluh), Zeisha's friend

Faylie (FAY-lee), Nora's former friend

Dani (DANN-ee), Nora's aunt and Ulmin's sister-in-law

Minister Sharai (shuh-RYE), Cellerin's Minister of Lysting

Hatlin (HAT-lin), New Therroan activist

Wallis (WALL-iss), New Therroan activist

T, New Therroan activist

Cage, dragon speaker

Osmius (OZ-me-us), dragon

Jushuen (juh-SHOO-en), royal guard

Taima (ty-EE-muh), dragon
Eira (EYE-ruh), trog
Liri (LEE-ree) Abrios, Nora's ancestor

Places

Cellerin (SELL-err-in), kingdom centered around Cellerin Mountain

Tirra (TEE-ruh), town on the southwest side of Cellerin Mountain

Cellerin City, capital of Cellerin, on the east side of Cellerin Mountain

New Therro (THAIR-oh), province on the north side of Cellerin Mountain

Deroga (der-OH-guh), large, preday city

Newland, nation northwest of Cellerin

1

Two years after the world ended, I was born.

-The First Generation: A Memoir by Liri Abrios

"Darling, your crown is crooked."

Nora turned to her father. "You're always telling me it's not a crown, it's a headdress."

"When it's just the two of us, it's a crown." His brown eyes twinkled as he pointed to the band of gold around his head. "One day, you'll wear the real thing."

Nora was only seventeen; she wasn't ready to think about the day when she'd become an orphan and a queen all at once. "That won't happen for a long time. Straighten the headdress for me?"

He grasped it with both hands, shifting it to the left. It scratched Nora's forehead, eliciting a wince.

"Sorry. Does it feel secure?"

"As secure as it gets." The headdress was crafted of fine silver, with delicate filigree extending high above Nora's head. She usually loved wearing it. But after weeks on the road, she had pimples from the molded metal that rested on her forehead. She couldn't be happier that they were approaching the last stop on their tour.

Unseen people began chanting, "Cell-er-in! Cell-er-in!" The open-topped steamcar was having a tough time making it up a steep slope. Beyond the hill lay the town of Tirra, where crowds awaited their king and princess. Nora wished they'd harness a couple of orsas to the car and let the beasts pull it up the hill, but that would ruin the effect of them rolling into town in the most modern vehicle available. Most rural residents had never seen a steamcar.

"Almost there!" the driver called over his shoulder.

"Thank you." Nora's father returned his gaze to her. "Chin up."

Before he could finish his admonishment, Nora did it for him. "Smile big."

Her father winked. A gust of chilly wind blew Nora's straight, dark-brown, chin-length hair into her face. She peeled a few strands off her glossed lips and curved her lips into a smile she hoped was sufficiently regal.

Windmills rose up on either side of the road as the steamcar puttered to the top of the rise. Chanting people came into view, hundreds of them, lining the road all the way down the hill and into town.

Nora and her father waved, and the chants turned into cheers. The rush of support filled Nora's chest and tugged her mouth into a wider grin.

Eight guards riding orsas surrounded the steamcar. Between them, Nora glimpsed a little girl perched on a man's shoulders, wearing a headdress made of—what was that, corn husks? Whatever the material, it was molded to look like Nora's. She blew a kiss to the cheering girl.

It didn't take long to arrive at the bottom of the hill. They drove a few blocks and pulled to a stop in a quaint town square. A wooden stage awaited them, decorated with large, fabric bows in blue and black, Cellerin's royal colors. A woman who introduced herself as Mayor Ashler showed Nora, her father, and several guards onto the stage. When the crowd calmed, the show began.

Nora awarded the town with a Cellerinian flag that had flown at the palace. Then King Ulmin began speaking, and Nora instantly grew bored. It was the same talk her father had given in every town they'd visited, except that somehow it got longer each time. He spoke of The Day, two hundred years earlier, when billions of humans on their planet, Anyari, had died. Then he looked up to the sky and said, "But we thank God that four hundred thousand people, one in ten thousand, survived. They were your ancestors and mine. And they rebuilt civilization."

Nora had to admit, her dad cut an impressive figure. He was tall, with a broad chest and slim waist. His beard, more silver than brown these days, was perfectly trimmed. Autumn sunlight reflected off the gold of his crown and the silver streaks in his hair as he continued his speech, extolling the nation of Cellerin that had risen from destruction. He praised his grandmother Onna, Cellerin's first monarch, who'd ended a terrible war.

At first, Nora's father's speeches had inspired her. Now, three weeks into their tour, she was sick of the stories. She tried to keep her face pleasant. At least her clothing was thick and warm, protecting her from the late-fall chill. Her blue-and-purple outfit—more of a costume, really—had belonged to her mother. The shirt and pants were crafted of high-tech, preday fabric that had been made to last for centuries. It was layered and molded into a structural wonder that hugged Nora's long legs, curvy hips, and slender torso. A massive collar of sorts, shaped like flower petals, extended up from her shoulders in front and back. The fabric was a visual reminder of the old days, and the collar represented Anyari's people, who had bloomed from devastating tragedy.

"Princess Nora."

Nora jolted but quickly recovered. Her father was facing her.

"The people of Tirra have a gift for you." He beckoned her forward, and Nora saw that Mayor Ashler had joined him onstage.

Nora raised an eyebrow. *Going off script, Dad? That's not like you.* The crowd cheered as she stepped to the front of the stage and waved.

"Princess Ulminora." The mayor had a closed wooden box in her hands. She was beaming. "We heard you ran out of ice on your journey. I'm an ice lyster too, and I just returned from the mountain last week to retrieve fuel for myself."

Nora's eyebrows shot up, and her gaze found Cellerin Mountain, which loomed in the distance. The mayor had climbed its icy heights herself, rather than sending someone else?

Mayor Ashler answered Nora's unspoken question. "I grew up climbing Cellerin's slopes, and I can't seem to break the habit." The people cheered, and the mayor continued, "Your Highness, we grow both grapes and bollaberries in our town greenhouse. I'd like to introduce you to one of my favorite things: shaved ice with bollagrape juice."

She opened the hinged lid. The box was thick, clearly insulated. Inside was a mound of shaved ice, colored with pale-purple juice.

The mayor handed Nora a silver spoon. "Care to try it?"

Nora grinned. "Thank you, Mayor." Year-round access to ice was one of the perks of being a princess. However, a few days into the trip, Nora had eaten the last of the ice from her personal ice chest. She'd then discovered that they'd left behind the large chest they'd meant to bring. It was the first time she'd ever gone two weeks without doing magic.

She dipped the spoon in the snowy concoction and brought it to her mouth. Instantly, she knew she'd have to beg the chef back home to find a source of bollaberries. The combination of the berries, which originated on Anyari, and grapes, which originated on Earth, was perfect. Like so many mixtures of Anyarian and Original produce, the flavor was complex and surprising, both sweet and tart.

Without thinking, Nora dipped the spoon in the ice again. She halted and flicked her eyes up to the mayor's. "I'm sorry—do you mind me going back for seconds?"

Laughter and cheers filled the square. The mayor's eyes crinkled. "Have as much as you'd like."

Nora ate several more bites, then turned to her father. She lifted her hands and wiggled her fingers. "May I?"

He nodded.

She took a step toward the edge of the stage, held her arms out wide, and turned her hands toward the sky. The crowd's murmuring stopped, the hush only broken by a baby's cry. Nora's arms, fingers, and throat started to tingle, the sensation delightfully chilly. She brought her arms in front of her and held her palms toward the crowd. With a bright smile, she pushed magic through her hands, shooting two puffs of snow over the front rows. The crowd cheered.

Nora took a deep breath, lifted her chin, and blew snow from her cold mouth. It arced into the air, then fell on a dozen grinning townspeople. She laughed, basking in the crackling energy of the masses. In a thousand ways, she dreaded becoming queen. But she savored moments like these, when she forgot the stifling responsibilities ahead of her and simply enjoyed the people of Cellerin.

Then, all at once, the crowd's gazes shifted. Fingers pointed high and to the right. Excited murmurs grew louder.

Nora lifted her eyes to the sky. When she saw what was distracting everyone, her focus broke, drying up the flow of snow. She dropped her arms to her side.

A man was soaring through the pale-orange sky, swooping up and down like a drunk bird. *This little town has a feather lyster? And he chooses this moment to put on a show?* She shouldn't be surprised; the feather lysters she knew were the vainest people in all of Cellerin.

Two royal guards were standing in front of the stage. One drew a pistol. The other lifted his bow and nocked an arrow. Both aimed at the flying man.

At the same time, the six guards who'd been standing at the rear of the stage rushed to surround Nora and her father. They faced outward, weapons pointed at the flying man. "Let's get you two off the stage," one of them said.

From outside the circle of guards, Mayor Ashler said, "I assure you, he's harmless. He's a show-off, but he won't hurt anyone."

"Let the mayor in," Nora's father said. Two guards moved apart, and the mayor joined the cramped circle. King Ulmin's authoritative voice boomed in the tight space. "I'm staying here. I want a guard on either side of me. The rest of you, take Nora off the stage."

"My office is next to the stage," Mayor Ashler said. "I'll take her there, and we'll lock the doors."

"Dad," Nora said, "the mayor said that man is harmless. He doesn't even have a weapon. Should we really run from him?"

"I'm not running. I'm keeping you safe."

Nora rolled her eyes as everyone followed the king's instructions. Two guards held her elbows. Another stood behind her, hand on her back, and the fourth positioned himself in front of her. Nora was tall, but the guard in front of her was practically a giant, his shoulders even with her eyes. His name was Ovrun, and he was the youngest guard, only nineteen. His muscular shoulders, clad in black livery with blue epaulets, distracted Nora as the guards rushed her across the stage, down a set of steps, and into a dark building.

Mayor Ashler locked the door. "My deepest apologies, Princess Ulminora."

"It's Nora."

"Pardon me?"

"No one calls me Ulminora."

The mayor flipped a switch. A light bulb came on, illuminating a small lobby with a large, curtained window.

Enough wind power for lights in public buildings. This town's doing pretty well. Nora took off her heavy headdress and set it down. She approached the window, but Ovrun and another guard were standing in front of it, their arms folded. A third guard stationed himself at the far edge of the window and pulled back the drapes just enough to look outside.

Nora gave Ovrun her most dazzling smile, and the corner of his lips quirked up. "I appreciate you trying to keep me safe," she said. "All I want to do is peek between the curtains. Please?"

The guards exchanged glances, and then Ovrun parted the curtains just enough for Nora to peer out with one eye. The lyster was still flying. Nora watched for any signs of his magic waning, but he was soaring in confident arcs. *Must've eaten plenty of feathers.* The crowd cheered as he flew in ridiculous figure eights, nearly hitting the tops of buildings every time he reached the bottom of the shape. Nora rolled her eyes. *Show-off.*

Finally, the flyer ended his flamboyant display. He stayed in the air, however, hovering over a three-story building that faced the square. Nora was close enough to discern a rough outline of his face. He looked like a teenager, but he couldn't possibly be that young. It took feather lysters decades to perfect their magical faculty.

His dark hair was long enough to cover his forehead, but the wind was lifting it into a messy mop. Despite how ridiculous this made him look, he beamed as he waved at the crowd. Then he alighted on the edge of the roof and dropped to his hands and knees.

Nora squinted, then gasped. A thick ribbon of smooth, white ice flowed from the man's hands, extending off the roof. *He's an ice lyster, too?*

The ice grew at an unbelievable pace. Within a minute, a gorgeous, curving ramp with banked edges extended from the roof to the ground. Nora's jaw dropped. Despite years of training (focused on one faculty, not two), she'd never made that much ice at once.

The young man sat on the ramp and grinned once more at the crowd. He pushed himself forward until the ramp grew steep enough for gravity to take over, sending him sliding at a dizzying speed.

Nora had just enough time to think, *I've got to learn how to make one of those ramps!* when the lyster reached the slide's halfway point, and everything literally fell apart. The entire slide broke into at least a dozen pieces. The young man's hands flailed in the air as he tumbled down, his fall cushioned only by massive, jagged shards of ice.

Nora's hand came up to her mouth. "Oh!"

The guards on either side of her tensed. Ovrun grasped her arm and tugged her away from the window. "What's wrong?"

"Nothing. The lyster just fell." Nora pulled away and stepped back to the window. It was clear what had happened. The man had lost focus, turning his ice brittle. She'd done it a thousand times, just never when she was depending on her creation to support her full weight.

"Come on, get up!" Nora urged under her breath. All the lyster's would-be rescuers blocked her line of sight. Her heart pounded and her cheeks grew warm as she tried to determine his fate. Sure, he was arrogant and lacked common sense, but he didn't deserve to die in a pile of his own ice.

The clock on the wall seemed to tick louder than it had before. Suddenly, the young man pushed himself up to stand atop his bed of ice. Nora couldn't see his expression, but his wave to the crowd was hesitant, his hubris gone. He dropped into a squat, then jumped into the air and flew again, soaring over the buildings of the square and dropping out of sight.

Nora laughed at the sight, then stepped back from the window and nodded at the guards. "Thanks for letting me watch."

"Is the feather eater gone?" Ovrun asked.

"Yeah. What a fool. He's lucky you didn't shoot him down." Despite her words, all Nora could think about was how fun it would be to make and use a slide like that.

Across the room, Mayor Ashler cleared her throat. "I'm very sorry about all this."

Nora grinned and crossed to the woman. "It's okay; this is the most fun I've had in weeks. Tell me, Mayor, what's that lyster's name?"

2

As soon as I could crawl, I started eating tree bark, a habit that annoyed my parents to no end. Not long after my fifth birthday, I chewed and swallowed a big bite of bark, ignoring my mother's commands to spit it out. Imagine her surprise—and mine—when I placed my hands on the tree and caused spring leaves to grow in the middle of autumn.

-The First Generation: A Memoir *by Liri Abrios*

WELL. *That didn't go as planned.*

Krey flew through Tirra's side streets. Due to the pageantry in the square, the streets were nearly empty. Despite that, he took the most challenging route, weaving between locked-up food carts and hitching posts, throwing his ire into one close call after another.

His body felt light, and not in a good, gravity-defying way. Clearly he'd burned up most of the feathers he'd eaten that morning.

Two more blocks. Trying to ignore his shaking limbs, he pushed himself, flying close to the ground.

Krey yelped as his talent petered out, and he plunged to the dirt road. He rolled, then lay there, moving each limb, testing for injury. Two falls in a quarter hour; could this day get any worse?

Thankfully, he'd only fallen a met or so this time. As a feather eater, he was used to that. He'd be bruised, but it didn't feel like anything was broken. He stood and glanced around to see if anyone had witnessed his humiliation. Of course not; they were all at the square.

He took off at a run and reached his house a couple of minutes later. Thank the sky, his aunts were at the two hundredth anniversary event, leaving him to nurse his disappointment in peace. He opened the door.

"Is that you, Krey, or is someone here to inform me that my nephew is incarcerated in the royal dungeon?"

How did she get home before me? Krey sauntered into the kitchen.

His Aunt Minona was seated at the table waiting for him, arms crossed over her ample chest, dark eyebrows raised so high, it was a wonder they didn't float away.

Krey greeted her with a sheepish smile. "Aunt Min, the king doesn't have a dungeon."

"He might decide he needs one after your display." She unfolded her arms and gestured at the chair across from her. "Sit."

Krey obeyed. "How did you get here faster than me?"

"When Evie and I saw you flying, we came to a quick agreement. I ran home to confront you if you made it back here, and she stayed in the square so that if the king arrested you, she could plead for your life." Min shook her head with a look of such disappointment, Krey was almost sorry for his failed mission. He opened his mouth to defend himself, but Min spoke first. "Krey West, do you know how old you are?"

"Uh—"

She pointed at him emphatically. "You are a seventeen-year-old magic eater with the talent of a forty-year-old and the judgment of a toddler."

"Oh."

"I have serious concerns that you'll kill yourself or get arrested before Evie and I die, and that's unacceptable, considering you're supposed to take care of us in our old age."

Krey couldn't prevent his lips from curving into a smile. "I'm fine, Aunt Min. I barely got hurt, and I promise you the king doesn't even know my name."

Her forehead knit beneath her tight, black curls. "All eight hundred people in that square know your name. I guarantee you the king knows it by now too." She reached her hand across the table, palm up, and when Krey took it, she squeezed his fingers. "Why did you do it, Krey? Do me a favor and tell me the truth the first time."

Krey sighed. At the same time, his stomach growled. That morning, he'd only eaten feathers and ice, magical fuel that provided no nutrition.

Min's eyebrows narrowed, and she stood. "You need a sandwich. Then we'll talk." Five minutes later, she set a plate and a cup of water in front of Krey, then returned to her seat.

Like all Min's sandwiches, it was a work of art—piles of greens, a slice of meat thick enough to be called a slab, and, dripping from the edges, the creamy, salty sauce she refused to share the recipe for. Krey picked up the sandwich and took a massive bite. Once he'd swallowed, he said, "I can explain."

"And you will. But you'll eat first. You've got dark circles under your eyes. I know you used more magic than you should've." Min watched Krey eat. When he was on his last bite, she said, "Looking better already. Let's move to the library."

Krey followed her. It was silly to call one room *the library* when books lined nearly every wall in the house. This room, however, had held the first bookshelf. Min and Krey entered and sat in cushioned chairs. They were upholstered in preday fabric, purchased from scavengers and pieced together like a quilt.

Even before he'd moved to this house, Krey had grown up hearing the story of his aunts' library. When Min and Evie had met a quarter-century before, they'd discovered a mutual love of preday books. They'd married, bought this house, and installed a shelf in this room, hoping they'd eventually have enough money to fill it with collectible volumes.

Then Evie found success as a fashion designer. It was crazy what rich people would pay for outfits like the one the princess had been wearing in the square. The two women had now spent twenty years building the largest preday library in Cellerin. The book-filled home attracted scholars who leafed through treasured tomes while sitting on the very chairs now occupied by Krey and his aunt.

Min propped her elbows on her knees, and her gaze snared Krey's. "Now, tell me why."

"I need to find Zeisha." Krey's heel tapped the floor, his knee bobbing up and down. "That means I need answers, and the capital is the only place to find them."

"Can you sit still for a minute or two?" Min asked, touching a hand to Krey's knee. He lowered his heel to the floor, and she continued, "What answers do you need? You know Zeisha is in Cellerin City."

Krey leaned back in the chair and rested his forehead in one hand, squeezing his temples. He took a deep breath and said, "She's not there."

"What do you mean?"

Krey shook his head and gritted his teeth against emotion he didn't have time for. "Those people who came into town, saying the king sent them out to recruit apprentices—have you ever heard of the king doing that before?"

"No, but there's no reason to doubt it. Zeisha has sent two letters to her parents." Min's voice was gentle. "She's apprenticing with a master vine eater. She's enjoying it."

"I've read those letters! She didn't write them, at least not willingly. For one thing, she used the term *plant lyster*. She's not a snob;

she calls herself a *vine eater*. And I know everyone thinks she's breaking up with me, but if she were, she'd tell me herself. There's something weird about all this."

"Let's say you're right. I still don't understand why you flew over the event today."

Krey gripped his armrests hard, like he was about to propel himself out of his seat. "Those people who took her to the capital claimed to work for the king. That means someone in the government is protecting them. So I decided to put on the best show I could. I figured if the king saw my magic, he'd invite me back to the city to work for him or something. Once I got there, I'd find someone with information on Zeisha. If I was working for the king, maybe people would actually talk to me."

"The resident cynic of our household willingly tried to impress the king." Min gave him a sad smile. "You must really miss her."

He ran his fingers through his tangled, black hair. "Do you have any idea how many damn letters I've written to government officials in the last six weeks, trying to figure out where Zeisha really is? Of course, nobody's answered me. They don't care about a girl from a small town!" Krey stood and turned away, swiping the palms of his hands over his wet eyes. "I'm catching a ride with the next trader who comes through. I'll go to the city and figure it out from there."

Before Min could respond, Evie's voice reached their ears. "Krey? Are you here?"

"We're in the library!" Min shouted.

Seconds later, Evie appeared in the doorway. Her full lips, so reminiscent of Krey's mother's, were pursed. "Krey, there are a couple of people here to see you." She stepped in, followed by a man and woman, both wearing the black-and-blue uniforms of the Cellerin royal guard.

Krey threw his hands in the air. "Oh, by the stone, it's not like I hurt anyone!"

"Well, you did take quite a fall," the female guard said. "I thought for sure you scraped up your ego."

The male guard coughed. Krey could swear he was covering up a laugh.

The female guard stood with her arms at her side, shoulders back. Her teasing voice turned officious. "Kreyven West, we're here to escort you to a meeting with His Majesty, the King."

IN THE DARK: 1

ZEISHA SHOOK the shoulder of the girl on the pallet next to hers.

Isla startled awake. "Huh?"

Not wanting to wake the others, Zeisha kept her voice low. "Did we already count tonight?"

"Oh . . . no. I don't think so."

Zeisha heard Isla sit up, though she couldn't see her friend in the dark room. As she took off her right shoe and sock, Zeisha squeezed her eyes shut, trying to picture Isla. For a moment, a dim, blurry image filled her mind—a short girl with long, black hair—and then it was gone.

"It's day seven," Zeisha whispered. She found the end of the string she'd looped around the big toe of her right foot. After carefully unwinding it, she wrapped it around her second toe.

"How many weeks?" Isla asked in a sleepy voice.

Zeisha knew the answer but counted just the same, rubbing her fingers along the tiny, crescent-shaped scars on her ankle. *One, two, three, four, five.* "Six," she said. Then she pressed her thumbnail into the skin above the previous week's mark, gritting her teeth. An involuntary yelp exited her mouth as her nail broke the skin.

Isla's hand found Zeisha's arm, then moved to her shoulder. Her grip was tight and comforting.

"Thanks," Zeisha whispered as she dug her nail farther into the skin, creating a deeper gouge. Then she pressed her index finger to the wound, releasing a long sigh.

Isla removed her hand, and her blanket rustled as she lay down.

When Zeisha was pretty sure the blood had clotted, she put on her sock and shoe and lay on her pallet. She placed the tip of her thumb in her mouth and used her front tooth, then her tongue, to clean out the blood under her nail. The metallic flavor made her gag, as it did every week.

3

Several other children in our community developed magical talents after I did. We got a lot of attention, and I'll admit, I enjoyed it.

But we had no magical experts to learn from. When we asked questions, our parents shrugged and said, "You'll have to figure it out together."

-The First Generation: A Memoir *by Liri Abrios*

———————

NORA SAT BEFORE A FIREPLACE, chatting softly with her father and the mayor, who was hosting them in her home for the night. A knock sounded at the front door.

The mayor left to answer it, returning with a member of the royal guard. He held both hands open in front of him, arms bent at the elbows, and briefly lowered his head. When the king nodded to acknowledge the man's bow, the guard dropped his arms and said, "Your Majesty, the guest you requested is outside."

"Bring him in," King Ulmin said.

Nora sat up straighter, fighting the smile that tugged at her lips. She'd asked her father if they could meet the poor lyster who'd fallen in his own magical ice. According to the mayor, the young man was seventeen, the same age as Nora. How had he gotten so good at magic at such a young age?

The guard returned, stopping in the doorway again. "Kreyven West, Your Majesty," the guard announced. He stepped back into the entry hall.

Kreyven West entered the room. He had a medium build, brown skin, a strong jaw, and thick, dark hair that was due for a cut. His clothes were simple, made of neocot fabric, but he wore them well. Nora kept her expression neutral as she took him in. Surely he had some lean muscles underneath his baggy shirt and pants.

The oddest thing about Kreyven was his expression. Most royal visitors were obsequious, giddy, or nervous. Not this guy. His lips were compressed into a sharp line, his arms folded.

All in all, Nora couldn't quite classify him as gorgeous or dashing. Rather, Kreyven West was . . . striking. Yes, that was it. A striking teenager with incredible magical faculties. *How intriguing.*

Nora completed her perusal of the young man, then realized her father had stood and approached Kreyven. She stood too, but didn't step away from her chair.

"Kreyven West, hmm?" King Ulmin said.

Kreyven didn't bow. He kept his chin high and met the king's eyes. "I go by Krey."

Nora watched her father. His eyes widened just a little, and she almost laughed, knowing the external reaction signified a pronounced internal one.

Before the king could say anything further, a middle-aged man spoke from the doorway: "Dinner is served."

The king shifted his gaze to the mayor, who was hovering near the door. "I'd like to have a conversation with this young man."

"And the dinner table is an excellent place to have it," Nora said, walking briskly to the mayor. "Can we accommodate one more?"

Her father's eyes found her, and he must've seen her fascination with Krey in her face, because his mouth twitched with a little smile.

By the sky, he was laughing at her! She raised an eyebrow at him and returned her attention to the mayor, who confirmed that Krey could dine with them.

Nora switched her attention to Krey and found that he'd turned toward her. He was squinting, studying her like he was trying to decode a book written in a foreign language. She returned his stare.

"Krey," Nora's father said, "tell us about yourself."

They'd all settled at dinner and were nearly done filling their plates from dishes of food passed around the table. Krey held a bowl of small, purple potatoes in one hand and a pair of tongs in the other. He placed five potatoes on his plate, ponderously arranging them. At last, he handed the bowl to the mayor, took the dish Nora was offering, and met the king's eyes. "What do you want to know?"

King Ulmin set down the bread he'd just served himself and speared a piece of meat. "I'd like to hear about your lyster training."

Krey lifted his chin and stared at the king. "I'm a magic eater."

A laugh escaped Nora's mouth. "Lyster, magic eater—they're the same thing!"

Krey smirked and barely glanced at her from the corner of his eye. "Okay."

For the next several minutes, the only sounds were clattering cutlery, a crackling fireplace, and chewing that seemed twice as loud as usual. Krey never once shifted his attention from his food.

Nora finished eating. Krey, who must be the slowest eater on Anyari, was still hunched over his plate, chewing. The king had cleaned his own plate and was watching their guest. The mayor cleared her throat.

"This," Nora said, scooting out her chair and standing, "is ridiculous." She placed her hands on the table and leaned toward Krey until he looked up at her with an expression that was somehow both combative and apathetic.

Nora straightened and clasped her hands behind her back, not releasing Krey's gaze. "Krey West, we, the royal family of Cellerin, would like to offer you an apprenticeship with master lysters."

The king coughed. Nora knew he hated being caught off guard like this. *Just go with it, Dad.*

Krey put his fork down. "An apprenticeship?"

"Yes. We'll connect you with an ice lyster and a feather lyster, some of the best in the country." She had his attention now, so she hazarded a smile at him. "Just don't call them magic eaters, okay?"

He stood, his average height putting him level with Nora. He folded his arms in front of his chest, and Nora's gaze darted down for a half-second. *Yep, definitely some wiry muscles in there.*

In a low voice, Krey said, "You saw my skills. You really think I need to study under a so-called master?"

Nora's jaw dropped, but she recovered quickly. "What I saw today was someone with sufficient skill to make an ice ramp and insufficient focus to keep that ramp together long enough to slide to the bottom. And speaking of bottom"—she pointed at his backside—"you okay after falling on all that sharp ice?"

His jaw tightened. "I'm fine."

"I bet a master lyster could help you develop your focus."

He swallowed, looked away, and sat in his chair. In a low, strained voice, he addressed his next question to the king. "Would this apprenticeship be in Cellerin City?"

Nora's father seemed to have recovered from his shock over his daughter's offer. His eyes were dancing as he looked between Nora and Krey. "Yes, I suppose it would."

Krey returned the nod, and his face relaxed a little.

Nora sat, then said, "Apprentices pay for their training by

working for the government. We could find somewhere in the palace for you to work. Right, Dad?"

"I'm sure we could arrange that."

Krey stared at her with cold eyes, and Nora wondered if she'd gone too far with the impulsive offer. But she was already dreading her return to the palace, where the modicum of freedom she'd enjoyed on this trip would be gone. Surely the strictures of palace life would be more bearable if she had a friend her age . . . one who could teach her to make an ice slide. If only Krey shared her enthusiasm.

"I'll do it."

His voice was so quiet, Nora wasn't sure she'd heard it right. "Pardon me?"

Krey squared his shoulders. "I'll do it."

Nora examined him. He'd acted like a carefree kid on that slide, but since arriving at dinner, he'd been surly and rude. *Who are you, Krey West?*

The king's voice, stately and official, boomed across the table. "Very well. You'll travel to Cellerin City with us."

4

One day, a scavenger came to town, trying to sell a hover scooter and a stash of new batteries. He demonstrated the vehicle, and I begged my parents to barter for it. Mom said we'd have to trade our whole house for it, and I don't think she was joking.

What I wouldn't have given to hover above the ground in that scooter just once before all the batteries in the world went bad. Sure, I could make plants grow, but to my eyes, a floating scooter was true magic.

-The First Generation: A Memoir *by Liri Abrios*

OVRUN PULLED a piece of hallep meat off its skewer. He let out a low groan as he chewed. It was tender, juicy, and seasoned just right with herbs, salt, and pepper. The food on this trip was the best he'd ever eaten. He'd expected their travel food to consist of dried meat and vegetables. He hadn't known the king would bring his personal chef along.

King Ulmin and his chef were sitting across the campfire from Ovrun, both of them laughing. At the palace, the king was usually hurrying from one responsibility to another. On this trip, he'd been much more carefree.

Ovrun took another bite and shifted his eyes to Princess Nora, who sat by her father, thoughtfully chewing her own food. Did she have any idea how lucky she was to have a dad she could depend on? Ovrun had never even met his father. Maybe *lucky* wasn't the right word, though. The princess had lost her mother years ago.

Before the queen's death, Ovrun had seen her at public events. She'd had glossy, black hair and a friendly smile. Queen Ambrel had been lovely, but her daughter was nothing short of stunning. Right now, Princess Nora didn't seem to notice Ovrun's attention, so he let it linger. The firelight flickered off her smooth, brown skin, shiny hair, and big eyes. Those eyes were spectacular—surrounded by dark lashes, with irises colored a deep brown that made Ovrun want to dive in.

He liked her eyes almost as much as her full lips, which he liked almost as much as her small waist, not to mention those rounded hips —*Stop*. He tugged his gaze away from her, but a few seconds later, it wandered back, settling on the forefinger of her right hand, which was currently tucked in between her pursed lips as she licked some food off it. Was she trying to torture him?

Of course she's not. She wasn't even aware of him, which was the problem. It hadn't always been that way. After Ovrun had started working at the palace a year ago, he'd often had short conversations with the princess. Then, a couple of months back, she was wandering the palace grounds at night, unable to sleep. He was on a night shift, patrolling. They started talking, then kissing—perfect, slow kisses under the bright stars. He'd always liked her, but after that, he was done for.

It wasn't like he'd never kissed a girl before. Nora was different, though. It was like tasting the chef's amazing food after a lifetime of eating plain bread. He didn't just want to kiss her again; he wanted to *know* her—her dreams, her pain, what went on behind those compelling eyes.

He'd tried to orchestrate more meetings with her, but after they kissed, she avoided him. Maybe, he'd thought, this trip would be different. He'd caught her looking at him plenty of times, and he could swear he saw admiration in that gaze, but they rarely talked, and when they did, it was always about his guard duties.

Nora's head swiveled in his direction, and their eyes met. She bit her bottom lip, which sent his mind spinning, then turned away and looked down, letting her straight hair cover her face.

"That dinner was amazing!" Krey's voice broke Ovrun's entrancement.

Ovrun turned to his new friend, who was just finishing up his skewer of meat. "I know. The chef's cooking is almost enough to make me wish this trip would last longer."

Krey scratched behind the ears of one of the guard caynins who'd accompanied them on the trip. He'd befriended both of the animals his first day on the road. "Almost, but not quite, right?"

"Yeah, I'm ready to get home." The royal caravan had been journeying for a month in the shadow of Cellerin Mountain, the largest freestanding mountain in the world. They'd departed from the capital, on the east side of the mountain. Over the course of three weeks, they'd traveled to about a dozen towns, finally ending up southwest of the mountain, in Tirra. After their final hurrah, they'd turned toward home, stopping only to buy supplies, eat, and camp out every night. Their return trip had lasted ten days, and they'd be back in Cellerin City by the next afternoon.

Once they were back, Ovrun would pick up his pay and ask for a day off. He'd go home to see what his mom and sister needed. Had his sister outgrown her winter coat? Probably; she'd gotten so tall over the summer. He'd look for a blue one; that was her favorite color these days.

Krey stood and walked off. That jolted Ovrun out of his reverie, and his attention returned to Nora. A couple of minutes later, Krey returned. "Here you go."

Ovrun turned. Krey had refilled both their water cups. "Thanks."

Krey's voice lowered. "You know, there are other girls in Cellerin City. Ones that would actually give you the time of day and not come with a bunch of royal baggage."

Ovrun chuckled and pulled his attention away from the princess, promising himself not to stare any more. *Not tonight, anyway.* He and Krey had talked a lot on this trip, and their conversations had often turned to the girl Ovrun liked and the girl Krey loved. Ovrun lifted his cup. "Here's to you finding Zeisha."

"And here's to the princess coming to her senses and realizing you're the best guy she'll ever come across." Krey clicked his clay cup against Ovrun's.

It was a nice thing for him to say, especially since Krey seemed to hold some grudge against Nora and never missed an opportunity to snub her.

Ovrun drank his water and stared into the fire. They'd arrive in Cellerin City the next afternoon. *Maybe things'll be different once we're home, away from prying eyes.*

Try as he might, Ovrun couldn't bring himself to believe his own pep talk.

"I'd hug you, but I'm dusty, and I stink." Nora grinned at her Aunt Dani, who'd come out of the palace to meet the returning travelers.

"Oh, don't be silly, you've smelled worse than this before." Dani, who looked as effortlessly put together as ever, gathered Nora into a tight embrace. She was several simmets shorter than her niece, and her wavy, brown hair, pulled up in a casual twist, rubbed against Nora's cheek. "I'm glad you're home."

"Me too. Now I need a hot bath."

Nora's father stepped up next to her. "Great idea. Right after you take your guest on a tour of the grounds." He gestured to Krey, who was bantering with the guards.

Nora positioned her body away from Krey and spoke in a hushed voice. "Dad, I'm dirty and cold."

"You're the one who offered him a job at the palace. Show him around, and then take him to the dorms. I'll have someone meet him there with his luggage in half an hour or so."

"Where are you going?"

"The chapel."

Nora pulled her knitted cap down lower, then approached Krey and stood behind him. He was telling a story to a group of guards, his voice and hands animated. At the sight of Nora, the guards stood up straighter, their smiles disappearing.

Krey's monologue trailed off, and he turned around. Seeing Nora, he lifted an inquisitive eyebrow.

"Welcome home." She shrugged and smiled. "I'm your tour guide."

"I don't need a tour."

"King's orders. Even I have to obey."

Krey held out his hands and lowered his head in a bow that Nora could swear was ironic. She stepped off the gravel of the circle drive into the grass. It still had some green in it, but patches were turning brown and dormant as winter approached. Krey walked beside her, leaving plenty of space between them.

The wagons and steamcar had stopped on the northern side of the palace grounds, in front of the main palace complex. Nora led Krey west, then turned south, pointing out various buildings.

A caynin ran up to them and nudged Nora's knee with its flat nose. She rubbed both the animal's large, triangular ears, which stuck out from the side of its face. Its maroon, compound eyes glinted in the sun. "There are about twenty security caynins roaming the property at any given time," she told Krey. "This one and the two we traveled with will take your scent back to the pack. By tomorrow, they'll all recognize you. But you'll still want to be cautious; they can be moody."

The caynin looked at Krey and opened its huge mouth so wide that its upper and lower jaws looked like an open book. It was an intimidation tactic, and even Nora shuddered at the animal's double rows of sharp teeth.

Krey smiled. "Hi, buddy!"

The beast closed its mouth most of the way, walked right up to Krey, and licked him with its forked tongue. Nora stifled a smile and glared at the caynin. "Making me a liar, are you?" The animal turned from Krey and rubbed against Nora's legs. She got down on his level and gave him a good scratch behind his ears. "Okay, all is forgiven."

They continued the tour, and Nora soon stopped at the door of a large, wooden structure. "Come on, I'll show you the stables."

"What do you keep in there, unicorns?"

Nora rolled her eyes.

"Dragons?" Krey asked. "Come on, I know the king would love to show off a royal dragon or two."

"No wild animals, magical or not. Being royal doesn't make us stupid. We only keep orsas here. Tame orsas."

She led him in. It was a huge stable, its dozens of stalls lit by skylights. With every step, Nora's heart beat faster. She hadn't seen her orsa in a month. Her mouth broke into a grin as she came to a halt in front of a stall near the back corner.

Past the chest-high door was a muscular, male orsa. His straight, shiny black fur was short everywhere but his chest and chin, where it grew long. Two bulging, blue compound eyes widened when he saw his visitors, and Nora could swear that, under his squat snout, his expressive mouth was sporting the beastly version of a smile. He greeted Nora with a mellow "OHH-AHH." The other orsas in the stable picked up the call, the building filling with gentle bellows.

Forgetting her guest, Nora laughed, swung open the door, and entered the stall. She reached up to wrap her arms around her orsa's broad neck, burying her cheek into the thick, soft fur hanging from his chin. He rubbed his head on hers, the rumbles of his continued greeting seeping into her chest.

"Guess you're pretty close to your orsa."

Krey's voice came from inside the stall. Nora pulled back, keeping one arm around the orsa's neck. Krey was running a hand along the animal's back, his chest and shoulders shaking with silent laughter.

Let him laugh; she was too happy to care. "I've had him since I was four. I learned to ride on him."

"What's his name?"

"Blue."

"For his eyes?"

"No, all orsas have blue eyes. I named him that because his fur looks blue in certain lights."

"Oh, you've got to be kidding me."

Nora wrapped both arms around Blue again. "Hey, I'm not asking for you to approve of his name."

"I couldn't care less what you named your pet. I do care that I just stepped in his crap."

It was Nora's turn to laugh. "I stepped in it too. It's no big deal. Come on, we'll wash our boots." She kissed Blue next to one of his big eyes, then led Krey back through the stables. Cries of "OHH-AHH" followed them the whole way.

Outside, they stopped under an elevated water tank attached to the building's roof. Nora retrieved two brushes from hooks on the wall and turned on a spigot. They cleaned their shoes under the flow of water.

Nora lifted her eyes to Krey a few times, but his attention was on his shoes. He was scrubbing the soles hard enough to take months off their lifespan. There was a strange fury in the action, and while she wanted to know what was going on behind that shaggy, dark hair, she didn't dare ask.

Whatever was wrong with him hadn't started today. Krey had been rude during the dinner in Tirra. And he'd ignored Nora during their entire, eleven-day journey. Perhaps she'd been naïve to expect him to become her friend. *Why can't I let go of that hope? Am I really so desperate?*

The only friend she'd ever had was Faylie, a talented fire lyster who knew more of Nora's secrets than anyone else. Faylie's mom had worked at the palace, and the girls had been friends since they were toddlers. Then, six months ago, Faylie had made it clear she wanted nothing to do with the princess. Nora still didn't know how she'd screwed up her only friendship.

Her chest tightened as pain from that day returned. She gritted her teeth and took a deep breath. She couldn't cry in front of Krey.

After Faylie had deserted her, the only person at the palace close to Nora's age was Ovrun. She genuinely liked him, but she'd messed up that friendship too. She'd let him get too close. There was no future with him, a fact she desperately wished she could change. She'd had to back away rather than lead him on.

When Krey came along, Nora had pinned her hopes for friendship on him. Like Faylie, he was a lyster. He was her age too, and while he was pretty cute, he obviously wasn't attracted to her. That should keep things from getting too complicated. He'd be a perfect friend . . . except that he seemed to think more highly of the crap on his shoe than of her. *What did I ever do to him?*

Nora took a deep breath, unwilling to give up on Krey yet. She turned off the spigot, stood, and hung up her brush. "There's something else I want to show you."

"Your wish is my command." Krey was facing away from her, hanging his own brush on the wall, but she could picture the sneer behind his words.

"This way." Nora led him through the open land in the middle of the property, skirting the southern edge of a pond. As they reached the eastern side of the palace ground, Krey pointed at a building tucked behind some trees near the southeastern corner. "What's that?"

"That's the chapel." Nora adjusted their route to walk north.

"*The* chapel? The one with the stone in it?"

"Yeah. It has its own gate, and it's open to the public a few hours each day. There's always a line. Everybody wants to see the stone that caused the apocalypse."

She continued walking north, and Krey kept up with her but glanced over his shoulder again. "So I can go there if I want to?"

"Sure. You can even go when it's closed to the public. But you can't visit now; my dad's there. He likes to worship alone." Nora slowed and studied Krey. "Are you curious to see the stone?"

"No, I want to worship."

Nora laughed for a second before realizing Krey wasn't joining in. "Oh—oh!" She swallowed. "You're serious." When Krey didn't answer, she said, "I wouldn't have pegged you as the religious type."

"I wouldn't have pegged you as a cynic."

"I turned into a cynic the same day my father turned devout."

Krey looked away before asking, "How many years ago was that?"

"Ten." She regretted the response as soon as it left her mouth.

He nodded, like that was what he'd expected.

Heat filled Nora's cheeks. Normal citizens could lose a parent without the whole world knowing, but not her. She sped up, nearly jogging. Krey kept up easily.

Nora was a little breathless by the time they halted at the stone wall enclosing the residential wing. The wall was four mets tall, over twice her height, and topped with barbed wire. She stopped at a stone gate, topped with the same wire. "This is where I live."

She unlocked the gate, walked in, and greeted two caynins. "The caynins who guard the residence are trained to attack when anyone enters unaccompanied by my family. No exceptions."

"How do the servants get in?"

"We call them household staff, not servants. They enter through an enclosed pathway between the residence and the palace."

Nora followed Krey's gaze as he looked up at the home. It was two stories tall, made of white stone. There were over twenty windows on the front of the building. Everything about the building was pristine. There was no moss or mold on the stone; the shrubs in front were meticulously trimmed; and the windows were so clean, they were almost invisible.

Krey let out a little laugh. "How do you, your dad, and your aunt manage to survive in such a shack?"

Nora ignored the question and continued around to the back of the house, where a small room jutted out. The stone walls there were paler than the rest of the house.

"What is this place?" Krey put a hand on the stone. "It looks new."

"It's been here for twelve years." Nora unlocked the door. They stepped inside, and she flipped a switch on the wall. A single bulb hanging from the low ceiling turned on, illuminating the tiny room. Large chests lined the walls, leaving a small, open passage of wooden flooring between them. On top of one of the chests sat a folded blanket. A door connected the room to the main building.

"No skylights in here, huh?" Krey asked.

"We don't want the sun shining in this building. The electricity comes from a solar panel array."

Krey's eyes widened. "Solar panels?"

"Yeah."

He shook his head, and Nora wished she hadn't said anything. The palace was the only place in Cellerin with solar panels. Before The Day, technology had been incredibly advanced. Most of it, however, couldn't be reproduced—not only due to the lack of infrastructure, but also because ancient digital storage systems had disintegrated long ago, taking much of the world's preday knowledge with them.

Engineers, funded by the royal coffers, had looked at old solar panels and experimented for years before successfully creating their own version. The king's goal was to spread solar power throughout the country.

Krey was examining the wall on either side of the open doorway. It was half a met thick. "Insulated?" he asked.

"Yes. Even the doors and ceiling."

Krey nodded. "Pretty sure I know what's in these chests." Without asking permission, he lifted the lid of one. It was full of ice chips, each about the size of a thumbnail. His face broke into a smile.

Nora grinned and opened a chest on the opposite side of the room. It contained much larger slabs of ice, as long as her forearm. "This is how they come to us. People break them apart as I need them."

He stiffened. "By *people*, you mean servants?"

"Staff." She gestured back at the chest he was standing in front of. "Go ahead, eat some."

He closed it. "That's okay."

"Consider it thanks for whatever job they give you at the palace. Any time you need ice, just find me, and I'll get you some."

"My apprenticeship is my compensation for working here." Krey folded his arms. "This place is cramped. Let's finish our tour."

Nora sighed and led him out of the room, locking the door. "We're both too dirty to go in the main palace. I'll show you your dorm."

Krey responded with a curt nod. They exited through the residential gate and walked east, soon entering a lush, manicured garden. There weren't many flowers in late fall, but it was still beautiful, with paths winding between Original and Anyarian plants.

Krey didn't comment on the garden. "You said the icehouse is twelve years old. I guess that was about the time you developed your magic?" He didn't wait for an answer. "A storage space just for your fuel. Nobody would want a princess to suffer for even a day without the means to practice her magic. This trip must've been torture for you." Underneath his casual tone ran a thick ribbon of scorn.

She swiveled her head, fixing him with a stare. "You seem angry. What's your problem, anyway?"

He didn't look at her, only muttering, "I'm fine."

They exited the garden into a small, forested area, full of evergreens. "Tell me, Nora," Krey said, "What happens if you don't need all that ice?"

"It melts. There are drains in the chests, and there's a pan under the floor that collects—"

"Got it," he snapped. "Your ice melts while poverty-stricken frost eaters in Cellerin City set out cups of water, praying for a freeze. Most of the year, they have to save up their coins just to get a block of ice every few weeks or months. I bet they use every bit of it before it melts." He stopped and looked up. They'd reached a blocky, two-story building with rows of identical windows. "I take it this is my new home?"

"Yes. You'll live here with some of the household staff and guards. I think there are a couple dozen residents." She gestured. "I'll take you inside; someone will be there to show you—"

Again, he interrupted her. "I can find my own way. I know you want to get home." He turned and locked eyes with her. "This dorm looks nice. It's almost as big as your house." He spun around and strode to the front door.

5

Once, when we were sixteen, my friend and I sneaked away to the abandoned city east of our community.

It wasn't the death in the city that scared me the most. It was the life— the person I saw out of the corner of my eye, peeking from a broken window. The man who crouched on a roof, watching us with wild eyes.

What kind of person prefers the company of millions of bones to that of fellow humans?

-The First Generation: A Memoir *by Liri Abrios*

KREY SHIVERED as he exited his dorm building. Winter would begin in a few days, and he could feel it in the air. He buttoned his coat, shoved his hands in his pockets, and walked toward the front gate. The lawns had a thick layer of frost on them. Krey scooped some up and ate it, then blew soft snowflakes out of his mouth, relishing the cold, magical tingle on his tongue and throat.

At the gatehouse, he greeted Ovrun and chatted with all the guards. They opened a pedestrian gate for him, and he ventured onto the street.

The sun was barely up, but nearly twenty people waited for the royal chapel to open. Krey wondered why each of them were visiting. Were they coming to curse the stone or honor it?

Rimorian religious leaders insisted no one should worship the stone. However, Krey had met plenty of people, mostly fellow magic eaters, who believed the artifact in that chapel was a gift from God. In bringing magic to Anyari, they argued, the stone had connected humans to their colony planet.

While he didn't agree with their reasoning, Krey understood it. Magic eaters could only use Anyarian fuel. Vine eaters, for instance, had to eat Anyarian, not Original, plants. Blood eaters fueled their healing talents with the yellow blood of Anyarian animals, not the red blood of fellow humans. Magic, it seemed, was a unique gift, given only to humans on this particular planet.

Dragons, unicorns, and sea serpents, which had appeared on Anyari after The Day, also figured into this belief system. These magical creatures played prominent roles in some of Earth's ancient myths. Those who honored the stone claimed that it had somehow tapped into humanity's tall tales, turning them into reality.

Krey wasn't sure how a fire-breathing reptid was supposed to make him feel connected to his planet, nor how people could worship a stone that had killed most of their ancestors. *To each their own, I guess.*

Other than the devoted, chilly souls waiting in front of the chapel, there weren't many people on the street. It was Sunday; everyone else was probably sleeping in. Krey hadn't even been tempted to sleep late. His apprenticeship and his job would both start the next day. He had one full day of freedom, and he'd put it to good use.

Zeisha's parents had shown Krey the letters their daughter had sent them. Krey knew they thought Zeisha was purposefully rebuffing him. Ignoring their pity, he'd copied every word of the letters, including the return address in Cellerin City. The palace grounds were on the outskirts of the city, surrounded by farms. According to the gate guards, Zeisha's location was several clommets away.

Krey picked up his pace. He passed preday buildings, constructed of man-made materials (such as stone grown in vats and weatherproof artificial wood), interspersed with postday structures built from natural substances.

Coming to the top of a small hill, he squinted into the rising sun. Cellerin City lay before him, but he couldn't quite see the crumbling, preday metropolis he knew existed in the distance. He'd seen drawings of ancient cities, with their tall buildings stretching into the sky. The huge structures stirred a desire in him, a longing to return to humanity's past when technology reigned and nearly anything was possible.

Well, anything except preventing an apocalypse. *Maybe it wasn't all that great.*

After Krey had walked for half an hour, the buildings of Cellerin City surrounded him. Compared to the ruins in the east, this place was hardly a *city* at all. About a hundred thousand of the kingdom's half-million citizens lived in the capital and its outskirts.

Krey followed the instructions the guards had given him, taking a right on a large thoroughfare. Shopkeepers were posting *OPEN* signs while vendors set up carts on the edges of the street. Even at this hour, a fair number of people were out and about. A woman on an orsa passed Krey, and he saw a small carriage driving farther up the road. Some pedestrians walked on the wooden sidewalks. Others, like Krey, stuck to the dirt road. The last thing he wanted was to be mowed down by someone zooming down the sidewalk on a push scooter.

To Krey's left, a food cart vendor tossed a handful of something into her mouth, then grinned and waved at Krey. "Good morning!" Gray powder covered her hand and teeth.

Ash eater. It was a convenient talent for someone who cooked food all day. The woman could create magical flames so long as she had a steady supply of ashes to eat. She probably got her fuel from other food vendors.

Krey returned the vendor's smile and kept walking until he found the large bank the guards had told him to look for. He turned left, then scrambled to the edge of the road to avoid an oncoming steam-car. *That's not something you'd see in Tirra.*

On his right was a park, mostly empty at this time of day. Krey's eyes narrowed. Despite it being the end of autumn, the trees, all of them deciduous, were covered in green fronds. That could only mean one thing.

His suspicions were confirmed when he spied a woman with her hands on a tree trunk. She had to be a vine eater, or what the pretentious royals would call a *plant lyster.* As Krey approached, he kept his gaze on the tree's branches. Long, green fronds sprouted and grew all over the tree.

Krey returned his attention to the vine eater, then halted, nearly tripping. The woman, whose back was to him, was short, with an hourglass figure clearly visible despite her coat. She had masses of black curls.

The figure, the hair—"Zeisha?"

The woman didn't turn. She peeled off a piece of bark and brought it up to her face. Krey knew she was eating it; he'd seen Zeisha do the same thing a hundred times.

Krey's breathing quickened as he moved closer. "Zeisha?" He tapped the vine eater's shoulder.

She turned. Her eyebrows were raised in a question, but her mouth was too full of bark to speak. The fine lines of middle age surrounded her eyes.

"Oh—sorry." Krey pivoted and ran back to the street. The encounter had left his chest tight with desire and disappointment. He swallowed against the lump in his throat. He kept running, Zeisha's hazel eyes and gentle smile filling his imagination.

Krey stood in front of a small house. Light-green paint adorned the siding in peeling, faded blotches. He reached into his back pocket and pulled out his copies of Zeisha's letters, double-checking the address.

This was the right house, but it didn't look like a vine eater's home. Zeisha's yard in Tirra had been lush and green year-round. Here, the only plants were determined weeds. Could she have gotten the address wrong?

He strode to the front porch. A small sign, hand-painted in sloppy lettering, hung next to the door. It read CELLERIN LYSTER APPRENTICESHIPS.

Apparently this is the place. Krey knocked and, a few seconds later, knocked harder. When no one came, he pounded at the door with the side of his fist, not stopping until he heard the slide of the deadbolt.

The door swung open, bouncing against the inside wall. A short, bald man, wearing nothing but a pair of patched drawstring pants with a hole in one knee, glared up at Krey with bleary eyes. "Whaddya want?"

Krey glanced inside the house, which was crammed with junk. He pointed at the sign. "Is this Cellerin Lyster Apprenticeships?"

The man stood up straighter and pulled his pants up over his sunken waist. "Sure is."

"I'm looking for a friend of mine who came here a couple of months ago. Zeisha Dennivan."

"What kinda magic does she eat?"

Krey raised his eyebrows. Hadn't Nora told him not to use such terminology in his own apprenticeship? "She's a vine eater. Are you her instructor?"

The man coughed without covering his mouth, and spittle flew onto Krey's shirt. "I'm not a magic eater," the man said. "This is the office. I do the paperwork."

"For all the apprentices in the city?"

"The ones like your friend. She's in a special program. But right now, the vine eaters are outta town, getting trained. Sorry." He backed up, grasping the doorknob.

Krey stepped over the threshold. "When will they be back?"

"No idea." The man made a shooing motion. "Get outta here! I told you, she's gone."

"I'd like to know how I can get in touch with my friend." Krey took a step closer to the man, who scooted back.

"What's your name?" the man asked.

"Kreyven West."

"Listen, Kreyven, every apprentice gives us a list of people we're allowed to give information to. Your friend—what's her name again?"

Krey took yet another step toward the man. "Zeisha Dennivan."

"I remember her." The man thrust his index finger at Krey's chest. "You're not on her list."

A disturbingly violent image invaded Krey's mind: him grabbing the man's index finger and breaking it. He shoved the thought to the side and tried to cover his fury with a calm voice. "Please check. Just to be sure."

The man's cheeks darkened to red. "I don't need to check! Nobody's on her list. She started a new life. You're not part of it!" His eyes flicked to the street behind Krey. "Oh, thank the stone." He sucked in a breath and yelled, "Get ridda this guy!"

Krey looked behind him, and the man shoved the door closed, forcing Krey onto the porch. He fell on his backside but quickly recovered, jumping to his feet as the bolt clicked into place.

Two men were crossing the street toward Krey. They strode across the dead lawn and stopped, trapping him on the porch. They were both tall, with broad chests and thick legs.

"This is private property," one of the men said.

Krey met the man's stony gaze with his own. "I'm looking for a friend. Get me some answers, and I'll leave."

The same man pointed at the door and said, "If Eb didn't give you answers, you don't get answers." With one hand, he grabbed Krey's shoulder and pulled him close. In a flash, his other hand moved to Krey's face. His meaty palm covered Krey's mouth as his thumb and forefinger squeezed his nose.

Krey tried to breathe against the man's hand. He couldn't. Panic replaced the air in his chest. He clutched his attacker's wrist with both his hands, but the second man grabbed Krey's elbows and pulled. Krey lost his grip. The second man wrenched his arms back, holding him with iron-strong hands.

Krey kicked. The man in front of him blocked the kick with his own foot. In the scuffle, his hand fell off Krey's face. Krey gulped in air as both men laughed. He tried to pull his arms free, but the man's grip was too tight.

The first man approached again, placing his face so close to Krey's, their noses almost touched. "Your friend doesn't want to see you. Neither do we." He grabbed Krey's mouth and nose again. "Next time, I won't let go." After squeezing Krey's cheeks hard, he let go and stepped off the porch, giving a little nod to the man holding Krey.

A foot connected with the back of Krey's knees, and as he fell to the porch, the man finally released his arms. Then a boot pressed against the back of Krey's neck, and the man growled, "Get outta here!"

As soon as the second man stepped off the porch, Krey leapt to his feet and sprinted away.

IN THE DARK: 2

"Do you know what I look like?" Zeisha whispered. She was sitting on her pallet in the dark room, swathed in blankets. Isla was in the same position, facing Zeisha. They'd pressed their knees together, and they were gripping each other's hands. It was a cold night, and their covers didn't provide enough warmth.

Isla was so close that her breath warmed Zeisha's face. "When I dream about the daytime, you're in those dreams. But then I wake up, and I only remember a little bit. I think you're short, like me." Isla's voice held a smile. "But . . . curvier?"

Zeisha laughed softly. "Yeah, I do have curves. Your hair is straight, right? And long?"

"Right. And yours—is it curly?"

"Yes."

In the long silence that followed, Zeisha wondered if Isla had fallen asleep sitting up. They wanted to stay awake at night, the one time their minds were clear, but their little-remembered daytime activities exhausted them. She squeezed Isla's hand gently. Isla responded by drawing her into a tight hug.

Zeisha swallowed against rising emotion. Every night, she craved the touch of people she loved. Her parents, her brothers, Krey. *Oh, Krey. Please come find me.*

Isla's body started shaking. When Zeisha realized her friend was crying, a loud sob burst from her own mouth.

A door creaked open. A bored, female voice commanded, "Back to sleep."

One night, they'd defied that voice, continuing their conversation. The woman had walked through the room, waking others by stepping on them. When she'd found Zeisha and Isla, she'd hit them both in the mouth, hard enough to make them scream. Since then, everyone slept when the woman came, or at least pretended to.

Zeisha and Isla stifled their weeping, but they didn't let go of each other.

6

When I was growing up, all my clothing was scavenged from closets of dead children. Sometimes when I got dressed, I closed my eyes and imagined the life of the girl who first wore my clothes. Other days, I imagined her death.

-The First Generation: A Memoir *by Liri Abrios*

NORA STOOD in her icehouse over an open chest, holding a handful of cold, magical fuel in front of her mouth.

She couldn't bring herself to eat it.

"Damn it, Krey West!" She threw the ice back into the chest and shoved the lid down.

The last time she'd lysted was twelve days earlier, onstage in Tirra. She was yearning to use her faculty. She could almost taste the ice, feel the snow shooting from her hands and mouth.

Krey's words, however, kept returning to her: *Your ice melts while poverty-stricken frost eaters in Cellerin City set out cups of water at night, praying for a freeze.*

She'd always known she didn't do anything to deserve all her luxuries, like year-round ice. But she also didn't deserve to have her career—her whole life, really—decided for her. It all evened out . . . right?

Nora pictured a poor frost eater parting with money he'd saved for months, exchanging it for a treasured block of ice. Such a man would give anything to have ice waiting for him in an insulated chest, and he'd laugh at her for whining about royal life. Nora let out a long sigh and walked from the icehouse into her bedroom.

She went to her closet, and Krey's words continued running through her head as she changed from her pajamas into a silky shirt and comfortable trousers, both tailored to fit her body. Next, she moved to her bathroom to do her makeup. A few minutes into her routine, an idea broke through her sobering, guilty thoughts. Her mouth widened into a smile that she had trouble taming when it was time for lipstick.

Skipping eye makeup, she threw on a pair of walking shoes and a jacket and left her rooms. She grabbed a hand pie from the kitchen for breakfast, then strode through the short hallway connecting the residence to the palace itself, greeting the guards at either end. By the time she reached her intended destination at the west side of the palace, she'd finished the pie, enjoying every bite of flaky pastry, soft vegetables, and spicy sausage.

Nora entered an office labeled *Ministry of Lysting* and approached the receptionist. "Hi."

The receptionist's only greeting was a pair of wide eyes and a mouth that dropped open under his neat mustache. Nora didn't usually visit this wing of the palace.

She smiled. "I'd like to talk to Minister Sharai, please."

The receptionist nodded and gestured to the door behind his desk.

"Thanks." Nora knocked on the minister's door.

"Come in."

She opened the door. "Is this a good time?"

Minister Sharai's eyebrows rose, but she recovered more quickly than her receptionist. "Of course, Your Highness. Have a seat."

Nora sat. "I'd like to chat about my icehouse."

The minister removed her reading glasses. "Do you need more catalyst than we're providing?"

Nora smiled. Most people called it *fuel*, but leave it to the Minister of Lysting to use the most formal term possible. "I have plenty, but I'd like to change how we do things. Every week before the ice delivery, I want someone to retrieve what I haven't used, then give it to ice lysters in Cellerin City."

The minister's brows rose even farther. "What a generous idea."

"I hate to see it go to waste."

"It will take some organizing, and funding, of course."

Nora grinned. "I know you'll be able to work out the details. I'd be happy to talk to my father if you need more funding."

"Very well. We'll make it happen."

"Great! I do have one more request. There's a new ice lyster living in the dorms named Krey West. Please send a medium-sized chest of chipped ice to his quarters every week."

Minister Sharai wrote the name down. "Krey West, very well. I'll add it to the order."

Nora thanked her and left the office, feeling lighter than she had all day. She had a niggling sense Krey wouldn't be satisfied with her gestures of goodwill. Then again, Krey probably wouldn't be satisfied with anything she did. She'd done what she could. Maybe later, she could do more.

She walked to the stables, where a groom had saddled Blue, just as Nora had requested the night before. She thanked the groom, greeted Blue with a snuggle, and mounted. Then she rode around the grounds, soaking up the sun and enjoying every minute of her meandering journey.

Nora stopped on the northwest side of the pond to let Blue grab a few bites of grass. In the distance, a guard exited the guardhouse and opened the gate. Someone dashed inside, running like he was fleeing a monster.

Is that—? Yes, his skin was a redder tone than usual, but she recognized Krey's shaggy, black hair. He ran northeast past the pond, then entered the garden.

Considering the tone of all their previous encounters, Nora had been brainstorming how she could get past Krey West's baffling grudge against her. She'd like to think he'd appreciate the ice she was sending to his room, but she doubted it. Another idea struck, and she turned Blue toward the residence, patting his rump. His legs broke into a smooth, loping run.

At the residence, Nora looped Blue's reins around a hitching post. She ran in the front door and asked the nearest member of the household staff to take Blue back to the stable. Next, she dashed to the kitchen.

She let out a victorious "Yes!" when she found a jug in the icebox labeled *BOLLAGRAPE JUICE*, with a little smiley face drawn next to the words. She'd asked the chef the previous afternoon to make the concoction she'd tried in Tirra. How he'd managed it so quickly was a mystery. She made a mental note to hug him for it.

Nora poured the juice into two mugs and took a sip from one, sighing with contentment. Then she carried the drinks through the house, outside, and to the garden, hoping Krey was still there.

She found him sitting on a bench, staring into the distance, his lips pressed into a tight line. When he heard her, he stood. "I know I'm probably not supposed to be here. I was cooling off. I'll go—"

"Have a seat, Krey. I saw you run in. I figured you were thirsty." Nora held out a mug.

His eyebrows drew together, and his eyes flicked down to the mug, then back up to her face. "I go for runs all the time. I don't need a drink."

She thrust the mug at him, and some juice sloshed out. "It's bolla-grape juice, not poison. Just take it!"

He grabbed the cup and downed it in one, long drink. "Thanks."

"Have a seat."

He did, and Nora sat next to him. The bench was small, and when her leg brushed his, he tensed.

She finished her own juice, then asked, "Did it taste like home?"

He gave a curt nod.

"I'll take your mug."

Krey handed it over, and she placed it on the bench next to hers. She'd hoped to tell him about her visit to the Ministry of Lysting, then convince him to practice magic with her. It didn't seem like a good time, though. What was going on behind those brooding eyes?

He turned his head toward her and stood. "I'm going back to my room."

"Wait!" She offered him a hesitant smile. "Can you sit—just for a minute? Please?"

He narrowed his eyes and furrowed his forehead, but complied.

"Are you okay?" Nora asked.

"Yes."

Definitely a lie. "Can you tell me what's wrong?"

"No."

His eyes were off somewhere in the distance again, and Nora studied him. What was that word she'd used for him the night they met? *Striking.* That was it. And it fit. His nose was a little big, his skin marked with a few scars from acne or a childhood illness. But his eyes were nice, jawline strong, hair thick. And the smile he was so hesitant to let her see? It was his best feature. Despite her assurances to herself that all she wanted from him was friendship and a little tutoring, she couldn't help thinking he was pretty cute. Maybe once he got over whatever his issues were with her . . .

Nora gave her head a little shake. *This is not the time for flirting.* Hadn't she learned anything from her mistake with Ovrun? Besides, Krey was upset. He probably needed a friend as much as she did, even if he wouldn't admit it. She swallowed. "I'm not sure what's going on, but it'll be all right."

His entire body swiveled to face her, his knees knocking against hers. This time, he didn't seem to notice the contact. "You have no way of knowing that," he said in a low, choked voice.

There were tears in his eyes. Anger too, but for once, he wasn't directing it at her. "Oh, by the sky, Krey. Whatever's going on, I'm sorry."

He blinked, and one shoulder lifted in a slight shrug. He looked so vulnerable. Only one thing came to mind that was sure to comfort him. Without giving herself time to reconsider the impulse, Nora leaned in and kissed him.

Her lips contacted his for a fraction of a second before he jerked his head back and stood up, nearly sending Nora tumbling off the back of the bench. "What the hell was that?" he demanded.

She looked up at him, her eyes wide, cheeks flaming. What was wrong with her? How had she gone from *not the time for flirting*, to throwing herself at Krey?

One of his arms swung up, pointing south, toward the gate. "What would Ovrun think if he knew you'd just tried to kiss me?"

Nora's mouth dropped open. *He knows about Ovrun?* In an instant, her single, brief tryst with her favorite guard rushed back into her mind, flooding her cheeks with heat. That night had been nothing short of divine. For one hour, Nora had forgotten that her entire future was already laid out for her. She'd felt truly free. Ovrun was a sweet, hot, perfect distraction from real life.

Then Ovrun had stopped kissing and started talking, and his adoring words made his stance clear: Nora was more than a diversion to him. His feelings for her ran deep. Too deep. Those perfect kisses had been a mistake.

Now this smartass apprentice was throwing that mistake in Nora's face. Avoiding Krey's gaze, she forced a denial through her tight throat. "There's nothing between me and Ovrun."

"Well, he certainly thinks there is."

Nora brought her hands up to cover her face and spoke into her palms. "Please, just sit down, Krey; I swear by the stone, I won't ever try to touch you again."

Krey didn't sit, but he didn't leave, either. Instead, he planted his feet in front of Nora.

She looked up, peeking through her fingers. Krey had folded his arms and was staring down, fire in his eyes. How had she managed to mess this up so badly?

"I—" Nora brought her hands down, forcing herself to lift her chin and meet Krey's gaze. "I regret giving Ovrun the impression I wanted a relationship with him. We . . . I thought we were just having fun."

That was sort of true. What Nora would never confess to Krey was that she liked Ovrun. A lot. But whoever she eventually married would rule alongside her. Her father had to approve the match, just like his parents had approved his marriage. In fact, Nora's parents had barely known each other when they'd gotten married. Her dad insisted his daughter would make her marriage work, just like he and her mother had.

Nora wasn't so sure. There was no getting around the strictures, though. She couldn't indulge in romance like other teenagers could. At least not with a royal guard who wasn't a lyster and knew very little about running a kingdom.

At first, Nora had assumed all Ovrun was looking for was an occasional tryst with the princess. They could probably hide a few midnight kisses. Then he'd opened up to her, and she'd realized he wanted the same thing she did: a real relationship. There was no way they could conceal that, and her dad would never approve. Not wanting to lead Ovrun on, Nora had forced herself to stay away from him.

With a start, she realized Krey was still watching her, one eyebrow raised. "So you kissed Ovrun to have a little fun," he said. "Is that what you were doing with me too?"

How was she supposed to answer that? *I acted without thinking, and it got me into trouble. As usual.* She shoved her hair behind her ears and murmured, "You just—you looked so sad. I wanted you to feel better."

Krey's mouth broke into a disbelieving smile. Laughter streamed out of him, and he sat next to her again, shaking his head.

"I wasn't trying to be funny!" Nora said.

That made Krey laugh harder. At last, he calmed and met her gaze. One more chuckle escaped his grinning mouth. "Sorry, I'm not trying to laugh at you. But—I just don't get—" He halted, then brought his fist to his mouth, tapping his lips lightly with his thumb and examining her.

"What?"

He dropped his hand. "Have you ever been around people your age?"

Faylie's sharp nose, high cheekbones, and long, straight hair flashed in Nora's mind. Her closest friendship, and she'd botched it. Just like she'd done with Ovrun, and now with Krey. She swallowed and shook her head. "Not . . . much."

"Well, consider me your tutor in how to be a teenager. Lesson One: Kissing. It's fun, don't get me wrong, but if you kiss a guy, he's gonna think it means something. Especially when you're a princess. Poor Ovrun is sitting in that guardhouse every day, dreaming of going to royal balls with you."

She stared at him. Nobody talked to her like this. She couldn't decide if it was refreshing or offensive.

He kept going. "And I can't believe I even have to tell you this, but you can't go around giving people consolation kisses. There are better ways to help someone in their time of need."

She wet her lips, though her tongue itself seemed dry. "Sorry. I just—you're right; I have absolutely no idea how to act around guys my age. I just thought you might like it."

Every trace of amusement left Krey's eyes. "And maybe I would've, if the source of my troubles wasn't my missing girlfriend."

Nora stared at him. "Your missing girlfriend?"

He released a loud sigh and turned to face the garden again.

"Krey—" Nora reached out a hand, then drew it back, remembering her promise to never touch him again. "Whatever's going on, I might be able to help."

He kept his gaze locked on the hedge across the path. "Thanks, but it's my problem."

It was her turn to sigh. "Don't be a martyr. You need help, and I'm bored out of my mind. Come on, bring some adventure to my life." She was smiling by the end of her statement, but she meant every word of it.

He turned back to her and narrowed his eyes. "Why did you invite me to work at the palace?"

She blinked at the sudden change in subject, then sighed. "I wanted you to teach me to do what you do with ice. The masters I work with are dull as table knives, and ever since I saw you slide down that ramp you made, I've wanted to know how to do it too."

He gave her the same incredulous smile as before. "Seriously?"

"Yeah. But based on how you've been acting, I figured you'd never willingly help me. I decided to kiss you so at least I'd get some benefit from your presence."

His eyes widened.

"That was a joke," she said with a smile. Then she sobered. "I told you my reason for inviting you here. It's your turn. Why'd you come here? I'm guessing it has to do with your girlfriend?"

He stared at her for a few seconds before giving her a small nod, like he'd made a decision. "Her name is Zeisha."

He told her about Zeisha's recruitment as an apprentice. That part wasn't too concerning. Then he told her about his experience in Cellerin City. The bald man in the little house sounded just plain odd, and Nora gasped when Krey described the brutes who'd threatened to kill him. When he finished, he let out a shuddering breath, clearly still shaken.

"Wow." Nora mulled it over. Krey had probably just encountered two overzealous guards who'd been instructed to keep some high-level apprentices safe. But he didn't deserve to be threatened, and he needed answers. The poor guy was out of his mind with worry. She laid a hand on his shoulder, not caring anymore about her impetuous promise. "I'll talk to my father today. We'll get to the bottom of this."

Krey shrugged off her hand. He crossed his arms and shook his head hard. "I don't want to get your father involved. Bureaucracy ruins everything. Besides, the government is obviously behind this."

Nora repressed an eyeroll. "If there's a government conspiracy—something I doubt, by the way—my father will bring a stop to it. At the very least, he'll figure out why those guards thought it was okay to threaten you." Seeing Krey's exasperated expression, she pushed forward, her voice turning shrill. "I'm offering to ask the king of Cellerin to help you. You're seriously turning that down?"

He unfolded his arms, swinging his hands wide and matching her elevated volume. "When you mentioned helping me, I thought you meant doing something useful, like breaking into some secret records room to look for information on Zeisha."

"The only place I know of where they keep files is the records hall, and it's guarded! How would you expect me to break in?"

"I don't know, you could kiss the guard and ask real nice."

She gaped at him. "That was low."

"Sorry, but I'm trying to find the girl I've loved since I was ten years old, and you're offering to help me by having a conversation with your father. You really think he'll believe me? The teenager who interrupted a royal event and fell on his ass in the process?"

"You don't know him!"

"You're right. But I've had a lifetime of experience living in this kingdom, and none of it has given me reason to trust you people." He stood. "Thanks for the juice."

He took off at a jog, not glancing back.

7

The school only had a few textbooks. Before The Day, most books had gone digital. Scavengers were happy to sell us ancient, paper books, but they were very expensive.

Our teachers read their few books to us, and we repeated the words as a class, one phrase at a time. Every once in a while, I got to hold a book and caress its pages with my hands and eyes. Those were some of my favorite days.

-The First Generation: A Memoir *by Liri Abrios*

AFTER DROPPING off the mugs in the kitchen, Nora returned to the main palace building and took the stairs to the second floor. "You can go in," her father's receptionist said.

Nora knocked, then opened the door. "It's me, Dad."

"Hey, sweetie, come on in."

She entered. Her father's office extended half the width of the building and included a large conference table and several windows overlooking the grounds. He had a desk, but he wasn't behind it. Instead, he was seated in his favorite overstuffed chair, feet on an ottoman, reading from a thick sheaf of papers.

Nora sat in the chair next to his. He put the papers on a small table, took off his reading glasses, and ran a hand through his gray-streaked hair. "The Prime Minister of Cruine is already planning her spring visit, and she wants to renegotiate our entire trade agreement. But you didn't come here to talk about that. Please, distract me from politics!"

Nora grinned. "Gladly. I just had a conversation with Krey West. He needs our help."

Her father lifted his feet off the ottoman, then leaned forward and propped his elbows on his knees. "Tell me more."

As Nora related Krey's story, her father's gaze never left hers. At several points, his eyes widened, but he didn't interrupt once. "I think this Zeisha girl is probably just an apprentice who's enjoying being away from home," Nora said, "but we should do something about the guards who threatened Krey. And I think it would be nice if we could get him some information about his girlfriend."

Her father nodded thoughtfully, then stood. "I'll be right back." A moment later, Nora heard him speaking to his receptionist. He returned and sat in his chair.

"Krey West is an impressive young man," the king said, "and if he's distracted by these concerns, we should try to help him."

"I knew you'd say that. Where do we start?"

Her father held out both hands in a familiar gesture of caution. "I didn't choose my words wisely. When I said *we*, I didn't mean you'd be involved."

"Dad, I want to help him! I have a lot more time to devote to this than you do."

"That's true. But you just told me he was attacked today. I'm not letting you get involved in that. And while I don't have time to look into this personally, I know who does." His gaze shifted, focusing behind Nora. "Dani, come in."

Nora turned to see her Aunt Dani entering the room. Her long, black, wavy hair was pulled into a low bun, and her full lips were smiling. She sat next to Nora.

"Nora just told me about a young man who needs our help," Nora's father said. "I'd like you to take the lead on this. She can give you all the details."

"Of course."

Nora returned her aunt's smile. "Thank you." It was just like Aunt Dani to commit without knowing what she was agreeing to. When Nora's mom had died ten years earlier, Dani had moved to the palace. In the early months after the tragedy, Nora had cried in her aunt's arms every day. Dani was grieving her own loss—the queen had been her only sister—but she'd always had time to comfort her niece. Dani had a bedroom near Nora's and an office near Ulmin's. The one thing she didn't have was a title. It would've been difficult to fit *Household Administrator, Advisor to the King, and Emotional Supporter to the Princess* on a nameplate.

The king cleared his throat. "I'm afraid I need to prepare for my trip. Tomorrow I leave for more negotiations with the New Therroans."

Nora stood and kissed him on the cheek. "Thanks for your help, Dad." She turned to her aunt. "Can we go to your office so I can give you all the details?"

Krey ran from Cellerin City back toward the palace. That morning, Ovrun had offered to loan him a push scooter, but Krey preferred running.

His first apprenticeship class hadn't gone well. The teacher, an old feather eater, had droned on and on about various catalysis hypotheses. Then he'd asked his few pupils to give their own input.

Krey hated such pointless discussions. Even supposed experts had no idea how magic worked. If Krey ate a meal of feathers and bread, both things landed in his stomach. How did his body turn his fuel into magic and his food into physical energy? Nobody could answer that question or any of the countless others he liked to ask. Why did magic eaters first display their talents around five years old? Why did they crave their fuel for years before that?

All the uncertainty tortured Krey. The technology needed to answer such questions had once existed. But the same stone that gave Krey magic had killed most of the world's scientists and returned Anyari to a pre-technological era. The universe could be maddeningly ironic sometimes.

As soon as Krey had discovered his talents, he'd started attending a weekly magical training course in Tirra, like all young magic eaters did. Within three years, he got fed up with the lack of answers to his questions. He convinced his parents to let him quit the course, promising to read books on magic instead. He usually chose practical tomes over theoretical ones. If he couldn't discover how his body turned feathers and ice into magic, at least he could learn to use his talents more efficiently.

This morning, he hadn't even tried to hide his lack of enthusiasm for his master's theoretical ponderings. The man hadn't appreciated his new pupil's attitude. Krey would have to behave better. If he got kicked out of the apprenticeship program, he couldn't stay in Cellerin City. And he had to stay if he wanted information on Zeisha.

After grabbing two sandwiches from the dorm's kitchen and eating them in his room, Krey walked down the hall to the bathroom. A hot shower washed away the last bits of frustration the run hadn't taken care of.

This was the first place Krey had ever lived that had hot, running water. According to Ovrun, ash eaters (or *fire lysters*, as people around here called them) worked in the basement under the palace, heating water in boilers. The water was used not only for showers and sinks, but also in pipes that warmed every room in the offices and residence. Krey wished heated air could be pumped into his dorm too, but with hot water available at a twist of the tap, it was hard to complain.

When he was done, he walked to the palace's rear entrance, where a guard waited. Krey greeted him and held out the medallion he'd been given. It was stamped with numbers that indicated where he could go on the palace grounds. The guard opened the door, and Krey walked down a set of stairs that led straight into the basement library.

The room was huge; Krey guessed it took up a quarter of the space underneath the palace's main building. He stepped past the empty reception area and stood between two rows of tall shelves, savoring the scent of paper and leather. Working afternoons in this place just might make up for his pointless morning classes.

A librarian approached and set him to work shelving books. The task gave Krey time to think about Aunt Min and Aunt Evie. He'd written a letter to them, but they wouldn't have received it yet. What if one of them got hurt or sick? It would be weeks before he got word of it.

Krey knew it was pointless to worry about such things, but after what had happened to his parents, dread colored all his relationships. When everything seemed to be going well, life tended to change for the worse. Zeisha's disappearance had confirmed that.

He picked up another stack of books. As he shelved them, he yawned. He'd had multiple nightmares last night, all centering on his attack in the city. Even now, his heart raced as he recalled that strong hand covering his mouth and nose.

Shaking his head, he distracted himself by remembering his conversation with Nora. He chuckled under his breath at her odd combination of brash action—trying to kiss a guy she barely knew who, let's face it, hadn't treated her that well—and innocence. Did she really not understand that flirting with the palace staff would cause more trouble than it was worth?

Krey was convinced that her impulsive kiss was motivated by

more than her strange combination of privilege and naiveté. Nora spent almost all her time on the palace grounds, around adults she had little in common with. She must be terribly lonely. In her shoes, he'd probably be making out with fence posts.

By the stone, do I actually feel sorry for her?

"Krey?"

Hearing the low voice, he turned from the shelf he was facing. His pace had slowed as he ruminated, and he figured the librarian had arrived to remind him to stay on task.

Instead, he saw Nora. His eyebrows leapt up.

"Sorry, I didn't mean to scare you," she said, her voice barely above a whisper.

He matched her tone. "It's fine, I was just—it's fine." He couldn't exactly tell her she'd caught him thinking about her.

She looked down at the cart and picked up a thin volume. "*Of Streets and Stars!* I've been waiting for this book to be returned! One of the staff had it for at least a month."

"You let staff check out books?"

"Of course. You can too. All the preday books have to stay in the library though." She gestured to one of the library's far corners, and he yearned to go check out the ancient books there. "We even have the original, handwritten version of Liri's memoir," she said.

"*The First Generation?* You have the original?"

Nora grinned. "Of course. Liri's my direct ancestor. Eleven generations back."

He shook his head. "I'd love to see that book."

"I'll show you sometime, when you're off duty." She lifted the book she'd picked up. "Have you read this one yet?"

"I haven't even heard of it."

"Really? It's very popular."

"I tend to read the classics."

"Oh—you'll have to tell me your favorites sometime."

He offered her a noncommittal nod. *Yep. Lonely.*

Nora tucked the book under her arm. "I came to give you an

update. My father asked my Aunt Dani to find information on Zeisha." She grinned, like she expected him to bow in humble gratitude.

"I know; she sent me a note last night requesting Zeisha's full name and the address I visited."

"Oh—right. She's very detail oriented, so she's the perfect person to help. In fact, she already sent two guards to that address. Nobody was home."

"Okay." He doubted Nora's aunt had sent anyone; she probably just wanted to get her gullible niece off her back.

"They'll try again in a day or two. Plus, Dani found out we do have a small, elite apprenticeship program that sends recruiters around the country. But we know you want to be sure that's where Zeisha is, so Dani put in a records request to confirm it."

"How long will that take?"

"Anywhere from ten days to three weeks."

"Three *weeks?*"

Nora held a finger to her lips.

Krey brought his voice down to a harsh whisper. "Your aunt's part of the royal family; can't she get information faster?"

"I asked her the same thing. But we have to go through the queue like everybody else. How would it look if we took advantage of the system?"

"Just like I said," he murmured. "Bureaucracy." He picked up another stack of books and turned back to the shelf.

"Uh . . . I'll keep you posted."

Nora stood there for at least a minute. He ignored her, then heard her walk away.

He shook his head. *Three weeks. Like I'm gonna stand for that.*

8

From my bedroom, I could see the little chapel that held the stone. Sometimes my friends asked, "Isn't it scary living so close to that thing?" I pretended it wasn't a big deal.

But when the chapel was closed to the public, I often stood before the broken stone, in awe of its power. Sometimes I even talked to it. I don't remember my words, but they were always variations on two questions: How? Why?

-The First Generation: A Memoir *by Liri Abrios*

AFTER DINNER in the dorm with a few other residents, Krey walked to the chapel.

The back door was painted black, and a silver Rimstar hung on it. Krey ran his fingers along the shape, tracing its eight points and the teardrop-shaped loops at the end of each one. It was the primary symbol of the Rimorian faith. Krey and his Aunt Evie attended a service at the chapel in Tirra every Sunday, and touching the cold, metal star made Krey feel a little more at home.

He knocked lightly. The woman who answered the door wore emissary vestments: tunic, slacks, and a long scarf, all in gray. Narrow bands of blue and black, Cellerin's royal colors, ran along the scarf's long edges. "May I help you?" she asked with a smile.

"I work at the palace, and I was told I could worship in the chapel."

"Of course. Come in."

He followed her into a hallway, brightly lit with several electric bulbs. She opened a door near the end of the hall. Krey's eyes took in the little chapel that attracted hundreds of visitors a week. The door opened onto a tiny stage, in front of which sat twenty chairs. In the middle of the stage was a large, stone pedestal. Atop it, enclosed in a thick, glass case, sat the stone itself. The cause of Anyari's apocalypse.

"I'm sure I don't need to tell you this," the emissary said, "but please don't touch the case. If it moves even a little, an alarm will sound. We can't risk anyone touching the stone. I know of two people who've handled it without gloves, and both died within a day."

"Of course."

"I'll lock up for the night at eight. And you're welcome to join us for a service every Sunday morning at ten."

"How do you decide who gets seats?"

"Sunday services are only for those who live on the palace grounds. The attendance is quite small."

A religious service only for the elite? Krey tried to keep the scowl off his face.

The emissary left, and Krey slowly approached the stone. It was broken into several irregularly shaped pieces. They were shiny and black, like highly polished obsidian.

The pieces were arranged to show how they'd originally fit

together, with several simmets of space in between each one. A layer of iridescent, orange material covered every broken face. The stone had cracked along those shimmering veins.

Much of the stone's history was unknown. Then again, the same could be said for humanity's history. Historians did, however, agree on the basic facts: over six thousand years ago, colonists had traveled to Anyari from Earth, humanity's home world.

Hundreds of people had landed on Anyari, but surely thousands had begun the journey. Apparently something had killed most of them along the way, also destroying the technology and records they'd brought with them. The only supplies the survivors salvaged were seeds from Earth.

The small group of colonists established a home on Anyari. Before leaving Earth, their DNA had been modified so they could eat Anyarian plants and animals. And genetic enhancement wasn't their only asset. They also benefited from the guidance of seers, mysterious individuals whose prophecies helped their growing population. Over millennia, Anyarians developed advanced technology. They lessened or eradicated war, hunger, and many diseases.

Then, two hundred years ago, preday archeologists had pulled a mysterious stone out of a cave. It broke apart, spreading orange light over all of Anyari, killing billions of humans and bringing magic into the world.

Everyone knew that story, but knowing *what* happened was different than knowing *how* it happened. Supposedly the stone had emitted some sort of radiation, but no one understood how radiation could cover an entire planet, much less create magic. Krey wondered if they'd ever have answers.

Some people claimed this very black-and-orange stone had also caused the tragedy on the colonists' ship, when it penetrated through the vessel's shields and hull. Nora's ancestors, who were some of The Day's well-known survivors, had defended that hypothesis. As Krey gazed at the deep, black pieces, with their orange edges that matched the sky, he could see why people believed the old story. It made sense that the otherworldly stone which had killed most of Anyari's humans two centuries ago had also decimated the colonists six millennia before.

Krey pulled his gaze away from the stone. As fascinating as it was, he had bigger problems than the unknowable history of a magical artifact. He sat in a chair in the front row, rested his elbows on his knees, and buried his face in his hands.

His prayer was silent and simple. *God, bring me to Zeisha, or bring her to me. May it be.*

"Fancy meeting you here." Krey grinned at Ovrun, who stood in a corridor in front of the records hall door.

"Any problems getting in?" Ovrun whispered.

"I told the guard at the back door I couldn't sleep and wanted to read in the library. Once I was in, I didn't have any trouble getting to the second floor."

"Good. Be quick and quiet in there, okay? I'd like to keep my job."

"I owe you."

"Big time." Ovrun looked both directions down the deserted hall, pulled a key out of his pocket, and opened the door. "Someone's coming to give me a break at two, and before I leave, he'll walk through the records hall. It's policy. So make sure you're out by quarter 'til, in case he's early."

"You bet." Krey slipped inside. Before pulling the door closed, he looked back and whispered, "You know how important this is to me. Thanks for helping."

As Krey had sat in the chapel on Monday night, an idea had struck him. He wasn't about to claim the plan came from God himself, but it did seem like a good one. He'd immediately left to find Ovrun.

He asked his friend to volunteer for night shifts guarding the records room—and to sneak Krey in. Ovrun was, understandably, hesitant. If he got caught, he'd be fired from a job he loved.

Krey hated putting Ovrun in such a position, but he hadn't been able to think of another way to get information on Zeisha. Seeing his friend's desperation, Ovrun had agreed to help.

Ovrun's first shift in this hallway had been on Thursday night, but that was Cygni 31st, the last day of the year. There were all-night celebrations on the palace grounds, and every guard post had double coverage. The two conspirators couldn't have gotten away with anything on such a night. Now it was early Sunday morning, Centa 3rd, and Ovrun was standing guard alone.

Krey turned on the light. The large room's wooden shelves were loaded with narrow file boxes. It looked like the dullest library known to man. He quickly navigated to a shelf labeled *APPRENTICESHIPS*.

The file boxes were numbered. Krey turned and walked along the room's perimeter, searching for a catalog that would tell him what the numbers stood for. At the back of the room, he found three doors. The first had a sign reading *ADMIN*. It was locked.

He moved on to the next door, labeled *SORTING*. It was unlocked. He turned on the light and found multiple tables, all covered with trays, many of which had papers in them.

Krey entered the third room, which was labeled *MAIL*. Crates of unopened letters sat on a table. Two additional tables held sorted mail. This wasn't what he needed.

He jogged to the front of the room and cracked the door open. "Hey, I need your key."

"Why?"

"For the admin room. I need a catalog to help me figure out this filing system."

"Sorry, man, only the filing director has the key to that room."

Krey sighed, closed the door, and returned to the shelves holding apprenticeships files. He pulled out box after box and at last found what he was seeking: lists of apprentices, filed by the years in which they'd begun their training.

He took the box to a desk at the front of the room and glanced at the clock on the wall. 1:30. He groaned. It didn't feel like he'd been here for an hour.

Krey frantically pulled papers out of the box. His knee bobbed up and down. At the back was a page labeled *CYON 200 PD*. That was the month Zeisha had been taken. She would've arrived in Cellerin City a week or two later.

The list was short. Just ten names. Krey read it four times. Zeisha wasn't there.

He brought his fist down on the table. "Damn it!" The exclamation must've been louder than he realized, because a warning knock sounded from the door.

Maybe she didn't get to Cellerin City until the next month. Krey looked for the page with records from the month of Cygni. It wasn't there. They probably hadn't filed it yet. He shoved the papers back in the box and replaced it on the shelf.

He ran to the sorting room, again opening the door and turning on the light. It didn't take long to find an overflowing tray labeled *APPRENTICESHIPS*. A list labeled *CYGNI 200 PD* was near the top. Zeisha's name wasn't on it. Krey looked through the other documents but found no mention of her.

Cursing under his breath, he looked through trays of financial statements, bills and receipts, documents related to public works projects, and more. With every pointless paper he perused, his ire grew.

He looked up at the clock. 1:50. *Ovrun's gonna kill me!* He left the sorting room but couldn't bring himself to go to the hallway just yet.

Instead, he entered the mail room. He didn't have time to look through the full crates of mail, so he ignored them. He moved past them to a table full of trays labeled with the names of minor officials.

They contained sealed envelopes. On the third table was a stack of unopened envelopes. Next to it were more trays, these labeled with the names of the king and his ministers. The letters in the trays were open. Krey stared, brows knitted together. Why had someone opened this mail?

Then it hit him. The government bigwigs didn't have time to go through every piece of mail. Even their assistants didn't want to read all the pointless letters people sent them. So underlings filtered the mail before it ever went to the offices.

Krey sifted through the king's letters but found nothing interesting. He scanned the rest of the trays. *What next?*

Something on the floor caught his eye. A trash can, overflowing with paper. He knelt before it. More letters, all addressed to the people whose names were on the trays. *What sorts of letters do they consider unimportant?*

He dumped out the papers and looked through them. Much of it was fan mail, gushing and sickeningly sweet. Then Krey picked up a page, and a word caught his eye: *apprenticeship.* He began reading.

Dear Minister Sharai,

I pray you can help me.

My son, a soil lyster, was recruited into the apprenticeship program four months ago. We've received two letters from him, but they were very short, and he's asked us not to visit him.

I worry that he may be struggling in his new position. Would it be possible for you to check on him for me? May I visit, despite his request?

The letter went on, but Krey stopped reading. *This is where the letters I sent about Zeisha ended up.* Hot rage bubbled in his chest, and he wanted to throw the trash can across the room. Instead, he sifted through the crumpled pages even more frantically, looking for similar correspondence. He struck gold with another letter, this one addressed to King Ulmin. It was from a father who was convinced someone had kidnapped his ash-eating daughter.

Krey folded the two letters in fourths, pulled his shirt tail out, and shoved the pages into the waistband of his pants. He glanced at the clock. 1:59.

He drew in a sharp breath. *Letters back in the trash. Lights off. Close the door. RUN.* At the front of the room, he turned off the light, panting. He reached out for the door, but it opened before he could grab the handle.

Ovrun was standing there, eyes wide, face red. "You gotta get out of here! Someone will be here—" He halted, glancing down the hallway. A low curse exited his mouth. "He's coming. He can see that I'm talking to someone."

Krey gaped at his friend. The open door blocked his view of the approaching guard—and the guard's view of him. Spurred on by an urgent impulse, he pulled the letters from his waistband. "Shove these in your shirt and arrest me."

"What?"

"Just do it. Get the papers to Nora."

Ovrun didn't argue. He took a step toward Krey, moving himself out of the line of sight of the other guard. Then he undid the two buttons of his black shirt and slipped the folded papers into the space.

A voice reached Krey's ears: "What's going on?"

"Turn around!" Ovrun shouted.

Krey obeyed.

"Sorry, man," Ovrun whispered. He grasped Krey's wrist and pulled him into the hallway. "Found this guy in the records room," he told the other guard.

The guard approached, eyebrows raised. "Want me to take him to the security office?"

"Nah, I got it." Ovrun marched his friend down the corridor.

"Button up your shirt!" the other guard called after Ovrun.

When they turned a corner, Krey whispered, "Any chance you can let me go?"

"Not without losing my job."

Krey sighed. "You better take me in."

IN THE DARK: 3

"Zeisha. Wake up."

"Hmm?"

"You need to count," Isla whispered.

"Okay." Zeisha didn't tell Isla that she'd already been awake.

They had an agreement: when one of them woke in the middle of the night, she roused the other one. With so many people tossing, turning, and snoring in such tight quarters, they were pretty sure one of them woke every night.

Tonight, Zeisha had wanted a few minutes alone to savor the dream she'd just had, of Krey soaring into this place and rescuing her.

She breathed deeply, trying to grasp the dream's details before they floated away. Krey had flown into a big room, where Zeisha, Isla, and the others were . . . *What were we doing? Where are we?*

"Everything okay?"

Zeisha's eyes snapped open at the sound of Isla's hushed voice. The images from her dream fled. She sighed. "I'm fine."

She took off her shoes and socks, then moved the string to the big toe of her left foot and slid her finger along her right ankle, counting the scars. "Eight weeks, five days," she said.

Once her socks and shoes were back on, she lay down and closed her eyes, praying for another good dream.

9

Our house had lightfilm panels in the ceiling, just like every preday building. At night, I used to hold a lantern up high, imagining what it would be like for soft, white light to glow in every room. No matches, no shadowy corners. Just pure light.

-The First Generation: A Memoir *by Liri Abrios*

A GENTLE KNOCK pulled Nora out of her dreams. Heart pounding, she turned on the light and walked into her sitting room. Someone had slipped two papers under her door. They were both letters. When she read them, she was instantly alert.

Despite Krey's concerns, Nora had remained convinced Zeisha was an apprentice in Cellerin City. The poor girl was probably avoiding her boyfriend because she was tired of his attitude.

These letters contradicted that narrative. They were from parents who were just as concerned about their children as Krey was about Zeisha. What was really going on with these apprenticeships?

Nora pursed her lips. She didn't know who'd delivered the letters. At first, she'd assumed it was Krey, but his medallion didn't allow him to enter the residence.

She read the letters again. Still stumped, she flipped them over. There, scrawled on the back of the second letter, was a message: *The new guy snuck into the records hall and got arrested. He's in the security office.*

Nora's eyes widened. Krey had gotten himself arrested? He was actually getting somewhere with his investigation. Now they'd send him home . . . or throw him in a cell for a few months to teach him a lesson.

I should let this go. Nora's father or Dani would advise her to let the immature Mr. West suffer his consequences. That would be the prudent route.

She tossed the letters on her bed. *By the sky, I hate being prudent.*

Krey West was rude, egotistical, and unpredictable. But his investigation had brought much-needed intrigue and excitement into Nora's life. She didn't want him to leave. Plus, she couldn't help but root for a lovesick fool who'd do anything to find his girlfriend.

Nora stared at the wall, searching for a solution. Only one idea presented itself. She folded up the letters, pulled off her pajamas, and ran to her closet to make herself presentable.

"You're telling me he broke into the records room on your orders?" The head of security stood behind the front desk of the palace security office, his thick eyebrows raised.

Nora glanced at the cell behind the desk. Krey was standing behind the bars, watching her, his forehead furrowed. Returning her attention to the head of security, Nora covered her mouth with her hands and set her face into a sheepish expression. "This is so embarrassing."

"Your Highness, you're gonna have to tell me the whole story."

She dropped her hands. "Okay—okay. Remember that groom we had a couple of years back? The tall one?"

He nodded.

"Well, he had a son. About my age. And, well . . ." She let out a nervous giggle. "We spent some time together, you know?"

The head of security smirked. "I remember."

"Oh!" And she thought she'd been so discreet. "Well, I've been thinking about him, wishing I could write him a letter. But my father won't tell me where he lives. I asked Krey to sneak into the records hall and find his address."

"Why would he risk his apprenticeship for you?"

She shrugged. "I promised him a chest of ice every week. He's an ice lyster, you know."

The head of security rolled his eyes. "You magic eaters. You'll do anything for fuel."

"Will you let him go?" She manufactured a shuddering breath and trembling chin. "I'd hate to be the one to ruin his life."

The man folded his thick arms. "If your friend there had actually taken records, I'd have to prosecute. You know that, right?"

She dropped her gaze to the floor and nodded.

"I suppose since he failed, and he was doing it on your behalf, I can be lenient. But if he gets in trouble again, I'm informing the king of what happened tonight. Including your role in it."

"Yes, sir. Thank you."

The head of security approached the cell and spoke to Krey in a low voice. Krey nodded earnestly, responding with "Yes, sir" and "I understand, sir." The big man unlocked the cell and ushered his prisoner out.

"You both better get to bed," the head of security said. "*In your own rooms.*"

"Yes, sir," they both said, before rushing out.

"Garden," Nora whispered.

Krey nodded once. They hurried past the palace and residence, the buildings' exterior lights illuminating their path. Nora led Krey to a far corner that was barely lit by a distant lamppost. They sat on a bench.

Krey immediately demanded, "Did Ovrun tell you I was arrested?"

"Somebody—I'm not sure who—slipped two letters under my door, along with a note. I read the letters, and—I hate to say this, but I think you may be right. I don't know where Zeisha and those others are, but something weird is going on."

Krey let out a harsh sigh. He fixed Nora with a stare. "Why'd you lie to get me out of that cell?"

Nora shrugged. "I guess I want to help you find Zeisha. If she loves someone as arrogant and rude as you, she must be pretty special." Immediately, she wished she could take back the words. *No wonder I don't have any friends.*

But Krey didn't get defensive. He laughed. "You're right about that."

Nora's mouth dropped open. She laughed too, then leaned in closer and said, "I have an idea."

The next night, Nora sat in her room. Everyone else was in bed. She was due to meet Krey in an hour.

Something was niggling at her, and she'd been trying to figure out what it was all day. She took a deep breath. Instead of her thoughts clearing, an image filled her mind: the letters Krey had stolen. Not wanting to alert anyone that she was awake, she lit a candle instead of turning on the overhead light. She pulled the letters from the unused journal she'd hidden them in. Was she missing something?

Reading through them, her eyes lit on a few words written by a worried father: *We've received two letters from him, but they were very short.* Krey had said something similar, that it seemed like someone else had written Zeisha's letters.

Nora drew in a sharp breath as her brain finally made the

connection it had been working on. She'd once gotten a short, confusing letter too. Well, more of a note than a letter. It was six months ago, and it was from her friend Faylie. Nora had burned it, but she could still remember every word.

Your Highness,
I no longer wish to be your friend.
Faylie Nett

The note had stunned Nora. She and Faylie had always agreed they were meant to be best friends. The ice lyster and the fire lyster. Opposites, yet a perfect match. They'd spent years whispering and giggling, sharing meals and dreams.

The cold words, written in stark, black ink, were so unlike Faylie. But the note was in her handwriting, so Nora hadn't questioned it. She figured she'd driven Faylie away and would never know why.

There had been two letters in the envelope. The second was to Dani, from Faylie's mother. She explained they were moving to the neighboring nation of Newland to join their relatives. She hadn't shared a forwarding address.

Like Zeisha, Faylie and her mother were talented lysters. What if they'd both been taken? It was a terrible possibility, but it came with its own sort of hope. *Maybe I didn't mess up our friendship after all.*

Nora mentally berated herself for the thought. Obviously it would be better for her former friend to be safe in Newland than to have been abducted. But she couldn't deny the possibility that Faylie and her mother might need rescuing. Just like Zeisha. Pacing in her bedroom, Nora promised herself, *We'll find the truth. Whatever it takes.*

A little less than an hour later, Nora tiptoed to the residential gate. She unlocked and opened it. Krey entered without a word. They hurried into the icehouse.

"Lock it, and turn on the light," Nora said.

He did.

Nora grinned. "You ready for this?"

"I still think I should go alone. I could skip all this covert stuff and walk out the front gate."

"You can't go alone," Nora said.

"Why not?"

Her theory about Faylie came out in a breathless monologue.

"Wow," he replied when she was done.

"Right? Your girlfriend, my best friend, and who-knows-how-many others, all together."

"Maybe," he said.

"Well, I know it's not a sure thing, but—"

"It seems like a big coincidence, you know? For both of them to be in the same place. And this story about your friend . . . it doesn't fit. Zeisha and the others, they're all young. They all told their families they're apprentices. Why would your friend's mom have disappeared too? And why would she say they were moving?"

Doubt seeped into Nora's excitement. "Well—I don't know."

"Sorry, I just don't want you to get your hopes up."

Nora swallowed. "It's fine, it was just a silly thought." She pulled her shoulders up in a shrug she hoped looked casual. She wasn't giving up on her old friend yet, but Krey didn't have to know that.

One thing was sure, they needed to get moving on tonight's goal. Nora pushed away thoughts of her old friend and knelt before a large chest. "How much should we eat?"

Krey joined her. "You've been trained by master magic eaters for over a decade, and you're asking me for advice?"

"They've never taught me to do anything like what you did in Tirra." Nora put a handful of ice chips in her mouth and began chewing. When Krey didn't follow suit, she looked up. He was staring at her with narrowed eyes, his forehead furrowed. "What?" she asked through her mouthful of ice.

"You getting me released last night—was that an excuse to get me to tutor you? Because you can skip the clandestine plans; I'll teach you what I know."

She swallowed her ice. "You will?"

"I suppose I owe you."

Nora rolled her eyes. "How kindhearted of you. But no, I didn't do this so you'd teach me to be a better lyster. Like I said last night, I want to help you." *And now that my friend might be involved, I want it even more.*

He nodded slowly. "Okay. We'll do this together."

"Great," Nora said. "How much of this should we eat?"

"When you're planning to do a lot of magic, you need to ingest as much fuel as possible. Then wait a few minutes, and eat even more. Gorge yourself."

"My masters always told me not to overdo it. It might make me sick. That's what my dad taught me too."

Krey smirked. "Nora, your father literally treats you like a pretty princess. Despite what he's told you, you can't overdose on fuel." He scooped up a huge handful of ice. "Eat up."

"We'll get cold eating that much ice." She pointed to the folded blanket on one of the chests. "You can wrap up in that one, and I'll get one from inside." Some people thought ice lysters were immune to feeling cold. Nora wished that were true. While the ice she and Krey created couldn't give them frostbite, the process of consuming fuel and creating ice would make them chilly.

He grabbed the blanket. "Thanks. Make sure you're quiet in there."

Once Nora was wrapped in a blanket she'd retrieved from her room, she sat next to Krey. They both ate until their stomachs were distended with ice. Nora lay back on the stone floor, her hand on her belly, groaning. "You sure we have to eat more?"

Krey, who was leaning back against the chest, burped. "Yeah. Give it a few minutes to settle."

"Okay." After a pause, Nora asked, "How'd you learn to lyst so well?"

"My aunts collect books. They're always on the lookout for rare books about magic eating. When I come across an idea I haven't heard of, I try it to see if it works for me."

"Are you close to your aunts?"

"They pretty much raised me."

Nora sat up and eyed him, but he was looking straight ahead. "What happened to your parents?"

His jaw tightened as he took a deep breath and released it. He pushed himself to his knees, turned, and opened the chest. "We can eat a little more now." When Nora didn't move, he turned to her, glowering. "We're in a hurry, you know."

They ate as much as they could, then left the icehouse and walked quietly to the perimeter fence at the edge of the garden. They saw a couple of caynins as they walked, but no guards.

"Okay," Krey whispered, "let's both turn our magic on."

In the same hushed voice, Nora replied, "You mean catalyze our fuel?"

He let out a quiet chuckle. "Whatever. Is yours on?"

"Yes."

"Move all your magic into your hands. It shouldn't be in your mouth."

"How exactly do you expect me to do that?"

He let out a sigh that, while still quiet, was annoyingly dramatic. "I guess we'll work on that skill later. Now form the first rung of the ladder right here." He pointed to a spot on the stone fence, about half a met off the ground.

"Um . . . okay." She knelt and, with a thought, sent magic into her hands and mouth. A chill infiltrated her body. On a night like tonight, she'd rather be a fire lyster. Then she could make fire and enjoy its warmth without being burned.

But this was her faculty, and right now, it was the one they needed. If she could get it to work properly. She held up her hands, her palms facing the stone. A lamppost a couple of dozen mets away shed dim light on the ice she shot from her tingling palms. The two icy streams joined to create a piece about as long as her hand and as wide as her finger, more the size of a pencil than a ladder rung. It sat in the mortar between two rows of stones before wobbling and falling to the ground.

She looked up and realized Krey was kneeling next to her. It was too dark for her to see his expression, but his words said it all. "That was . . . small. Did you lose focus?"

She didn't want to tell him that, while she was good at creating snow, she'd just demonstrated the extent of her ice-making talent. "I guess," she whispered. "I'll try again."

The next attempt was worse than the first; the ladder rung she made was only fit for a bug to climb on. It immediately fell off.

"I think I'm seeing why you wanted my help," Krey said.

Nora blushed, but she could hear the laughter in his voice. It was better than the disdain she'd grown used to.

"We need to hurry," he said, "but try one more time. I want to see what your hands are doing."

Nora took a deep breath and pushed her magic with all her might, tightening every muscle in her body. *I'm so glad he can't see my face.* She was finishing up another pencil-sized piece of ice when Krey reached around from behind her and grabbed both her hands.

Startled, she jerked her hands away. Her ice turned to little chips, which fell to the ground.

Behind her, Krey coughed. She was pretty sure he was laughing again. "Sorry—should've warned you."

"It's okay." It was more than okay; now that Nora was over the shock, she wished he'd grab her hands and press his chest against her back again. She shook her head. Was one touch all it took to turn her into a puddle of romantic goo? *I've got to get out more. Amazing what being starved of normal social interactions does to a girl.* Maybe Krey had been right during their first garden conversation. She didn't just need tutoring on magic; she needed tutoring on how to be a normal teenager.

He was next to her again. "Your hands felt really tense," he said. "We'll work on you relaxing more, but we don't have time tonight."

"I think you'd better make the ladder."

"I think you're right."

She watched as he held his hands near the stone, just as she had. But clearly he was doing something different, because ice flowed from his palms as easily as water from a palace tap. His fingers moved a bit, guiding the shape of the ice, forming it into a perfect ladder rung, attached to the stone.

When he started forming the next rung, she ran her fingers along the one he'd just made. It was covered in ridges so their feet wouldn't slip. *Ingenious.*

He made the upper rungs more like long handles, attached to the stone on two ends and arcing out in the middle. When he got high enough, he stood on the ice ladder, hanging on with one hand while he used the other to form rungs. At last, the ladder went all the way to the top, an impressive feat. The fence was four mets tall, as high as the one around Nora's residence.

He climbed down carefully to stand next to Nora. "I need to focus to keep these solid. Can you climb up and watch for the guard?"

"Sure." She began the climb and was instantly glad she'd chosen shoes with rugged treads. The ice was still slippery, but her soles gripped it well. Holding onto the top rung with hands that were getting numb, she peeked through the thick coils of barbed wire atop the fence.

A guard was approaching, lantern in hand. Nora scrambled down. She whispered in Krey's ear, "There's a guard about to pass us. We'll probably have a few minutes before another one comes by."

Krey nodded and climbed the ladder he'd made. Nora watched him peek over the fence. As they'd discussed, he waited until the guard was distant enough not to hear them. Then he held one hand up to the barbed wire. Ice gushed from his hand, covering the wire in a thick mound. He lifted himself one step higher.

Nora held her breath as he leaned out over the blob of ice covering the wire, extending both hands. Now that they could get to the top of the fence, he had to create a way down. Nora braced herself, one foot back, as if she could catch him if he fell.

After about half a minute of silent work, Krey scampered up the rest of the ladder. He sat on the ice mound and dropped out of sight.

Nora's heart thudded in her ears. She climbed the ladder, hands shaking. The backpack she carried wasn't that heavy, but she felt like it would send her tumbling to the ground at any moment. Somehow she made it to the top. She pulled herself into a seated position on the mound of ice.

The fence blocked out the dim light from the garden. Beyond, the night was black. Nora held her breath and pushed herself off, trusting that Krey had succeeded in his magical mission—and that his focus was better than it had been at the event in his hometown. A fantastic thrill pulled at her gut as she went down the steep ice slide he'd made.

As soon as she tumbled onto the cold grass, the ice slide cracked with a sound that made her cringe. Chunks crashed to the ground. Without a word, Nora began groping in the dark, grabbing the ice pieces one at a time and heaving them over the tall fence. She heard Krey doing the same. When they were about halfway done, Krey tapped her shoulder.

Nora gasped. Far in the distance was a bouncing light. Another guard with a lantern.

They worked even faster, throwing one block of ice after another. Each one resulted in a *thud* on the other side of the fence. As the guard drew closer, Nora became convinced he'd see or hear them. "We gotta go," she whispered.

They had a plan for this. Nora reached down, feeling around for more ice. She knew Krey was doing the same. She found two blocks and pushed them along the grassy dirt until they hit the fence. They had to make sure the guard didn't trip over their evidence. Hopefully his lantern wouldn't reflect off the icy chunks.

Nora was tempted to run, but she knew she'd make too much noise and probably smash into a tree in the wooded area beyond. So she walked as briskly as she dared, hands extended, until she found a tree trunk. She secreted herself behind it, watching the lantern-wielding guard pass.

A minute or so later, she heard Krey's quiet voice. "You still alive?"

She wanted to cry with relief and scream with excitement. Instead, she whispered, "Alive and free. Let's go."

By the time they reached the street that ran in front of the palace, Krey was complaining of a hole in his pants, and Nora was pondering how she'd explain her scratches and bruises to Aunt Dani. They hadn't dared light a lantern in the woods, concerned a distant guard would see it. The trees and roots hadn't been kind to them.

But once they turned onto the road, they were just two ordinary people taking a late-night stroll. Nora opened her backpack and retrieved a lantern. She poured in some oil from a stoppered bottle and handed the lantern to Krey, who lit it with a match. They'd agreed he should carry the lantern, keeping it as far from Nora's face as he could.

"Is your hood up?" Nora asked.

"Yeah."

While the temperature was above freezing, it was chilly. Nora pulled the drawstring of her hood, thankful for the warmth and relative anonymity it provided.

They walked so fast, they were almost jogging. Krey led them through the rural outskirts of Cellerin City, then into the city itself.

"Are we almost there?" Nora asked after they'd made several turns.

"Getting close."

Halfway down the next street, Krey extinguished the lantern. They walked in silence. Once Nora's eyes adjusted, starlight provided a little illumination.

"It's the next house," Krey whispered. They crept around to the back door. He tried the handle. "Locked."

"What do we do now?"

"I have this thin metal piece that might get us in—if there's no deadbolt."

"You have a lot of experience breaking into houses?"

"None at all. I read a lot of books."

Again, Nora could hear his smile. Her breaths grew shallow as he used his tool, which seemed extraordinarily loud in the silence of the residential street. After a few seconds, the knob turned, and the door squeaked as Krey pushed it open.

They tiptoed in, and Krey locked the door. Nora wondered if he could hear her heart's urgent beat. The house was completely dark.

"Take my hand," Krey said.

This time, the touch of his hand didn't stir any desire in Nora, but she savored the physical reminder that she wasn't alone. They walked carefully through the room and soon reached a wall. An opening led them to the next room, and they felt their way along its walls.

"This is wrong," Krey soon whispered.

"Shh."

"No, listen. This house was crammed full of stuff last time I was here. We shouldn't be able to take a step without running into something."

"That's weird."

Nora and Krey kept walking and soon turned into a hallway. There were two open doors, one on each side.

Krey spoke softly, so close to Nora that his breath tickled her ear. "You go right. I'll go left." He let go of her hand.

Nora entered the room and walked along its entire perimeter, encountering no furniture. She met Krey back in the hallway.

"Nothing," she whispered in his ear.

"Me, either." His voice, now a normal volume, made Nora jump.

She heard him rummaging around. The distinctive sound of a

match strike was followed immediately by the light of a flame. Krey lit the lantern and returned the matches to his pocket.

He was shaking his head, his mouth tight and forehead furrowed. "I suppose you think I was lying, and now you're done with all this."

She reached out and took the lantern, then walked back to the front room. The light illuminated the door, a grimy window, and a room empty of all but a few pieces of trash. The place felt like it could be the setting of a thriller novel.

Nora turned back to Krey. "I know you're not lying." She grinned. "And we're just getting started."

10

I came home from school one day, bawling. Dad must have seen my shaking shoulders from the field where he was planting, because he ran and picked me up before I reached the front door.

"What's wrong, baby girl?"

I told him one of my friends had said he and Mom were snobs because they were leaders in our community.

Dad laughed, then held me close. "If they knew how often I wish someone else was leading, they might see things differently."

-The First Generation: A Memoir *by Liri Abrios*

KREY GRITTED HIS TEETH. This entire stupid adventure—gorging themselves on ice, making a ladder and slide, breaking into a house—was all pointless.

"Did you hear me?" Nora's waving hand caught Krey's attention. "I said I'm still in."

He stared at her, wishing the lantern was closer to her face so he could determine what she was really thinking.

She placed her free hand on her hip. "Why are you glaring at me?"

"I'm glaring because I'm not getting any closer to finding my girl-friend. I'm looking at you because I'm wondering . . . who are you trying to find? Zeisha or your friend?"

She looked away, confirming his hunch that she still thought her friend had been abducted. "Does it matter?" she murmured.

"It might! If you find out your friend is truly enjoying her new life with her family in Newland, will you decide none of this is worth it? Maybe you'll go tell your father all about how I broke into the records hall and sneaked you out of the palace?"

"What the hell, Krey? I've been supporting you for the past week, and I didn't even figure out that Faylie might be involved until tonight! Is it that hard for you to believe I want to help you?"

"Yep."

Her voice rose in pitch and volume. "I want to help because if I were missing, I'd want people to look for me. And I was serious when I told you I needed to get out of the palace. Call me shallow, but you have no idea what it's like to be locked up in that place with my aunt and an orsa as my only two friends!" Krey responded with a cynical shake of his head, and Nora huffed. "By the orange sky above, don't you trust anyone?"

"Sure. But not royals."

"Why?"

He shifted his gaze away from her. "We need to look around, see if we can find anything."

Nora sighed. "Fine."

She sat the lantern in the middle of the small room and walked the perimeter, examining pieces of trash then dropping them. Krey did the same. It didn't take long to determine there was nothing useful in the room.

"Bedrooms?" Nora asked.

"Yeah." Krey took the lantern and led her to the bedroom on the right. It was empty.

They were searching the bedroom on the left, which faced the front of the house, when someone started pounding on the front door. Nora and Krey cursed in unison.

"Back door?" Nora asked.

"They'll be watching it. Wait here."

"Wait? For what?"

Krey was already running. He set the lantern in the hallway so it would shed a little light into the living room. Having learned a lesson from his previous trip to this house, Krey had eaten a few feathers before leaving his dorm. He urged his flight talent to turn on. His entire body filled with a tingling lightness, and he flew the last few mets to the front door. He reached down and threw the bolt, using the motion to push himself up to the ceiling.

The door crashed open. One of the brutes who'd threatened him earlier charged in, passing right beneath him. Krey didn't give the man time to find him. He swooped down and captured the man's neck in the crook of his arm, squeezing as tight as he could. He'd never done anything like this, but he'd read about it plenty of times.

The guard reached up to pry Krey's arms off his neck, but Krey held on with furious strength. The man's big boot kicked backwards, which might have worked if his attacker weren't hovering two mets off the ground.

After a brief struggle, the man slackened. Krey released him, and he dropped to the ground.

Krey flew to the bedroom where Nora waited. He landed. "Let's go! Leave the lantern!" They both sprinted into the living room, out the front door, and into the street.

As soon as they reached the street, a male voice behind them shouted, "Stop!"

"Keep running," Krey shouted. He stopped, turned, and shot a large ball of ice at their pursuer's chest. The man went down with a grunt.

Krey took to the air just long enough to catch up with Nora, who was still sprinting away. He landed and ran alongside her. After about a minute, he touched her arm. "We should walk. People will be suspicious."

They slowed to a panting walk and stayed in the shadows, away from streetlamps. When they'd caught their breath, Krey glanced at Nora. "Damn it, put your hood up!"

She pulled it up, then turned her head to look at him. "Did you kill the man in the living room?"

"No. He just passed out."

"Good. Why'd you come back for me? You could've flown away by yourself"

That was a good question. Nora could've told those men she was the princess, and they probably wouldn't have hurt her. He shrugged. "I didn't think about it."

She let out a short laugh. "I've seen you cry over your girlfriend, Krey."

"Almost cry. And what's your point?"

"I know you're not coldhearted."

"Whatever."

"Okay, so we've agreed that you didn't leave me because deep down, you're a decent human being." There was laughter in her voice. "So why didn't you pick me up and fly us both out of there?"

He swiveled his head to give her an incredulous look. "How many feather eaters have you known?"

"A few."

"How many of them could carry passengers?"

"All of them."

He laughed. "You're lying."

"No, really. All the ones I've met were masters."

"Oh, of course. I imagine you don't often associate with normal magic eaters." He glanced at her again. "Carrying someone else while flying is really hard."

"I assumed you were as talented with flying as you are with ice."

"Well, I'm not."

"Do you practice flying every day?"

"Of course not."

"The masters I work with always say there aren't any shortcuts to becoming a better lyster. *If you want greater powers, practice for hours.*"

He knew she was right, but frost magic was easier than feather magic. Once he'd gotten decent at flying, and done it enough to get over the initial insane thrill of it, he'd switched a lot of his focus to his other talent.

"You know," Nora said, "I could have someone order feathers for you to practice with."

Heat filled his face, and his hands clenched. "Your Royal Highness, I don't need your charity. In fact, I don't need the ice you had delivered to my room the other day. I can buy my own fuel."

"Oh! You . . . you can?"

"Just because I don't show off my money doesn't mean I don't have any. My Aunt Evie is a successful fashion designer. It's ridiculous how much people pay for her stuff. I don't think anything she makes costs less than five hundred quins." He immediately wished he'd kept his mouth shut. Nora didn't need to know any more about his personal life than he'd already told her.

It was too late. "Evie Designs? I love her clothes! I buy her entire collection every season!"

"Well . . ." Krey cleared his throat. "I guess that means you were already providing my fuel to me."

"So you come from a wealthy family. I wouldn't have guessed that after you got on my case about poor people who can't afford ice."

"You don't have to be underprivileged to care about those who are."

For several minutes, the only sound was their footsteps on the packed dirt. When Nora spoke again, her voice was soft. "That conversation we had in the icehouse? The day you came? It made me think. I even—well, I—like I said, it made me think."

He turned to study her, but she was looking off into the distance. He kept his gaze on her. In so many ways, she was exactly what he'd imagined a royal would be: privileged and clueless. But she'd sounded so genuine just then. And she was helping him, when all he'd expected from the monarchy was apathy or hostility.

"I almost forgot." Nora reached in her pocket and pulled out a crumpled piece of paper. "I was picking this up when that man started pounding on the door. This street's empty. Let's stop under that light and see what this says." They stopped, and she smoothed the page, then read aloud.

"NEW THERROAN LEAGUE
(NTL)

presents

AN EVENING OF LECTURES AND DISCUSSION
on the topic of
TRUE FREEDOM AND INDEPENDENCE
Wednesday Centa 13TH
7-9 PM – Alit's Pub"

Nora's eyes were wide, her breaths shallow and quick. "This is it."

"What?"

"New Therroan extremists—that's who's behind all this."

Krey's forehead screwed up. "New Therroan extremists?"

"We can't keep standing under this light." She set out at a quick pace, and Krey ran to catch up. "You've heard of the New Therroan movement for independence, right?" Nora asked.

"I've heard of it, but it's not big news in Tirra."

"Okay, a brief history lesson. After The Day, about a thousand people gathered in this area. They named their community Cellerin.

A hundred years later, about half the community moved out to the lake in the North Forest, northwest of here. They started their own nation: New Therro."

"Named after Therro, the preday country," Krey interjected.

"Right. From the beginning, New Therro and Cellerin had constant trade disputes. Almost fifty years ago, in 153 PD, New Therro's army attacked us. But our top legislators were stuck in a power struggle. They gave our generals contradictory orders, and we were losing almost every battle. So Cellerin's population rose up and named their mayor, Onna, as queen."

"Your grandmother," Krey said.

"Yes. She was a brilliant strategist. She not only won the war; she negotiated a truce that required New Therro to become a Cellerinian province."

"I know all this," Krey said, not trying to hide his impatience. "Talk to me about these New Therroan extremists you mentioned."

"A lot of New Therroans believe they should still be independent. They hold protests in Cellerin City all the time, sometimes at the palace gates. For the last couple of years, there's been real concern that they're gearing up for a civil war."

"What?" Krey stopped, expecting Nora to do the same, but she kept right on walking. Again, he ran to catch up. "I've never heard anything about impending war!"

She shook her head hard. "I shouldn't have said anything. This isn't public knowledge." She met his eyes. "You can't mention it to anyone. Okay?"

"I won't. I swear."

Slowing her pace, she watched him, her brows drawn together.

"Nora, I'm not gonna tell anyone. I just want to find Zeisha." He sighed and added, "And there are other people that need to be rescued too. I doubt your friend is one of them, but if she is, we'll find her. Please, tell me what you know."

She nodded slowly and released a loud breath. "My father has been traveling about once a week to negotiate with New Therroan leaders. He's keeping it quiet. The last thing we need is for this to turn public and political. The negotiations haven't been going well."

"Why doesn't he just let New Therro have their independence?"

Nora gaped at him. "If we did that, they'd think we were weak. They'd try to take over our government. What they really want is power—and revenge for being under our thumb all this time. Onna brought unity and stability to our nation. We aren't giving that up! If you can't see that . . ." She shook her head. "I never should've told you all this."

Krey didn't believe a word of her reasoning. King Ulmin wouldn't give independence to New Therro for one reason: he didn't want to lose any of his power. None of that mattered, though, not while Zeisha was still missing. "I appreciate you telling me," he said. "I swear on the stone, I'll keep it quiet. But I still don't understand . . . how does Zeisha fit into all this?"

"I don't know, but it can't be a coincidence that we found this flyer in that house. Think about it. Most of the people who left Cellerin for New Therro weren't magical. There's still not much magic in their province. It makes sense that they'd want some lysters on their side."

Krey clenched his fists, and when he spoke, his words were louder than he intended. "Nora, open your eyes. I don't care what that flyer says. Someone in your government is behind all this. New Therro is a poor province; what makes you think they have the resources to send people out to kidnap magic eaters? And to keep it quiet?"

Nora shoved the paper in front of his face. "*This* makes me think it! What are the chances your grudge against the monarchy is blinding you to the truth? Be honest, Krey!"

Krey tried to brush off her words, but he couldn't. Uncertainty twisted his stomach. *Maybe the government is hiding my girlfriend. Maybe a band of extremists abducted her. How am I supposed to fight against either one?*

Nora turned, and when she saw his face, her blazing eyes softened. "Are you okay?"

He covered his mouth. "I feel sick."

"We'll get to the bottom of this, you know."

He nodded and tried not to throw up.

The sky was still black when they arrived back at the palace grounds. Krey breathed a quiet prayer of thanks when he had enough frost magic in his reserves to create another ladder and a slide. They slid to the ground in the garden, and he let go of his mental hold on the ice, this time allowing it to break into tiny, frozen pebbles. Hopefully the guards out there wouldn't notice the ice chips left behind by the ladder rungs.

They walked through the garden, and Nora stopped and gestured toward Krey's dorm. "Hope you can get a little sleep."

"Actually"—he couldn't believe he was saying this—"I'll make sure you get back to your house safely."

"Krey, my dad is overprotective enough. I don't need it from you too. I'll be fine."

"I know you will, but we just evaded palace guards at the fence and two goons in the city." He swallowed. "I . . . I appreciate your help tonight. I'm still not sure why you're doing it, but I appreciate it. Let me walk you home, okay?"

She paused, then nodded. "Okay."

They walked back to the residence. As Nora struggled to unlock the gate in the dark, she whispered, "When you get off your library shift tomorrow, let's meet in the garden. We'll talk about what to do next."

"Sounds good."

She opened the gate and took a step in. Two caynins greeted her. "I appreciate you walking me here."

Before he could respond, a voice spoke from several mets away. "So do I."

A bolt of alarm shot through Krey, and he grabbed Nora's arm to keep her from going in farther. "Who's that?" he whispered.

Nora tugged her arm away and spoke at full volume, her voice thick with resignation. "Hi, Aunt Dani."

11

My neighbor, a survivor of The Day who is five years older than me, married at seventeen. She was pregnant within two months. In the next sixteen years, she had eleven babies, eight of whom survived infancy.

Perhaps the most defining feature of my generation is our desperation to rebuild Anyari's population. We pressure young people to marry early and procreate quickly and often, just as our parents did after The Day. We encourage unmarried individuals, same-sex couples, and other childless couples to adopt children in need of families. In our society, which lacks modern medical technology, far too many parents die young.

We also instruct teenagers not to have sex until they're married. Unlike preday society, we have no contraception or protection against sexually transmitted diseases. In an effort to build strong, healthy families, postday culture encourages lifelong, monogamous relationships.

Of course, whether in procreation or in chastity, there is often a gap between intention and reality.

-The First Generation: A Memoir *by Liri Abrios*

Nora's Aunt Dani had an uncanny ability to catch her when she broke the rules. Thankfully, Dani was sometimes willing to keep secrets from Nora's father. Holding onto that hope, Nora stepped toward her and fixed a wide smile on her face. "Didn't expect to see you here!"

Dani's voice was stern. "Come in. Both of you."

Krey was still outside, swathed in shadows. He heaved a sigh and entered. Nora locked the gate.

"Let's go in through the icehouse so we don't wake anyone." Dani led them around to the back. Once they were in Nora's room, Dani turned on the light and pointed at four upholstered chairs by the unlit fireplace. "Sit."

Nora and Krey both sat. Dani walked to the fireplace and faced them, folding her arms over her chest. She locked her gaze on Krey for several seconds, then shifted it to Nora. "Are you two having sex?"

They answered at the same time:

"What?"

"I have a girlfriend!"

Dani's stance didn't change. "I need to know if you are. While I'd advise against it, I want you to protect yourselves—"

"Ma'am," Krey interrupted, "I didn't come to this city to seduce a princess. I came here to find my girlfriend. I've never even had sex with her; you really think I'd jump in bed with someone else?"

Nora's brows leapt up. That was . . . more information than she'd expected. She recovered and turned to her aunt. "Give me some credit. I'm smarter than that." She wanted to add, *If I was gonna sleep with anyone, it wouldn't be a moody teenager with a grudge against me.* But a spark of common sense shut down the impulse. She didn't want Dani to keep an even closer eye on her.

Dani's shoulders relaxed. She walked to Nora's desk and returned with a plate of cookies, which she set on a low table in front of the chairs. "Please, eat."

Krey's confused gaze found Nora.

She shrugged and whispered, "Just take one." Cookies served multiple purposes in Dani's world. They could be expressions of love, edible apologies, or icebreakers at negotiations. Right now, Nora figured these cookies were a sign of Dani's trust. And maybe a little attempted bribery too. Dani wanted answers.

As Nora and Krey chewed, Dani scooted a chair to face them. She sat and leaned forward.

Before her aunt could say more, Nora asked, "How did you know I was gone?"

"A guard found a large pile of ice blocks inside the fence. Knowing you're an ice lyster, he woke me to inform me of it."

Nora chewed and swallowed. She hadn't realized the guards inside the grounds ever checked that area. Good information for later. "Does Dad know?"

"Not at this point."

Whew. Nora's father had always been protective, and his wife's murder ten years earlier had multiplied his natural tendencies exponentially. It didn't matter that the queen's killer had been a deranged woman with no organizational ties. The king lived every day of his life in fear that someone would take either his daughter or his crown from him. After Nora's last escape attempt, he'd threatened that if she tried it again, he'd take away the modicum of freedom she had.

Dani gestured to Nora's and Krey's faces. "You're both scratched up. What happened?"

"We were in the trees outside the fence," Nora said. "It was dark."

"Tell me where you went. And be honest."

Out of the corner of her eye, Nora saw Krey eyeing her. She had no doubt he wanted her to keep her mouth shut.

"We were at that house Krey visited last week," Nora said.

Krey's huff drew Nora's gaze. *Seriously?* he mouthed.

"Why?" Dani asked.

Nora almost blurted out the truth about the letters Krey had found. But then he'd be in trouble for breaking into the records hall. She bit her lip and stared at her hands.

Dani didn't say a word. She'd mastered a particular type of silence, designed to elicit true confessions through pure awkwardness.

It was Krey who finally spoke, after brushing cookie crumbs off his fingers. "I wanted to get into the house at night while the guy who lives there was sleeping. Just to look around."

Dani turned her attention to Nora. "And you went with him because . . . ?"

For a silent moment, Nora considered bringing up her suspicions about Faylie. But something told her Dani would find the assertion preposterous. She settled for, "I think he's onto something. I wanted to help."

"And you wanted an adventure?" Dani asked with a small smile.

Nora shrugged.

Dani sat up straighter. "Let me guess. You found an empty house."

"How did you know that?" Krey demanded.

Dani picked up a cookie, eating it thoughtfully, then turned to Krey. Her gaze and voice were gentle. "As I promised, I've been looking into this, but the king asked me to keep the details confidential." She shifted her gaze to Nora. "After Krey's experience with those guards, he feared something similar would happen to you."

Nora was glad she hadn't mentioned the man Krey had left lying on the floor. Or the one he'd toppled with a high-speed ice missile. "Can you please tell us what you found out?" she asked. "It's very important to Krey."

Dani shook her head, releasing a sigh. "I want to be open with you, Nora, but I also want to honor your father's wishes."

Nora kept her mouth closed and her eyes fixed on her aunt. Dani was infallibly loyal to her family. She'd spent the last ten years of her life caring for Nora and Ulmin. These days, however, her devotion to her impetuous teenage niece often conflicted with her allegiance to Ulmin. Usually, her soft spot for Nora won out.

Sure enough, Dani finally said, "I suppose I made things worse by hiding the truth. I'll tell you what I know."

"I'd appreciate that," Krey said softly.

"This is highly confidential information, and I expect every bit of it to remain in this room. Are we agreed?" When Krey and Nora confirmed it, Dani said, "As I mentioned before, Cellerin does have a secret, elite apprenticeship program. Even I didn't know about it until I asked."

"Who did you ask?" Nora interrupted. "The Minister of Lysting?"

Dani nodded. "Your father approved the program but hasn't kept up with the details. Minister Sharai confirmed that the house you visited was a private home used as an administrative outpost. She didn't want to route correspondence through the palace. The administrator you met is eccentric, but trustworthy. Because the program is secret, he was given permission to hire two guards. They lived across the street. I told her what happened to you, Krey, and I made it clear that we can't have ruffians attacking teenagers in the king's name. Rest assured, those guards are no longer employed by the monarchy."

Nora narrowed her eyes. *They're still working for someone.* She could almost feel Krey's relief when she kept that thought to herself.

"Why was the house empty?" Krey asked.

"After your first visit, the administrator moved to avoid any further confrontations with you. He told Sharai you were threatening and pushy."

Krey scoffed, but Nora didn't have trouble buying the description.

"Krey," Dani said, "my records request was fulfilled today. I confirmed that Zeisha is, indeed, part of the elite apprenticeship program."

A question burst out of Nora's mouth. "Is Faylie part of it too?"

Her aunt's response—a tilted head and merciful eyes—reminded her why she'd declined to bring up Faylie in the first place. "Nora," Dani said softly, "Faylie is in Newland. I know you miss her, but there's no mystery to her departure. People come and go from our lives. I hate it as much as you do."

Nora's shoulders fell. Her aunt hadn't seen the note Faylie sent, but it wouldn't make a difference if she had. Dani was convinced nothing weird was going on. If Nora used the note to make her case, Dani would comfort her, but she wouldn't believe her niece's speculations.

Krey's strained voice interrupted Nora's brooding. "If the apprenticeship program is such a secret, I'm surprised your records request was successful."

Nora raised her eyebrows. It was a good point. Besides, why hadn't Krey found any information when he'd broken into the records hall?

"When Sharai told me how confidential the program is, I asked her about my records request," Dani said. "She told me the files are kept in a locked office within the records hall. She sent the administrator a note instructing him to release the information to me."

Nora nodded, but the answer didn't really clear things up. If everything was legitimate, why had Krey found letters from other concerned parents? Why were the supposed guards still watching an empty house? And what about that New Therroan flyer they'd found? She was tempted to mention it, but she'd seen Dani's response to the question about Faylie. Her aunt would view any further theories as pure paranoia.

Krey stood. "I can't tell you how much it means to me that you shared all this." His voice, tight and low, didn't match his words.

Dani looked up, her forehead wrinkled in compassion. "Krey, I'm terribly sorry Zeisha hasn't contacted you. I know this is hard to hear, but if she'd wanted to get in touch with you, she could have. Minister Sharai assured me of that. I can't imagine how difficult that must be." She stood. "Now that you know the truth, I think you need to make the most of your own apprenticeship and move on. Can you do that?"

"I guess I don't have a choice."

"And you, Nora? Can you let go of the friendship you lost and appreciate what you have now?"

Nora tried to look contrite as she stood. "Of course. I'm sorry about tonight. It was a stupid thing to do."

"I'm glad you realize that." Dani smiled. "Now get to bed. Tomorrow's Monday, and we'll all be busy." She placed a hand on Nora's shoulder, then one on Krey's. "I remember what it's like to be young. I'll keep your adventure tonight secret. But I can't keep hiding things from your father, Nora. Please don't try anything like that again. That goes for both of you."

They murmured acknowledgements, but as Krey walked to the door, his squared shoulders screamed of determination. Nora fought to keep her expression neutral.

There was no way they were letting this go.

12

I was ten years old, playing outside with my siblings, when I caught sight of a bird in the distance. As it flew closer, I realized it was too large to be a bird. I thought perhaps it was a dragon.

When I saw that it was a child about my age, soaring on the wind, I screamed. I guess a flying human was a lot scarier to me than a fire-breathing dragon.

-The First Generation: A Memoir *by Liri Abrios*

KREY RAN TO THE GARDEN. Nora was pacing there, her jacket hood up against the early winter breeze.

"Sorry," he said. "I lost track of time in the library."

"Apparently so." She yawned. "I was considering taking a nap on this bench."

"Yeah, I've been tired all day too. Did your aunt say anything else after I left last night?"

"She reminded me about ten more times not to sneak out or have sex." Nora let out a short laugh. "How was your day?"

So, we're at the "How was your day?" phase of our friendship? As Krey mulled that over, a more important question struck him. *Did I just call this girl a friend?* He realized he'd waited too long to answer Nora. She was staring at him like she doubted his sanity. "Uh, it was fine. I listened to a horribly boring frost eater tell me things I already know. Then I worked in the library, which was much more interesting. How about you?"

"I had school all day."

"School?"

"Well, private tutoring. Unlike every other teenager in the kingdom, I didn't graduate when I turned seventeen."

Krey supposed that made sense. As the eventual queen, she'd need an advanced education. "So you haven't practiced your magic today?"

She groaned. "No."

"But you do practice every day, right? Like you told me to do?"

"Uh . . . most days."

Krey laughed. "I knew it!"

She yawned again. "Let's talk strategy."

"Absolutely. But we should practice magic together too. Your aunt's gonna get suspicious if we keep spending time alone in the garden."

Her tired eyes brightened. "You'll really teach me more about ice lysting?"

"I told you I would."

She grinned. "Let's go to my icehouse. And you should practice both your talents. Do you have feathers?"

He patted his pocket. "Right here."

Nora led the way to her icehouse. They wrapped blankets around their shoulders and sat on the floor. As they ate fuel, Krey said, "Whatever's going on, your aunt's in on it."

Nora choked on her ice, coughing violently.

Krey sat up straight. "You okay?"

She nodded, still coughing.

"I, uh . . . take it you disagree?"

She got control of her coughing and said, "It's the most insane thing I've ever heard."

Krey swallowed a small piece of feather. Feathers were notoriously difficult to chew, so he always diced them first. "We've eaten enough fuel. Where do you want to practice?"

Nora crossed her legs and leaned toward him. "Why do you think Dani's involved?"

"Let's talk as we walk. How about we practice by the pond?"

"Fine. But I haven't dropped this topic." Outside, Nora set a quick pace and asked in a low voice, "Why do you think Dani's involved?"

He cleared his throat. "Well, I'm not really sure. I just wanted to see your honest reaction."

"I could've choked to death!" Nora cried.

"On ice? It would melt first!" He chuckled, then grew serious. "Who do you think is behind it?"

Nora slowed, her anger seemingly forgotten. "I could barely sleep last night thinking about that. Clearly it's Minister Sharai."

"I agree she must be involved. But she can't be doing it alone."

"Maybe. But Aunt Dani has nothing to do with it."

Krey wasn't so sure, but he let it go. It wasn't like he had any proof. "What about your father?"

Laughter burst from Nora's mouth. "Not a chance! My dad's a rule follower, not a risk taker. Plus, if this is some sort of New Therroan plot, like we talked about last night, he's the last person who would support it. He's been doing all he can to negotiate with them."

Krey wasn't about to rule out any possibilities. For now, though, he'd move on. "Speaking of the New Therroans, I found a book in the library about their exodus from Cellerin. A bunch of the settlers shared one very familiar name."

Nora stopped, and so did Krey. Her eyes were wide. "Sharai?" she whispered.

"Good guess."

"Whoa."

They began walking again and soon reached the lawn north of the pond.

Nora looked across the pond. Several dackas were floating on the water, their green feathers gleaming in the early-evening sun. "So . . . Sharai is New Therroan. Or at least her relatives are."

"Yep. We can keep talking, but let's practice too. Turn on your magic."

Nora turned to him, a small grin on her lips. "Can't do that. I can catalyze my fuel, though."

"Snob." The word was out of his mouth before he could stop it. *And just when things were going smoothly.*

Her grin didn't disappear; it grew larger. "Ass," she said. She lifted a hand and, quick as lightning, shot a small ball of ice at him.

She'd probably been aiming at his face, but it hit his neck. He couldn't stifle a laugh. "That was fair."

"The name calling or the ice?"

"Both."

She laughed too. "My magic is *turned on*, as you like to say. Is yours?"

He responded with a snowball to her neck, in the same spot she'd hit him.

That led to an all-out snowball fight. From the start, he was the clear victor. About two minutes in, Nora shot a snowball over his shoulder then cried, "We have to stop! I think I've catalyzed half my fuel."

A male voice reached them. "Glad to see you both putting your faculties to good use."

Krey spun around. King Ulmin was watching them, his shoulders shaking with silent laughter. "I'd like to join you," he said, "but I make stone, not snow. It wouldn't exactly be a fair fight." He was still smiling as he turned to his daughter. "I'll see you at dinner, Nora. I'd like to spend a few minutes in the chapel first."

They watched him leave, and Nora stepped up to Krey. "Truce?"

"Truce."

Krey held out a hand, and she reached out as if to shake it. At the same instant, they both lifted their hands and shot one more snowball, each hitting the other's face.

Nora started giggling, and her response brought out the same in Krey. They both ended up on their backs in the grass. Krey laughed harder than he'd done in weeks, maybe since before Zeisha disappeared.

It was probably wrong to have fun when Zeisha was in such trouble. But the laughter cleared his mind and somehow made it easier to hope. *I'm at the palace, laughing with a princess who's kind of snobby but really not all that bad. When did my life get so weird?*

When he finally sat up, his laughter spent, Nora was watching him, a relaxed smile on her face. "Back to business?"

"Definitely." He stood, and she followed suit. "You're good at turning your magic on," Krey said, "but if you've already used half your fuel, you're not very efficient. Fuel doesn't last forever; eventually our bodies flush it out if we don't turn it into magic. But if you can learn to only use a little bit at a time, one big serving of ice will last you hours."

"I've never been good at conserving my fuel," Nora said.

"Clearly. And sorry to be rude, but your aim sucks."

She rolled her eyes. "I know. Can you fix me?"

He smiled. "You're not broken. But I can probably teach you a few things." He showed her how to change the position of her hands and fingers, adjustments that gave her greater control over how she used her magic.

Nora's forehead furrowed as she practiced. When she was out of fuel, a row of small ice spheres sat in the grass at her feet. "That helped," she said. "Thanks."

"The masters don't teach you this?"

"Well . . . they probably want to. But they spend so much of their time talking about the theory behind lysting, and I've never had patience for that. I suppose I'm not very cooperative. We always end up parting ways. Then another teacher comes along, and we start the whole thing over. That's why I'm good at initial catalysis; I've practiced it until my hands fall off. We just never get to the advanced stuff."

Krey nodded. He understood. Just as she'd plateaued in her frost eating, he'd stopped growing as a feather eater. He'd been told he had more instinctive talent than any other magic eater in his hometown. How much more could he have learned if he'd really tried? He couldn't blame boring masters, though. He simply hadn't had the patience to move further.

Like she'd read his mind, Nora said, "You should practice flying with weights. Build up your tolerance." She pointed at the eastern edge of the pond. "There are some rocks over there. Fly over, pick up the biggest one you can manage, and return to me."

He lifted his eyebrows. *Bossy much?*

She matched his expression and asked sarcastically, "Please?"

Krey turned his feather magic on and flew. The rock he retrieved was about half the size of his head. It weighed him down immediately. After a few mets, he dropped it in the pond, humiliated by the splash it made. He flew back, picked up a rock a little bigger than his fist, and returned to Nora.

He could swear her eyes were dancing with laughter, but she just smiled and said, "We both have a lot of work ahead of us."

Krey grunted. "We need to talk about what's next in our search for Zeisha."

"And the others."

Oh yeah, she still thinks her friend is involved. Krey supposed if his best friend had turned into a jerk overnight, he'd want an alternate explanation too. "And the others. Have a seat?"

She joined him, sitting on the grass about a met in front of him.

Krey still had plenty of ice magic, and as they talked, he used it to create a pile of snow between them.

"I think you need to go to some New Therroan meetings," Nora said. She pulled the flyer out of her pocket and held it out. She'd folded it into a neat rectangle, though the paper still held evidence of being crumpled. "Maybe over time, you can build up trust and get some leads."

Krey didn't take the paper. "The people at this meeting might be holding my girlfriend hostage. You want me to make friends with them?"

"I know it's asking a lot. I'd go there if I could, but . . ."

Krey sighed and took the paper. "I guess I can pretend to be friendly." Seeing Nora's eyebrows lift, he said, "Believe it or not, I can be polite when I want to. I'll go to the lecture. But Minister Sharai is our best lead. We need to find out what she knows."

"Yeah. I wish Dani could help with that. Everybody trusts her." Nora paused, biting her bottom lip as she studied Krey. "You know, I think we could tell her about the letters you found and ask for her help."

Krey sat up straighter, suddenly tense. "You've got to be kidding."

"She's trustworthy, Krey! I honestly don't think she'd turn you in."

He shoved his hands into the snow he'd just created. Clenching and unclenching his fists, he compacted handfuls of the stuff. He knew there was acid in his voice, but he couldn't help that. "Nora, she wouldn't even pressure the records people to move her request up the queue. She'd send me to the security office in a heartbeat if she knew I broke in. And she clearly trusts Sharai. I know you're extra-attached to her because she's the closest thing you have to a mother, but I don't trust her. You shouldn't either."

Nora's mouth dropped open. She looked away and snapped it shut, jaw tightening. He was pretty sure there were tears in her eyes.

Oops.

Nora stood and spoke in a low, controlled tone. "I'll find a way to get into Sharai's office." She strode toward her house. As she passed him, she muttered, "Ass."

IN THE DARK: 4

Zeisha pressed her finger against the bloody spot on her ankle. With her other hand, she shook Isla.

Isla sat up.

"Nine weeks," Zeisha said.

"Nine." Isla sounded hopeless.

A couple of mets away, a male voice slurred, "I don't . . . lemme sleep . . . tired of fighting." His voice trailed off into incomprehensible muttering.

"Shuddup," someone hissed.

Zeisha sucked the blood off her finger and thumb, then lay down. She shook Isla, who was already asleep again.

"Huh?" Isla murmured.

"That guy who was just talking—it sounded like he was dreaming. He said he was tired of fighting."

Isla's groggy voice grew excited. "We need to listen for that stuff. And when we wake each other up, let's do it gently. See if we can catch those moments when we're still half-dreaming."

"Good idea." Zeisha lay on her pallet, staring into the blackness.

After a few minutes, she whispered, "*Tired of fighting*, he said. Is that why we're so exhausted?"

Isla was already asleep.

13

My parents, as leaders and keepers of the stone, were more respected than anyone else in the community. The next-most-respected citizen was Connel. He was our brewer.

-The First Generation: A Memoir *by Liri Abrios*

"Give us your address, and every quarter, we'll send you a calendar of our events."

Krey turned to a friendly young woman who was holding out a notebook. *Mail from the New Therroan League—yeah, that would go over real well at the palace.* "Sorry, I'll pass."

She shrugged and moved on to someone else.

Krey walked through the crowded pub, stopping at the bar. "Do you have any bollaberry juice?"

"No, I've got bollaberry wine," the bartender said.

Krey flashed back to the night a couple of years back when he and some friends had raided his aunts' wine cabinet. He'd downed a whole bottle of bollaberry wine. It made him feel great . . . until it didn't anymore. His friends had fled when his loud vomiting woke his Aunt Evie. Tonight, he needed a clear head and a settled stomach. "I'll have water."

As Krey waited for his drink, he examined the attendees. *Who's hiding their guilt behind a beer mug and a laugh?* He tried to see past their relaxed smiles and find someone with . . . with what? Evil eyes betraying a tendency to abduct young magic eaters?

Krey shook his head. He'd have to actually talk to these people; there was no getting around it. When he had his water, he walked up to a small table. Two men, both with goatees typical of New Therroans, looked up. "Is that seat taken?" Krey asked.

"It's yours," one of them said with a smile.

They all introduced themselves, and the second man asked, "Have I seen you here before?"

"No. I'm not even New Therroan. But I've been reading a lot about current events, and I don't see why a province can't claim independence if they want to." It was true that he'd spent the last eight days reading all he could. He was still on the fence about independence, however. It was hard to be objective about the group who might have Zeisha.

Another goateed man stepped onto the pub's small stage. He gave the first lecture, and two more speakers followed. They all spoke passionately for New Therroan independence, but none of them seemed extremist. After the third speaker wrapped up, the first man returned to the stage to facilitate a discussion.

There were two major camps within the crowded pub: those who advocated for peaceful diplomacy, and those who spoke in vague terms about the need to *do what it takes* and *stand up for our rights.*

Several people railed against the government's unwillingness to even consider their claims. Clearly the king had succeeded in keeping his negotiations confidential, but his secrecy was backfiring.

Once again, the monarchy is totally out of touch, Krey mulled. *Shocking.*

Krey took note of the attendees who seemed to be advocating for violence. If anyone would kidnap magic eaters, it would be them. After the meeting, he crossed to a table where several vocal, angry protestors still sat, engaged in a heated discussion. He stood back and listened.

"I'm telling you, I'd love to live in a world covered in purple flowers, where everyone cares about everyone else, and we can find solutions by hugging each other real tight." The man speaking was tall and broad, with a fighter's crooked nose. He allowed a few seconds for laughter, then raised his voice. "But that's not how things work! We aren't gonna get anything done unless we FIGHT—FOR—IT." He emphasized the last three words with hard slaps on the heavy, wooden table.

Krey nodded, and the man caught his eye and pointed at him. "See? This guy gets it!"

Everyone looked at Krey. "Sure do," he said, his voice hard.

"You been here before?" the man asked.

"First time." Krey took a small step forward. "I got tired of watching the king take people's money and then take advantage of them." That much, at least, was true.

"Well said. What's your name?"

"Krey."

"Pull up a chair, Krey."

Just like that, he was in—at least with one man. It might take longer to convince the others. He stayed quiet unless someone asked his opinion. At those times, he asked questions instead of giving hard answers. Gradually, glimmers of trust entered some of the suspicious eyes.

When they'd been talking for an hour, a woman said, "I say it every time we get together, and I'm saying it again. The king's more powerful than us. We gotta find a way to level things out if we're ever gonna take what belongs to us."

"Do you agree, Krey?" It was the man who'd first welcomed him to the table.

"I've been thinking about this a lot," he said. "I've got a question. Is it true there aren't many New Therroan magic eaters?"

The woman said, "Yeah, and we need to change that. We can't win without some lysters on our side."

A woman who'd been silent until then said, "We've got a few."

The first woman's voice rose. "The king's got thousands!"

Krey's eyes roamed the group as the discussion continued. No one, however, seemed to have an answer for the New Therroans' magical shortages. If anyone knew about a scheme to abduct magic eaters, they were hiding it well.

The discussion broke up, and the man who'd first spoken to Krey pulled him to the side. "My name's Hatlin," he said. "Some of the folks around this table get together every Saturday night at nine. A few others join us too. You'd be welcome."

"Here at Alit's?"

"Yeah, in the back room."

"Thanks for the invite. I'll try to make it."

Hatlin clapped him on the back, then moved toward the door.

"Oh, I should tell you something," Krey said.

The big man turned around.

Krey took a deep breath. Better to be honest than have the truth come out later. "I'm a magic eater. An apprentice. I live and work at the palace."

Hatlin's mouth went slack, then widened into a grin. "That could all be very convenient."

Krey followed Hatlin out of the pub. They shook hands and parted. As he walked through the city, Krey mulled over his experience in the meeting. The people had been friendly, and he admired their willingness to stand up against the monarchy. But he'd barely repressed his disgust as he'd contemplated who in that pub might be holding Zeisha captive.

It was late and had been dark for hours. Before the meeting,

Krey had filled his pockets with pre-diced feathers. He ate his fill as he walked. When he reached the outskirts of the city, he took to the air.

He soared through the peaceful dark. Every time he came near a house with lantern light shining through the windows, he swooped low and used the illumination to scan for rocks. In front of a small cottage, he spotted the perfect one—oval in shape, as long as his forearm. He landed and picked it up.

Okay. Now fly with it. His gut clenched. He tried to laugh off the nerves. Why was this so hard?

Like all feather eaters, he'd learned to fly naked. Clothes could weigh him down. At age five, he hadn't been the least bit embarrassed to soar above the ground with nothing between him and the breeze. He'd driven his mom nuts, peeing in her flowers from an altitude of five mets. The memory lifted the corners of his lips. It also pinched his heart.

It had taken him a couple of years to learn to envelop his clothes in his magic. He'd started with underwear. In his head, he knew his little shorts weren't actually part of him. But in his gut, where his feathers turned into magic, he had to believe that the soft, neocot fabric was just as much *him* as his hair or his teeth.

Once he'd mastered that, he added more clothing, then shoes. These days, he automatically integrated his clothes into his magic. As he flew, he was aware of every fiber, seam, and button. He could even sense the soft leather of his shoes, despite the socks between his shoes and his feet.

He'd progressed to flying with small items in his pockets, but he'd never been able to carry anything else. Over the last few days, he'd tried flying short distances holding little rocks, but they hadn't felt like part of him. He could only overcome their weight through sheer will, which didn't work for long. He felt his talent nudging him, saying, *There's an easier way.*

Krey held the rock. *If I can do this with clothing and shoes, I can do it with a rock.* Confidence swelling in his chest, he pushed off into the air—and promptly came back down, dropping the rock and nearly falling as his feet scrambled on dry grass.

He gritted his teeth and picked up the rock. *This rock is me.*

The second flight was even shorter than the first.

"By the stone!" He whispered it to avoid waking anyone in the nearby house, but he wanted to shout with rage. When he looked at the rock he'd dropped, the humor of it hit him. "By the stone," he repeated, laughing.

He retrieved the rock and closed his eyes. In one long exhale, he released his anger, his drive, his analytical mind. All but his desire to grow in his talent.

He pressed the rock against his chest, feeling its firm, irregular surface. All at once, it was like the rock was no longer on top of his shirt. It *was* his shirt, which meant it *was him.* He could sense every little divot in its surface, every sharp bump and smooth curve. It was dense but no longer heavy, and the winter chill left it as it integrated into his warmth.

Krey opened his eyes and pushed himself into the air. He held the rock against his chest with one hand, lifted his other fist into the air, and hollered a wordless victory cheer. Below him, a young boy who was walking to an outhouse looked up. Krey laughed and waved.

He returned his attention to the air, and his laughter turned into a shrill scream. A large, black carribird was flying straight at him. He swerved to the right, barely avoiding the bird, who hadn't changed course at all. The action broke Krey's focus, and suddenly he was falling through the dark air, weighed down not only by the rock, but by his own body. His magic was gone.

"No!" Krey cried as he dropped the rock and threw every bit of focus and energy into turning his magic back on. It worked, sort of. His landing was rough, but not hard enough to break anything. He bounced along the road for at least fifty mets, his talent switching on and off like an electric bulb gone bad. When at last he skidded to a stop in front of a small farmhouse, the young man and woman sitting on the lamplit front porch gaped at him.

Krey brushed dirt off his clothes, picked up another stone, and grinned at the couple. "I am the rock!"

He took to the air again, smiling the whole way back to the palace.

14

After The Day, millions of pets were left homeless when their owners died. Most of the ones that survived turned feral. Our family kept three caynins as pets. We needed them to protect us from their wild cousins.

-The First Generation: A Memoir *by Liri Abrios*

NORA USUALLY LIKED ECONOMICS. Today, she could barely listen to her tutor. There was snow on the ground, the first of the season, and it had been beckoning to Nora all day. She had all the ice she could wish for, but there was something magical about fresh snow. She wanted to shove it in her mouth, let it melt on her tongue and in her throat, and catalyze it.

As soon as her lesson was over, she grabbed her coat. As she slipped it on, she heard Dani chatting with the tutor in the hallway. Next, her aunt would stop by to make sure Nora was completing her school assignments. Groaning, Nora removed her coat. She was sitting at her desk when Dani peeked her head in the room.

An hour later, Nora had made progress in three subjects. She bundled up in waterproof boots and a hooded coat, then headed outside. Her boots made a satisfying *crunch* on the snow. She scooped up a handful of it and took a bite, shivering with cold and pleasure. She continued eating it as she jogged to the pond.

Once she got there, she gathered more soft snow off the top of the stone bench. She'd eaten half a handful of it when someone behind her spoke.

"I saw that."

She turned. Krey stood a few mets away, grinning. Nora compacted the rest of the snow in her hand and threw it at him. He caught it and took a bite.

"I didn't hear you coming!" Nora said.

"I flew."

"Of course you did. And speaking of flying, you've been flying with stones for a week. Ready to carry me yet?"

"We could try, but I'm ninety-percent sure I'd drop you."

"I think I'll wait."

"What if I promised to drop you in the pond instead of on land?" Krey used his hand to sweep snow off one side of the bench.

Nora sat in the area he'd just cleared off. She shot a small ball of ice at his forehead.

He screwed up his face and rubbed the area. "Good aim."

"Thanks to your tutelage."

He gestured at the bench. "You could return the favor and clear off some snow so I can sit down."

"You said I'm a snob; I'd hate to disappoint you now."

Smirking, he wiped off the bench and sat. "Any ideas for getting into Sharai's office?"

"I asked if I could apprentice with her. My dad and Dani said that while they appreciate my interest in the workings of government, I need to focus on my other studies."

Krey sighed. "I wish something had come of that meeting I went to with Hatlin on Saturday. I don't think anybody there knew anything. I need to meet their leaders, but it may be a while before they trust me enough to introduce me." He stared out over the pond, his hands tightening into fists. "I need answers."

Nora frowned. "I wish I knew how to help you."

"So do I." Krey stood. "Come on, let's practice some magic."

"Okay. I want to learn to catalyze my fuel more efficiently so I can make more ice. Like you do."

He gestured to the ground. "Better start eating."

Nora gorged herself, then took a break and ate a little more. Krey showed her how to burn less fuel by tightening muscles in her chest, neck, shoulders, and arms. The actions didn't feel natural, but she worked on them all the same, making compact balls of ice and shooting them into the ground.

By the time her fuel dried up, she'd made twelve ice spheres, more than she'd ever done at once. They were bigger than usual too. "Not bad, right?" she asked. There was no response, so she turned around. "Krey?"

He was pacing behind her, his face flushed.

"What is it?" she asked.

"Nothing." It came out almost as a growl.

"Yeah, I know what *nothing* looks like. That's not it."

"Look behind you."

She did. In the distance, Minister Sharai was walking toward the front gate.

"In four days, it'll be four weeks since I got here," Krey said. "Zeisha's been gone for over two-and-a-half months! And apparently I'm incompetent to find her!"

By the end of his speech, he was shouting. Nora drew back. "Hey, it's not like I took her!"

He stared at her like she'd sprouted horns. "I know you didn't take her!" he yelled.

"Then stop screaming at me!"

"I'm not screaming at you!" He stepped right up to Nora, and his voice lowered, but it was no less harsh. "I'm pissed at Sharai, and whoever else is behind this thing! Is that not allowed, Your Highness?"

Nora shot back, "Of course you're allowed to be pissed, but don't take it out on me! I hate that my friend is gone, but I'm not taking it out on you!" She turned away, picked up two of the ice balls she'd made, and threw them as hard as she could into the pond.

Then she heard it: a staccato *uh-uh-uh* sound. It wasn't loud; she might not have even noticed it if she hadn't grown up hearing the sound. She spun around to see a caynin sprinting across the grassy lawn, straight toward Krey. "Stop!" she cried.

The beast didn't seem to hear her. It repeated its harsh *uh-uh-uh*, much louder this time. Krey turned toward the noise. The animal leapt, his wide-open, toothy maw aimed at Krey's neck.

"STOP!" Nora screamed. The caynin, who'd known her since she was born, snapped his jaws closed. He couldn't stop his momentum, though. He slammed into Krey, knocking him to the ground.

The animal immediately dismounted and ran to Nora, his huge ears pinned back in a submissive position. She rushed to kneel next to Krey. "Are you okay?"

His eyes were wide. For several seconds, he said nothing. Then he moaned, "I thought those things liked me."

Laughter, more nervous than amused, escaped Nora's mouth. "Let me help you sit up."

He waved her off and stood, coughing and rubbing his chest where he'd been hit. "What the hell was that about?"

"Those big ears have a purpose, you know," Nora said. "He heard you shouting, so he protected me. Yes, he likes you, but he's been loyal to me for seventeen years." She turned to the animal and rubbed his head, then pointed. "Go." He loped away.

"It's not like I was attacking you." Krey sat on the bench, still rubbing his chest.

Nora sat next to him. "It felt like you were."

He turned to her, his eyes wide. "What?"

"You were yelling at me! And your eyes, they were . . . enraged!"

"I told you, you weren't the one I was mad at."

"I couldn't tell the difference."

He fixed his gaze on the pond. After several seconds, he said, "I'm sorry."

It wasn't the most eloquent apology ever, but she got the feeling those two words meant a lot coming from him. "Thanks." She took a deep breath. "Listen, I still want to get into Sharai's office, but I don't know how. I need your help."

He chuckled, shaking his head.

"What's so funny?"

"I never dreamed a princess would ask me for help."

"You know, being royalty doesn't make us a different species. We're just people."

He met her gaze. "I almost believe it about you. The jury's still out on your dad and aunt."

She sighed. "I'll take what I can get. So . . . any ideas?"

"We'll have to sneak into her office."

"Because it went so well the first time you sneaked in somewhere?"

"I didn't say it was a good idea. It's just all we've got. The offices will be empty on Anyari Day, right?"

"Right."

"Then all we need is the keys."

"Where are we supposed to get keys, Krey?"

The corner of his mouth rose, and he looked across the pond.

Nora followed his gaze to the guardhouse. "Ovrun won't help you again. Not after the records hall."

"Maybe not . . . but he'd help you."

Nora spun to face him. "I'm not asking him for anything!"

Krey's eyebrow quirked up. "You're blushing."

"My cheeks are just cold!" As she said it, warmth spread to her neck and ears.

"The princess is afraid of the lowly commoner she kissed. Now this is interesting." There was laughter in Krey's eyes.

Nora reached down, grabbed a handful of snow, and ate it. She catalyzed it, welcoming the chill it brought to her face, then blew snow at Krey's face. *This is not a conversation I want to have*, she thought.

Krey chuckled. "I know you don't want to have this conversation."

She gaped at him.

"Can you think of a better way to get keys?" he asked.

She shook her head.

"Then come on. I'll walk with you, and we'll see if he's working."

The only argument Nora could think of was *Please, please don't make me face the hot guy I kissed.* She knew that wouldn't work.

She stood. "I'll go alone."

Ovrun was in the guardhouse with two coworkers when someone knocked on the door. He looked in the peephole and immediately drew in a sharp breath. Ignoring the queries from the other guards, he opened the door and performed a bow, holding out both hands and dipping his head. "Your Highness."

The princess gestured for him to lower his hands. When he did, she stammered, "Would you—would you like to go on an orsa ride?"

His mouth dropped open. "Uh . . . sure. Let me see if I can take a break."

From behind him, his shift supervisor said, "It's fine, Ovrun."

Laughter in his voice, the other guard said, "You might wanna get your coat first, unless you have other plans for staying warm."

Nora's smooth, light-brown cheeks darkened with a blush. Ovrun glared at the two grinning guards as he bundled up. When he returned to the door, Nora extended a hand. He reached out for it, then realized she was beckoning for him to exit, not offering to hold his hand. He shoved both hands in his pockets. *Smooth, Ovrun.*

They walked to the stable, having a single, brief conversation about the weather. As a groom saddled Blue and another orsa, Ovrun said, "Thanks for asking me to do this, Your Highness."

"I've told you, call me Nora." She briefly met his gaze, then looked down at her feet.

After an awkward silence, they had yet another discussion about the snow. Ovrun pointed out the salmon-and-scarlet sunset, but Nora barely glanced at it. She was shifting on her feet and chewing a nail, like she wanted to be anywhere in the world but there with him. *Why did she ask me to ride?*

The groom emerged with the orsas. Nora and Ovrun mounted and set off at a slow pace. Even in profile and with her hood up, Nora was beautiful. Ovrun tried not to stare too much at the curve of her lips, but his eyes kept wandering there.

He squeezed the reins tighter. *We're nineteen and seventeen years old. We should be able to have an adult conversation about how we feel.* He wet his lips and spoke. "Nora, that night we met up? That was, uh, really nice." *Great. So eloquent. How could she ever resist you?*

Nora leaned over and stroked her orsa's head. "Yeah, we should probably talk about that. The thing is, when I kissed you, I . . . well . . . it can't go any further. We can't be in a relationship." After blurting out the last sentence, she sat up straight, meeting his gaze.

An ache filled Ovrun's chest as he looked into her gorgeous eyes. "You're saying I read too much into it?"

"No!" Nora shook her head hard. When she spoke again, her voice was choked. "It meant a lot to me. But . . . oh, by the sky, Ovrun, I'm so stupid. I thought you just wanted to have some fun, and then when I realized you liked me as much as I liked you—" A sob burst from her mouth.

I made her cry! If Ovrun hadn't been riding an orsa, he'd have pulled her into his arms again. Then her words sank in. *She said she liked me.* "Your High—I mean, Nora—if we both like each other, what's the problem?"

Nora took a deep breath and wiped her nose on her sleeve. "I can't be in a relationship with anyone unless my dad allows it."

The words punched a hole in Ovrun's chest. He'd hoped no one would subject Nora to such an old-fashioned tradition.

"I can't date, not like other people do," Nora said. "The man I marry will become the king. My dad will help me find that person, just like Queen Onna helped my dad choose my mom. I suppose I'll do the same for my heir. My dad assures me he'll do all he can to help me find someone kind, but . . ." She trailed off and shrugged.

"But it won't be someone like me who wouldn't know the first thing about leading a country."

Nora didn't contradict him. The waning sunlight glistened off the fresh tears in her eyes. "I've kissed a few boys before," she said softly. "None of them really liked me; they all just wanted to be able to say they'd kissed a princess. So I thought you and I would have some fun, and it would end there." She turned her head to look straight at him. "I assumed you'd take advantage of me, and instead, I ended up taking advantage of you. I'm sorry. It was no way to treat a friend."

Her regret was stark and genuine. Ovrun forced a smile. "So . . . you consider me a friend?"

Nora laughed and sniffled. "Don't get too excited. I've only had one friend before, and I drove her away. I doubt you'd want a friend who's this much of a mess."

"But I do, Nora." He tugged his orsa's reins. Seeing it, Nora did the same. Both beasts halted. "I meant everything I said to you that night," Ovrun said. "I like you, not just because you're gorgeous, but because you're *you*. I've missed talking to you lately. If we end this conversation as friends, we're at a better place than where we started it. Right?"

"Right." The word emerged as a croak.

Ovrun reached out a hand. Nora took it and squeezed it. After a few seconds, she smiled. "Don't take this the wrong way, okay?"

He gave her a wary look. "I'll try not to."

She blushed. "Those were really good kisses. Like, exceptional."

He laughed, even as his chest ached with desire. "I can't say I disagree." He turned his head toward the guardhouse, knowing if he looked at her any longer, he'd kiss her again. "I should get back."

"If you could wait a little longer . . . I need to ask you a favor. And I'll understand if you say no." She patted her orsa's backside. Ovrun followed suit. When the beasts were walking alongside each other again, Nora said, "I need the keys to the ministers' offices."

His eyebrows leapt up. "I can't give you those. Why would you even need them?"

"I'll let Krey tell you the details if he wants to. Long story short, it's the best chance we have of finding Zeisha."

Ovrun glanced to the east, toward his family's little house in the city. His mother and sister were probably having dinner. He'd bought the chicken they were eating. He'd also saved their family from eviction twice. Ovrun had never met his dad, and when his sister was five, her father had disappeared. Their mother had sacrificed so much, taking care of them. Now that he was a guard, he was returning the favor. If he got caught loaning out his keys, he'd get fired. He might never get a job this good again.

Then he thought about Krey, who'd been in love with Zeisha since he was too young to know what love was. He was going mad with worry and wanted nothing more than for her to be safe.

Ovrun had great reasons to say no to this request. But what was a job compared to the life and safety of a human being?

He took a deep breath. "I'll do it, Nora. Because you're my friend. Krey is too."

Nora smiled. "I could almost kiss you."

"I can't believe I'm saying this, but please don't."

She laughed, and they turned back toward the stable. The groom took the orsas, and Nora gave Ovrun a tight hug. He didn't want to let go. He could feel her reluctance too.

As he watched her walk back toward the palace, he unbuttoned his coat. An odd combination of contentment and desire had banished the evening chill.

15

*My neighbor, Vosh, liked to tell about how he'd nearly starved after
trading all his food for a wooden flute. He said he never regretted it.*

*Every year on Anyari Day, the entire community gathered together.
Some years, we feasted; other years, we were still hungry at bedtime.
Regardless of the status of our crops, Vosh played his flute from
morning until night, bringing joy to our gathering.*

-The First Generation: A Memoir *by Liri Abrios*

CENTA 25ᵀᴴ, Anyari Day, dawned sunny and warm. All the snow
from a few days before had melted, and now a warm front had
ushered in spring-like weather.

Nora ate breakfast, smiling as she chewed. She washed it all
down with coffee, went to her closet, and chose one of her favorite
shirts, crafted from preday fabric in several shades of green. She
looked at the tag and smiled. *Evie Designs.*

She'd woken early, and the house was still quiet. Her father and Dani rarely slept in, and she couldn't begrudge them their laziness. After putting on her makeup, she poured another cup of coffee and sat at the kitchen table with a novel. Her mind, however, was too busy to focus on a book.

Silently, she reviewed the plans she and Krey had made for later that day. *Is late afternoon really the right time? Will anyone notice we're missing?* She chewed on the inside of her lip, then stopped and took a few deep breaths, shifting her thoughts to the day's festivities.

Anyari Day was the one holiday still in existence that the colonists themselves had celebrated. Many historians speculated that it was related to some sort of winter holiday on humanity's home planet, Earth. It couldn't be proven, but it was a nice idea.

On Anyari Day, people around the world honored the planet's colonists. It was a day of celebration and speculation as people remembered their brave ancestors and considered the mysterious history of their race.

"You woke up early!" Dani said from the doorway.

"Pretty sure you woke up late."

Dani laughed, got a cup of coffee, and sat with Nora. "I'm glad I caught you alone. I've been wanting to talk to you."

Nora's heartbeat accelerated into a rapid trot. Did Dani suspect something about her niece's plans for the day?

"You've seemed a little down the last few days," Dani said, smiling gently.

"Have I?" Nora knew she'd been moody since her conversation with Ovrun. She had a friend again, a fact that brought a smile to her face at the most random times. *If only he could be more than a friend.* She'd been born into an invisible cage, and these days, its bars were squeezing her tighter than ever.

Dani's kindness was hard to resist, though Nora wasn't ready to tell her aunt everything. She drank the last of her coffee and stared into the cup. "Lately, my future has felt so real. And honestly, I don't want to be queen. I know I'll never feel ready for it." That was more than she'd meant to say. She lifted her eyes to her aunt, expecting a lecture.

Instead, Dani reached out and tucked Nora's hair behind her ear. "Oh, sweetheart. It says a lot about you that you're taking it so seriously. But it'll be decades before the crown is yours. I know I push you to be responsible, but I also want you to enjoy being seventeen years old. Maybe I don't tell you that often enough."

Nora blinked back unexpected tears. She'd held back much of what was on her mind, yet somehow her aunt had said just the right thing.

The conversation might have continued, had Nora's father not chosen that moment to enter. "Happy Anyari Day!"

Nora smiled, hoping her eyes weren't too moist, and returned the greeting.

When the king sat down, he took Nora's hand and gave her that sweet, sappy smile she'd gotten used to in the last ten years. "Your mother loved this day."

Now Nora didn't feel the need to hide her tears. She squeezed his hand. "I know. Do you recognize my shoes?"

Her dad looked down at the foot she was extending, and his eyes, too, filled with tears. "They're the ones she wore once a year, on this day. You remember that?"

"Of course I do, Dad."

He kissed her forehead. Across the table, Dani sniffled loudly. An easy silence fell over the table as all three of them used their napkins to wipe away tears.

After a few minutes, Ulmin stood. "I'd better get ready. I'd like to spend a few minutes worshiping in the chapel before the festivities begin."

" 'Bye, Dad."

He smiled and kissed her forehead again, then left. She'd never understood his sudden devotion to God that began right after her mother died, but it seemed to comfort him. Sometimes she envied that.

Dani excused herself to get ready, leaving Nora alone with her thoughts again. She pulled one foot into her lap and ran her fingers along the soft leather of her mother's shoe. When tears filled her eyes, she let them fall.

At eleven, the celebration began with live music on an outdoor stage set up east of the pond. Nora went outside to soak up the joy of the small crowd. The only palace staff expected to work on Anyari Day were guards, and they rotated on short shifts so no one had to work more than five hours. Caterers from the city took care of the food, leaving the household chef free to join the celebration. He was sitting next to the king at a table close to the stage.

Nora found a seat at an empty table and listened to the music. Five string musicians and a trio of percussionists played music that had been popular thirty years ago.

Krey pulled out a chair. "Mind if I sit?" He didn't wait for her response.

"Actually, I was saving the whole table for my large group of age-appropriate friends."

"Oh, good. I'm the same age as you."

"Yeah, but I wouldn't call you appropriate."

A laugh sputtered from his mouth. "So, when are all your friends coming?"

An image of Faylie flashed in her mind, but she banished it. She'd had enough tears today. "Well," she said, "Ovrun is my friend now, but he's working. It took me seventeen years to find him, so at that rate the table will fill up in"—she counted chairs and did some quick figuring in her head—"over a hundred years. You'll have to give up your seat when the last one shows up."

Krey propped his feet on one of the empty chairs. "This music sucks."

"Right? My dad chose it. I chose the after-dark band, though, and you'll love it."

"Assuming we aren't locked up in the security office," he murmured.

She glanced around. "That's enough of that."

"Want a drink?"

"I thought you'd never ask."

He stood. "Get it yourself."

She scowled and followed him as he laughed all the way to the drink table. It was good to hear him laugh. She knew Zeisha was never far from his mind, but hopefully he could enjoy the holiday.

Nora's table did fill up, not with people her age, but with palace staff she'd known for years. They ate lunch together, after which King Ulmin took to the stage and gave a short, rousing speech honoring Anyari's colonists.

Another band began playing, and many celebrants rose to dance. Krey, the only one left at the table besides Nora, spoke quietly. "You nervous?"

"Of course."

"Me too. Just a few more hours."

Nora gave a slight nod. "Know what the best remedy for nerves is?"

"What?"

"Dancing to terrible music." She grinned, stood, and grabbed his hand.

He groaned, but didn't resist too much as she pulled him toward the joyful mob.

Nora and Krey knew it was four o'clock when the king announced the bar was open. He and Dani always served the first round of drinks. Their distraction, combined with a general air of excitement, made it a good time to escape.

Not wanting to attract attention by leaving with Krey, Nora

slipped away first. She strode to the residence gate, praying that neither her dad nor her aunt looked her way. Their backs were to her, but the key still shook in her hand as she opened the gate. A couple of minutes later, she heard a quiet tap. She swung the gate open so Krey could join her.

After leading Krey through the large residence, Nora opened a door, revealing the hallway that led to the palace. She smiled brightly at a guard. "Krey wants to show me a few books in the library," she said. Krey held up his medallion.

The guard lifted an eyebrow. "Tired of this music already?" He gestured for them to pass. The guard at the other end of the hall had heard the exchange, and he didn't give them any trouble, either.

When the door closed behind them, Krey pulled a handful of feathers from his pocket. He threw a couple of them in his mouth and started chewing. "Just in case."

Nora's stomach knotted as they walked through the dark building, but she couldn't keep a smile off her face. "If I wasn't a princess," she whispered, "I think I'd be a spy."

They reached Minister Sharai's office. Nora pulled out the keys Ovrun had loaned her. The key turned easily in the lock. They closed the door and walked past the receptionist's desk. Nora unlocked the minister's door.

The room had a window, but the drapes were closed. Once he'd closed the door behind them, Krey reached for the light switch. Nora covered it with her hand and whispered, "Desk lamp."

"Good call."

They approached the desk, and Nora turned on the small lamp. As they'd planned, Krey started searching drawers while Nora looked through the papers on top of the desk. There wasn't much to go through. Minister Sharai, it seemed, was a minimalist.

Nora was glancing through a neat stack of letters when Krey said, "This drawer is locked. Can you hand me the keys?"

She did, then continued looking through the letters as Krey tried one key after another.

"No luck," he said, setting the keys on the desk. "I'll have to use my magic. Glad I ate those feathers."

"How can flying help with a locked drawer?"

"I'll try to incorporate the drawer into my magic as if I were flying with it. I should be able to sense what's in there."

Nora's eyes widened as she turned to him. "You can do that? That's amazing!"

"Shh. Let me focus." He placed both hands on the front of the drawer. After a moment, he lowered them with a frustrated groan. "It's a big stack of papers. I can feel them, but I can't see them. I have no idea what's written on them, if anything." He jostled the drawer. "I'll see if I can get it open just like I did at that house in the city."

Nora sighed. The letters she'd been looking through were innocuous. Ignoring Krey's grunts and curses, she moved on to other things on the desk. She found a pad of paper, sealed at the top with thick glue. The first few pages contained notes on educational initiatives for rural lysters and reminders about upcoming events. She flipped through the pages once, then again. That's when she noticed writing on a page about halfway through the pad.

"Did you hear that?" Krey whispered.

"What?" she asked, eyes still on the page.

"Shh."

A male voice reached them from the receptionist's office on the other side of the door. "Minister Sharai?"

Nora gasped, her eyes wide. She'd forgotten to lock either of the doors from the inside.

She had barely enough time to turn off the desk lamp before Krey grabbed her arm and practically dragged her to a door in the corner. He threw it open, and they rushed in and pulled the door shut.

The little room was dark, but Nora had seen enough to know it was a bathroom. They had to hide. She groped around the room, though she knew finding a hiding spot in a tiny bathroom with only a toilet and a sink was hopeless.

Her hand hit a metal doorknob, rattling it in a way that made her suck in her breath. She turned the knob and groped around the space with both hands. Shelves, piled with towels and supplies, were on either side. A small space in the middle contained a mop and broom.

Nora reached behind her, and her hand found Krey's shirt. She grabbed it and pulled him close. "Linen closet!" she hissed in his ear.

She stepped in and stood on one side, expecting Krey to join her. Instead, a current of air tickled her skin, and a whisper from above reached her. "I'm up here. The ceiling's high. Hide under some towels."

It was a good plan, as there was only room for one of them to crouch on the floor. Nora pulled the door closed, then crouched and covered herself with towels.

The bathroom door opened. There was a click from a light switch, though little illumination entered the closed closet.

"Minister?" the voice asked again. "Are you in here?"

Nora stayed as still as she could, but her breaths were coming too quickly. Then she heard the sound she'd been dreading—the metal twist of a doorknob and the squeak of hinges as the man opened the linen closet. Panic squeezed Nora's chest, but she didn't dare breathe.

"Huh," the voice said.

The door closed.

Nora didn't take a breath until the light turned off. When the bathroom door closed, she started counting in her head. She planned to count to one hundred, then say something to Krey. When she reached her goal, she didn't think speaking was worth the risk. She kept counting and reached 286 when a hand tapped her through the towels, making her jump.

"Sorry," Krey whispered from where he floated above her. "I think he's gone. We better go in case he calls security."

Back in the dark office, Nora asked softly, "Where'd you put the keys?"

"Right here." Krey rummaged around on the desk. "They were here, I swear," he whispered, tension tightening his voice. He turned on the desk light.

There were no keys.

They searched every bit of the desktop and looked through all the unlocked drawers. Krey crawled under the desk. Nora held the lamp so he could search.

Krey cursed. "They're not here. We have to go."

"But the keys!" Nora's heart, which had calmed a little after the man's exit, resumed its urgent pounding.

"Whoever was here must've taken them. Do you know who it was?"

"Minister Sharai's receptionist. I recognized his voice. Krey, those are Ovrun's keys! We have to return them!"

"You don't think I know that?"

"What are we gonna do?"

"First, we're leaving. Then we'll figure it out."

After turning off the lamp, they left the office and rushed through the building until they reached the hallway leading to the residence. By unspoken agreement, they slowed their pace. Krey opened the door.

The first guard raised his eyebrows. "Where are your books?"

Krey's eyes widened. Nora giggled and said, "We were looking at old books. The ones that stay in the library." She reached her hand up and patted her hair, which was messy, thanks to the towels. She pushed it behind her ear and grinned at the guard.

He chuckled. "Better get back to the celebration."

The other guard let them go with nothing more than a knowing smile.

When they were well past the guards, Krey said, "We should go outside."

Nora grabbed his arm. "Wait—I have to tell you something. Right before the receptionist came in, I saw something on that pad of paper. On a page in the middle, like she didn't want anyone to come across it."

"What was it?"

"A list—food and blankets and stuff. There was a heading on it that said *Militia Supplies*."

"Militia? We don't have a militia. We have an army."

Nora raised her eyebrows. "Sharai doesn't have anything to do with the army. She's in charge of lysters. It's gotta be a New Therroan militia." She left off the obvious conclusion: *A lyster militia.*

Krey's whole face tightened, and he rammed his fingers through his hair. "We've got to find them!"

"Hey." Nora waited for him to meet her gaze. "We will."

He clenched his teeth and shut his eyes, then took a deep breath and released it. "We should go outside."

Nora nodded, and they walked silently back to the celebration. They stopped at the drink table, where Nora asked for two cups of grape juice. When she turned to give Krey's to him, she found him standing a few mets away, staring at a spot behind all the tables.

"Here." Nora handed him his drink, following his gaze. Minister Sharai's receptionist was talking to the head of security and a second guard. "Oh no."

"Is that the receptionist?" Krey murmured.

"Yes."

"We can't both keep staring that direction; someone will notice." Krey walked toward an empty table, followed by Nora. She sat with her back to Sharai. Krey positioned himself so he could see the minister over Nora's shoulder. They pretended to have a normal conversation.

The band played two full songs, and Nora began to hope all was well. Maybe the head of security wouldn't trace the keys back to Ovrun—or to her and Krey. The two of them were keeping up appearances by chatting about something inconsequential when Krey's eyes widened. Nora drew in a sharp breath. "What is it?"

"The other guard left a while ago. He just got back." Krey swallowed. "Ovrun's with him." He was silent for several seconds, and then his shoulders dropped. "The head of security just grabbed Ovrun's arm. It looks like they're walking to the palace."

IN THE DARK: 5

ZEISHA WAS FALLING THROUGH BRIGHT, syrupy air, a broken vine in her hand. The ground drew gradually closer. She wanted to cry out, but all that she could manage was a moan.

Something brushed her shoulder, and a whisper cut through her fear: "What do you see?"

She tried to say, "Help," but it came out as "Hehhuh."

The ground, which had been approaching so slowly, was suddenly beneath her. "Ow." She reached up to her head, closing her eyes against the pain.

"What happened?" That same whisper again.

"Fell. Ow . . . I fell."

"What did you fall from?"

"My vine." She could just sleep here on the ground, right where she'd fallen. It was dark now. She mumbled something that was supposed to be "Good night" and rolled over.

"Zeisha." That insistent whisper. "Did you make the vine?"

She didn't answer; couldn't the person see she had a headache and wanted to sleep?

"Did you, Zeisha?"

Zeisha opened her eyes. Blinked against the darkness. Brought her hand to her aching head.

"Did you make the vine?"

"Yeah," she mumbled. Where was she? Why wasn't the vine in her hand? "I made it. Oh, my head." Her fingers connected with a large, tender lump, and pain jolted her to alertness. *I'm in the dark place where we sleep. Isla's talking to me.* "I think I hit my head today."

"You said you fell from a vine you lysted," Isla said.

"That doesn't make sense. I can't make a vine strong enough to hold me."

"I can't create a huge hole in the ground, but that's what I dreamed about a few days ago."

Zeisha sat up, gasping when the throbbing in her head worsened. She reached out for Isla's hands. They were cold, and Zeisha rubbed them between her own hands. "Why don't they want us to remember, Isla?"

"I don't know." Isla sighed. "You need to count."

Zeisha moved the string and ran her fingers along the ridges on her ankle. There were two columns of them now. "Eleven weeks, six days."

"Good night," Isla said.

Zeisha lay down. Even her pounding head didn't keep her from sleeping.

16

Mom and Dad often talked of their preday lives. It was strange hearing them speak of grandparents, aunts, and uncles. Nobody in our community had such relatives; they were all dead. But an elderly lady who lived nearby let us call her Granny, and some of my friends' parents seemed like aunts and uncles.

When my own children interacted with their aunts, uncles, and grandparents, it brought a fullness to my life I hadn't realized was missing.

-The First Generation: A Memoir *by Liri Abrios*

As Nora had promised, the after-dinner band she'd chosen was great.

But dancing was torture for Krey. His limbs were stiff, his smiles forced. He could tell Nora felt the same, but they were determined not to attract attention. That meant they had to celebrate.

Moving her hips and feet to the music, Nora brought her mouth to Krey's ear. "The head of security is talking to my father."

A dozen curses were on the tip of Krey's tongue, but he stifled them and whispered to Nora, "Dessert time."

They walked together to the dessert table, grabbed cake that didn't look remotely appetizing, and found seats with a good view of the king's table.

Away from the crowd of dancers, the evening breeze hit Krey's sweaty body, chilling him. He put on his jacket and pulled up the hood. Nora did the same. They watched the king's table wordlessly. It wasn't long before the head of security left.

Krey took one bite of cake. He held his fork between two fingers, tilting it up and down like a seesaw, tapping the table over and over.

Nora brought her hand down on the fork, silencing it. "We have to help Ovrun."

"I know, but I'm all out of bright ideas."

She looked away and folded her arms. He tapped his fork again, this time in rhythm with the music. Nora twisted to face him and grabbed the fork, slamming it on the table, out of his reach. "We need to tell Dani everything. She'll save Ovrun's job if she knows he stole the keys for me."

"No—no!" Krey was so overwhelmed with the sheer *terribleness* of the idea that he momentarily forgot how to form coherent sentences.

"But—" Nora began.

"No! Listen, it was one thing for them to give *me* a break when I went into the records hall. They thought I was just a stupid apprentice going on an errand for you. It's different for a guard! They won't care that he was helping you!"

"Then what can we do for him?" Nora's chest was rising and falling rapidly, and the lamp in the middle of their table illuminated tears in her eyes. "You know I wasn't joking when I said he was my only friend, right?"

Krey just looked at her, pressing his lips together. The confession made his heart ache, a sensation he didn't particularly like.

Nora shook her head hard. "If he gets fired, I'll never forgive myself."

Krey sighed. "Me either."

Nora went to the kitchen the next morning, drawn by the smell of savory sausage.

"You're up early, Your Highness!" the chef said. "I was making breakfast for your father, but there's enough for two."

"Thanks." She poured two cups of coffee. "I'm going to my father's rooms. Will you please bring the food there?"

"You bet."

Nora walked to her father's quarters and knocked. "It's me."

"Come on in, sweetie."

Nora entered. "I brought you coffee. I thought we could have breakfast in here."

Her father was buttoning his shirt collar in front of a mirror. "Perfect! Why don't you set it on the table? I'm almost ready."

She sat at his small, private dining table and watched him, trying to figure out how to bring up the subject of Ovrun. Guilt had kept her awake most of the night. Ovrun had risked his career to help her. She should've guarded those keys with her life.

Ovrun had filled a place in her heart that had been empty for months. The thought of losing him so soon after realizing his value—of letting him down when he'd given her way more than she deserved—was unbearable.

Her father sat and sipped his coffee. "Delicious. I needed this; yesterday wiped me out." He chuckled. "In fact, I need all the help I can get with the New Therroans today."

"How do you think your negotiations will go?"

He gave her a kind smile. "I'm glad you're asking. One day, you'll be the one working on this. I'm sure things will be more stable by then, but right now, it's rough. Some of their leaders want to compromise, but others will only settle for immediate independence."

"I'm sorry it's not going well." She was also sorry she'd asked. As important as the topic was, right now she couldn't focus on anything but Ovrun's fate.

The chef entered and set a plate in front of each of them containing chepple sausage, bread, and fruit. They thanked him, and he exited.

"I don't want you worrying about New Therro," her father said. "Dani told me you've had a rough week. It was good seeing you enjoy yourself at the celebration yesterday."

"It was a lot of fun!" Nora lied. She eyed him over her coffee. "Did you feel like everything went smoothly?"

"Overall, yes. Though I didn't care for the bands you chose." He grinned at her; it was an ongoing topic of ribbing for both of them.

Nora laughed, hoping it sounded natural. They ate for a few minutes in near silence. *Well, if he isn't gonna bring up the break-in, I will.* "I saw you talking to the head of security. Is everything okay?"

He set down his fork and wiped his mouth with a napkin. "Nothing you need to worry about."

"Did something happen?"

"Always the curious one." He gave her a fond look. "I don't suppose it hurts to tell you. Someone found one of the ministers' offices unlocked. Inside was a set of keys belonging to a guard."

"Oh, really? Which guard?"

"Ovrun. Do you know him? He came on our trip with us."

Nora widened her eyes in mock surprise. "Yeah, I do know him. Nice guy."

"He does seem nice. He claimed he lost his keys and didn't report it because he hoped he'd find them. Unfortunately, someone used them to sneak into an office. It's not a mistake we can overlook."

"Is he in trouble?"

The king gave her a helpless shrug. "We had to fire him. It might have been different if he'd told us as soon as he lost the keys. I don't like letting him go, but I'm sure he feels lucky we didn't arrest him."

"Oh." Nora was glad she still had a little food on her plate. She took a bite, chewed, and swallowed through a tight throat. Her quickening heartbeat pressed against her shirt, the rhythm whispering, *No! No! No!*

She glanced up at her father, who was watching her with a concerned expression. "Was he a friend of yours?"

Friend. The word struck Nora like a blow. She brought her coffee cup to her lips, but it was empty. "Yeah. He was."

"I'm sorry, sweetie. I'm sure he'll find another place to work. He just needs to mature a bit."

It took an awful lot of effort to nod and smile.

Ulmin stood and went to Nora. He leaned down and gave her a hug. "I'm going to visit the chapel before I head out. I'll be home late tonight."

"Aunt Dani?"

Dani looked up from the book she was reading. "Good morning. Enjoying your day off?"

Nora suddenly found it impossible to hold back tears. She pressed her lips together and covered her mouth.

Dani stood. "Oh, honey, come in. Sit down."

Nora sat in the chair next to Dani's. The downstairs living room was lit with bright electric lights, plus a crackling fire. Nora's sobs echoed off the papered walls. Dani leaned over and enveloped her niece in a hug. "That's right, let it out."

Nora shook her head, trying to calm herself. She didn't want to cry; she wanted to *talk*. But her aunt's soft arms and soothing words made her even more emotional.

After a couple of minutes, Nora said, "I'm okay." Dani sat back. Nora sniffled and blurted, "A guard got fired yesterday."

Dani nodded. "I heard. Why are you so upset?"

"Because it was my fault."

Dani's eyes widened. "I think you'd better tell me what that means."

A spear of guilt entered Nora's stomach. Krey would hate that she was sharing this with her aunt, but who else was she supposed to talk to? At least she could keep him out of it. She wiped her eyes and told her aunt about her suspicion that Minister Sharai's elite apprenticeship program was something more.

"Nora, what would make you think such a thing?" Dani asked.

Good question. Nora couldn't tell Dani about the letters Krey had found, or about the New Therroan connection. "Just . . . just a feeling," she said. Then she confessed that she'd befriended Ovrun and convinced him to give her the keys to Sharai's office.

"I went into the office yesterday, and I left the keys there," Nora said, her chin trembling again. "He'd still have his job if it weren't for me. I messed up the rest of his life because I was careless!"

Dani reached out and took Nora's hand. "You did mess up, but Ovrun did too. He knew better than to go along with such a scheme. In fact, if the head of security knew he loaned his keys out rather than misplacing them, he'd be in even more trouble."

"Please don't tell him!" The words came out as sobs.

It was a minute or two before Dani responded. "Against my better judgment, I'll keep this private. More to salvage your peace of mind than to save Ovrun." She locked her gaze with Nora's. "Krey West was with you when you broke in, wasn't he?"

Nora stopped crying. Stopped *breathing*. At last, she recovered enough to say, "No." But she'd never been good at lying to Dani.

"You left the celebration yesterday afternoon. Krey was gone too."

Nora looked at her hands. "I'm sorry."

"Oh, Nora." Dani's hand came up and rested on Nora's cheek.

"This boy . . . this *young man* . . . as nice as he is, he's not a very good friend. He's gotten you into trouble twice now, trying to find his girl-friend. And she isn't even missing; she just doesn't want to talk to him! He's even making you question why Faylie moved. Sweetheart, he's dragging you down."

"It's not like that!" But Nora didn't know how to convince Dani without disclosing Krey's visit to the records hall.

"Krey needs to live somewhere else."

"What?" Nora's voice turned shrill.

"Other apprentices live in boarding houses around Cellerin City. We'll find him a job at a public library instead of our private one. It'll be better for him, Nora. For both of you."

"No!" Nora wiped fresh tears off her cheeks, but they kept coming. "Ovrun was my friend, and he's gone! And Krey—well, he's infuriating, but I think he might be my friend, too. I won't have anyone left! And besides, he needs my help—"

"No, Nora! He doesn't need your help. He needs to focus on his apprenticeship. I'll try to find some other young people to work at the palace; I know you need friends. But you don't need *him* as a friend! I'm sorry, but I'm not budging on this."

Nora knew when she'd lost a battle with Dani. She continued to protest anyway, but none of her arguments left a divot in Dani's stone resolve. Finally, Nora whispered, "Can I tell Krey goodbye?"

Dani considered it for long enough to convince Nora the answer would be no. But at last, her aunt nodded. "Five minutes. That's it."

Krey was pacing in his room, trying to figure out how to get word to Nora that Ovrun was gone. He'd heard it from a guard earlier that morning.

Movement outside his window caught his eye. Nora and Dani were walking toward the dorm. Their postures—square shoulders for

Dani and slumped ones for Nora—told him all he needed to know. *She told her aunt we broke into the office. By the stone, she told her; I know she did!* He stomped down the stairs and into the yard, ready to give Nora a piece of his mind.

But when Nora approached him, leaving her aunt standing several mets away, she was crying. Not a few elegant, royal tears; this was all-out bawling with hiccups, snot, and sobs. All Krey's angry words fled. "What happened?"

"You—I—" She couldn't get more than that out.

Krey stood motionless. Then a memory of his Aunt Evie's voice echoed in his brain: *Best piece of advice when Zeisha's crying? Just hold her.*

Could he do that with Nora? Would she take it wrong? Since her ill-fated kiss attempt, she hadn't even flirted with him. Surely it was safe to give her one hug.

He held out his arms, and she rushed into them. When she wiped her nose on his shirt, he didn't flinch. *I deserve major points for that.*

Nora's tears soon slowed. She pulled away, took a deep breath, and told him the truth. She'd been so upset about Ovrun getting fired that she'd talked to her aunt, trying to keep Krey out of it. Her shrewd aunt figured out his role anyway.

Now Krey had to leave the palace. *I should've known better than to trust a royal. I did know better.* Maybe Nora had good intentions, but telling her aunt had been just plain stupid.

Dani's gentle voice reached them. "Nora, you need to wrap it up."

Nora leaned in close and spoke softly, her voice hoarse from crying. "I still want to help you. If you find out anything, write me a note, fold it as small as you can, and throw it over the fence. Right where we climbed over. I'll check every morning and afternoon."

The offer struck a gentle blow to his hard-earned cynicism. Was she really that kind? Or just that lonely? *Does it matter?* "Okay," he whispered. "You do the same. Don't write too many specifics. I'll fly over to look for notes as often as I can." His eyes flicked up. "Your aunt's coming."

Nora gave him another hug and said in his ear, "You're an ass, but you're my friend."

A laugh broke through his frustration. He let go of Nora, then turned to Dani. "I'll get my things."

17

When I was four, someone in our community learned to make candles. Before that, our bedrooms were dark as the stone at night. My siblings sometimes felt scared, but not me. I looked out the window and talked to the stars like they were my friends.

-The First Generation: A Memoir *by Liri Abrios*

KREY CLAPPED Hatlin on the back. "This round's on me."

Hatlin grinned. "I'm not gonna argue with that!"

Krey went to the bar and came back with grape juice for himself and beer for Hatlin.

Hatlin took a big gulp of his drink. "You ever gonna drink anything more exciting than juice?"

"Hey, we're discussing important stuff. I don't want to slow my mind down."

"Lucky for me," Hatlin said, "I can drink and think at the same time."

Krey chuckled. Hatlin wasn't very smart when he was sober, and by the end of a meeting, the group counted themselves blessed if he made sense at all.

This was Krey's third private meeting with the rebels, and he still hadn't heard one reference to a magic-eater militia. Every week, he became less convinced that the New Therroans had Zeisha. And he became more convinced of the righteousness of their cause.

Most of the people at these meetings had grown up in New Therro, where they were treated like rebellious children. In the half-century since the advent of the Cellerinian monarchy, there'd never been a minister from New Therro. (Minister Sharai's parents were from there, but she'd been born in Cellerin City.)

It wasn't fair, they all argued, to pay taxes when no one in the government advocated for them. Plus, New Therro had trouble getting the same goods and services as people closer to the city. That particular issue struck close to home for Krey.

Above all, Krey admired these ordinary people who were willing to work for something big, something they believed in. Their lives had meaning beyond putting bread on the table. That was what he'd always wanted for himself: To affect the world for good. To *matter*.

"Let's get started." Wallis, a man who had no title but was clearly the group's leader, stood at the head of the long table. He was of average build and height, but his hazel eyes were fierce and intense. When everyone quieted, he said, "I'd like to continue our discussion on our lack of magic eaters. Anyone come up with any recruitment ideas?" He looked straight at Krey, the single talented person in the room.

Krey almost tested them by saying, *We could abduct magic eaters and start a militia.* But they'd think he was crazy—or they'd kill him for finding out their secret. He shook his head and shrugged, keeping his ears open and his mouth closed.

It was past midnight when the meeting ended, but Krey needed to see if Nora had left him a message. He walked through the cold streets, wearing both a hat and a hood, eating diced feathers. When he thought he'd had enough, he took to the frigid air.

He landed inside the wooded area east of the palace, then walked through the dark trees, keeping his eyes fixed on the ground. The moonlight soon illuminated the item he was seeking: a fallen branch.

He lifted it. It wasn't that heavy, but it was nearly as tall as him. Flying with a stone clutched to his chest was second nature now, but was he ready to support an item's weight all along his body? Krey held the branch upright against his left side and, as he'd been doing with stones, enfolded it into his magic.

A gasp escaped his mouth. The base of the branch pressed against his booted foot. They were all one—sweaty foot, soft sock, broken-in leather, rough bark. It was the same all the way up his body where the crooked branch pressed into his thigh, waist, arm, and shoulder. He could sense the miniscule holes of early rot throughout the wood. He shivered with the sensation of dozens of tiny bugs crawling in those spaces. There was a beauty in this fallen branch, one he'd never have seen with his eyes.

Continuing to clutch the branch, Krey flew above the trees. He stopped when he neared the palace perimeter fence. Two guards were patrolling with their lanterns. He doubted they'd spot him against the dark sky.

When the guards were far enough away from the area Krey was targeting, he swooped in, landed, and set down the branch. He lit a small candle he'd carried in his pocket and began looking for a note from Nora.

Several minutes of careful searching yielded nothing. He held the candle close to his chest. Blocking most of its light with his gloved hand, he rose into the sky and looked for the guards. One of them was nearing the corner. Cursing, Krey returned to the ground. He was about to blow out the candle when an idea struck. *What if Nora wrote a note but didn't throw it far enough?*

Still blocking most of the candlelight, he flew up. He surveyed the top of the thick, stone fence. *There!* A compact, folded piece of paper was stuck in the twisting barbed wire.

Krey pinched the candle wick with two gloved fingers and put it in his pocket, just as a guard turned the corner and started walking his way. He reached between the wires and grabbed the note. As he lifted it out, barbs snagged his glove, holding it fast. *Damn it.* He withdrew his hand from the glove, leaving the note where it lay and wincing when the sharp metal cut him. There was no way to retrieve the glove without further injuring himself. At least it was a tall fence; the guards shouldn't find the glove any time soon.

The guard was close now. Krey adjusted his position so he was hovering over the garden, inside the fence. A caynin came running. *Must've heard me.* It drew closer, and a loud *uh-uh-uh* emerged from its gaping mouth. Krey grabbed the note with his still-gloved hand. He pulled it out, avoiding the barbs.

Gripping the note tightly in his bleeding hand, he soared away, pursued by the caynin's staccato call.

Back at his boarding house, Krey washed his hand in the outdoor water pump. If it weren't so late, he would've found the blood-eater apprentice who lived down the hall. The young man could've easily healed Krey's wounds. The cuts weren't too bad, though. They'd heal quickly.

Krey rushed into his room and pulled the note from his pocket. In neat print, it read, *Our friend:*, followed by a Cellerin City address.

A smile tugged at Krey's lips. *Our friend.* That had to be Ovrun, and this must be where he lived. Nora had probably gotten the address from another guard. *Flirting again, Princess?*

Krey's long day caught up with him, and when he lay in bed, he fell asleep immediately. The note with Ovrun's address filled his dreams, waking him at dawn. His first inclination was to go straight to

Ovrun's house, but the former guard might still be sleeping. It was Sunday, so Krey set off instead to find a Rimorian chapel. Since leaving home, he hadn't been to any services. He hadn't wanted to attend a snooty, private service only for the palace residents.

The streets were almost empty, and Krey soon found a small chapel. He joined about a dozen other early risers at the first service of the day. The music started, and he soaked in the songs he'd grown up with. He held back tears when he imagined his aunt, hundreds of clommets away, hearing this same music. After the emissary's short message, the music started again. Krey slipped out, more at peace than he'd been in weeks.

After half an hour of walking, he knocked at the pale-green door of a small, well-kept house. No one came, so he knocked again. The door opened, revealing a bleary-eyed Ovrun.

"Krey!" Ovrun's eyebrows pulled together. "What are you doing here?"

"I got kicked out of the palace."

Ovrun folded his arms.

"I know you're pissed," Krey said, "and you have every right to be. But can we talk?"

Ovrun eyed him warily, but stepped back and beckoned him into a small, tidy living room.

"Are your mom and sister here?" Krey asked.

"They're at chapel services." Ovrun sat on a small couch and gestured to a chair.

Krey spoke as soon as he was seated. "Ovrun, it's my fault someone found your keys. I left them on the minister's desk." Ovrun wasn't looking at him, but he kept talking anyway. "I know apologizing doesn't come close to making up for what I did, but I had to tell you . . . I'm sorry."

Ovrun met his gaze. "I loved that job."

"I could tell."

"I *needed* that job. My family needed me to have it."

"Have you found anything else?" Krey asked quietly.

"No. I've tried. I'm thinking about joining the army, if they'll take me. And if I can convince my mother. She says it's dangerous, even though we've been at peace since before she was born. But even if I do enlist, it doesn't pay much. I'll have to find something else too."

Krey pressed his lips together and nodded. Cellerin's army was small and only trained a couple of weekends a month. *It's my fault he's scrambling for work.* Krey felt like a fool, coming here to ask for Ovrun's help again. But Zeisha's freedom, and possibly her life, were at stake. *I'm happy to be a fool for her.*

He took a deep breath. "I know I shouldn't be here, but—" He swallowed and spread his hands helplessly. "By the stone, Ovrun, I just want to find Zeisha."

Ovrun's expression softened a little. "I know. That's why I helped you. That, and because I considered you and Nora friends."

"I considered you a friend too. I still do." Krey leaned forward, resting his elbows on his knees. "In fact, I trust you enough to tell you why we needed your keys. We should've told you this from the beginning."

He started talking, and the only detail he skipped was Nora's suspicion about Faylie. That part of the story was hers to tell.

Ovrun's eyes widened as Krey told him the Minister of Lysting might've started a secret militia. "Can you tell me anything about Sharai?" Krey asked. "Maybe people who visit her, or specific times she leaves? I don't really know what I'm looking for, but with all the time you've spent at the gate . . ."

Ovrun was looking down at his folded hands, flicking one thumbnail against the other. After a minute or so of this, he looked up. "Some guy delivers a thick envelope to her every week. It always seemed weird to me that he doesn't use the regular mail system. He's got permission to go inside the gate and bring it straight to Sharai."

Krey's mouth dropped open, then widened into a smile. "That's exactly the type of information I need."

Ovrun shrugged. "I can't imagine what you're going through with

Zeisha missing. And maybe I'm stupid for saying this, but . . . I have some time on my hands these days. Do you still need help?"

Krey gaped again. "Are you serious?"

"Yeah." Ovrun smiled for the first time since Krey's arrival. "Yeah. I want to help."

Krey blinked against an influx of emotion. He covered it with a laugh. "I need all the help I can get."

18

My mom used to talk longingly of the days when a woman could take one pill a month to suppress her period. If she preferred not to take medication, she could use high-quality, inexpensive hygiene products. After The Day, scavengers gathered as many of these pills and products as they could find, hoarding them and requiring such valuable goods in return, only the wealthiest could afford them.

-The First Generation: A Memoir *by Liri Abrios*

NORA TAPPED her pencil on the table and gazed out the window behind her father's desk. It was such a nice day, barely cold enough for a light jacket. Inside, heaters made the air stuffy and thick. She longed to leave the palace and practice magic.

"How's the math coming?" Nora's father's voice yanked her attention away from the window.

"Great!" She turned her gaze back to the problem she'd been stuck on for fifteen minutes. *Pointless, pointless, this is pointless.* It was a refrain that had been running through her head constantly. She'd even made up a little tune for it.

Dani hadn't revealed Nora's role in the break-in. She had, however, told the king that his daughter needed more structure. Now he forced Nora to sit in his office every weekday, doing school work. He'd temporarily halted her training with master lysters. Tutors came every afternoon, assisting her under her father's watchful eye. It had been less than a week, and Nora was already sick of it.

"How close are you to being done with that assignment?"

Nora flinched. She hadn't heard her father come to stand behind her.

"I still have a whole page of problems."

"I want it done by the time I return from my Board of Ministers meeting."

"I could go with you." Nora flashed him a hopeful smile. "I'd learn a lot there."

"Great idea." When Nora started to rise, her father placed his hand on her shoulder and gently pushed her back down. "When you graduate, you can start attending the meetings with me." He winked and left the room.

Nora stared at the paper without focusing on it. She'd gotten a note from Krey a few days earlier, and she could think of nothing else. *Sharai gets top-secret papers delivered to her every week.* Surely they had something to do with the militia. They might contain information on Zeisha.

They might contain information on Faylie too.

Nora knew her friend had almost certainly moved to Newland. But what if she hadn't? What if she was in trouble? The possibility seemed more real as the days progressed. Whether that was due to some inner instinct or misplaced hope, Nora didn't know.

Still, it was one thing to know about Sharai's secret papers. It was another thing to actually get to them. It wasn't like Nora could break into the minister's office again.

She sat up straighter. Sharai would be at the Board of Ministers meeting. Maybe breaking in wasn't necessary. A plan quickly formed in her racing mind.

She'd brought a small ice chest with her, hoping to practice outside at lunchtime. She opened it and fueled up, just in case. The ice sent a chill through her body, a welcome sensation after being so warm all day. She put on her hooded jacket and waited a couple of minutes, reviewing her plan. Then she ate more ice.

That done, she rushed into her father's receptionist's office. She grabbed the edge of the desk, leaning close to the startled woman. "Do you have a tampon?"

The receptionist, who acted as Nora's jailer while the king was away, gave Nora a pitying smile. "Of course." She opened a desk drawer and handed Nora two paper-wrapped tampons. "One for later."

"You're the best." Nora smiled, then winced and brought her hand to her belly. "I might be a few minutes." She shoved both tampons in her pocket and rushed out.

Instead of going to the bathroom, she descended the stairs as fast as she dared. She strode into Minister Sharai's office. "I'm here for my appointment with the minister."

The receptionist's eyes were as wide as they'd been last time Nora came to visit Sharai. "I . . . uh, I'm sorry, she's in a meeting."

Nora stepped toward the minister's office door. "It's all right; she asked me to come by."

The receptionist stepped between Nora and the door. "I'm sorry, Your Highness, but she's not in there."

"Oh." Nora frowned. "Is she in the palace?"

"Yes."

"Hmm. It sounded like it was urgent when we spoke." Nora squared her shoulders and spoke imperiously. "I'll write her a note to let her know I'm here. You can deliver it." She bent over the receptionist's desk, grabbed a piece of paper and a pen, and started writing.

"Your Highness?" The receptionist's voice was hesitant. "You want me to bring her a note . . . during the Board of Ministers meeting?"

Nora paused in her writing. "Of course. My father won't mind. Or at least . . . I don't think he will." She let out a nervous laugh. "Don't say who the note is from, okay? I mean, I've gotta live with the guy."

When she was done writing, she handed the note to the receptionist. He walked away, fidgeting with the paper. As soon as the outer office door was closed, Nora rushed to the inner door and found it unlocked. She stifled a giddy laugh. Whatever the results of this adventure, it beat doing math problems.

Listening through the open door for the receptionist's return, she dashed to the desk. Sharai's secret communications were probably in the locked drawer Krey hadn't been able to open. Nora grabbed the handle, but the drawer was as immovable as before. She scanned the desktop and looked through the three unlocked drawers. No keys.

Breathe, Nora. She surveyed the room, though she didn't know what she was looking for. Her gaze fell on the cardigan draped over the back of Sharai's chair. Was that . . . ? Yes! *Pockets!* Nora reached in one pocket, then the other—and drew out a ring of keys.

The third one opened the desk drawer, revealing hundreds of papers, covered in typed text. She didn't have time to read any of them, nor space to carry them all, so she grabbed a handful, folded them in half, and shoved them into the waistband of her pants. Her jacket was loose enough to cover the bulge. She closed the drawer and locked it, then put the keys back.

Again, hysterical laughter threatened to emerge from her mouth. She shoved it down and rushed back into the outer office—just in time for the receptionist's return.

The man nearly jumped when he saw Nora. "What were you doing in the minister's office?"

Heat entered Nora's face, but she shrugged, trying to stay relaxed. "I thought I'd wait in there. I was checking to see if you were back." Noting the suspicious look in the receptionist's eyes, she catalyzed her magic. Just a precaution.

The receptionist took a step back, his body blocking the outer doorway. "Due to last week's break-in, I've been instructed to report any intruders to the minister's office. Sky above, why didn't I lock that door?" He pointed at a chair. "Please sit, Your Highness." His gruff tone belied his polite words.

Where'd the intimidated receptionist go? Nora forced her mouth into a calming smile. "I'm sure that edict doesn't cover a member of the royal family."

"*Anyone.* It doesn't matter who your father is."

Nora's breathing turned shallow as she stared at the man in front of her. He was close to twice her size and could overwhelm her in seconds if he wanted to. He wouldn't go that far though . . . would he?

"I'm going to fetch a guard," the receptionist said. "But first, sit." He stepped toward her with one arm extended, like he was about to guide her—or force her—into the chair. His eyes were alive with panic. He'd messed up by leaving her alone. He'd make things worse if he let her go.

Almost before Nora knew what she was doing, she lifted her palms and shot a stream of ice downward. A small, slick spot formed in front of the receptionist's feet.

His forehead furrowed, but he didn't stop coming for her. One of his big boots hit the ice. He slipped, his foot continuing forward while the rest of him toppled backwards. He landed with a crash and a grunt.

Immediately, he started to push himself up. Nora ran toward the door, aiming a ball of ice over her shoulder at him, hoping it hit him somewhere—anywhere.

His groan was a lot louder this time. Nora rushed out. As she slammed the door behind her, she glimpsed the man holding his groin. *Oops.* She hadn't been aiming there in particular, but it had done the trick.

She ran down the hall, her mind racing as fast as her feet. *I broke into the office and hurt the receptionist. They'll find these papers on me. I'll be grounded for eternity. Maybe disinherited.* Within seconds, her thoughts all converged on one point. *I have to get out of here.*

The first hallway was empty, but the next one wasn't. "What's wrong?" multiple staff members asked as she ran by them.

"Minister Sharai's receptionist!" she replied, panting. "He's sick!"

She kept repeating the message as she ran, leaving chaos behind her. Several people responded by hurrying toward Sharai's office.

Guards at the front doors stood up straighter as Nora approached. "What's wrong, Your Highness?"

She stopped long enough to repeat the message about the receptionist, adding, "I know someone who can help! I'll be back!" She threw open the front door and continued her sprint. The outdoor guards yelled questions, but she ignored them. Before long, they'd know what happened. Everyone at the palace would be looking for her. She had to be gone by then.

Nora didn't have time for a fancy escape plan. She couldn't hide her tracks or create an alibi. Instead, she ran, all the way through the garden and to the stone fence.

It loomed above her, tall and intimidating. Ignoring a caynin who loped up to greet her, Nora knelt before the fence, the papers in her waistband crinkling.

Krey's advice ran through her mind. *Keep your magical passages tight.* Just as she'd been practicing, she tensed her chest and arms.

Aim. She'd been working on that too. Fingers bent at ninety degrees, she shot a narrow ladder rung onto the stone wall. *It worked!*

She moved up, setting the rungs as far apart as she dared, glancing behind her every few seconds. Her handle-shaped rungs were lopsided and small, not nearly as pretty as Krey's. But they were thick, and they stuck to the stone.

She began to climb, adding handle-rungs as she went. Her mind insisted she was about to fall. Her heart hammered madly. She tried to ignore them both.

When she reached the top, she was so out of breath that she

feared she'd pass out. Stopping, however, wasn't an option. Nora covered the barbed wire in a wide, rough blob of ice.

"Princess Nora! Come down!" a distant voice called.

Trembling, Nora grabbed onto the ice covering the wire. Her stomach lurched with effort and anxiety as she pulled herself up to the last ladder rung. There were no guards in sight on the other side of the fence, thank the sky.

She didn't have anywhere near enough fuel to make a Krey-style slide. Her mind had chewed on this problem the whole time she was making the ladder rungs, and only one idea seemed doable.

Despite the shouts, which were getting closer, Nora leaned over. Her belly rested on the ice blob she'd created over the barbed wire. Dizziness overtook her, but she ignored it. She held her hands out, pointed her fingers, tightened her pathways, and aimed.

She used every bit of her remaining fuel to create a small ledge halfway down the outer face of the fence. It was just big enough for her to crouch on. Hopefully it was strong enough to hold her.

"Your Highness! Stop!"

The shout was just mets away. Nora scrambled to crouch on the ice topping the fence, turning herself around as she did so. She found two slick handholds and dropped her body over the opposite side. Her gut screamed at her, insisting she was about to fall.

This time, her fears were well founded. Her fingers slipped, and she dropped.

She landed hard, but she was on the ledge, not the ground. Her knees would be bruised, but nothing was broken.

"Climb!" one of the guards shouted from the other side of the fence.

A high-pitched moan exited Nora's throat as she gazed down. She was still two-and-a-half mets off the ground, and she didn't dare jump off. With brisk, sure movements, she repeated her action from before. *Turn. Hang on. Dangle. Drop.*

Now her knees weren't just bruised; they were bleeding. And her wrist hurt. But her ankles were fine; that was what mattered. Nora turned to run, then heard a guard shout, "Stop!" This time, the fence didn't muffle the voice. Nora turned and saw a guard pulling himself up, trying to get on top of the mound of ice she'd left behind on the fence.

She halted and shouted, "I'm going to let the ice go! It'll crumble! Climb back down! I don't want to hurt you!"

"Why are you running?"

She didn't answer.

"Come on, Nora!" The guard was one she'd known for at least ten years. He smiled. "Please, come back. Running'll just make it worse."

"I'm sorry!" she shouted, and she meant it. "I'm releasing the ice in five seconds. One—"

"Help me down!" the guard shouted to his colleague behind him.

Nora gave him more than five seconds. When she figured he was close enough to the ground not to hurt himself, she released the ice. It crumbled into tiny chips.

She sprinted into the trees.

19

My parents flew across the world in great machines called solarplanes. Such trips were inconceivable to children who'd never traveled in anything faster than a wagon pulled by two lazy orsas.

We couldn't visit the rest of the world, but we did learn about it through the stories of traveling traders. Many had traversed our entire continent. We even met two who claimed to have sailed across the ocean.

The traders' tales confirmed that magical people and creatures exist all over the planet. Some storytellers claimed to have visited magical places too. They described meadows that sang, rivers that divided so the worthy could cross, and fruit that would extend the life of the one who ate it.

I don't know if I believe in such magical locations. I hope some of them are real.

-The First Generation: A Memoir by Liri Abrios

THERE'S *no way I can reach the city before the guards do.* Lungs and legs burning, Nora ran through the wooded area, toward the road. *Some of them will search the area around the palace. Others will go to the city. They'll find Krey, because Aunt Dani will think that's where I'm going.*

How long would it take for them to start chasing her? The guards who'd seen her go over the fence would run to tell the others. Some would set out on foot; some would take orsas. She had a three- to five-minute head start, not nearly enough time to stay ahead of mounted guards.

She quickly reached the road. When she got there, she looked to the right, toward the palace gate.

No one was coming. Yet.

She crossed the road and kept running into a field of hardy, winter greens. A farmhouse and outbuildings sat beyond the field. The barn beckoned her, but there was no way she'd reach it before guards entered the road.

Only one thing to do. She ran a couple of dozen mets, hopping over one row of greens after another. Then she lay flat on the cold soil between two rows, parallel to the road, praying the guards wouldn't see her.

Her breathing hadn't had time to slow before she heard the rapid footsteps and urgent voices of guards. They approached—and passed her.

Nora lifted her head and watched through the plants as three guards ran to the farmhouse. They entered the house for several minutes. During that time, six mounted guards passed on orsas, likely headed toward the city.

The guards exited the farmhouse and separated, walking into various outbuildings. When they finished, they'd probably search the field. *Where can I go?* She scanned the area, her gaze fixing on a long line of people waiting to enter the chapel. Did she dare?

I don't have another choice. Nora stood, put up her hood, and swiped dirt off her clothes. She jogged to the road, joining the back of the line and keeping her head down. Before The Day, the daughter of a nation's leader would've had her face plastered all over screens. Now, newspapers published drawings of various quality, but Nora knew from previous escapes that people often didn't recognize her. Her hood should help too.

Soon, a group of three people on push scooters pulled into the line behind Nora. She ignored them, keeping her arms folded and gaze low.

Within half an hour, another mounted team of two left the palace. The guards who'd gone into the farmhouse split up, moving toward neighboring properties. Nora stepped out of the line. The people behind her glanced up, then returned to their conversation. She crossed the street and entered the field of greens again.

This time, she walked farther into the field, keeping her back to the palace. When she was confident the fence guards were too far away to recognize her, she turned at a furrow between two rows and walked parallel to the street.

Most of the searchers had gone to the city, and for good reason: they knew she'd have a hard time surviving by herself, out here in the country. If she walked far enough, she'd encounter the river that fed ancient canals still used by farmers. Eventually, she'd reach the massive mountain in the west. *Where I'd die of starvation.*

Staying outside wasn't an option. She needed an alternate route into the city, one the guards might not immediately search. After a clommet or so of walking, she saw a country road running north-south. She turned to parallel it, staying under the shade of scattered trees as much as she could.

This area was unfamiliar to Nora. She wished she had the time to enjoy her walk. She hurried through fields both cultivated and fallow, finally seeing a narrow, east-west road leading into the city. *Maybe no one's searching that road.* Her heart lifted. As she'd done countless times already, she glanced behind her, just to make sure no one was coming.

Far in the distance, a rider was approaching on orsaback. Nora drew in a sharp breath.

A group of trees stood just ahead, their branches bare. Tree climbing had been one of her favorite solitary pursuits as a child, especially in the first few years after her mother's death. There was something peaceful and healing about sitting far above the world, unobserved by the people below.

She rushed into the trees and scrambled up the one farthest from the road, her eyes locked on the approaching rider. *Please, please don't look this way.* After a quick, daring climb, she settled in a branch about three mets up, close to the trunk.

The sound of the orsa's running feet grew nearer, finally overtaking Nora's position. The rider had his back to her briefly, until he turned onto the east-west road. Once again, she'd be in his line of sight if he looked this way. Squinting to hide the whites of her eyes, Nora tried to blend into the tree, as if she could do so by pure force of will. Her skin tone was similar to the medium brown of the tree bark, and her clothes were navy and dark tan. *Not the greatest camouflage. I hope it's enough.*

The guard once again passed her position—and kept riding.

Nora released a long sigh, considering her predicament. Clearly she couldn't go into the city in the middle of the day, not even if she used a minor road. The guards were probably still searching nearby farms, which ruled out the possibility of hiding in someone's barn. *I have to find a place to hide outside. I'll move tonight.*

From her high perch, Nora scanned the area. South of the narrow road, far in the distance, was a copse of trees. They looked like fan trees, which had large, evergreen leaves. Their spindly limbs weren't the best for climbing, but she'd done it before.

After scanning both roads and finding them empty, Nora scrambled down and sprinted toward the trees. After another thrilling climb, she was surrounded by minty-smelling, fan-shaped leaves and the occasional grumbles of birds. She got as comfortable as possible and waited.

Time passed slowly in a tree. It had been early afternoon when Nora climbed it. Within an hour, she was all too aware of her acute thirst, growing hunger, and boredom. But she didn't dare move.

The papers in her waistband begged to be read, but she had one arm looped around a tree branch. She wasn't confident in her ability to retrieve and read the papers without dropping any. They'd have to wait.

Hours crawled by. Nora shifted position often, creating heart-stopping noise each time. She was despairing of the sun ever setting when at last the sky began to darken, bringing with it a chill that made Nora wish she had more than a light jacket.

Not long after darkness truly settled, Nora couldn't wait any longer. She had to find water. Ironically, she also needed to pee. She descended and took care of the second need first, squatting by a tree. *Hooray for new experiences.*

As she walked through the trees, her excitement returned. This was the longest she'd ever been away from the palace by herself. Freedom filled her limbs and chest with a delightful buzz. At the edge of the trees, she stopped, listening for voices or riders. It was quiet.

Windows in a distant farmhouse glowed with lantern light. A farm would surely have water. The moon hadn't risen, but the stars helped a little as Nora navigated across a meadow and several fields.

She went straight to the dark barn and walked around its perimeter, looking up. There it was, blocking out the stars: an elevated, rain-collecting water tank attached to the roof, just like the one at the palace stables. Nora groped around and found the tap. She crouched, opened her mouth, and turned the handle. Once she'd had her fill of cold water, she stood.

Where to now? Did she dare travel this early in the evening?

The creak of the farmhouse's back door, followed by approaching footsteps and the glow of a swinging lantern, answered her question. It was too early to walk to the city. She circled around to the back of the barn and returned to the trees. *Just a few more hours.* She knew it would feel like eternity.

Several hours later—or at least she hoped it had been hours; she had no confidence in her concept of time—Nora descended again. She exited the woods and paused, taking in her surroundings. The farmhouse lights were off, and she could no longer see any buildings. A half-moon sat low in the sky, barely illuminating trees and bushes. Some sort of nocturnal bird grumbled. Bugs buzzed. Nora knew she was still in danger of being caught, but at that moment, it felt like the palace and its guards were worlds away.

She'd heard stories of how, in the early decades after The Day, certain places on Anyari were enchanted. These days, most people agreed that if sentient trees or healing ponds had ever existed, their magic had long ago faded to nothing.

In the silver moonlight, however, surrounded by a peace so thick it was almost tangible, Nora could easily imagine the land itself was imbued with the magic of the stone. After drawing a deep breath of cold air to break the lovely spell, she set her feet toward Cellerin City.

In the dark, it took longer than usual to reach the city. Along the way, she tripped twice. Her knees, which already hurt from her jumps outside the fence, got even more banged up. To make things worse, her nose was numb with cold. But the dim sight of city buildings made her forget all that.

She knew Ovrun's address, and she couldn't think of a better place to go. Guards might be watching his house, but she thought they'd be more likely to keep an eye on Krey. Everyone had seen the two of them practicing magic by the pond.

Nora had never been more grateful for her geography tutor, who'd often used a map of Cellerin City in their map-navigation lessons. She easily moved through the city. Within half an hour, she was gazing up at Ovrun's tiny, two-story house.

There were no guards in sight, but she still had to be careful. Ovrun's mother and sister might turn her in. It wasn't exactly normal for a princess to show up at your house in the middle of the night. And what about Ovrun? She didn't think he was the type to turn on her, but how could she be sure? After all, she'd cost him his job. *This is a genuinely bad idea.* Problem was, she couldn't think of a better one.

Nora crept around the house and identified two upstairs windows that probably led to bedrooms. Both were covered with drapes, leaving no indication which room belonged to Ovrun. With a sigh, she chose one randomly. She groped around, found a rock, and threw it at the window. It hit with a clatter that sounded incredibly loud in the still night.

Nothing happened. *Okay, maybe it wasn't that loud.* Nora tried again. And again. After she'd thrown six rocks, she gave up. She'd try the other window.

She didn't get a chance. The bottom half of the window moved, pulled inward and upward on a hinge.

Nora gasped and scrambled backward. Her heel caught on a rough patch, and she fell. She kept her eyes glued to the window as she tried to scoot farther back.

A shadow appeared in the window, followed by a male-sounding grunt. The shadow moved, like it was looking around. The window began to swing back down.

"Wait!" Nora called in a hissing whisper as she stood up. "It's me!"

"Who?" The voice definitely belonged to Ovrun.

"Nora."

She heard his sharp intake of breath. Then he spoke four words that made all her nighttime travails worth it: "I'll be right out."

When he arrived, he grasped her shoulder. "What are you doing here, Nora?"

She patted her waistband, and the papers rustled. "I got into Minister Sharai's office. I found her secret papers."

"What do they say?"

"I don't know. I got caught, and I had to run away. I haven't had a chance to read them."

"You ran away?"

"Yes."

Ovrun's breath came out in a long sigh. "Then they're looking for you."

"Yeah, that's why I didn't go to Krey. My aunt knows I was working with him on this."

"But she knows I helped you too. It won't be long before they come to find me. You can't be here."

Nora's stomach twisted with disappointment. Perhaps he wasn't going to turn her in, but he wouldn't help her either. She couldn't blame him. "You're right." Gently, she removed his hand from her shoulder. She forced her words through a tight throat. "Ovrun, I'm so sorry. For everything." She turned to leave, but stopped short when his hand grasped hers.

"Wait!" he whispered. "I'm helping Krey, didn't he tell you that? When I said you can't be here, I meant we both need to leave. Give me ten minutes to grab some things and leave a note for my mother."

"You . . . you're coming with me?"

She heard the smile in his voice. "Friends, remember? I'll be right back." He squeezed her hand and ran back inside.

It felt more like twenty minutes, but at last he returned. "Here," he said. "It's a coat."

He helped her put it on. The sleeves totally covered her hands. "Is this yours?" she asked.

"Yeah." He laughed softly. "It doesn't fit me anymore. I'm sure it's big on you."

"That's okay. Thank you."

"I packed two backpacks. Mostly clothes. Can you carry one?"

"Sure."

He handed her a pack. "Come on, let's go."

"Where?"

"A park near Krey's boarding house. I'll drop you off there, and then I'll go get him. If the guards haven't beat me to it."

As soon as Krey opened the door to his room and saw Ovrun there, he was wide awake. He ushered his friend in. "What is it?"

Ovrun updated him, and Krey walked to the door. "Let's go."

"Hang on. There are two royal guards out front. I'm sure they're watching the door for you to come or go."

Krey muttered a curse, then lit a lantern and started pacing. After a couple of minutes, he stopped. "I've got it. Wait here; I'll be right back." He grabbed the lantern and some coins, rushed to the room next door, and knocked.

A sleepy male apprentice opened the door. "Krey? What time is it?"

"I need you to do something for me, and I can't explain why. But I can pay you seventy quins." Krey held out the coins, enough to eat at pubs for a full week.

The young man's eyes widened. "What do you need me to do?"

Krey explained, eventually reaching a deal when he upped his offer to a hundred quins.

Back in his room, he loaded up a backpack, explaining the plan to Ovrun. The two of them led Krey's neighbor to the front door. They watched through a window as the young man, holding three bottles of warm beer, approached the guards.

One of the guards refused the drink. Krey ground his teeth together while the second guard waffled back and forth, then took the beer. When the first guard reluctantly followed suit, Krey allowed himself a small smile.

The apprentice started an animated conversation with the guards

—a conversation that did nothing to take their diligent eyes off the front door. Krey drummed his fingers on the doorframe.

Then the apprentice pointed at the horizon, away from the door. His voice grew louder and more excited. Krey heard him say something about a great pub he'd found.

As one, the guards turned their heads away from the boarding house.

Without a word, Krey and Ovrun rushed outside, leaving the door open. They ran to the front door of another boarding house, two buildings down, before daring to look back.

The guards were just turning back around. Krey and Ovrun walked casually away from the second boarding house, as if they were residents leaving for an early morning shift. Their movements didn't catch any attention. Krey could've screamed with relief.

They hurried to the park and approached the stone table and benches where Ovrun said he'd left Nora. It was too dark to see much, but there were no princess-shaped silhouettes in sight.

"Nora?" Ovrun asked.

There was a shuffling sound and a loud "Ow!" Nora emerged from under the table.

"You okay?" Ovrun asked.

"I hit my head. What took you so long?"

"We had to get past the guards." Krey stepped close, speaking softly, though no one else was around. "Ovrun said you found the papers in Sharai's office?"

"I couldn't bring them all, but I have some."

He lit his lantern and sat. His heart was beating so hard, he could feel it in his stomach. "Let's see what you got."

Nora and Ovrun sat, and within seconds, they were all perusing different papers.

Krey scanned his quickly. "This is a supply list—Oh, wait. It's all fuel. Vines, ice, ash, animal blood, milled rocks, soil, feathers."

"That makes sense if they're abducting magic eaters," Ovrun said.

"What's on yours?" Krey asked.

"More supplies," Ovrun said. "Food, blankets, things like that."

Nora held up three sheets in a trembling hand. "I think . . . this is a list of all the militia members. It's got updates on how they're doing."

Krey held his breath.

"Zeisha's on there," Nora said softly.

Krey squeezed his eyes shut as tears filled them.

"Faylie's not," Nora whispered.

Krey opened his eyes and saw that her chin was trembling. Ovrun just looked confused. "I'm sorry, Nora," Krey said.

After a moment, she spoke, the words seeming to strain her throat. "No, it's—it's okay. It means she's safe. Here, um, let me—let me read you what it says about Zeisha." The papers rustled, and she read in a stronger voice, *"Zeisha, a plant lyster, showed great improvement this week. The vines she creates are now strong enough to hold her whole body weight, though she still struggles with focus, often falling when her vines lose strength. We've just begun working on her throwing ability. Within the next month, I hope she'll be able to throw vines with enough accuracy to strangle someone from three mets away."*

A hush fell over the table, broken only by Krey's loud, rapid breathing. Suddenly, he brought his fist down on the table. "Zeisha would never hurt someone."

He grabbed a handful of pages before anyone else could. With furious eyes, he scanned and discarded a supply request and an inventory list. He stopped when he found another document with updates on the magic eaters. After reading Zeisha's, which was older than the one Nora had read, he reviewed the others. One in particular caught his eye.

Ruli, a stone lyster, can still only create a small mound of palm-sized rocks each day. In the past week, we have continued to struggle to control her. She still has occasional breakthroughs of awareness, asking where she is or what she's doing. Considering her lack of improvement and the other issues, I suggest eliminating her. We can find someone to replace her or make do with the other stone lysters on our team.

Krey set the paper down between Nora and Ovrun. "You both need to read this."

Nora read it aloud. By the end, she sounded horrified.

Ovrun's voice intruded into the subsequent silence. "What do you think it means, *occasional breakthroughs of awareness?*"

"They're controlling them." Krey's voice sounded hollow in his own ears. "That's why they think Zeisha will be willing to strangle someone with her magic. They've abducted magic eaters, and somehow they've turned them into . . . into . . ." He trailed off.

Nora finished his thought. "They've turned them into mental slaves."

IN THE DARK: 6

"THIRTEEN WEEKS," Zeisha said.

"Oh," Isla said. The word sounded hoarse. She followed it with a pained moan.

Zeisha reached out and found Isla's knee. "What is it?"

"My throat."

"You sound sick!"

"No. Not sick. Something happened to my throat. My neck—feel my neck. Be gentle."

Zeisha's hands grasped into the darkness and found Isla's face, then her neck. It was sticky. When Zeisha pulled her hands back, she smelled herbal ointment. "What happened?" she whispered.

"I don't know."

An image invaded Zeisha's mind, one she was certain had come from the dream she'd just had. She began to sob, eliciting angry mumbles from two nearby sleepers.

"What, Zeisha?" Isla found her hands. "I'll be okay, really. It's just a little sore."

"It's—it's not that." Zeisha struggled for breath. "It was—it was me. My vines. I did that to you."

Across the room, a door opened, the hinges creaking. "Back to sleep!" their nighttime guard yelled.

Zeisha lay down and swallowed her sobs, but she knew she couldn't sleep.

20

My daddy held me on his lap and pointed east. "There's a big city out there, with buildings that almost reach the sky. Before The Day, our whole community could've lived together in one of those buildings."

I looked at all the space around me and my daddy. The wind blew through the trees, and our corn was almost tall enough to play chase-and-hide with my friends. One of our caynins brushed against my leg. "That old city sounds like a terrible place to live," I said.

-The First Generation: A Memoir *by Liri Abrios*

"Krey," Nora said, "we have to find a place to stay. There are guards in the city looking for me. You too, probably."

Krey was the only one still sitting. He was hunched over, eyes closed, rubbing his temples with both hands. When Nora placed a hand on his forearm, he pulled away. She gave Ovrun a helpless look.

"She's right, Krey," Ovrun said. "I know where we can go, but it'll take a while to get there. We should travel in the dark."

"Fine." Krey stood so forcefully that if the bench hadn't been bolted down, he would've toppled it. The dim lantern light shone on his tight jaw. He gathered up all the papers, folded them, and shoved them in his pack. "Lead the way, Ovrun."

"Where are we going?" Nora asked. "I don't have money for an inn."

Ovrun grabbed the lamp and laughed. "We're not staying at an inn. They'd find us by lunchtime. Come on, this way." He gestured, and Nora and Krey followed him farther into the park.

Nora jogged a few steps to catch up with Ovrun. Krey clearly needed time alone to brood.

"So you didn't bring any money?" Ovrun asked.

"I don't have any."

Ovrun swiveled his head to gape at her. "You don't have money?"

Nora shrugged. "When I need something, someone else buys it for me. And when we visit a business in the city, we don't carry coins."

Ovrun nodded. "Oh yeah, I escorted your aunt to the city once. She bought everything on credit."

"The merchants know we always pay on time."

Behind them, Krey spoke. "It's easy to pay on time when your coffers are full of money earned by hard-working citizens."

Nora forced her voice to stay level. "Yes, Krey, we collect taxes. Like every other government in history. That's how we pay for this park."

"And for designer clothes and a full icehouse," Krey added.

In response, Nora pulled up the hood of her jacket, which she was still wearing under Ovrun's coat. She wished the hood were soundproof. The lining, made of soft suede, rubbed against her ears. The warmth it provided was tinged with guilt. How many loaves of bread would a baker have to sell to purchase a garment like this?

"Nora," Ovrun said, "you mentioned Faylie. I remember her and her mom."

Nora nodded and bit her lip.

"Did you think she was in the militia?"

"Yeah." Nora swallowed. "But she wasn't. She just moved away."

"Oh good. I'd hate for her to be caught up in all this. She seemed nice."

Nora nodded, holding back tears. "She was." *Until she wasn't.* A tear slipped onto her cheek. Was it possible to feel both relief and grief, all at once? Nora would've been devastated to learn that her former friend was a mental slave. But she'd half-convinced herself that Faylie's departure wasn't actually a rejection. Now, the pain of it slammed into her all over again.

A good cry in her soft bed was in order, but that wouldn't happen any time soon. As Ovrun led them into a wooded area at the park's border, Nora gave herself an internal pep talk. *Focus. Faylie's gone. You have new friends now.*

It didn't work; the loss still sat like a stone in her throat. When Ovrun spoke, his words jolted her back to the present.

"On the other side of these woods is the manufacturing sector of the city. It's pretty much deserted this time of night. Once we get through it, we'll pass through a residential area before we reach the Eastern Road."

Nora's head swiveled toward him. "The Eastern Road? Don't tell me you're taking us . . ." She trailed off.

Krey wasn't so hesitant. "We're going to Deroga? We need to hide, not get killed!"

"Exactly," Nora muttered, eyes glued to Ovrun. Deroga was the pre-day capital of the nation of Therro. Nearly fifteen million people had once lived there. A city that size was unimaginable now. The population of the entire planet was currently estimated at twenty million. Only half a million lived in the kingdom of Cellerin.

"We won't go anywhere near the trogs," Ovrun said with a quiet laugh. "I'm guessing neither of you have been to the ruins?" When they confirmed it, he continued, "Think how big a city had to be to fit millions of people. Deroga's locked in by the bay on its eastern border, so it grew in every other direction. We'll only have to go about twenty clommets to get to the western outskirts. There are a bunch of little cities and towns there. Suburbs, they used to call them. That's where we're going. The suburbs are a little creepy, but they're deserted."

Nora's heart pounded harder, and not just from physical exertion. In hours, she'd be inside the Derogan ruins, surrounded by memories and old bones. She shivered at the thrilling thought.

"We're almost back to the road," Ovrun said as he held back some branches from a scraggly bush, letting Nora and Krey pass. "Let's keep our voices down."

They walked through the quiet manufacturing sector at a rapid pace, made more difficult by the heavy backpacks they carried. Nora soon had sore feet and was short of breath. She was pretty sure her companions would've gone even faster without her. Krey, after all, went running for fun—something Nora couldn't fathom. And when Ovrun had worked at the palace, he'd worked out in the weight room before every shift. Nora suppressed her complaints. *Maybe I'm a spoiled princess, but I don't have to act like one.*

They didn't talk much as they continued through the city's dark residential streets, only stopping to refill their glass water bottles at a neighborhood pump. At last, they reached the Eastern Road. Without pausing, Ovrun turned onto it.

"The suburbs are still twenty clommets from here?" Nora asked. Even at their quick pace, it would take over three hours to walk that far.

"Yeah," Ovrun said. "By the time it gets light, we'll be far enough out of town to avoid any guards or search parties. I hope."

They'd been on the Eastern Road for half an hour when Ovrun asked, "You feeling okay, Nora?"

She would've turned red if she weren't already flushed from exertion. *Apparently he noticed that I'm panting like this is the farthest I've ever walked.* Which, to be fair, was true. "Yeah, I'm fine."

Krey handed out some fruit he'd packed. Nora devoured hers and didn't argue when Krey offered her another piece. After they'd eaten, they all fell silent. Nora wondered if her companions found the dark road and their rhythmic steps as hypnotizing as she did. At least her rapidly developing blisters kept her awake.

After some time, Krey thought he saw light behind them. He took to the air and discovered a small group traveling with a lantern. He couldn't tell if they were guards, but nobody was taking any chances. He, Ovrun, and Nora hid in a tree until the other travelers passed.

Ovrun led them to a narrower road, and they continued walking for hours that felt like days.

By the time they neared the first suburb, they were squinting into the morning sun. Ovrun turned to Nora, whose lips were pressed into a thin line. He was pretty sure she was holding back tears.

He wished he could reach out to her, but he wasn't sure how she'd respond. It had been a tough journey for her. Unlike her companions, who both wore boots, Nora had on simple, leather shoes. They'd stopped a couple of hours earlier to bandage her bleeding toes and heels.

Ovrun gave her an encouraging smile. "Nearly there. You got the bad end of this deal, Nora. I'd let you use my boots if they weren't so big." Wanting to distract her, he pointed. "See all those skinny lines in the sky? Those are Skytrain tracks."

She lifted her eyes to his and managed a small smile. "What I wouldn't give to be on a Skytrain right now." After several seconds, her smile disappeared. "Are you sure trogs don't live in the suburb ruins?"

"I'm sure. It's too close to civilization. The main city is their territory—where the buildings are tall and crammed together."

"I don't understand how they survive there," Nora said.

"They grow food on roofs," Krey said. "I've read about it. Then they trade with each other. Some of them even venture into inhabited areas for supplies."

"But it's illegal to trade with trogs," Nora said.

Krey laughed. "Lots of things are illegal."

"So they have their own society?" Nora asked. "I thought they were recluses."

"They were in the early years. Back then, there weren't many of them." He chuckled. "I guess it takes someone special to live among millions of decomposing bodies. Once there were only bones left, more people moved in, enough to build communities."

"More like gangs," Ovrun said.

"True. There's a lot of violence between the different groups. And none of them like outsiders to intrude on their turf."

The road led them past a few buildings, marking the start of the suburbs. Before long, hundreds of structures surrounded the travelers. Two-hundred-year-old solarcars and solarbuses, some of them now host to weeds, bushes, and even trees, populated the dirt streets. All ecophalt paving had disintegrated long ago, but vehicles had been made of sturdier stuff.

"I'm surprised there weren't more vehicles on the road into town." Krey's voice was quiet, like he feared waking the ghosts.

"I think the early scavengers moved them to make it easier to transport their wares," Ovrun said. "They probably sold as many as they could, until the batteries all went bad." He led them around several solarcars that had run into each other. "Most of the ones in the cities got smashed up when the drivers died."

"How far into this suburb are we going?" Krey asked.

"A couple more clommets. The farther we go, the harder it is for search parties to find us. I have a building in mind."

Ovrun's eyes shifted toward Nora, as they seemed to do every couple of minutes. She was gaping at the surrounding buildings, shaking her head. While most of the structures were still standing, many were covered in graffiti, everything from angry words to beautiful art to obscene cartoons. "Why aren't there very many doors or windows?" Nora asked.

Krey turned to her. "You've heard of polymus, right?"

"I know what it looks like, but that's about it."

"It was a renewable preday substance, made from fungi. Researchers are trying to figure out how to recreate it. It eventually breaks down, so preday builders only used it for parts that were easy to replace, like doors and window frames. See that?" He pointed to a door riddled with cracks and holes that was, miraculously, still hanging. "That's polymus." He gestured to another door that was still intact. "That one's probably faux wood."

Ovrun turned to Krey. "How do you know all this, man? I've been here a bunch of times, and I never knew why the doors were gone."

Krey shrugged. "I read a book about it."

The three travelers were silent until Nora pointed to a sign in front of a small, green building. "*FLEX REPAIR*," she read. "Flexes were communication devices, right?"

"Yeah," Krey said. "Flexscreens. They used them for about a million other things too."

"And there was a business just for repairing them? They didn't repair anything else?"

"You think that's unbelievable, check out the yellow building." Ovrun gestured across the street to a sign reading, *SIMPLY SOCKS*.

"Is that a store? Just for socks?" Nora asked.

"I think so."

Nora shook her head. "How many types of socks do you need?"

He gestured to her blistered feet. "Wish we could get you some new ones, but scavengers got there first." He pointed ahead and to the left. "See that building with all the graffiti? We're turning there."

When they arrived at the building, they all stopped. Ovrun watched Nora shaking her head slowly as she took in the graffiti, which consisted of a single word, repeated in countless colors and styles:

WHY? WHY? WHY? WHY? WHY?

"It's a chapel," Krey said softly.

Ovrun nodded. A large Rimorian star, covered in layers of paint, still hung above the open doorway.

Nora ran her fingers along the thick layers of painted *WHY*s. "Wonder if they ever got an answer," she murmured.

"Does anyone get an answer to that question?" Krey asked.

Ovrun turned to look at his friend, who was standing with his arms folded tight and eyebrows drawn together. Their eyes met for a second, and then Krey turned away.

The distant call of a caynin rang through the air, jolting them all out of their distracted states. "Let's go," Ovrun said.

Ten minutes later, he led them onto a street full of large, plain buildings. Most were only one story, with blocky construction and minimal windows.

"These are preday factories." Ovrun pointed at the roofs. "See, no smokestacks. Everything was done with clean energy. We're headed for that blue one on the right."

He led them to the building's front doorway, which had hinges but no door. They walked inside a large room, full of dusty machines.

"What is this place?" Nora asked.

Ovrun ran his hand along the machinery. "Some sort of food factory. The first time I came here, I found a container under one of the machines. It didn't have a label, but it looked like those food jars they have in the Cellerin City Museum." He pulled out his matches and lit the lantern. "We're going to the room behind this one. It's dark back there."

Ovrun led them past the machines to a metal door. It had held up well through the centuries. He held it open, and they entered a room with no windows. Holding up the lantern and closing the door behind them, he said, "This was a warehouse. I'll show you around."

They walked around the huge room. Ovrun pointed out empty crates and pallets. When Nora sneezed, he said, "Sorry about the dust. But it's better than most places around here. That door keeps animals out."

He led them to the center of the room, and his lantern illuminated a pile of blankets and pillows, along with two more lanterns. Off to the side, a ring of stones surrounded charcoal and ashes.

"Is this your stuff?" Krey asked.

Ovrun glanced at Nora, who was staring at the bedding. "Yeah," he said, trying to keep his tone casual. "Have a seat." When they were all settled, he lit the two extra lanterns and cleared his throat. "I used to come here with, uh . . . my friend."

"You used to walk over thirty clommets from your house to cuddle up around an indoor campfire with a *friend*?" Krey asked dryly.

Nora lifted her eyes to meet his.

Ovrun swallowed. "We didn't walk; we took her family's orsas."

Nora stared at him. "Her? You have a girlfriend?" He could hear her other question as clearly as if she'd asked it aloud: *And you kissed me back?*

Ovrun didn't get easily embarrassed, but this definitely qualified as awkward. Ignoring Krey's smirk, he held Nora's gaze. "*Had.* She broke up with me a year ago."

"Oh. Okay." There was a long silence, and then Nora said, "The pillows and blankets look . . . comfortable."

"Um, yeah, we were always tired after being on orsas for so long." Ovrun gestured to the circle of stones, anxious to draw Nora's gaze away from the blankets. "As Krey guessed, we used to make fires in here. Just for cooking, though. We figured with a room this big, the smoke would dissipate pretty well. Outdoor fires might attract attention."

Nora's gaze was still on the blankets and pillows. Ovrun wanted to hold her and assure her that Joli, his ex, meant nothing to him now. He wanted to insist that, while Joli was pretty, Nora was gorgeous; while Joli made him smile, Nora made him laugh; while Joli's kisses were nice, Nora's were—

He cleared his throat. He could write a whole list of what was wrong with that train of thought. *Number one: she just wants to be friends, you idiot.*

"Anyone hungry?" Krey asked.

Ovrun flinched. *Number two: there's another person in the room.* "Yeah," he said, "we should get some food and rest. I know we're all exhausted. We can talk more in the morning."

There was little conversation as they all ate fruit and dried meat. Nora didn't even wait for the lanterns to be extinguished before she curled up in a blanket and rested her head on a pillow.

Ovrun left the lanterns to Krey and lay with his head half a met from Nora's. "Sorry it's so uncomfortable," he whispered.

She propped herself up on her elbows and smiled softly at him. "Don't be silly. I was just thinking how amazing this is, lying on the floor of a preday warehouse with the two people in the world I can actually consider friends."

Krey extinguished the lamps, and Ovrun was struck with a powerful urge to reach into the darkness, draw Nora close, and kiss her. Resisting was the most difficult thing he'd done all night.

21

When I was fifteen, a five-year-old boy in our community developed an ability to heal others. It explained why he'd been sneaking into his parents' kitchen to consume blood from uncooked meat.

People traveled from distant communities to beg for this boy's help. He could heal cuts and broken bones but not internal illnesses and cancers. However, in our grieving world, any amount of healing represented hope—a commodity that was all too rare.

-The First Generation: A Memoir *by Liri Abrios*

"DON'T FORGET LAMP OIL," Ovrun said.

"Oh, right." Krey's comment was followed by the light scratch of a pencil on paper.

From her cocoon of blankets, Nora decided it was time to join the conversation. "I need socks," she said. "And boots. Please. I never want to look at those other shoes again."

"You're up!" Ovrun said. "Sleep well?"

Nora stretched and yawned. "After all that walking, I could've slept well in a dragon's den. What time is it?"

"Mid-afternoon," Ovrun said.

Krey looked up from his list to stare at Nora.

"What?" she asked.

He smirked and brought his pencil back to the slip of paper. As he wrote, he said, "Hairbrush."

"You're so kind." Nora peeled a few strands of hair off her cheek, where her drool had glued them down. She tried to run her fingers through her tangles, then gave up. "Here, take one of my shoes with you so you can find boots that fit. I assume you're flying to a store somewhere?"

"Yeah, Ovrun gave me directions to a little town west of Deroga, northwest of where we are now."

"My cousin lives there," Ovrun said. "It's not too far from the ruins, and trogs visit the store sometimes. The owner's not the type to ask questions. Or to cooperate with search parties."

"Can I see the list?" Nora asked. Krey gave it to her, and she scanned it. "A bow and arrows? Are we forming our own militia?"

"We should all be able to defend ourselves," Ovrun said. "And we'll be hunting for our meat. The only money we have is Krey's. It won't last forever."

"There's only so much I can carry," Krey said. "Is there anything else you absolutely need?"

Nora took the pencil and tapped it on the floor as she considered the question. She scrawled a few necessities at the bottom of the list:

Shirt, pants, underwear
Soap
Food. PLEASE.
Box of tampons

She handed the page back to Krey and watched his face.

"This last item," he said. "When do you need it?"

"In a couple of weeks or so."

"Okay, I'll get it on this trip. I don't know when we'll go back."

Her lips curved into a small smile.

Looking up, Krey raised an eyebrow. "What?"

"I expected that to be a lot more uncomfortable than it was."

"You do realize I grew up with two women, right?"

"True. What about the clothes; do you have space for them? My pants have blood on the knees, and my shirt's dirty. When I wash them, I'll need something to change into—" She halted and turned to Ovrun. "Do we have a water source?"

"There's a creek about half a clommet away. And if it snows, we can melt it."

Nora shivered at the thought. She dreaded the possibility of huddling in this unheated building during a snowstorm. Sometimes they went an entire winter with nothing more than occasional flurries. Maybe they'd have that kind of luck this year.

Back to the task at hand. Nora gestured to the list. "You know, I might be able to do without new clothes. I hate asking you to spend that much money on me." She studied Krey. "Obviously I can't borrow Ovrun's clothes, but yours might work."

The two guys turned to each other. "I think what she's saying," Krey said, "is that your muscles give my muscles an inferiority complex."

"I was referring to his height." Nora suppressed a smile. Krey was in great shape, but Ovrun was a lot bigger than him—and not just taller. Ovrun's arms drew her gaze. Even though he was wearing a jacket, the lantern in front of him illuminated his muscles. She could imagine them flexing, no, *rippling* was more like it—

She realized she'd been ogling Ovrun's biceps for several silent seconds. A warm flush rose to her cheeks as she dropped her gaze to the floor. "So, uh, anyway," she said, her voice louder than it needed to be, "Krey, can I borrow some of your clothes?"

Maybe no one had noticed her wandering eyes. She glanced at

Krey. He was watching her, holding back laughter. *Of course he noticed.* She didn't dare look at Ovrun.

Apparently Krey had a shred of empathy in him, because he picked up the thread of the conversation and ran with it. "Sorry, but I only brought one change of clothes. I don't mind buying you some, as long as you don't mind that they'll be way cheaper than anything you've ever worn. I'll get you a new coat too. Ovrun's is huge on you. I think I can probably fit everything in two packs. I can always go back later if I need to."

"Sounds good," Nora said. "I'm not sure what size clothes you should get for me."

"You don't know your size?"

"My clothes are all custom-made or tailored to fit me." She didn't miss Krey's raised eyebrow. "I know, I know. Taxes. Just—tell the storekeeper I'm about your height, slender on top, and pear-shaped."

"Pear-shaped?" Ovrun asked.

That infuriating heat rushed back into Nora's face. She'd never been much of a blushing type; what was wrong with her today? "It's a fruit. Original, not Anyarian. Small top, big bottom. I mean, big—" She racked her brain for an alternate term besides *bottom* but failed to come up with anything.

"I know what a pear is; I've seen pictures in books. I just hadn't, uh, hadn't heard the term used to describe, uh, shape. People shape, I mean. You know."

Now it felt like someone had turned on a furnace. Nora patted her round hips. "Yeah, well, if the fruit fits . . ." She made her best effort to smile and laugh.

Ovrun's laughter sounded as awkward as hers. "One of these days, maybe I'll get to try a pear." His eyes grew as round as coins, and he sputtered, "The fruit, I mean. I'd like to try . . . the fruit. Not . . ." He finished the thought with a shrug.

"Well," Krey said loudly, and when Nora looked at him, he was sporting a massively amused grin. A piece of feather was poking out of his teeth. He had more diced feathers in his hand. "I know we're all hungry." He raised an eyebrow at Ovrun. "The sooner I get out of here, the sooner we can eat some lunch. I'll leave the two of you alone to continue your fascinating discussion about Original botanicals."

Ovrun held out his pack, which he'd emptied. Krey took it and walked off, laughing and popping another feather piece in his mouth.

"Maybe we should keep looking through Sharai's papers," Ovrun said, his eyes anywhere but on Nora.

"Good idea." Nora scanned through more supply lists and updates on the lysters but didn't see any information that could help them.

After a little while, Ovrun held up a sheet of paper and said, "This is different. It's a report on the militia as a whole, not the individual lysters."

Nora sat next to him and started scanning it.

"Look at this." Ovrun pointed to a paragraph, reading it aloud. *"We've asked repeatedly, and we're asking again. We need at least one more blood lyster. The one we have is ineffective and can't keep up with daily training injuries. Last time the general visited, I mentioned this, but nothing changed. Surely in this entire nation, we can find one or two healers to join us! Otherwise, I fear we will start having fatalities."*

"I guess when you're teaching people to kill, there's bound to be injuries," Nora said. She shuddered. She'd never envied healers. Like all lysters, they had to consume Anyarian fuel—in this case, the blood of native animals. She didn't think any amount of healing ability would make that worth it.

"Who do you think this *general* is that they mentioned?" Ovrun asked.

"I figured it was Sharai."

"This report is directed to someone named S. See?" He pointed to the top of the page. "That has to be Sharai. The general must be someone else."

Nora's eyebrows drew together. "Maybe a New Therroan leader. I don't know."

They continued reading, but they found no clues to the militia's location. Nora finished reading the last sheet and looked up at Ovrun. What could they talk about until Krey returned? *Welcome to Awkward Town, folks.*

"Do you miss your family yet?" Ovrun asked.

"A little." Nora smiled. This time, it felt natural. "Is it weird that I miss my orsa?"

He laughed. "Not weird at all. Ever since I got fired, I've missed the caynins."

"What about you? Do you miss your family?"

"I'm sure I will. But right now, I'm just glad they only have two mouths to feed, not three. Without me bringing in a paycheck, things are tight."

Nora closed her eyes briefly. When she opened them, a tear rolled down her cheek. "I'm so sorry I got you fired."

"Hey." He wiped the tear away with his thumb. "I chose to give you those keys, and I'd do it again. When we find Zeisha, it'll be worth it."

Their conversation continued in a remarkably comfortable manner. When they heard Krey opening the metal door, Ovrun gave Nora a smile and a wink. "Nice talk."

"Yeah," she said, trying to keep the surprise out of her voice. "It was."

The next morning, Nora changed clothes behind a screen made of two pallets and a blanket. The new underwear, shirt, and socks fit fine, but the pants were shapeless and hung low on her hips due to the too-large waist. Krey had explained that the store was small, with few clothing options. Nora pulled the pants up, but they slid back down. *We had that whole conversation about pears for nothing.*

At least she'd gotten the chance to wash up. Krey had bought two metal buckets, which Ovrun had filled with water. After dark, they'd all do laundry at the creek.

Past the makeshift changing screen, Krey said, "Way to go, man!" Nora gathered her dirty clothes and emerged. Ovrun was holding up a bow in one hand. In the other, he held a dead animal by its stubby tail. An arrow had penetrated the creature's skinny, bright-blue body.

Nora wrinkled her nose. "Is that a shimshim?"

"Sure is!"

She eyed the creature. Like all reptids, its smooth, shiny skin grew in a basket-weave texture. Shimshims were pests, known for sneaking into pantries and picnics to steal food. "I've never eaten a shimshim," she said.

"There's not a lot of meat on him, but what's there will taste pretty good, especially with those spices Krey picked up. Who wants to help me skin it and clean it?"

Nora swallowed and looked at Krey, silently begging him to volunteer. He held up his hands. "Not me. I'll cook all day long, but I'm not touching any part of that thing except the meat." He picked up the book he'd been reading and opened it pointedly.

Nora laughed. "You never struck me as the type to get grossed out by dead animals."

He didn't look up from his book. "Just keep it away from me, Ovrun. Bury the parts we won't use, and don't even tell me where you put them. I don't want to come across that stuff."

Ovrun shrugged and turned to Nora. "I bet most princesses don't know how to clean a shimshim."

She squared her shoulders, swallowing her hesitation. "You'd better teach me, then."

Two days later, Nora had cleaned three shimshims with Ovrun's help and one on her own. She hated the process, but everyone had to do their part out here. Krey continued to be squeamish about hunting or cleaning shimshims, so he was their cook. Ovrun was their hunter, but he was teaching Nora to use a bow. Before too long, maybe she'd be accurate enough to take on some of the hunting shifts.

Hunting helped them stretch their funds, but Krey had also purchased various dehydrated foods. After a lunch of fresh shimshim and dried vegetables, Nora and Ovrun practiced with the bow. Krey read through Sharai's papers for the millionth time. Later, he'd get his own lesson with Ovrun. He didn't want to hunt, but he needed to be able to defend himself.

"Your feet are too close together," Ovrun said.

Nora widened her stance.

"Good. Now stay in that position. Don't move around."

She nocked the arrow and pulled back the string.

"Wait!" Ovrun said. "Rotate your elbow out, remember? No, the one holding the bow."

"Like this?"

"A little more." He reached out like he'd touch her arm, but all he did was gesture. "Rotate just a smidge more."

"You know," she said, trying to keep her voice casual, "if it would help, you can move me into the right position. Might be easier than giving me all these verbal instructions." *And,* she added silently, *it would be a lot more fun.*

He returned the smile but said, "I think that's probably a really bad idea. Want me to demonstrate one more time before you go?"

"Sure." Nora handed him the bow and arrow, and he showed her the proper form, narrating every little move. She tried to pay attention, but when he pulled the string back, all she could focus on was his arms. *Get ahold of yourself, Nora. You're setting yourself up for heartbreak.*

Out here, however, it was easy to forget that she was supposed to be considering her future as a queen. She was wearing pants that didn't fit, shooting arrows, and looking forward to a dinner of wild shimshim meat. Life at the palace felt impossibly far away. *Would it really hurt to have a little fun?*

An arrow flew through the air, and Nora looked toward the lantern-lit pallet at the end of the room. Faux wood was incredibly hard, but Ovrun was strong. The arrow pierced the pallet near its center, and it stayed there.

"Did you see how I held my elbow?" Ovrun asked.

"I think so." She took the proffered bow. "I'll give it another try."

Before she could loose an arrow, however, Krey's voice interrupted them. "It's Saturday!"

Nora turned. "And?"

"Tonight's the New Therroan meeting!" Krey tossed the papers on the floor in front of him. "I should go to it. These papers aren't telling me anything useful."

"I thought you'd decided the New Therroans weren't involved," Ovrun said.

Nora's eyes widened. "You decided what? Sharai's family is from there! It's got to be—"

"Hang on, Nora," Krey interrupted. "I've started questioning it, yes, but I'm still open to the possibility. I want to keep up my relationship with them, just in case."

"Good, because I know they're behind it," Nora said. "Can you fly that far?"

"I think so, if I do it in stages. I'll fly low, far from any travelers. When I need to, I'll rest and eat more feathers. The only thing is, I'll probably use up my entire feather stash on this trip."

"Tons of birds live in the buildings around here," Ovrun said. "I see them all the time when I'm hunting. I'll start collecting feathers for you."

"I can help," Nora said.

Krey shoved a handful of diced feathers in his mouth. "Time to fuel up."

22

My parents often let my siblings and me roam around outside. I could always tell it made Mom and Dad nervous, though. They talked long-ingly of how their own parents had checked up on them through the electronic devices they all carried. That sounded silly to me. When it was time for dinner, they just had to stand outside and yell our names. We always came running.

-The First Generation: A Memoir *by Liri Abrios*

KREY APPROACHED the back of the pub, his legs feeling heavier with every step. Magic rarely tired him out, but he'd never pushed himself like this. Frequent rests had made the journey take longer than expected. The meeting might already be over. If it was still going on, Krey doubted he'd stay awake through it.

Where am I supposed to sleep? I was naïve to think I could fly home tonight. He didn't want to pay for a room at an inn. When he'd come to Cellerin, he'd thought the money he packed was more than sufficient. After all, his internship included room and board.

That was before he'd started buying feathers in bulk so he could practice outside his normal apprentice hours. Before he'd paid inflated prices for supplies at that store two days ago. His coin purse was getting uncomfortably light.

Krey pushed the thoughts to the side and knocked on the back door in a pattern: three knocks, then two, then three again.

The door opened a crack. Wallis, the unassuming guy who led the Saturday meetings, fixed one hazel eye on Krey. "You're late."

"I know, I'm sorry. I had to flee the city, and I flew over twenty-five clommets to get here." Krey hadn't planned to blurt all that out, but exhaustion had obliterated his caution.

Wallis's eyebrow rose. "You had to flee the city? Why?"

"Long story."

The door swung open. "Come on in and tell it."

Krey followed Wallis into the pub's back room. Several hanging lanterns shone on the old table, emphasizing its divots and scratches. Twenty or so beer mugs were scattered around, but only three men remained in the room: Wallis, Hatlin, and a short, thin man Krey had never met.

Wallis sat. "Krey, this is—" He gestured to the new man with a questioning look.

"Call me T." The man didn't stand or offer to shake Krey's hand. "Have a seat."

"It's good to meet you, T."

"You're our feather-and-frost eater?" the man asked in a reedy voice. He pronounced each word with precision.

"Yes, sir."

"An apprentice?"

Krey hesitated, then admitted, "Former."

T nodded. "Did I hear you say you had to flee?"

Krey briefly closed his eyes and fought the temptation to take a nap, right there. "Yes. I left the city early Wednesday morning."

"The princess has been missing since Tuesday afternoon." T examined Krey with narrowed eyes that looked like they would slice through any attempted lies.

Krey considered several possible responses but discarded each one. He'd wanted to ask Wallis about the militia tonight, but for all he knew, this guy T would kill him for bringing it up. For the first time, an aura of danger filled the cozy back room. Tonight, Krey had no problem believing these men could've hired someone to abduct Zeisha.

His gaze drifted to Hatlin, the one person here he'd almost consider a friend. The big man wasn't wearing the half-drunk, gregarious expression Krey had grown used to seeing on him. Instead, he was watching Krey with eyes nearly as incisive as T's.

"Why don't you tell us what's going on, Krey?" Hatlin said, his voice low.

Krey pulled his glass water bottle out of his pack and took a long drink. *Tell the truth, just not all of it. Build trust with these men.* He wiped his mouth with the back of his hand and said, "Nora—the princess—we became friends. Her aunt thought I was a bad influence. That's why I got kicked out of the palace. Nora is . . . well, I guess she's bored. She ran away on Tuesday, and I helped her leave the city. We're living in the Derogan suburbs now."

He'd directed his words at Hatlin, but it was T who responded. "Is she sympathetic to our cause?"

"She wants peace between the monarchy and New Therro, but if she had to choose sides, she'd choose the monarchy. She trusts her father."

"Just not enough to keep living with him." T steepled his fingers in front of his mouth. "Krey, where do your loyalties lie?"

With Zeisha. He couldn't say that aloud though, not to the men who might've imprisoned her. "I want the monarchy to stop taking advantage of people who can't fight back."

"And if they won't stop?" T asked.

"Then we make them."

T's thin lips lifted in a small smile. "Pleasure to meet you, Krey. I look forward to talking more." Without another word, he stood and left.

Krey looked between Hatlin and Wallis. When neither of them said anything, he ventured, "So, T's important to the cause?"

Wallis chuckled. "He is."

"Who is he?"

Hatlin stood. "You look tired. Want me to ask Alit for some blankets and a pillow? You can take a nap in this room, then get back to your princess."

Krey knew he wasn't getting any answers about T tonight, and he didn't have the energy to press. "Alit wouldn't mind?"

Hatlin was already headed to the door. "Not a bit."

Five minutes later, Krey curled up on the floor of the dark room. He wanted to mull over the odd meeting, but within seconds, his eyes fell closed, his breath slowed, and he drifted off to sleep.

When Krey opened the metal warehouse door, Nora ran to him and gave him a tight hug that nearly knocked him over. "Why did it take you so long to get here? We were worried!"

"Flying that far is hard. I need a nap." He walked toward his pile of blankets.

"Did you find out anything?" Ovrun asked.

Krey dropped to the floor and mumbled into his pillow, "We'll talk when I get up."

He woke a few hours later and visited the "outhouse," which was a deep hole hidden behind a couple of pallets they'd leaned against the building's exterior wall. When he went back inside, Nora handed him a plate. The meat was cold, but after all that flying, he was hungry enough to eat anything.

"How did the meeting go?" Nora asked. As he shared the story, she froze. "The New Therroans know where I am?"

"They know we're in the suburbs. This place is huge; they can't find us."

Nora turned to Ovrun. "Do you think that's true?"

He hesitated. "Probably."

"Why did you tell them, Krey?" Nora asked, her voice shrill.

"I'm sorry, I wish I could've avoided it. But if they're behind the militia, I have to build trust with them."

"I understand that. And I want to help you find Zeisha—but preferably not at the expense of being abducted by terrorists!"

"Abducted? They'd never risk taking a princess!" Krey waved both hands wide. He was still holding his meat skewer, and grease dripped on the floor. "Whoever's putting this militia together is obviously trying to keep a low profile!"

"Krey, they'd abduct me *because* I'm the princess! Nothing like a little blackmail to push the negotiations along!"

Krey's breathing grew shallow. "I didn't think of that. I—I was exhausted. I said more than I wanted to, and he guessed the rest."

Ovrun cleared his throat, and both Nora and Krey turned toward him. "Krey, are you sure none of the New Therroans followed you here?"

"It would've been pointless to try. They couldn't keep up with a feather eater."

"Then we should be okay," Ovrun said. "There are thousands of buildings in the suburbs."

"You don't think we should move?" Nora asked.

"I can't think of a safer place," Ovrun said. "If we go too far into the city, we'll run into trogs."

Krey watched Nora, whose face was pale in the lantern light. "I'm really sorry."

She sat and pulled her knees to her chest. "I was sick of the palace, but at least it was safe. Out here, I'm constantly afraid someone will find us. Royal guards would just bring me home. The New Therroans—I don't know what they'd do to me." Her voice turned pleading. "We're all sacrificing to be here. This isn't some fun campout! We need a plan. Something more detailed than you going to meetings and coming home with no information." She took a deep breath. "I think I should reach out to Dani. Now that I've been gone a few days, I bet she's desperate enough to listen to what we have to say."

Krey sat up straighter. "Dani? That's your plan? Listen, Nora, I don't care how nice she is; I don't trust her, not for one second!"

"She's my aunt, Krey! She's like a mother to me! How would you like it if I said I didn't trust one of your aunts?"

"If you had good reason for it, I'd listen to you."

Nora let out a humorless laugh. "Sure you would." She turned to Ovrun. "What do you think we should do?"

He sighed. "Nora, I always liked Dani, but I don't think we should bring in anyone at the palace. Someone's got to be helping Sharai. Dani's probably not involved, but what if she talks to someone who is?"

"Then what?" Nora exclaimed. "What do we do?"

"I have an idea," Krey said. "But it'll require a lot more feathers."

This isn't getting any easier. Krey was flying low in the dark sky, trying to make it to one of the farms near the palace. His whole body shook, reminding him he needed more fuel. *Come on . . . so close.*

He flew over a group of dark trees and suddenly felt himself dip down. Branches scratched him through his shirt. He cursed and pushed himself higher. As soon as he passed the trees, he performed a half-controlled landing, tumbling into a graceless somersault as he skidded into the cold dirt.

"Well," he mumbled, brushing off his clothes, "that worked. Sort of."

Clouds covered most of the stars, leaving the area nearly as black as the stone. Krey rummaged around in his pack for some dried fruit. He gnawed off a bite, then set off on foot.

Every step was a chore. This flight had been even longer than his trip to the pub for the New Therroan meeting. It didn't help that he'd only had a little over a day to recover between the journeys.

One step at a time; you got this.

After about twenty exhausted steps, he realized that no, he didn't have it. He headed for a nearby structure, praying he'd make it there in time. Too tired to think, he stumbled into the dark building, toppled into a heap, and fell asleep.

"Funniest-looking orsa I ever seen."

Krey's eyes snapped open, and he looked up at the source of the booming voice—a broad-shouldered, middle-aged woman with a scowl on her face.

He looked around, barely remembering lying down in this empty stall the night before. Around him, orsas were lowing, and he couldn't believe their *OHH-AHH*s hadn't woken him.

He returned his attention to the woman. "Uh . . ." he said.

"Just get outta here, and don't let me catch you in here again."

"Yes, ma'am."

"There's a well on that side of the barn." She pointed. "You got a bottle you can fill?"

His eyes widened. "I do."

"Get on with it, then." Her mouth curved into an understanding smile.

"Thank you." Krey exited, filled his bottle, and jogged away. The sky was pink and orange in the east. He'd meant to approach the palace in the dark, but it was too late for that now.

Less than a quarter-hour later, he huddled behind a tree in the middle of a fallow field. From there, he had a good view of the palace gate. As he watched it, he munched on feathers and dried vegetables. Hours passed, and he drew pictures in the dirt to keep himself awake.

It was almost noon when he saw the man Ovrun had told him to look for: short, with a thick mustache, shoulder-length black hair tied in back, and a broad-brimmed hat. He was riding a bored-looking orsa.

The man approached the gate, and the guards let him in. A few minutes later, he exited and returned the way he'd come. Krey took flight, praying the guards didn't look up. He didn't want to find out how far their firearms could shoot. He flew in random patterns, like he was merely practicing his skills, but he always kept the man on the orsa in sight.

In Cellerin City, the man stopped at a public stable. Krey landed nearby and waited. After the man returned his orsa, Krey casually followed him down the street, keeping plenty of distance between them. The man turned, then stopped at a small, green house.

Krey strolled through the neighborhood. While some houses were well kept, others looked like they hadn't seen a paintbrush in years. Across the street and a couple of houses down from the man's house was a vacant, boarded-up home. *Perfect.*

Krey flew out of the city, looking for a good place to rest and refuel. A smile kept coming to his mouth. The next time the man with the mustache left to pick up reports on the magic-eater militia, he wouldn't be alone.

23

One day, a man who'd been living in Deroga, the great, preday city, showed up in our community. He was cold, hungry, and ready to rejoin civilization.

He stayed about three weeks, and then one morning he was gone. Someone saw him walking toward Deroga.

I guess he missed the bones and ghosts.

-The First Generation: A Memoir *by Liri Abrios*

"AT LEAST IT'S INSIDE."

Nora turned a baleful glare on Ovrun, who was still cheerful after their long, nighttime trek to Cellerin City. Yes, they were inside, but the tiny, vacant house they'd broken into reeked of urine and body odor. They weren't the first squatters to find this place.

On top of that, a light snow had fallen on them as they walked through the night. They all changed into somewhat dry clothes, but cold air blew inside through poorly boarded-up windows. Maybe once the sun rose, it would get warmer. Until then, they'd huddle up in blankets.

The courier always brought papers to Sharai on Tuesdays. He probably wouldn't pick up the package from the militia until shortly before then. Whenever he left, Nora, Krey, and Ovrun would follow him. It was only Friday, but they'd decided to set up camp a few days early, just in case. They might have to follow him on a few trips to the market or his workplace, but at least they wouldn't miss the pick up.

"What I wouldn't give for a seer right about now," Nora said. "We just need one prophecy telling us when this guy is leaving his house."

Krey laughed. "If we had a seer, I'd skip this whole spying thing and ask them where the militia is."

"Do you think seers really existed?" Ovrun asked.

"I do," Krey said. "There's a lot of written history about them, too much to be mythical. Prophecy was the one form of preday Anyarian magic."

"There was one final seer," Nora said. "She tried to stop the apocalypse."

Krey raised an eyebrow. "You think that story is true?"

"Definitely. Liri wrote about it in *The First Generation*. You don't believe her?"

He shrugged. "There are so many stories about those final days. It's hard to know what's true and what isn't. Anyway, we'd better settle in and watch for this guy to leave. Unless one of you is hiding your prophetic abilities."

"I'll take the first watch," Ovrun said. "If I see the courier, I'll wake you both."

Nora and Krey used their booted feet to sweep away little bits of who-knew-what from a patch of floor. They set out their blankets and pillows and lay down.

Nora had read in novels about teeth chattering, but she'd always thought it was a figure of speech. Nope. Her own teeth were clacking against each other like a tiny percussion section.

From about a met away, Krey spoke softly. "I'd offer to cuddle up together, but that might be kind of weird."

Nora didn't care if it was weird; sharing body heat was the best idea she'd heard in days. "Well—" she began.

"Of course," Krey continued, his voice soft enough to reach only Nora, "I suppose there are weirder things. Like trying to kiss someone you just met who's not even available, all because you feel sorry for them." There was laughter in his voice.

She tried to hold back her own smile and whispered, "If I'd known you had a girlfriend, I wouldn't have tried to kiss you. In fact, if I'd known anything at all about you, I would've stayed far, far away."

He laughed loudly.

"You two should sleep," Ovrun said from his spot at the window. "You'll both get shifts tomorrow night."

"In all seriousness," Krey said, "even Zeisha would tell us to cuddle up. When you're the one on night watch, I'm gonna make the same offer to Ovrun."

"Oh good. I was afraid I'd wear my teeth down to nubs by morning." Nora scooted over, her back to Krey, and he pulled her close, wrapping an arm around her. It wasn't as weird as she'd expected.

***

Friday, Saturday, and Sunday, they took turns watching the courier's house, peeking through boards nailed over the broken window. He never left it.

Days in the cramped house were boring. Ovrun often did push-ups and other calisthenics. Nora tried not to be too obvious when she watched him. Krey had brought a couple of books, which he and Nora read. The two of them also practiced their ice lysting, using snow from the overgrown back yard. Ovrun was the recipient of more than a few well-aimed, magical snowballs.

They divided the night into two shifts. One person got the whole night off, while the other two took turns keeping watch. The weather remained cold, so the two who weren't on duty cuddled together while they tried to sleep.

Nora gave Krey high marks for snuggling. He was relaxed and still. She slept well with his chest against her back and his arm over her. It felt good and totally unromantic, which she figured Zeisha would appreciate.

Ovrun, on the other hand, was tense and shifted position every few minutes. Finally, an hour or so after they'd gone to bed Sunday night, Nora turned to face him. "You're awfully wiggly," she whispered.

"Oh, uh . . . sorry."

"It's okay, just relax. If you can. I know the last thing you want to do is touch me, but—"

Ovrun's soft laugh interrupted her. "That's not it, not even close," he murmured. "You know that, right?"

She swallowed. He didn't clarify, not that he needed to. Nora glanced toward the window, where she could barely see Krey's silhouette. *Good thing he's here to keep us out of trouble.*

Except she kind of wished Krey were anywhere but here.

"Good night, Ovrun," she whispered. She turned over. This time, he held her close, his strong arm pulling her into his firm chest, his breath warm on her neck.

She never should've told him to relax. This felt way too good.

As the sun rose on Monday morning, Nora disentangled herself from Krey to take her shift at the window. The cold snap was finally coming to an end, and she was watching an icicle drip when movement caught her eye. Her gaze snapped back to the courier's house. A man in a wide-brimmed hat stepped out the front door.

"He's leaving!" Nora gasped.

Krey and Ovrun rushed to the window. They all watched the man walk to the street.

"He's walking in the direction of the stable," Krey said. "I'll fuel up." He pulled a few pieces of feather from his pocket and shoved them in his mouth.

Ovrun grabbed his backpack. "If he rents an orsa, I'll get one too."

"Remember, big enough for two," Nora said.

Ovrun shoved a knitted cap on his head and wrapped a scarf around his neck and mouth. Hopefully he wouldn't encounter any sharp-eyed royal guards who recognized his eyes and nose. Krey handed him a coin purse. Ovrun grabbed his backpack and archery supplies and exited through the back door. Krey ate a quick meal of feathers, gave himself the same hasty disguise as Ovrun, and left. Nora put on her backpack, watching out the front window.

Perhaps half an hour later, Ovrun rode up on a large, reddish-brown orsa. Nora met him at the back door. She smiled behind her scarf, took Ovrun's proffered hand, and pulled herself onto the back of the orsa's long saddle. Not sure which direction to go, they rode slowly through the residential streets.

A few minutes later, Krey flew down and hovered next to them. "He turned. Take the second left up ahead, then the first right."

Nora gave the orsa two gentle slaps on his backside. She tightened her hold on Ovrun's waist as the beast broke into a gentle run.

It wasn't long before Nora and Ovrun had the courier in sight. They followed at a distance.

Krey descended again. This time, he landed and walked with them. "If he leaves the city, I'll follow first." He shoved more feathers in his mouth.

Nora nodded. They would take turns following the man if and when he left town. When it was Krey's turn, he'd fly high above while

Nora and Ovrun stayed just out of the courier's sight. Hopefully the man would mistake Krey for a bird, if he noticed him at all. When Krey stopped to rest and refuel, Nora and Ovrun would get close enough to keep track of the man until Krey was ready to pick up the pursuit again.

As the man continued to the edge of town, the traffic in the streets became sparser. Krey took to the air. Nora and Ovrun couldn't follow without being noticed, so they waited in a park.

Krey returned half an hour later. "He left the road, and he's riding through the middle of nowhere. I'll lead you to him so I can refuel. It's hilly out there, so you should be able to stay out of sight most of the time."

They continued their back-and-forth following pattern. Nora was chilly and tired, but she couldn't stop grinning. This was the most excitement she'd had since the day she fled the palace.

Mid-morning, Krey approached Nora and Ovrun. He'd just taken a break and was still chewing on a feather. His eyes were locked on the horizon. "I think we know where he's going."

Ovrun nodded. "He's headed straight for Deroga."

Krey ate as many feathers as he could tolerate, and then he choked down a few more. It would be impossible for two people on an orsa to follow the courier through the deserted streets of a ghost town without being seen. He'd have to finish this quest on his own. He stuffed his pockets with as many diced feathers as he could manage, strapped the bow and arrows to his pack, and took to the air.

Nora and Ovrun headed back toward the warehouse, where Ovrun would drop off Nora before riding back to Cellerin City to return the orsa. They'd been tempted to abandon it, but Ovrun had paid a hefty deposit. They needed the money back so Krey could return to the store to buy more food and supplies. After returning the orsa, Ovrun would once again walk from Cellerin City to the suburbs.

Krey performed a lazy loop in the sky, then glanced down at his belly, which was overly full of feathers. *I look several months pregnant.*

As the mounted man made his way through the suburb, Krey positioned himself so the sun would be in the man's eyes if he looked up to see what was flying above him. Then he took in the sight of the massive city stretching beneath him.

The distant buildings were impressive, some of them rising dozens of stories into the sky. Even more incredible were the Skytrain tracks that crisscrossed the city skies, like a vast network of blood vessels. Many of the tracks stopped abruptly, where large sections had fallen to the streets below. A few Skytrain cars still sat on the tracks. One waited at a passenger tower, forever stalled at its final stop. *I can't believe any of it's still standing. That's good engineering.*

The courier had entered the suburbs several clommets away from where Krey, Ovrun, and Nora were staying, so Krey didn't recognize the area. However, after following the man's path through city streets for about half an hour, two things became clear: First, they were uncomfortably close to the actual city of Deroga—and the violent trogs who lived there. Second, despite all the fuel he'd taken in, Krey's body was exhausted from using so much magic.

He cursed and dropped to the roof of a building. In his recent extended trips, he'd gone as far as he could, then rested for as long as he needed. Today, he'd been experimenting with shorter flying shifts and shorter rests.

Without Nora and Ovrun to take over the search, however, he couldn't afford to rest for long. He threw several pieces of diced feathers into his mouth and swallowed. He coughed, nearly choking. *You've got to chew, Krey. You know this.* He drank some water and chewed the next batch of feathers.

Time to try something new. He'd fuel on the go, keeping his belly full of feathers. Maybe he could compensate for his exhaustion by keeping his magic topped off.

He ate more feathers and some dried fruit, then took to the air again, quickly finding the man he was following.

Krey fell into a rhythm: *Pull feathers out of pocket. Shove feathers in mouth. Chew. Swallow. Repeat.* Meanwhile, he increased his altitude and kept a close eye on the mounted man below, who was still riding at a rapid clip.

The first evidence of trogs that Krey noticed was a building with a green roof. He squinted and saw several more like it: rooftop farms, just as he'd read about. He shook his head and smiled. *Incredible.* All the green roofs were near the wide river that ran through Deroga. It made sense that the city's populace would center itself around fresh water.

When Krey drew closer, he saw his first trog. The man, who was wearing earth-toned clothes, exited a building and walked toward the courier. They engaged in a short conversation before the courier rode on.

The encounter had gone a little too smoothly. *The people behind the militia must have an agreement with the trogs. Maybe they're even working together.*

Krey considered the possibility as he flew higher. It would make sense for the New Therroans to ally themselves with another group. More people meant more power. But what was in it for the trogs? Were they tired of living outside society?

More trogs appeared in the city streets. Each time the courier encountered one, he stopped briefly, then continued.

Despite his constant feather eating, strength slowly seeped from Krey. His thoughts shifted into a prayer. *Please, God, if you've ever heard me, hear me now. I need to keep following this man. I have to find Zeisha.*

The man continued on for another half-hour. Krey was getting shaky and having a hard time controlling his altitude when he noticed the man had entered an area that, for a couple of blocks in every direction, appeared to contain no trogs.

The courier stopped next to a huge, metal building in a street that was free of broken-down vehicles. The building looked like a ware-house. He dismounted and set to work hitching his orsa to a nearby light pole.

Krey alighted on top of the three-story building across the street, lay on the roof, and examined the warehouse. Across the front of it were five bays. Four were covered by huge, metal doors, each one about seven or eight mets wide and at least six mets tall. They looked like the garage doors he'd seen at some preday houses and at the warehouse in the suburbs. These, however, were bigger, and they had skinny, horizontal windows set at eye level.

The fifth bay was open, its door up. Krey squinted to see past the yawning entrance, but darkness shrouded the area. Next to the open bay was an ordinary-looking, metal door, sized for people rather than preday delivery vehicles.

The man finished tying his orsa, then walked all the way to the other side of the street. He stopped right under Krey's perch. Krey kept his breathing quiet and shallow as the man stepped into the street and picked up a rock. He threw it as hard as he could toward the single, small door. When it didn't hit its mark, he sighed, then picked up another rock, stepped about a met closer, and tried again. He missed. Krey felt his brows knit together as he scrambled to decipher the man's actions.

For his third try, the man stood in the middle of the street. He brought his arm way back behind his head, stepping forward as he hurled one more rock toward the building. This time, the rock bounced off the metal door with a *clang*. Before the echoes died out, the man pivoted and sprinted back across the street. Once again, he halted below Krey.

A deep, resonant growl emanated from the open bay. The source of the horrific sound came into view—first its snout, narrow at the end, broadening as it connected with a face as tall as a person. Small, rounded ears extended from the sides of the thing's face. Its compound eyes were gleaming half-orbs of faceted gold. Krey's pulse accelerated as he imagined the beast taking in every detail with those eyes—including the teenager lying on top of the building across the street.

The creature continued to step forward, revealing a short neck and a massive, powerful chest. While its front legs were small compared to its overall size, they would nonetheless dwarf Krey. The beast was clearly reptid, with sleek skin that grew in a basket-weave pattern. It was iridescent grey, and where the sunlight hit it, little rainbows seemed to bounce off.

The rest of the creature emerged. Its golden, translucent wings were folded against a long, sleek body reminiscent of a grotesquely overgrown shimshim. It had muscular, powerful back legs. Its tiny, nub-like tail would've been cute on a small animal. On this beast, it looked out of place.

Krey absorbed all these details in the five seconds that it took for the gray monstrosity to exit its hiding place. As soon as it was out, it halted. Its head and chest strained forward, but it progressed no farther. That's when Krey noticed the massive, black chains on the creature's back legs.

Krey's befuddled mind formed a single thought: *I've never seen a dragon before.* Then the reptid unfolded its golden wings and opened its massive mouth. Its craggy, knife-edged teeth flashed in the sunlight. It roared, and a surge of red-and-orange flames accompanied the earth-shaking sound.

Below Krey, the courier released a high-pitched moan. The dragon had clearly aimed at him, but its flames didn't reach that far. Krey knew some dragons could belch streams of fire up to a quarter-clommet long. However, he'd also heard that, just like lysters, dragons needed fuel—in their case, a particular type of leaf. Whoever controlled this beast also controlled its fire-making competence.

The building's small door opened, and a bored-looking, bald man emerged. He pulled up his jacket hood and sauntered into the street, stopping right in front of the dragon. Hands on his hips, the man stood wordlessly for several seconds. The dragon then backed into its dark den.

A dragon speaker. Krey had never encountered such a person before, though one had lived in Tirra before he was born. According to stories he'd heard, she hadn't been a magic eater. One day, she'd been hanging laundry out to dry when a dragon had flown overhead and spoken directly into her mind. She'd communicated with that single dragon, who lived in a cave near Tirra, for the rest of her life.

Dragon speaking was different than other talents. While magic eaters were more likely to parent talented children, the ability to communicate with dragons was a seemingly random gift. It was also the only talent that didn't require any fuel.

Krey held his breath as he continued to watch the street. He had no idea what telepathic message the man had given the dragon, but it had worked. As soon as the dragon was out of sight, the dragon speaker gave the courier a contemptuous look and beckoned him toward the warehouse. The courier followed him in.

Krey was sweating profusely, and his heart felt like it would sprint out of his chest. *I think I understand why the trogs leave this area alone.*

A soft *whoosh* reached Krey's ears. He couldn't quite place it, but he knew he'd heard the sound before. Recently, even.

Another *whoosh.* This time, an arrow flew past his head, near enough for him to feel the tiny gust of wind it created.

Krey stifled a scream.

IN THE DARK: 7

ONCE AGAIN, a memory-dream had Zeisha in its grasp. This time, however, she didn't relive her daytime activities. And it certainly wasn't a nightmare.

In the dream, she and Krey stood on a lookout a half-hour's hike up Cellerin Mountain. He'd promised to take her to a spot she'd never forget, and he'd delivered. Below them, the town of Tirra looked like a collection of carved miniatures. The smoke rising from chimneys was reduced to tiny, gray ribbons. People were barely more than specks, and for a moment, she imagined that she and Krey were the gods of Anyari, all their responsibilities gone. They could stay on this mountain forever, enjoying each other. No school, chores, or parents, just gorgeous him and beautiful her.

That was one of the things she liked most about Krey. He made her feel beautiful. Sometimes it was his words, but more often, it was the way his dark eyes looked at her. The way his brown skin took on a bit of pink when she caught him staring. She might doubt her loveliness at other times, but not when she was with Krey.

His arm snaked around her shoulder, and she brought hers around his waist, looking up at him, hoping. They hadn't kissed yet, and she'd wanted it for weeks. He smiled but didn't dip his head to her. Instead, he pointed at the sky.

She'd been so busy watching the town below that she'd missed the start of the sunset. Flowing bands of gold, pink, and purple extended up from the horizon. As she and Krey watched, the colors deepened, multiplied, and spread—up, and up, and farther still across the orange sky. For a few blissful minutes, wisps of pink floated even in the east, like the sun's paintbrush had slipped off its evening canvas, getting a head start on the morning sunrise.

As the colors faded, Krey's hand found her chin, and she met his gaze. His skin was flushed, his eyes hopeful. Movement caught her attention, and her eyes dropped to his mouth, just in time to see his pink tongue lick his perfect lips.

She returned her eyes to his and whispered, "Now would be a good time."

Finally, he pulled her close and bent his head. She stood on her toes, and his lips pressed hers, just barely. It was his first kiss; she knew that. Hers too. So while she understood his hesitation, it didn't fit with the strong, aggressive Krey she'd known all her life.

She brought her hand to the back of his neck, pulled his head back down, and kissed him. A real kiss this time, sweet but urgent. She felt his lips smile under hers, and then his mouth opened, reducing her whole body to throbbing perfection—soft lips, eager tongue, trembling legs, racing heart.

She'd had no idea it would be like this. If kissing was this amazing, how did people work, eat, and sleep? How did they not stand on mountainsides all day and all night, freezing or sweating or starving, lost in each other's lips?

With that delightful thought, Zeisha's dream ended.

Rather than wake Isla, she sat, huddled in a blanket, trying not to lose the thrill of the memory, fresh on her mind and her lips. Had their first kiss, up there on the side of the mountain, really been that incredible?

Yes. Yes it was. And more.

"Krey," she whispered, "please come."

24

I was thirteen, and the boy down the street had finally noticed me. "He held my hand," I told my mom.

Mom smiled. "Was it magical?"

"Totally," I said with a happy giggle.

"You know one of the reasons I love you?" She gave me a tight hug and whispered, "You remind me how much this world hasn't changed."

-The First Generation: A Memoir *by Liri Abrios*

KREY SCRAMBLED TO HIS KNEES. Another arrow flew past him. He leapt into the air, cursing himself for not eating more feathers while on the roof. He was wobbly, but his magic hadn't quite petered out.

He scanned the rooftops and met the gaze of a slender girl holding a bow and reaching for an arrow. She was wearing loose tan pants and a black shirt, similar to clothes he'd seen on trogs in the streets. She looked about thirteen. *Guess trogs start training young.*

The girl let the arrow fly. Another miss. Krey cursed under his breath. He urged himself to fly higher. Every cell in his body screamed that he didn't have enough fuel. He dropped a dozen mets, leaving his stomach somewhere in the air above him. With a burst of stubborn will, he pushed himself higher. Again, he took an unplanned dive. He reached into his pocket as he flew upward again, into the mist of a low cloud.

His magic gave out all at once, and he fell through the chilly air. Desperate, he pinched his fingers together and yanked his hand out of his pocket. He'd managed to grab one piece of diced feather, but too many additional pieces fluttered into the air, riding the wind with more grace than him.

City roofs were rapidly approaching. Krey shoved the feather in his mouth and swallowed. Fear of death must be working to his benefit, because this time, he didn't choke.

The tiniest bit of magical lightness seeped into his body. Despite that slight lift, he landed hard on an ancient, pitched roof. His right shoulder and hip hit first. His breath shot out of his lungs. He rolled across the roof's steep surface, into the sharp valley between two peaks.

Unfortunately, the valley itself was steep too. Krey began to slide down. His fingers turned into claws, but the roof's smooth surface provided no handholds. His feet slid off the roof first. The rest of him followed. Once again, he fell through the air—but only for a moment. He slammed into a metal railing and landed on a balcony with a *thud* and a groan.

He lay still, evaluating his body's signals. They were loud, strong, and all of one sort: *pain.* He'd have more bruises than he could count if he got out of Deroga alive. He methodically tested each limb, finger, and toe. Nothing felt broken, which meant every bone in his body owed a debt of gratitude to that one, tiny piece of feather.

Sleep. It wasn't a desire; it was an urgent demand. Krey closed his eyes, then pried them back open. *First—fuel. Just in case I have to get out of here fast.*

With a pained moan, he sat up, then rummaged in his pockets. If only he hadn't lost those feathers while he was falling. He still had some, but it might not be enough to get him back to the suburbs.

Well, he'd make the best of what he had. He put two pieces of feather in his mouth. Even chewing hurt. He didn't think he'd bruised his jaw, but his exhausted body protested against any movement. Despite the pain, he forced himself to eat one feather after another.

At last, it wasn't a full belly or an empty pocket that made him stop. It was fatigue like no other, one that put an end to every movement except gravity's pull on his torso. His head hit the balcony floor.

Whispers interrupted a lovely dream in which Krey had been kissing Zeisha for the first time. With a quiet huff, he forced his eyes open. The still air was dark and cold. Krey peered through the balcony's metal rails and saw two lanterns and the silhouettes of three people. *Trogs. Did they somehow see me?*

The whispers below continued. Krey bit back the curses he wanted to hurl at the trogs, then pushed his hands against the balcony floor. His bruised body begged him to stay put, but he rose into the air. His foot caught the railing, making a hollow, metallic sound. The trogs cried out, but this time, they didn't shoot any arrows.

It shouldn't have taken too long to fly to the warehouse campsite, but Krey could tell that his tired body was expending magic faster than usual. As he reached the suburbs, he once again dipped dangerously low. After recovering, he landed, this time on his feet.

From here on out, he'd have to walk. Every simmet of his battered body hurt. It would be a long, slow trip.

"If he doesn't come back, I think we should still find Zeisha," Ovrun said.

"I agree," Nora said.

Ovrun watched her pace in a big circle around their campsite, as she'd done for much of the night. "You could sit," he said, patting the floor next to him.

She shook her head. "I might fall asleep."

"Would that be so bad?" Ovrun was having trouble keeping his own eyes open after returning the orsa and walking hours back to the suburbs.

"I'd feel like I was betraying Krey if I slept. When you only have two friends, you've got to be loyal to both of them." She let out a short laugh, but Ovrun didn't think she was joking.

"So you didn't have any friends before you met me and Krey?" he asked.

"Just one." Her voice was almost too soft to hear. "You know . . . Faylie."

"Oh yeah." Ovrun looked down at his hands, then up at Nora. "Do you mind telling me where she went? I used to open the gate for her and her mom all the time. Then they were just gone."

"Her mom quit her job in the residence so they could move to Newland. Faylie sent me a note ending our friendship." Nora shrugged, but her voice sounded choked. Her pacing had turned to speed walking. "It was so out of character. That's why I thought she might be in the militia. But she's not. She just didn't think I was worth being friends with."

Ovrun cursed under his breath. He wanted to tell Nora just what he thought of someone who'd hurt her like that, but he didn't think it would help. Instead, he said, "I think you're worth being friends with."

Nora's head was down, her bobbed hair covering her face. She nodded and sniffled. Several seconds passed, and Ovrun added, "We should eat something."

"I'm not hungry. You need food though. Sleep too."

Ovrun rummaged through his backpack, stood, and approached Nora. He took her hand.

She stopped walking and looked down at his hand on hers. Then she lifted her gaze to his, and he saw the sheen of tears in her wide, brown eyes. Her lips parted.

He turned her hand over, placed two pieces of dried fruit in it, and gently closed her fingers over them. Then, with regret disproportionate to the action, he let go.

"Thanks," she whispered, her eyes still locked on his.

He could get lost in those eyes. If only she were just *Nora*. Not Princess Ulminora Abrios. He let out his breath in a sigh that was louder than intended. "I'm gonna take a nap."

Nora nodded.

Ovrun didn't know how long he slept, but he woke to the sound of the metal door opening. He watched Nora rush to Krey, who held both his hands up. "No hugs this time, please. I'm pretty sore."

Yawning, Ovrun stood and approached. He shook Krey's hand. "I'm glad you're okay."

"*Okay* is relative," Krey said, wincing as he walked forward. "I need to eat something, and then I have to sleep. At least a couple of hours."

They all sat. Krey tore into a pile of dried fruit with ravenous gusto.

"Did you find the militia?" Nora asked.

Krey swallowed. "I think so." He took another bite.

"Come on, Krey," she said. "Tell us about it."

He shrugged and kept eating, not saying a word until he'd finished several strips of dried fruit. Then he lay down and covered himself in blankets. "When I wake up," he said in a voice that was barely more than a mumble, "I'll tell you about the dragon." His mouth curled into a smile, and his eyes closed.

Krey told his story as they all ate yet another lunch of skewered shimshim—or rather, as the skewered shimshim on their plates grew cold. When someone was describing a dragon, food became an unnecessary distraction.

Ovrun's mouth hung open as he pictured the huge beast. When Krey finished summarizing his escape, Ovrun asked, "Have you ever seen any magical creatures before?"

"Not until today," Krey said.

"What about you, Nora?"

Nora leaned forward. "People say there's a unicorn in that little forest next to the palace. Once when I escaped for half a day, I thought I saw it from far off. But it could've just been a cervida. It looked like it had a horn, but it might've been a tree branch." Cervidas were quiet animals that lived in forested areas. Ovrun's uncle liked to hunt them for their meat.

"A lot of people think unicorns are related to cervidas," Krey said. "Unicorns are much bigger though."

"I know, but from that far away, I couldn't tell how large it was."

"Back to the dragon," Ovrun said. "If that thing is guarding Zeisha and the others, how are we gonna get past it?"

"We have to get help," Nora said.

Krey put his meat skewer down. "Please don't say we should bring in someone from the damn monarchy."

"The *damn monarchy* is my family!" Nora cried. "Maybe taxes are too high, but we genuinely want what's best for every citizen of this nation. Whether or not they appreciate it!"

"You honestly think I hate the monarchy because of taxes?"

Nora stared at him, eyes flashing, and dropped her voice. "I want to help you, Krey, and the best resources I have are within the monarchy because—news flash—I'm part of the royal family. If taxes aren't the root of your concern, then get over yourself and tell me what is."

"No." The single word shot out of his mouth like a bullet.

"You won't tell me?"

He shook his head.

Silence fell, and Ovrun looked back and forth between his two friends. Neither of them seemed likely to budge. At last, he said, "Before we make a plan, I think we should visit the militia site again. We know there's a dragon, but we need more details."

Nora raised an eyebrow. "There are trogs all over the city. How are we supposed to get past them?"

"We'll go at night," Krey said. "I'll fly us. I think I'm ready to carry someone with me."

Nora raised her eyebrows. "You *think* you're ready?"

He shrugged. "Obviously we'll practice first."

"Great idea," Ovrun said, "except I'm—kind of big."

A short chuckle left Krey's chest. "I noticed. I'll practice with Nora first. Once I know I can fly safely with her, I'll practice with you. We'll go at night so the trog archers don't see us. I'll drop off one of you and come back for the other one."

Nora caught his gaze. "And when we complete our reconnaissance and realize we can't break into a dragon-guarded facility, we'll talk about reaching out to my aunt."

Krey sighed. "We'll see."

25

Sometimes when I place my hands on a plant and make it grow, I believe, just for a moment, that I'm a plant too. My hair feels like tree fronds, and my feet seem to grow roots. At those times, magic feels like bliss.

-The First Generation: A Memoir *by Liri Abrios*

KREY SOARED IN THE CHILLY, dark sky above the warehouse. Nora was on his back, her arms tight around his chest, her legs circling his waist. Flying with a passenger was more amazing than he'd dared hope.

He'd been practicing with stones and pallets. Every time, he felt united to the object he carried. It was the same with Nora; it seemed she was part of him, rather than being a weight on his back. He could sense her head, her features, her limbs, just as he sensed his own. Her clothes, too, felt like part of him—every fiber of her shirt, the supple suede of her jacket, even the sweat soaked into her socks.

He supposed it should feel odd to be aware of every aspect of her distinctly female form. It didn't, though. It was like he'd found the most natural way to understand a woman's body.

"This," Krey said as he spiraled higher, "is incredible."

Nora's only response was a little squeak. He hoped that didn't mean she was as frightened as she'd been when they took off. As soon as he'd started flying, when all they were doing was hovering over the warehouse floor, she'd demanded he stop. She'd jumped off, saying that while he felt weightless, she did not, and she couldn't imagine flying above the city like that.

Krey had assured her it had been weeks since he'd dropped something he was carrying. He'd explained how aware he was of her form, which would allow him to make tiny adjustments to keep her as stable as possible.

While his words about being connected with her body elicited a creeped-out grimace, his confidence convinced her. "Okay, let's go," she'd said. Since then, she'd been silent.

"I'm headed back," Krey said. "Don't want to use up too much of my fuel." He, Nora, and Ovrun had been collecting feathers from the buildings near the warehouse. After his recent experience running out of fuel, he was determined to build up a large stash. He'd even skipped last Saturday's New Therroan meeting, unwilling to eat that many feathers.

Krey flew through the machinery room and into the warehouse. He performed a smooth landing. Nora jumped off his back as soon as he let go of her legs, and he turned to her with an expectant smile.

Her eyes were wide, and she was panting. That didn't surprise him; he'd felt her physiological reactions as if they were his own. The flight had been indescribably thrilling. She must be just as excited as he was.

"That," Nora said, "was the most terrifying thing I've ever experienced, and I'd rather fight a gang of trogs than do it again."

Krey laughed before he could stop himself. A silly smile remained on his lips as he said, "Sorry. I hoped you were enjoying it."

"I wasn't."

"Clearly." Another little chuckle escaped. He was still on a high from the incredible trip.

"I'm glad it's funny for you." Nora stomped off.

Krey sighed and followed. It wasn't like she could go far in this place. He stayed a few steps behind her, doing his best to wipe the grin off his face. "Hey, I really am sorry. If I'd realized you hated it that much, I would've come back sooner."

"It's fine," she said, her chin high. "The trip to the militia will be a lot longer. I guess I have to get used to it."

"Or, you know, train to fight a gang of trogs."

She turned and gave him a scathing look.

"I love this, man!" Ovrun said.

Krey laughed. "You keep saying that." He performed a couple of quick dips, eliciting a "Whoop!" from the passenger on his back.

He'd practiced carrying passengers for a week now, and they'd all agreed it was time to go to the militia warehouse. Since Ovrun had the best bow skills, Krey would drop him off first. Ovrun would wait, hopefully without incident, until Krey returned with Nora.

The flight felt nothing like Krey's previous journey into the city. He was well-rested with plenty of feathers in his system, and a small pouch in his sleeve stored additional fuel that he ate on the go.

As passengers went, Ovrun was vastly different from Nora. He was enthusiastic, and his body was nothing like hers—or like Krey's, for that matter. When Krey incorporated Ovrun's physique into his own, he was awed by his friend's bulk and strength. Krey's frequent runs kept him in good shape, but he'd never have big biceps or a broad chest like Ovrun. *Maybe I should do more push-ups*, Krey thought. By the sky, even Ovrun's neck was thick and powerful, though Krey wasn't sure how much use a big neck was on a daily basis.

After a flight they both heartily enjoyed, Krey dropped Ovrun on a rooftop within view of the militia warehouse. It was the tallest building in the vicinity. *Good luck finding him up here, archers.*

Krey returned to the dark sky. He hadn't been flying long when he passed over the thick, metal lines of a Skytrain track. He could live here for a hundred years and never lose his sense of awe. Ordinary people had designed and built that track, those buildings. People like him.

The world was different these days, but Krey figured their simple society had enormous potential for growth . . . if the right people took leadership. He would be one of those people; he was sure of it. He'd contribute something big, something good, to his world.

What would that big, good thing be? He wasn't sure yet. He'd often dreamed of starting a network of public libraries, something larger and more accessible than Cellerin's hodgepodge of local facilities.

When Zeisha is safe, we'll build something as impressive as those buildings below me. Something that will outlast both of us.

That thought carried Krey back to the warehouse, where he refueled and rested for about half an hour. Nora was quiet, and when he stood, she reluctantly got on his back. They had a silent, uneventful flight to Ovrun.

As soon as he landed, Nora got down, dropped to her knees, and vomited her dinner onto the roof.

"You okay?" Ovrun asked.

She shuddered. "I can't believe you actually enjoy flying with him."

"Give yourself some credit," Krey said. "Not everyone could've waited to puke until they got off my back."

"I won't be so kind next time," Nora muttered.

Krey popped another feather piece in his mouth. "I'll fly down and find somewhere we can hide near the warehouse."

It didn't take long to find several spindly bushes alongside the building. He returned to Ovrun and Nora. "I'll take you one at a time."

"Do you need to rest first?" Ovrun asked.

"Maybe I should. Wake me up in half an hour, okay?"

His short nap brought him back to full energy. After two short flights, they were all huddled between the scratchy shrubs and the building.

"I think we should take turns walking around the building," Ovrun whispered. "We might all spot different things." When his companions agreed, he said, "Stay low; someone could be looking out the windows." He pointed at an eye-level window on the side of the building. Like the windows on the bay doors, it was horizontal and too narrow to crawl through. "I'll go first."

He was back in less than a minute. "Someone holding a lantern just left the front of the building. They're walking our way. Probably a night guard."

"We could hide between the buildings across the street," Nora said.

"Okay." Ovrun crouched and led the way.

When they'd almost reached the front corner of the building, he stopped. Nora bumped into him with a soft "Oof."

He spun around and whispered, "Other way."

They all turned and ran toward the back of the building. Once they'd turned the corner, Ovrun said, "The guard was walking faster than I thought. She would've seen us."

They sprinted all the way around the huge warehouse and straight across the street. Without a word, they huddled between two buildings. They were all panting, the sound intolerably loud in the tight space.

When their breathing slowed, Krey said, "That was close."

A hand clutched his arm, and Nora's soft voice let loose with an impressive collection of curses. "She's coming this way."

Nora was right. The guard was walking across the street, her pool of lantern light shifting with every step.

"Come on," Ovrun said. He moved on quiet feet, leading them

farther into the dark space. Within seconds, they reached a fence. "Get into a ball. Hide your head."

Sandwiched between a wall and Nora, Krey drew his knees to his chest. Nora was trembling—or was that him? His breaths came even faster as he tucked his chin and tried to stave off panic. *I should be facing the fence, not the street! Idiot!* Too late to change position now.

He kept his eyes open, peeking between his knees at the ground in front of him. The guard's footsteps were audible now. Krey tried to slow his breaths.

Lantern light entered the space between the buildings. Krey stopped breathing, and the sudden stillness told him Nora and Ovrun had done the same. The guard's footsteps continued to approach, accompanied by the creak of the swinging lantern, echoing off the walls on either side. Yellow light crept closer every second. It illuminated the dirt a met from Krey's boots, then closer still, until mere simmets separated him from the light.

The light stopped moving. The footsteps stopped too.

Then the steps resumed, and the light shifted away from them, retreating toward the street.

As soon as it was safe, Krey gulped in air. He heard the others do the same. He lifted his head, wiped frightened tears from his eyes, and watched the street.

"Let's get closer," Ovrun said, his voice impossibly calm.

He led the way, stopping when they had a wide view of the street. Nora's hand, damp with sweat despite the cold, found Krey's. He squeezed it in wordless gratitude.

Krey watched as the guard continued down the street and disappeared in between two more buildings. The pattern repeated a few times before she headed back across the street, toward the warehouse.

The guard halted.

"Did you hear that?" Nora breathed.

"What?" Ovrun asked, just as softly.

Then Krey heard it too. It was a very loud sniff that could only have come from a very large nose.

The guard dashed back to their side of the street and extinguished her lantern. Krey silently laughed. *Guess the dragon keeps even the bad guys on their toes.*

In the scant starlight that bled through the clouds, Krey could barely see the dragon's massive form emerge from the warehouse's open bay.

Nora's mouth was wide open, but she wasn't breathing. How could she breathe, watching that huge, moving shadow and hearing the rattle of its chains?

"Cage!" the guard screamed.

The sound somehow jolted life back into Nora's lungs, and she gasped as the guard cried out again.

"Cage, get out here!" The woman kept screaming until the warehouse's small door opened with a creak.

Someone emerged, holding a lantern. He stood in front of the beast, his light reflecting off shiny scales and horrifyingly large, faceted eyes.

"He's the dragon speaker," Krey said in a bare whisper.

Seconds passed, then a minute, or two, or maybe ten.

With a jangle of chains, the dragon returned to its prison, swallowed up by the darkness of the bay. The man turned to the guard. "Come on."

"You sure, Cage?" she asked in a tremulous voice.

"We have an agreement with him." Cage's voice was clear in the still, winter air. "He's not gonna hurt you; he just likes messing with you. I keep telling you; ignore him, and he'll ignore you."

"That's what my mom always said about the rats in our house, and then I'd wake up to them gnawing on my toes."

Cage laughed, but the guard didn't join in as she followed him inside.

"What next?" Ovrun asked.

Krey responded, but Nora couldn't tell what he said, because another sound distracted her.

Well, not a sound, not exactly. It was a voice, smooth and treacherous as flowing lava, born of the earth and fire. A voice that, in its depth and otherworldliness, reminded Nora of *something*, though she couldn't pinpoint what. A voice carried not on the air but on waves of thought, penetrating her mind.

Who are you?

Every muscle in Nora's body stiffened, including her tongue.

ANSWER ME.

The voice held the same authoritarian tone Nora's father sometimes spoke with, but it was exponentially more demanding.

"Nora?" Ovrun's whisper intruded into Nora's reverie.

"Shh."

"But—" Krey began.

"Shh!" she insisted. Krey and Ovrun both sighed, but they stopped talking.

I saw you in the street, human, the voice said. *Who are you?*

The second she'd heard the sound (was it even considered *hearing* when it didn't involve the ears?), Nora had known it was the dragon. Who else could speak directly to her mind? And something about the voice seemed almost familiar, though she'd certainly never heard it before.

She focused her mind on the dark beast and did her best to send a thought in his direction. *My name is Nora.*

That is not what I asked.

The reply caused Nora to jump. She'd forgotten she was holding Krey's hand until he squeezed hers tighter.

"What's wrong?" Krey asked, but she ignored him.

I asked who you are.

I'm the princess of Cellerin.

NOT WHAT I ASKED.

Nora took a deep breath, trying to calm the whirlwind of her mind. She sent him one more response. *I'm a friend.*

Whose friend? the smooth, terrifying voice asked.

The two young men I'm with. One of them wants to save the girl he loves. We think she's in that building. She's a slave.

Silence fell for several seconds, and then the dragon's voice returned, lower still. *Many slaves dwell here.*

Can you help us free her? Nora asked.

He didn't respond.

Please answer me!

The silence lingered, broken finally by Ovrun whispering, "Nora?"

"Wait!" Again, she reached out to the dragon. *Who are you?*

After a pause, his voice reached her. *I, too, am a slave. Return tomorrow, Nora-human. We will speak again.*

Wait—it was hard to get here. Can we talk more tonight? Please?

The dragon was silent. This time, it didn't matter what Nora said. The conversation was over.

Realization flooded her, from her fingertips to her earlobes. Her skin thrilled with it.

She was a dragon speaker.

It was a gift she'd dreamed of having. She supposed most Anyarian children had that fantasy. A massive surge of gratitude brought tears to her eyes, and she covered her mouth with her free hand to keep her cries from escaping. But there was no hiding her emotion; her breaths were out of control, and her body shook with the rhythm of her quiet sobs.

"Nora!" Krey's voice, quietly urgent, broke through. "What is it?"

She couldn't tame her breaths, couldn't talk.

"Back to the fence!" Ovrun whispered.

They all scampered back.

Nora's crying gradually subsided. At last, she was ready to speak, though her whispered words didn't feel real.

"I just had a conversation with a dragon."

26

One in ten thousand people survived The Day.

Who was left? Thousands upon thousands of childless parents and orphaned children. Perhaps there was an exception somewhere, one child who survived alongside their parent. Statistically, it's unlikely.

Adults took children in, stitching together new families with threads of grief, trauma, and desperation. Even now, I can tell whether someone was born before or after The Day. Orphans of the apocalypse grew up too quickly. The evidence remains in their eyes.

-The First Generation: A Memoir *by Liri Abrios*

KREY SAT UP, wrapped a blanket around his shoulders, and stared into the darkness of the warehouse. He needed rest, especially after all that flying, but his mind wouldn't allow him to sleep.

Nora could speak to dragons.

The first time he'd seen the huge, gray-and-gold creature, Krey was scared to death. Getting shot at by trogs afterward hadn't helped his mindset. It wasn't until later, after he'd rested, that he'd allowed himself to think about the complications the dragon presented.

How was he supposed to save Zeisha if her captors could sic a dragon on him? Like taking down a bunch of militia leaders wasn't enough . . . now they had to deal with a fire-breathing creature the size of a small house?

Going to the warehouse last night had been a long shot; he hadn't thought they'd learn much. He certainly hadn't expected Nora to strike up a casual conversation with the dragon.

This changes everything. If they could get that creature on their side, they might actually have a chance to save Zeisha.

Warm hope took root in Krey's chest. For the first time in weeks, he let himself imagine what it would be like to reunite with Zeisha. He could almost feel her soft curls in his fingers, her full lips on his, her—

He brought the reverie to a halt and dropped the blanket from his shoulders, letting the cold air calm his passions. *There are two other people in this room with you, Krey. Not the ideal time to get all worked up.* He tried to shift his thoughts back to the dragon, but Zeisha's eyes and curves anchored themselves in his imagination, like she was begging him from afar to think about her.

Krey wasn't sure whether to be resentful or grateful when Ovrun interrupted his reverie. "You awake too?"

"Yeah," Krey murmured. "Can't sleep, thinking about the dragon." *Among other things.*

"Crazy, right?" Ovrun yawned. "You nervous about taking Nora back there?"

"A little."

"You know, I've been thinking. Some of the other royal guards would join up with us if I asked. You'd be surprised how many—"

"No."

"Krey, they're guards. They're not part of the monarchy."

"Yes, they are. They work for the king."

"I worked for the king. You trust me."

"Only because you've shown me that you're willing to stand against him. If you hadn't done that, we might be friends, but there's no way I'd trust you."

"Is that why you trust Nora? Because she broke the rules?"

Krey released a short laugh, then reminded himself to keep his voice low. "Who said I trust her?"

After a long pause, Ovrun said, "I don't love the monarchy either, but it's different with you. It's like you really hate them."

Krey gritted his teeth and swallowed. "You could say that."

"Why?"

Breathe. In, out, repeat. Every time Krey thought about this, his system went straight into rage mode. He wanted to throttle Ovrun or risk his life doing crazy stunts in the air. *Breathe.*

"Come on, man," Ovrun said. "You can't keep holding this stuff in."

Maybe Ovrun was right. It was exhausting, hanging onto the awful truth. These days, Ovrun was the closest friend he had—who better to share with?

"Okay." Krey let out his breath. "This goes no further than the two of us, right?"

At the same time that Ovrun said, "Of course," Nora's voice filled the room.

"Wait!"

Krey jumped. "You're awake?"

"Well, I was trying to sleep, but with you two chatting it up like it's the middle of the day—and then I didn't mean to listen, not exactly, but I heard you, and . . . I didn't want you to say anything you didn't want me to hear. I mean, I did want you to, but . . . I'd feel bad if I kept listening."

"I get what you mean, man," Ovrun said. "She's totally untrustworthy."

Krey didn't laugh. "Nora, I trust you as a friend. Just not as a royal."

"Why?"

Her voice held a vulnerability Krey wasn't prepared for. Was she in tears?

"If you're gonna hate part of me, at least you could tell me why," she said.

Yeah, definitely tears. Oh, by the orange sky above, he couldn't handle this. Couldn't he just hang onto his reasons and continue the nice little friendship he and Nora were building? She was more than her royal title; he knew that. In fact, he'd been doing a pretty good job forgetting she was a princess. Most of the time, anyway.

"You know, I can't help that I'm a princess," she murmured.

Krey flinched.

Her voice sounded stronger now. "Whatever it is you've got against me or my family, I'm sick of you carrying it around like some portable wall between us. Doesn't it get heavy, Krey?"

The question hit him deep inside. *Yeah. It does get heavy.* "Okay," he blurted.

"Okay?" Nora and Ovrun asked in unison.

"I'll tell you," Krey said. "I'll tell you both."

"Let me light the lantern," Ovrun said.

As Ovrun groped around for matches, Krey tried to calm the ferocious ire blazing in his chest. When he heard the match strike and soft light illuminated their space, he turned to Nora. He wanted to direct his words straight to her, but there was too much compassion shining in her eyes. He blinked and focused on the cold coals in their firepit.

"It's not a long story," he faltered. "I don't know why I've never told you." *Fantastic, start with a lie. You had plenty of reasons for keeping this secret.* He drew in a deep breath and started fresh.

"Fourteen years ago, there was a bad bout of orange plague." He glanced up just long enough to see Ovrun and Nora nodding. They'd all been young, but nobody forgot orange plague epidemics. The disease got its name from the crusty sores that afflicted plague sufferers for months. Half of all untreated cases progressed to internal bleeding. Half of those people died.

"Well," he continued, "The plague hit Tirra early. We think a trader spread it around a pub. Twenty people got sick in the first week. My mom came down with it a month later. As soon as she saw the first sore, she sent me to my aunts' house. But my dad stayed to care for her. He got sick too."

Krey's tongue felt like dry, rough rope. He swallowed and pushed forward. "My mom started coughing blood about six weeks after she got sick. Dad got bad a couple of weeks later. He died first, and she was gone the next day. I think she was holding on for him."

He stopped. Not because he wanted to, but because his throat was too tight to push more words through. He blinked rapidly and took a few big gulps from his water bottle.

"The antibiotic . . . it didn't work?" Nora asked. "For either of them?"

Krey forced himself to meet her confused, sympathetic gaze. It was a fair question. The medication used to treat orange plague was a simple one, manufactured using an Anyarian fungus that grew near Cellerin City. Nora had every reason to believe Krey's parents would've been given the medicine they needed.

His parents had every reason to expect that too.

When Krey could speak again, he did so in a low voice. "We didn't get any antibiotic in Tirra. Not for almost a year."

"What? Why? I remember my mother giving it to me every night to prevent me from getting sick."

"Me too," Ovrun said.

Their words stoked Krey's rage. "Because the king hoarded the medicine!" he shouted. "Because your father"—he leaned forward and pointed at Nora, barely noticing when she drew back—"was so concerned about the plague spreading through his precious capital that he refused to send out any antibiotic until everyone in Cellerin City had been dosed, whether they were sick or not!"

Nora released a high, disbelieving sound, then stammered, "Oh no—he wouldn't—oh no!"

Krey leapt to his feet. "Oh yes, Your Highness, he most certainly would. He sent couriers all over the country. Told us as soon as he had medicine, he'd send it. But my Aunt Evie has friends with money and power, and they told her the truth. Cellerin City is five times the size of any other city in our kingdom. The king said a plague there would devastate our society. Who cares if he was destroying families in towns like ours, as long as everyone near the throne was safe!"

He realized his glass water bottle was still in his hand, the liquid inside sloshing with as much violence as his emotions. He drew it back and threw it hard across the room. It smashed into the floor, shattering.

It wasn't enough. A strong compulsion flooded over him, to run to the wall and punch it with all his might. He settled for a roaring scream, the type that stung his throat and would make him hoarse.

Even that didn't tame his fury. So Krey ran out of the building. Rocks, sticks, and ancient shards of polymus poked through his socks, and he relished the pain. It matched what had taken over his heart.

The eastern sky was slowly brightening, giving Krey just enough light to navigate by. After he'd been running through the deserted city for ten minutes, his anger morphed into tears. Uncontrolled, heaving sobs forced him to halt. He fell to his knees in the middle of the dusty street. The cold ground pressed against his knees, and he covered his face with his hands and let the tears fall.

Why did he tell that story? *Stupid. Pointless. Humiliating.* He couldn't go back and face them, his friends who'd asked a simple question and gotten little-boy screams in return.

His sobbing slowed after an eternity. A caynin's cry rang through the air. It sounded close. Still Krey sat, not caring that he had no way to protect himself. *Let it attack me. The fury of grief is a powerful thing.*

He didn't feel very powerful, though, not with bruises and small cuts on his feet. Not with eyes swollen to twice their size and a throat sore from screaming.

Footsteps approached, and Krey leapt to his feet and spun to face his attacker. It was Ovrun, his bow strapped to his back, his hands held high in a calming gesture.

"Just me," Ovrun said. "We were concerned about you."

Krey folded his arms. He almost said, *I'm leaving. I'll find Zeisha myself.* He was rational enough, however, to remember that only Nora could talk to the dragon. Did he want to spend more time with two people who knew how weak he really was? No way. But he'd do it for Zeisha.

Ovrun reached him and put an arm on his shoulder. He spoke just five words—"No wonder you're pissed, man."

That was enough to bring Krey's tears back.

After Nora cleaned up the broken glass, she walked slowly around the warehouse. She didn't want to be crying when Ovrun and Krey returned, but she couldn't stop.

It was her father's fault that Krey's parents had died. Had her dad thought his decision was best for the nation? Of course he had.

That didn't change the fact that families were torn apart when thousands of people took medicine they didn't need. When *she* took medicine *she* didn't need.

If she were Krey, she'd hate the monarchy too. A little part of her hated it now.

And she'd be the one making these life-changing decisions when she became queen?

"Why?" she sobbed. "Why does everyone else get a choice about what they do with their lives, and I have to rule a country, whether I want to or not?" Nora had always known that being a royal was more than parades, a pretty headdress, and fancy clothes, but Krey's story had driven home the reality of it like never before.

She forced herself to take deep, calming breaths. She couldn't fix Krey's painful past. But she could be there for him now. If he'd let her.

By the time she heard two sets of footsteps, she'd stopped crying. She knew what she needed to say. Then Krey appeared in the doorway with dirty socks and pants and his eyes pinned to the ground, and her tears returned. She'd just have to talk through them.

Nora took the lantern and approached Krey. Ovrun saw her, gave her a smile and a nod, and walked past them both.

As soon as Nora got close, Krey started talking. "I shouldn't have told you all that. I know it's not—"

"Wait, Krey, please." She wanted to reach out and hold his hand or touch his face, but she wasn't sure how he'd take that. Instead, she put the lantern down and stood in front of him, giving him plenty of space.

"What my father did to your family was wrong. I know there's nothing I can do to make it right, but I do want to tell you something." Tears rolled down her cheeks. Her sobs begged to return, but she refused to let them. "Krey, your king failed you. As his daughter, I'm sorry. I know an apology doesn't fix anything. But it's real, and it's deep. I'm crying for you, because you lost people you never should've lost. I don't expect you to ever talk to me again. I won't even be mad if you don't. But I want you to know that I'll still help you save Zeisha. And when I'm queen, I'll do anything in my power, anything at all, to make sure what happened to you never happens again. That's my pledge, Krey West."

He hadn't looked at her the whole time she talked. She didn't blame him. She'd said what she needed to say. Maybe it was even what he needed to hear, though Nora doubted it. How could a bunch of words blurted by a spoiled, teenage princess do anything to mend his heart?

She turned away, but she only took two steps before Krey stopped her with a word: "Wait."

Nora slowly pivoted to face him. He held out his arms. She swallowed hard, walking into them.

They held each other tight and cried.

27

An elderly lady in our community walked across the ridgeline of her roof every morning. It was a steep roof. People told her it was unsafe, and she laughed.

My dad shook his head and said, "Some survivors of The Day are afraid of everything. Others know the worst has happened, so they fear nothing."

When I was eight, the woman fell to her death.

-The First Generation: A Memoir *by Liri Abrios*

AFTER NORA and Krey stopped crying, they found Ovrun wiping away tears too. Without discussing it, they all lay down for a long nap.

Sleep was slow to come for Nora. She watched Krey in the light of the single lantern they hadn't extinguished. His face was calm, his hands relaxed. She'd never seen him look so peaceful. Maybe he'd finally broken down that wall he was carrying, or at least set it down for a while.

At last, Nora slept. When she woke, Ovrun was assembling a simple meal of dried foods. Krey sat up, rubbing his eyes.

"Eat up," Ovrun said. "I checked outside, and it's almost dark. You two can fly to the warehouse."

Nora's limbs buzzed with energy. *I have an appointment with a dragon.*

Minutes later, cold wind tangled her hair as her arms and legs kept a rib-crushing grip on Krey. She didn't suppose she'd ever enjoy flying, but at least her mindless terror was gone. Now, she half-believed she might survive the flight. That was progress, right?

They arrived safely and settled in the same crack between buildings where they'd waited the night before. This time, they'd brought a blanket along, in case they needed to hide from the night watch. Nora didn't think a guard would ignore a lumpy, black blanket, but she supposed it was better than their previous strategy of curling into frightened balls.

As soon as Nora got off Krey's back, the dragon spoke. *You returned.*

Again, the voice was weirdly familiar. She mulled that over, then remembered the dragon was waiting for a response.

Before she could come up with one, the dragon spoke again. *You asked for my help.*

Yes. Her pulse accelerated.

I know not if you are trustworthy.

She bit back a shrill sales pitch about how she, Krey, and Ovrun were the most trustworthy humans he'd ever meet. Something told her such arguments wouldn't work with him.

If I wish you to return, I shall invite you, the dragon said.

Invite us? How? When she didn't get an immediate response, she barreled on. *How will you contact us? Do you—*

245

NORA-HUMAN. In my two hundred years, I have learned patience. Perhaps one day, you shall learn it as well.

Two hundred years. That meant he'd existed since The Day, or shortly thereafter. Had any magical creatures been born since then? Were all the dragons, unicorns, and sea monsters two centuries old?

As she mulled over his words—*In my two hundred years*—a realization forced the air from her lungs. She knew what the dragon's supernatural voice reminded her of: the stone in the chapel. The one that had caused the apocalypse, brought magic to the world, and created glorious new creatures. The dragon's voice was dark and smooth, like the deep-black surface of the artifact. His sonorous tone resonated with magic, like the still-luminous orange seams between the stone's pieces.

He's a creature of the stone.

Apparently she'd sent that thought to the dragon, because he laughed, a sound rippling with deep, bright magic. *As are you, little frost eater.*

Wait . . . he preferred the term *frost eater* over *ice lyster*? Nora glanced at Krey. She'd keep that tidbit to herself.

The dragon's voice resounded in her mind again. *Now go. You are not safe here. Go unless I bid you return.*

I have a question. We know there's a general in charge of this place. Can you tell us who it is? Or describe them to us?

Silence extended for long enough to convince Nora the dragon was done talking. Then he responded in an odd tone, *You don't know?*

I don't.

I shall determine if you and your companions are trustworthy. If you are, I shall bring you back. Soon.

But how will you know if we're trustworthy?

The dragon didn't respond.

Nora woke the next morning to the smell of sizzling shimshim meat. Ovrun was cooking, and Krey was gone. She figured he was at the little outhouse.

After a few minutes of waiting, she muttered, "Doesn't he realize three of us are sharing that outhouse?"

Ovrun's brows jumped up. "Oh, by the sky, Nora, I forgot you didn't know. Krey and I were talking last night after you went to sleep. It's Saturday. He's flying to the New Therroan meeting."

"What? If the dragon somehow contacts me, I need Krey to take me into the city!"

"He'll be back tomorrow."

"That's true."

"He didn't want to wait on a dragon who might never contact you again. He decided it was time to ask the New Therroan leaders about the militia."

Nora sighed. Maybe the dragon should've lectured Krey on patience too. "That sounds risky. They barely know him."

"I know. I couldn't talk him out of it."

"If he doesn't come back tomorrow morning, we'll go after him." She stood. "I'm going to the outhouse."

After breakfast, Nora suggested they go hunting for shimshims and feathers. Ovrun readily agreed. It was a warm day, and they left their jackets behind, letting their easy jog warm them up. "Let's stop here," Ovrun said, pointing to a house they'd never searched.

Wedged into the corner of the front room, next to a decaying couch, sat a human skull. A few more bones were scattered around the room. Nora shuddered.

This place didn't smell like a shimshim den, but maybe they'd find some feathers. Birds sometimes roosted in cabinets. In the kitchen, Ovrun reached up to a top shelf. As he stretched, his shirt did too. The muscles of his back shifted in enthralling waves, capturing every bit of Nora's attention.

Ovrun turned and gave her that dazzling smile that would've

melted her heart if it weren't warm and soft already. He held up three feathers. "Found some!"

Oh yeah. We're searching for feathers. She knelt. "I'll check down here."

She found one feather. When she held it up to show it to Ovrun, she caught him watching her. His expression was full of *something*. She wanted to think it was desire, but whatever it was, he replaced it with a casual smile.

"A feather!" he said, clapping her on the shoulder. "Way to go, bud!"

She raised an eyebrow at him. "Bud?"

He turned with an adorably awkward laugh, and they walked to the next house.

About an hour and a half later, they had a good stash of feathers, and Nora had shot a shimshim for lunch, a feat she couldn't have been prouder of. Ovrun offered to clean it.

Nora went inside to start the cook fire. The blaze was growing when a familiar, rumbling voice entered her mind.

Nora-human.

She jumped, nearly burning herself. When she'd regathered her wits, she responded with a thought of her own. *Where are you?*

You know where I am.

How are you talking to me?

I can breathe fire. Is it difficult to believe I can talk over long distances?

Good point. *Have you been listening to us too? Did we prove we're trustworthy?*

Nora tapped her foot while she waited for the dragon's response.

At last, he said, *We shall discuss that when I see you.*

Okay. Would tomorrow night work for you?

Tonight.

I can't come tonight. Krey's gone. He's the one who flies me there.

I know. You must find another way.

Can't we talk from here?

248

You must come.

Nora considered his request—or was it a demand? Her breaths quickened as horror stories about trogs filled her imagination. She and Ovrun could travel at night, but even that was dangerous. She sent her thoughts to the dragon. *It's too far, and it's not safe. Please, can we wait until tomorrow?*

It must be tonight. At dawn tomorrow, the general will arrive.

Nora drew in a breath. *The general? Just tell me who it is! Please!*

His voice was adamant, pressing into her mind. *Nora-human, this is something you must see with your own eyes.*

28

My first kiss with the boy down the street was awkward and totally disappointing.

It was our second kiss that convinced me I was in love. For a few weeks, anyway.

-The First Generation: A Memoir *by Liri Abrios*

"I THINK WE CAN DO IT." Ovrun was pacing, his chest moving up and down with his rapid breaths.

He's just as nervous as I am. Great. "What about the trogs?" Nora asked.

"We'll walk through the suburbs during the day, then enter trog territory when it gets dark."

"It's not like there's a line marking where their territory starts. We could run into them."

Ovrun stopped next to her and knelt. "I know. And if they did anything to hurt you . . ." He shook his head. "You know what? The general will return another time. We don't need to go today. Let's wait and see if Krey finds out anything."

Nora drew her bottom lip between her teeth and dropped her gaze to the floor. She, Krey, and Ovrun could try to save Zeisha and the others without knowing who the general was. They might even succeed. Then what would happen? Whoever was in charge would try again, somewhere else, with new lysters.

She lifted her head and looked in Ovrun's eyes. "I don't just want to save the people in that building. I want to stop this from ever happening again. To do that, we have to find out who's in charge."

Ovrun nodded slowly, then squared his shoulders, lifted his chin, and took her hands in his. "We can do this, Nora. If we encounter trogs, we'll defend ourselves." His lips curled into a little smile. "You're really good with that bow, you know."

She laughed. He'd be the one carrying the bow; he was still a much better shot than her. But it was a nice thing for him to say.

They put out the fire, left a note for Krey, filled their water bottles, and loaded their packs with food. They'd have to throw out the shimshim meat. Neither of them wanted to take time to cook it.

Nora watched Ovrun strap the bow and arrows to his broad back, then sling his pack over his shoulder. *I guess if I'm gonna get murdered by a gang of trogs, at least I'll have a hot guy at my side.* The thought made her smile.

He caught her eye and returned the smile. "Let's go."

Nora looked up at the broken Skytrain track Ovrun was pointing out. He recognized it from his flights with Krey.

"I'm glad you know how to get there," Nora said. She usually had decent navigational skills, but she had no clue where the warehouse was. On her flights with Krey, she'd been busy trying not to shower the city with her stomach's contents.

Ovrun spoke in a low, serious tone. "See how much taller the buildings are about to get? I think we're getting close to trog territory. We should find a place to hide out until it gets dark."

"Oh good, I'm ready for a break." They'd been walking for hours.

They considered where to wait and soon chose a heavily treed area. It had probably once been a small park. Once they were both seated, leaning against two neighboring tree trunks, they ate quietly. Nora stole glances at Ovrun, whose alert eyes were gazing through the trees. She wanted to reach out and run her finger along his sharp jawline.

She'd done that before, the night they kissed. That night, she'd felt so lucky to spend time with someone who actually listened to her. Before they'd touched at all, they'd talked for a good hour, mostly about Nora's frustrations with tutors and the upcoming two-hundredth-anniversary trip.

Her cheeks grew warm as she realized she'd done most of the talking that night. Relieved to have a friend, she'd monopolized the conversation. *I was spoiled back then. Self centered.* And really, how much could she have changed in the six months since?

A lot. Out here with Krey and Ovrun, Nora felt like she was finally growing up. She was part of the real world now, rather than the perfect-yet-banal world of the palace. *It's been over three weeks since I wore lipstick or used a flushing toilet.* The thought made her laugh softly.

Ovrun turned to look at her. "What?"

She swallowed her last bite of dried fruit. "I was thinking about how different things are out here. How different I am. I'm not sure I like who I was a few months ago."

"I liked who you were then, and I like you now."

She released a soft laugh. "Why?"

His eyes left hers, slowly taking in her whole form. Normally, she'd bask in that gaze, but she wasn't sure she wanted it now. Her hair was tangled and greasy. Her clothes never got very clean in the creek water, and now they were damp with sweat. She tried to stay relaxed, though the feel of his eyes and the anticipation of his answer had her on edge.

Ovrun's eyes returned to her face. "You're so—" He swallowed. "You love living, Nora."

She blinked. She wasn't sure what she'd expected him to say, but it wasn't that. It was like he'd seen her heart and reflected it back to her. Many people at the palace were comfortable and content, but for Nora, that had never been enough. To truly *live*, she needed adventure and passion.

She reached out and found his hand, lacing their fingers together. "Thanks," she whispered.

His eyes dropped to their hands, his expression inscrutable.

Nora scooted closer and laid her head on his firm shoulder. A minute or two later, she tilted her head to look up at him. He was watching her, and this time, the look in his eyes was unmistakable: hot desire.

"Kiss me," she whispered.

She felt his chest fall, heard the air leave his lungs. Then he let go of her hand. "We can't."

She drew back, begging him with her eyes.

"We can't," Ovrun said, "because I enjoyed it way too much last time."

A smile pulled at her lips. "Isn't that the point?"

"Nora . . ." The word was a soft sigh. "We could have a lot of fun out here." His smile was both sweet and wicked, and Nora thought her racing heart might leave her chest. He turned toward her and brought his hands up to her cheeks. "And then before too long, you'd go back to the palace, and I'd go back to my little house to find a job. The problem is, you'd take my heart with you."

She raised her own hands and cupped his face, just as he was doing to her. "I'm not sure if that was supposed to make me want you less, but if so, it totally backfired."

He shook his head helplessly, his stubble rough against Nora's palms. "We've talked about this," he said. "There's no future for us."

He was right. One of these days, she'd go back home. Once again, her life wouldn't belong to her. But until then—oh, by the stone, until then, couldn't she pretend she was normal? "I know we don't have a future," she whispered. "But we do have right now."

Neither of them moved their hands. Nora observed the battle raging in Ovrun's dark eyes. She wasn't going to initiate a kiss, not when he'd just told her no.

All at once, something shifted in Ovrun's expression. In one motion, he slid one hand into her hair and drew her to him, capturing her lips with his. There was no build-up, no gentle kiss leading to something more. No, this was like standing on a cliff one second and leaping into a bottomless pool the next. In one moment, his mouth undid all the cautious words he'd just spoken.

Rationality fled Nora's mind. All that was left was Ovrun's mouth, melding with hers; his arms, gripping her like they'd never let go; her hands, roaming over his chest, his shoulders, his neck, his hair. A little moan exited her mouth, and then her mind was ten steps ahead, and she didn't care that they were in an overgrown park, hiding from people who might kill them on sight. All she knew was that she wanted Ovrun, more of him, all of him.

She reached for the buttons on his jacket, unfastening the top one, then the next. She was fumbling with the third button when he pulled back, and the strong arms that had been holding her to him pushed her away, gently but firmly. "We can't do this."

Every cell of her body disagreed, and her mouth dropped open in wordless protest.

His breaths were coming just as quickly as hers. "By the sky, Nora, don't look at me like that. Last time we kissed, it was great, but what we did just now, it was . . . well . . . I was lost in you. If I didn't stop right then, I wouldn't've stopped at all. Unless you didn't want it, of course—I'd never—"

"I didn't want to stop." Her fingers found his lips. "I still don't want to stop."

Ovrun closed his eyes, like he was gathering whatever strength he could. "Do you have any idea what you do to me?" he murmured, his breath hot on her fingers. He took a deep breath, met her gaze again, and gently removed her hand from his mouth. "I'm not getting a princess pregnant. I mean—I'm nineteen, I'm not getting anyone pregnant."

The word *pregnant* broke through the delicious haze she'd wanted to stay in forever. Her first inclination was to protest that all she was doing was unbuttoning his jacket, and if he thought that would lead to pregnancy, well, he needed some serious education.

Just before the words traveled from her mind to her mouth, Nora pressed her lips together. She'd had no intention of stopping with his jacket, and they both knew it. Bringing her hands to her warm face, she shook her head. "This is a terrible time for you to be logical."

Ovrun's laugh sliced through the tension hovering between them. "One of us should be."

"You know," she said, trying to pull her eyes and mind away from his stupidly perfect lips, "before The Day, men and women had these tiny devices implanted in them to prevent pregnancy. Even now, there's a pharmacist in Cellerin City who makes pretty effective, uh, creams." She felt a blush on her cheeks, which seemed silly considering what she'd been ready to do with him.

He nodded. "I know. And if we had any of those things now, well . . ." He shook his head with a little shudder and a sigh. "I want you. In case that wasn't obvious."

"Yeah? I mean, I was feeling ambivalent about the whole thing."

"Sure you were." They both laughed, and he locked gazes with her again. "I can be honest with you, right?"

"Um . . . sure."

"I told you if I kissed you, you'd take my heart back to the palace with you. The truth is, you've had my heart since I met you."

She smiled. "You've had my heart since I saw what your muscles looked like in your guard uniform."

He groaned, but he was grinning. After a moment, his expression turned serious again. "Nora, sex is a commitment, at least to me. And we can't commit to each other; we both know that. I can move on from a couple of kisses. I don't want to have to move on from more."

She filled her lungs with air and let it out in a big sigh. "Why do you have to be so sweet?"

He chuckled. "Sorry."

"Was that our last kiss?"

"I guess so." He sighed, and his shoulders lifted, just a little.

Nora knew she shouldn't read anything into his response, but she couldn't help it. *He shrugged. And he didn't really answer the question.*

29

When I was a teenager, my mother became the mayor. One day, she told me about some angry constituents.

"I don't see why they have to blame you for everything," I said.

She got a sad smile on her face and said, "I fail them all the time, Liri. It's unavoidable. I can only hope I'm helping them more than hurting them."

-The First Generation: A Memoir *by Liri Abrios*

OVRUN SQUINTED, trying to identify a building. The nearly full moon cast light on its smooth sides.

"Recognize that one?" Nora whispered.

He sighed. "Nope."

They'd been walking in the dark for hours, and they'd gotten off track somewhere. Ovrun wanted to blame the darkness, but he knew the truth. He'd gotten distracted because he was thinking more about the girl at his side than the city surrounding them.

Even shrouded in night's gray hues, she was beautiful. He couldn't prevent his eyes from drifting her way. Each time that happened, his thoughts returned to their time under the trees. Kissing her was the best thing he'd done in a long time. The stupidest too.

Focus, he chided himself. He examined their surroundings again. "I feel like we're too far east. Let's turn here."

Several minutes later, Nora whispered, "What's that?"

Ovrun's eyes widened. "I think it's the landmark I was looking for."

They approached a round fountain in the middle of the wide street. Moonlight reflected off its crumbling sides. A broken, unidentifiable statue sat in the middle.

"Maybe eight or ten clommets to go," Ovrun said, turning left. "A couple more hours, tops."

Throughout the night, they'd heard a few footsteps and seen lights in some windows, but so far, they hadn't encountered any trogs. Now that they were back on the right path, Ovrun dared to hope their expedition would end well.

They walked several more blocks, and Ovrun pointed into the distance. "See that building, the one that looks like stairsteps against the sky? I recognize it."

"Oh, good. So you think—ow!"

Ovrun gripped her shoulder. "What happened?"

"Something hit my back." Nora looked frantically in every direction.

Ovrun knelt and came back up with a spherical stone. "Think it was this?"

She took it. "Looks about right."

"We better get outta here." He took her hand, and they turned and started jogging the way they'd come.

Another stone bounced off the street in front of them. Nora cursed, then pointed at a figure in between two buildings. "There!"

Ovrun grabbed Nora's hand. They ran, but rapid footsteps followed. A rock hit Ovrun's ear at an angle, eliciting a pained grunt. With better aim, the rock might've cracked his head open. *Or Nora's.* Fury flared in his chest, and he released her hand. "Stay here." He turned to give chase. Half a second later, he heard Nora's footsteps behind him.

Ovrun quickly caught up to the rock thrower. His first instinct was to tackle the attacker, but his better judgment reigned when his hand closed around a very thin arm. This little twerp probably wasn't even a teenager yet. He caught the kid up in a tight bear hug, trapping both skinny arms.

Nora reached them and halted, panting.

"Who are you?" the trog screamed in a high-pitched voice that sounded female. The sound echoed on the dark street.

"Shh!" Nora covered the kid's mouth with her hand, then yelped and pulled away. "What the hell? Do you sharpen your teeth?"

Ovrun thought back to the rock he'd picked up. It was perfectly round, too uniform to be natural. "I think she's a stone eater."

Nora huffed. "That makes sense."

Ovrun didn't envy Nora the bite she'd received. The girl's teeth were probably broken, ragged, and sharp. Rich stone eaters, like the king, could afford finely milled rocks, ready to be stirred into water and downed like a thick tea. Those without means to buy such fuel, or the patience to mill it themselves, had to swallow small stones whole or do their best to chew them up. Some types of rock worked better than others, and Ovrun had heard that many stone eaters sacrificed their teeth to grind particularly effective fuel.

The young trog started screaming again. "INTRUDERS! INTRUDERS!"

Keeping one arm tight on his captive's torso and arms, Ovrun reached out his other hand and grabbed the kid's face, his fingers under her jaw and his thumb on her ear, forcing her mouth closed.

"All we want to do is leave!" he said. "We aren't here to hurt anyone. Okay?"

She nodded, and as soon as Ovrun released her jaw, she shouted again. "INTRUDERS!"

"Let her go," Nora said as Ovrun forced the girl's mouth closed again. "We can run faster than her."

It would've been a great idea, had the moonlight not revealed an adult approaching them from the left . . . and two from the right . . . and a fourth from behind Nora. Three of the four held knives.

"Nora!" Ovrun shouted, just as strong hands grabbed her arms and wrenched them behind her.

Nora screamed.

The man to her right stepped close and twisted her ear. "Shut it!" he barked.

Nora stayed quiet, and when the man let go of her ear, she started sobbing. Ovrun's breath caught as he refused his instinct to drop the trog and go to Nora, who was still being held tight from behind. *I can't. They have knives.*

A woman, the only one not holding a knife, stepped closer. "Let go of my girl! You want us to kill you while you hold her? We will!"

Ovrun's eyes met the woman's. "You tell her to stop making stones and throwing them at us, and I'll let her go."

"You lie!" the woman screamed. "She doesn't attack intruders! You lie! You come to take her to new city!"

Ovrun's voice rose above hers. "How would we know she was a stone eater if she hadn't thrown stones at us?" He had to repeat the question twice before the woman finally stopped screaming at him. Then he made his point once more, in a lower voice.

The woman propped her hands on her bony hips and crossed to her daughter. "You throw stones at them? You do that?" An indecipherable murmur came from the girl, and the woman yelled, "You got stones for brains? Girl, I tell you over and again! Let my girl go, intruder. She won't throw stones at you now."

Ovrun watched the woman warily. He could hold the girl to

bargain for their freedom, but it would require threats he wasn't willing to follow through with. He released the young trog, and her mother pulled her across the street and out of sight.

"Let my wife go," Ovrun said. Nora flinched at the term.

"Why are you here?" the man holding Nora asked. He sounded young, his voice absent the gruffness of the man who'd told her to *shut it.*

"We were exploring," Nora said through continued tears. "We got lost."

The gruff man spoke again. "Stupid new-city folk."

The third man, who'd been hanging back, stepped toward Ovrun. He spoke slowly, his voice menacing. "You are in Deroga. This city belongs to trogs."

"We know." Ovrun kept his voice calm. "We're sorry. We thought we were headed out of the city, but we got turned around."

"New-city folk don't know stars," the gruff man said with a laugh.

"Do new-city folk know knives?" The slow-speaking man walked right up to Ovrun and held the blade to his throat. "If you move, I move."

He was a small guy. Ovrun could take him in a fight, probably even steal the knife. Where would that leave Nora, though? He kept his hands at his sides. "I know bows and arrows. You want the ones on my back? Let us go, and you can have them."

The man threatening him with the knife said, "Nice bow, that. I'll take it off you after I kill you."

"Wait!" Nora cried. "I'm the princess, and my father knows I'm here. I left him a note. If I don't come back, he'll send the army in here. Your whole way of life—it'll be gone by next week. You have to let us go!"

The man behind her laughed. "Nice try."

"It's true," Ovrun said. "I was one of her guards. We . . . ran away together. I mean, can you blame me? She's hot as hell." He grinned, trying to lighten the mood.

No one said anything for at least fifteen seconds, the longest quarter-minute of Ovrun's life. Then the gruff guy laughed, a loud guffaw. "Maybe they lie. Maybe they tell the truth. I say, we take his bow, let them go. Stupid new-city folk, too dull to waste sharp blades on."

Just like that, the man removed his knife from Ovrun's throat and stepped away. Ovrun slid the bow and arrows off his back, and when he spoke again, his voice was deathly serious, every trace of humor gone. "Let the princess go, and I'll give you the weapon."

The man released Nora, who was still crying. Ovrun handed over his bow and arrows, put his arm around Nora's shoulder, and started walking. Nora's entire body shuddered with sobs, and he tightened his grip, whispering, "You're okay."

"Hey!" the younger man shouted. "New city is that way!"

Ovrun looked at the man, then shifted direction, leading Nora away.

When they were several mets away from their attackers, he whispered, "Shh, we don't want to attract anyone else's attention."

Nora put her hand over her mouth. Her breathing soon steadied.

Ovrun led her to the next street over, then back in their original direction. He kept his arm tight around her shoulder as they walked in silence for at least a quarter hour. Finally, he spoke in a bare whisper. "You okay?"

"I think so." They kept walking, and then she turned her face up and whispered, "I have a question."

"What?"

"You really think I'm hot?"

He shook with silent laughter. "As hell," he whispered back.

Over the next three hours, they repeatedly got lost and had to backtrack. Once, they made a complete circle. Nora couldn't complain, though. They avoided trogs and arrived down the street from the warehouse well before dawn. Nora wiped tears off her cheeks as they halted. "You got us here."

Ovrun didn't sound as relieved as her. "Now we have to find a place to hide. Somewhere no one will see us once it gets light."

A voice entered Nora's mind. *Go to the roof you waited on when you first came here.*

"I was thinking—" Ovrun said.

"Wait. I'm getting advice from a dragon." She gave Ovrun a quick smile, then sent out a thought. *How are we supposed to get up to the roof?*

Don't humans use stairs? There was a hint of laughter in his tone.

Was he making fun of her? *We'll give it a shot*, she returned.

The tall building's back door wasn't made from polymus; it was still sturdy and locked. However, there was a broken window nearby. Ovrun gave Nora a lift, and she pulled herself through.

Once inside, he lit the lantern he'd packed, and they found an open doorway leading to the stairs.

"How many floors do you think are in this building?" Nora asked.

"I don't know, maybe twenty?"

They started up the stairs. Scattered bones awaited them on two of the landings. Nora didn't want to see them but couldn't help looking. *So many people, all gone at once.* Two hundred years ago, her ancestors and Ovrun's had beat the odds and somehow avoided dropping dead when the stone killed their neighbors, friends, and families. The bones were creepy, but they also reminded Nora that life was immeasurably precious.

They were panting by the time they reached the top of the stairs. Ovrun shoved his strong shoulder into a metal door. After a few tries, it opened. He extinguished his lantern, and they stepped onto the same flat roof they'd been on before.

It was cold up there, without any other buildings to block the winter breeze. They lay next to each other on their bellies, near enough to the edge to watch the street and warehouse below, far enough that Nora didn't feel like a good gust of wind would blow her off.

She sent out a thought. *We're on the roof.*

I know, the dragon returned. *Dawn will break soon. I sense it. Now is the time to ask me if I trust you.*

She laughed. *Do you trust us?*

I have listened to you over the past two days, he said in that low, luminescent voice. *Since your first visit here.*

Had that really just been two nights ago? No wonder she was so tired. *What did you hear?*

I heard three people who are risking themselves to free slaves. There was a long silence, and he continued, *I heard three people who care about one other.*

Nora reviewed their recent conversations in and around the warehouse. Krey had revealed his parents' deaths. She'd comforted him. She and Ovrun had searched for feathers and hunted shimshims.

Ovrun shifted, and his shoulder pressed against Nora, briefly reigniting her desire for him. Then her eyes widened. Had the dragon listened in on their moment of passion and their discussion afterward? She decided not to dwell on the possibility.

Yes, we care about each other, Nora told the dragon. The statement sent warmth into her core.

I want to help you, the dragon said. *However, my assistance comes with a cost.*

She waited, heart pounding.

My mate is imprisoned in Cellerin Mountain, he said, and his grief resonated in Nora's heart. *If I do not continue guarding this place, she will be killed. You must free her. She will then help you free me. Together, we shall help you free the humans.*

Nora drew in a deep breath and pushed it out. How would they rescue a dragon?

"You okay?" Ovrun asked.

"Maybe."

He took her hand, and she sent a thought to the dragon below. *I want to say yes, but I need to know more. Where is she? How can we free her?*

Nora flinched as a picture entered her mind. It was like a map, but it wasn't drawn by a pen. This was a memory, taken from the mind of a dragon who'd soared above the land of Cellerin. There were wispy, floating clouds, gently curving roads, and squiggly, flowing rivers.

She saw Cellerin Mountain, with Therro Lake to the north and Cellerin City to the east. Deroga, the ancient city where she now waited, was even farther east. Beyond that, Burig Bay's blue waters beckoned.

The view suddenly zoomed in, as if Nora were a dragon diving through the sky. It was so realistic that she gasped, her stomach lurching. Ovrun squeezed her hand.

She was high over the main road that extended west of Cellerin City. There was the palace, and next to it the small forest. Across the road, crops grew in neat, square fields. The dragon continued to direct Nora's consciousness at a dizzyingly fast speed, farther down the road, across the river, and all the way to Cellerin Mountain.

Everything slowed. In her mind, she dropped lower, and the dragon began to narrate. *You must not fly once you reach the mountain. If you do, the guards shall see you. Follow the footpath. It looks like it ends here, but if you climb over this rock, the path continues. Look for these two trees, twined together. Take the path to the left. Almost there, Nora-human. See the dark spot? That is the cave where they hold my mate. You do not see her, for when I flew here, she was not yet imprisoned. Now, she is chained as I am. She tells me that four large men guard her.*

You can talk to her from here? Nora asked.

I cannot. Our thoughts do not travel that far. For a time, I was imprisoned near enough to her to communicate.

The vision faded, but every detail of it was imbedded in Nora's mind, branded there by the dragon's magic. *Can you tell me anything else?*

As you approach, speak to my mate. Tell her my name. No human has ever heard it. When you speak it, my mate shall know I sent you.

Your name? What is it?

The silence that followed made the dragon's previous hesitations seem short. Tears came to Nora's eyes as she pictured him—his magnificent legs held by huge chains, his ability to breathe fire limited by his captors. He was about to share the secret of his name with a member of the species who'd enslaved him. She sent a thought to him: *I'll hold your name close. It's a treasure to me.*

In her mind, she heard his sigh, and somehow she knew it was a fiery one. *My name, Nora-human, is Osmius. You may tell your two companions. Do not share it with anyone else.*

She wiped a tear off her cheek. *Thank you, Osmius.*

Look at the eastern sky, Nora-human.

She turned and looked. A bit of golden light greeted her eyes. The rest of the sky had turned gray.

Dawn is nigh, he said. *When the general comes, we can speak no longer.*

Why not?

My mind shall not be my own.

Her heart felt as if it would crack open. *How do they enslave your mind?*

That is a question I cannot answer. My knowledge of humans is limited.

Can't you listen to other humans, like you've been listening to me?

I can only listen to those with whom I have already spoken. People such as you, Nora-human. After a brief pause, he said, *The carriage approaches.*

Nora looked but saw nothing. *Where?*

You shall see it soon. Your vision is less acute than mine.

Before long, Nora saw two tiny lights approaching from the end of the street. Lanterns on a carriage, she was sure of it. She pointed.

"Ovrun, the general is coming." She sent one more thought to the captive dragon below. *Thank you for helping us, Osmius.*

He didn't respond.

———

Hatlin clapped Krey on the back. The two of them and Wallis were the only three left in the pub's back room. "Don't you need to get back to where you're staying?"

Krey met Hatlin's gaze. "I'd like to stick around."

Hatlin looked over at Wallis, who nodded. "Okay," Hatlin said, his voice low and serious. "But if T says you gotta go, you gotta go." Once again, Krey got the feeling there was a lot more to Hatlin than the guy usually let on.

"Thanks," Krey said. "Who is T, anyway?"

Two knocks sounded, then three, then two more. Hatlin raised his eyebrows at Krey and walked to the door.

T entered, looking even smaller and less impressive than the last time Krey had seen him. They all sat. "Krey," T said in his reedy voice, "Hatlin tells me you weren't here last week."

"It takes a lot of feathers for me to fly that far," Krey said. "I didn't gather enough."

"Good to have you back."

Krey had thought of Zeisha the whole way here. He was finally desperate enough to be straightforward with these people. "Who are you, T?" In his peripheral vision, he saw Wallis sit up straight. Good; they all needed to know he was serious.

The question didn't phase T. "I'm a New Therroan leader."

"*A* leader or *the* leader?"

T's face broke into a smile. It looked like an expression he didn't wear often. "Now, that's a good question. I'm *the* leader, Krey. The real leader."

Krey nodded. The New Therroans had a governor, but T held the true power. Knowing that, Krey wanted to bring up the militia.

But there was too much tension in the room. None of them seemed to know quite what to make of this teenage outsider. What if he tested them with a different question? One that would show them he knew more than they thought, without making them too wary?

T watched him through narrowed eyes. "Do you have another question?"

Krey leaned forward, eyes locked on T. "I know you've been in secret negotiations with the king. Why can't the two of you come to an agreement?"

T's forehead furrowed, and he shook his head slowly. "I admit to being a bit . . . baffled. I assume your information comes from the princess?"

Krey nodded.

"Fascinating," T said. "You might ask her where she got the impression we're negotiating with her father. I've asked to meet with him at least once a month for the last year. In all that time, I've received a single, one-word response: *No.*"

Krey stared at T. Had Nora lied? She said her father left town frequently for his meetings with the New Therroans. If he wasn't meeting with T, where was he going? All the suspicions he'd been harboring, the ones he'd genuinely wanted to disprove for Nora's sake, dug their claws into his mind again.

I have to ask.

"T," Krey said, his voice strained, "this question might sound strange, but please, I have to know. Are you building a militia of magic eaters to fight the king?"

T's head tilted slightly to one side, and his eyebrows formed an understated arch. "Absolutely not."

The carriage pulled up in front of the warehouse. Nora squinted, trying to see through the glass windshield, but they were too far away.

The door to the rear compartment opened, and a man stepped

out. He was tall, and the dawn light reflected off streaks of silver in his dark hair. Nora squinted, and her heart began to race.

"He looks—" Ovrun said, and Nora heard him swallow. "I know it's crazy, but he looks like . . ." He trailed off.

Nora swallowed a sob and whispered, "It's my father."

IN THE DARK: 8

Zeisha always seemed to wake in the middle of the night, but this —this was different. *What's changed?*

There: a narrow sliver of pale, gray light. *The sky. It's dawn.* The truth hit her with a jolt of joy. *There's a window in this room!* Whatever was covering it had slipped down just enough for her to glimpse the outside world.

She didn't think she'd ever woken this close to morning before. Her body seemed to crave sleep in the early hours, and judging by all the deep breathing she heard around her, that was the norm.

Zeisha used the tiny bit of light to step over sleeping bodies. She had to get to the window and peel back whatever was covering it. *I need to look outside.*

Pain entered her head, driving her to her knees. She barely avoided landing on someone's arm. The ache was so intense that she couldn't reason, could hardly breathe.

Then a wash of peace overtook not only the pain, but every conscious thought in Zeisha's mind.

Seconds later, the curly-haired plant lyster was on her feet, straight and still, just one among a roomful of standing compatriots.

Faces blank, they waited for instructions.

30

One of our neighbors was a bitter woman who snapped at us every time we walked past her house.

"Her whole life fell apart, all in one day," my mother told me. "She doesn't trust the world anymore. She doesn't trust people."

"Everyone's life fell apart," I said. "Why aren't more people like her?"

"I can't speak for everyone. But for me, it's simple. I choose to live." She looked out at the little chapel on the edge of our property. *"And as irrational as it sounds, I choose to trust."*

-The First Generation: A Memoir *by Liri Abrios*

KREY FLEW THROUGH THE CRISP, dawn air, anger propelling him to dangerous speeds. But the faster he went, the more focus he needed. After dropping his backpack for the third time, he landed on a dusty plain and released a string of curses as he put the pack on. When he returned to the air, he forced himself to fly at a reasonable speed.

The meeting the night before had gone late. T and the others had demanded to know what Krey meant by *a militia of magic eaters*. He'd had to tell them more than he wanted to, but in exchange, they'd answered many of his questions about their relationship with the king. After that, he'd gone to sleep, exhausted.

Only now, with his head cleared by a few hours of sleep, could Krey process what he'd heard. Nora's father, the likeable king who'd joked with Krey about bringing a stone to a snowball fight, was a malicious liar. His Majesty King Ulmin might even be in charge of the magic-eater militia.

And Nora's been on his side the whole time.

Krey indulged in a loud, growling cry. It disappeared into the clear air. There weren't even any structures or mountains near enough to give him the satisfaction of an echo.

She betrayed me, like I knew she would. She was deceiving me from the beginning. I'd leave her to rot in that warehouse if it weren't for Ovrun. I'm pretty sure he's still on my side. Or is he? The way he looks at her—I've never seen a guy so besotted after one stupid kiss. Was that part of her whole plan? She earned his worship by locking lips with him, and then they both fooled me by pretending to help me. All this time, they've been on her father's side, sabotaging my efforts, making sure I never rescue Zeisha.

A large bird approached. It seemed to glare as it passed Krey, as if it couldn't believe a human would take up its airspace. The booming flap of its wings brought Krey back to reality. Who was Nora, really? He'd never expected anything from her but pure pomposity. He'd moved to Cellerin City knowing full well that royals didn't care for anyone but themselves.

And Nora had spent the last two months debunking his assumptions.

Well, most of his assumptions. She'd had her privileged, snobby moments, just as he'd expected. But then she'd risked herself to get him out of trouble when he broke into the records hall. Later, she sneaked into Sharai's office with him. Sure, she wanted to do it because it was exciting and she hoped to find her own friend, but something told him she also cared about him and Zeisha.

When Dani expelled Krey from the palace, Nora cried, a display that was either genuine or an award-winning counterfeit. Then she broke into Sharai's office again, in the middle of the day this time. It was reckless and probably stupid, but she did it, and when she got caught, she left behind her life as a princess to find Krey and bring him the papers she stole.

When she realized her old friend didn't need saving, he expected her to run back to the palace. She didn't. Later, he was shocked when she didn't flee from that awful, drafty house across the street from the courier. Her warm, comfortable bedroom was a few clommets away, yet she stayed with her new friends.

Then, in a moment of weakness, Krey told her and Ovrun the truth about his parents' deaths. Nora didn't defend her father like he expected her to. She apologized, and she let Krey grieve.

He'd been thinking of her as a friend for several weeks now. It wasn't like he'd been looking for a friend. He'd left home to find Zeisha, not to socialize. No, he'd started considering Nora a friend because she acted like one, despite him doing his best to push her away.

Ulmin Abrios had lost any right he'd ever had to Krey's loyalty.

And Nora Abrios, despite her unfortunate last name, had earned Krey's trust. He could latch onto his own anger and blame her for her father's actions. Or he could accept her help, if she still wanted to give it.

When she finds out about her dad, she'll be devastated. Tears stung Krey's eyes. Yes, Nora would be a wreck, and it had taken him half an hour of flying to even consider that. *Krey West, you are a first-class ass.*

At that thought, he felt his magic flicker. He hadn't been eating feathers on the go, and his fuel was almost out. He got his feet beneath him just in time for a hard landing, right into a thorn bush. "Oof . . . ouch." He carefully extricated himself, wincing as he pulled out one thorn after another. "I suppose I deserved that."

"No." It was the only word Nora could push through her sobs. "No, no, no."

She was still on the roof, lying on her side with her knees pulled up to her chest. Ovrun was lying behind her, holding her tightly like he'd done back at the little house in Cellerin City. "Shh," he said as she cried into her knees.

It wasn't long before Ovrun murmured, "He's leaving."

Nora lifted her head from her knees, her weeping tempered by the words. She flipped onto her belly and looked down at the street. Sure enough, her father was exiting the building. "He was"—a hiccup broke through her words—"he was only there a few minutes."

"Yeah." Ovrun flipped onto his belly next to her and placed a warm hand on her back. They watched as the King of Cellerin entered his carriage and began his journey toward the capital.

Tears threatened to spill out of Nora's eyes again, but she was tired of crying. She squeezed her eyes shut until the inclination subsided. Then she opened them and watched the carriage get smaller and disappear from sight. "My father," she whispered.

"I'm sorry," Ovrun said.

Another voice, low and grieved, reached her mind. *As am I, Nora-human.*

Why didn't you tell me?

Would you have believed me?

She almost insisted that of course she would've, but she knew that wasn't true. She trusted her father and Dani more than anyone else in the world. Osmius was right; she'd needed to see this with her own eyes.

Why?

If you wish to know why humans betray each other, the smoldering, smooth voice replied, *I am not the one to ask.*

Nora gave voice to the suspicion, both unbelievable and unavoidable, that filled her mind. *Osmius, is my father the one controlling you and the militia?*

Yes.

How?

Such knowledge is beyond me, Nora-human. When he comes, a cloud covers my mind, replacing my thoughts with the desire to protect him and the others from intruders. I remember little of his visits afterward.

And the militia? Nora asked. *He controls their minds too?*

Your father shares his strength with a woman called The Overseer. She controls the soldiers at all times, except when they sleep.

What's her name?

I know not. She has visited me but once. Late at night when I first arrived, she touched me and attempted to control me. I resisted her. She controls the soldiers from a room deep within the structure. When soldiers arrive, they are brought to meet her. She touches them once to establish her control over them. After the initial touch, The Overseer controls them from her quarters. Others without mind-stealing abilities work directly with the soldiers.

You said my father shares his strength with The Overseer. How can he do that?

I do not understand the mechanics of human magic. I only know your father is stronger than The Overseer. He is the only one who can control me.

Nora let out a long breath. Her father was stronger than a dragon, using a faculty Nora hadn't known existed. How could he embrace such an evil use of magic?

Her sobs returned, shaking her whole body. Ovrun laid his arm over her and held her tightly. No amount of determination could dam the tears that flooded her cheeks.

Weeping was even more exhausting than walking for hours

through a dark city. In time, despite the bright sun and the cold roof, Nora fell asleep.

Soft voices woke Nora, but she was too exhausted to open her eyes.

"I got your note," Krey said. "Did the general come?"

"Yeah," Ovrun responded quietly. "It was—"

"Was it the king?" Krey interrupted.

Ovrun's volume rose. "How'd you know that?"

"I found out something at the meeting that made me suspect him. Damn it, that means Nora knows already. How did she take it?"

Eyes still closed, Nora snapped, "How do you think I took it?"

She heard someone moving. The sound terminated right next to her. Squinting her eyes open, she saw Krey, lying where Ovrun had been before. His forehead was furrowed in an expression she couldn't decipher.

"You were right all along," she said. "My dad—" Her voice broke. *Crying? Again? I'm sick of crying!* "Just take me home," she blurted through her sobs.

"Home?" he asked softly. "To the palace?"

"No! The warehouse!"

He gave her a sad smile. "It's too bright out. Two trogs shot arrows at me as I flew here. Besides, I need more fuel. I brought some water, food, and blankets, plus plenty of feathers. Let's stay until dark, and then I'll fly you both home."

Nora's tears subsided. "Fine. I'm going back to sleep. As soon as I find a place to pee."

From the other side of her, Ovrun said, "There's some sort of big, metal box in the center of the roof. You can go behind there."

Nora rose into a crouch and scurried to the place Ovrun had indicated, which already smelled like pee. She squatted in the cool wind. *How did my life get to this point?*

When she finished and rounded the metal box, she found that

Ovrun and Krey had set up camp closer to the center of the roof. She joined them, took a sip of the water Krey offered, and lay down. Ovrun covered her with a blanket, and she slept again.

When Krey woke her, it was dark. Despite the rest, Nora's body and mind screamed with fatigue. *All that stupid crying. It's so tiring. I'm done with that for now.* Without a word, she put on her backpack and got on Krey's back.

"You ready?" he asked.

"I'm never ready to fly. But let's go."

As they flew, Krey said, "I know you don't like to talk while we're in the air, but can I tell you what I learned at the meeting?"

Tonight, flying wasn't as bad as usual. She was too numb to be terrified. "Go for it." As Krey told her about the nonexistent negotiations between Cellerin and New Therro, Nora felt heavier and heavier with the weight of accumulated grief.

When he finished talking, the rest of the trip was silent. Krey ate feathers the whole way. At last, they arrived back in the warehouse. Krey set Nora down and lit a lantern. She sat in front of it and again pulled her knees to her chest. To her surprise, Krey sat next to her.

"How are you?" he asked, in a tone that told her it was a real question, not an inane attempt to make small talk.

"Don't you need to pick up Ovrun?"

"He can wait. How are you?"

She examined his face in the golden lantern light, expecting to see smugness there. King Ulmin himself had proven that the monarchy was untrustworthy, just as Krey had always said. But there was no superiority in his expression. Instead, it was twisted with what looked like grief.

Nora took a deep breath. "I don't know my father at all. Maybe I never have. I'd already lost one parent; today I lost the other one!" Tears pressed at her throat, but she held them at bay. "Do you have any idea what that's like?" Immediately, she realized what a stupid question it was. "Krey, I'm sorry. Of course you do."

He moved the lantern to the side, got up, and sat right in front of her, folding his legs and resting his hands in his lap. He was close enough for her to see the film of moisture shining in his eyes. "I do know, and I wish no one else ever had to go through it. I'm sorry." His voice cracked on the last statement.

Nora reached out and took one of his hands. "How'd you survive when your parents died?"

He squeezed her hand. "I'm still figuring that out. But it's gotten easier."

They sat silently, hands still clasped together, until Nora urged Krey to fly to Ovrun. When she was alone, she slowly chewed dried fruit and contemplated what she'd learned.

My dad is controlling minds. Such a reality was unthinkable. In this corner of the postday world, Nora's ancestors had served as mayors, legislators, and, for the last two generations, monarchs. Through that time, they'd built a tradition of benevolent leadership. Nora's father had often pointed out that he was a king, not a dictator. *Lies, all lies.*

Filled with sudden ire, Nora stood. She wanted nothing more than to throw balls of ice from her hands, fueled by snow and fury. While she had plenty of the latter, she had none of the former. Instead, she sprinted through the warehouse and skidded to a stop near a metal wall. She swung her foot back and kicked, hard.

A loud *twang* sounded, and a jolt of pain traveled into Nora's toes and up her leg. She repeated the gesture, pairing it with an angry roar. "Why?" she screamed. "Why would you do this?" She kicked the metal wall one more time, even harder, grunting as it bruised her toes through her boots.

She flopped down to the hard floor, lay on her back, and gave in to weeping, despite her intention not to. "You're the king," she cried. "That should've made you think twice. And even if it wasn't sufficient, you're my father. Couldn't that've motivated you to do the right thing?"

Her choice was heartbreakingly simple. She could return to her father, give him her loyalty, and forget about the militia members whose lives he'd stolen. Or she could fight for a bunch of strangers and permanently rip apart her relationship with her dad.

It wasn't a decision any daughter should ever have to make. Regardless of what she chose, she didn't know if she'd ever forgive her father for putting her in this position.

"Dad," she said through her sobs, "I don't want to hurt you. But you're the one who taught me to fight injustice. What am I supposed to do when you're the cause of it?"

As her crying slowed, the answer became clear. *If I go back to live with my father, I won't be able to live with myself.* Nora had taken the first step away from him when she'd chosen not to tell him about Krey breaking into the records hall. She'd moved farther away when she'd continued helping Krey. And she'd created a huge gap when she'd left the palace.

This last step, though, would be the worst. She wouldn't be creating more distance between her and her dad. Instead, she'd move in close and confront him—not to reconcile, but to stop him.

The decision felt like a knife in her heart. Despite everything her father had done, Nora knew he still cared about her. Even his treatment of Krey proved that. Back in Tirra, he'd probably wanted to put the talented double lyster in his militia. But he'd known his daughter needed a friend. When she'd invited Krey to the palace, he'd humored her—because underneath it all, he loved her. Her resistance would hurt him. She'd be taking the knife out of her own chest and thrusting it into his.

How did it come to this point? Nora had gotten involved in Krey's quest to find Zeisha because she'd wanted an adventure. Then she'd made friends with both Ovrun and Krey, and she'd grasped onto a dream of finding Faylie. It had become even easier to take risks and give up privileges. For a while there, it had all been so fun.

"I like to dance and kiss and throw magical snowballs," Nora said to no one in particular. She wiped her hand across her runny nose. "Nothing in my life has prepared me to rescue a group of mind-controlled lysters and confront my father. On top of all that, I'm supposed to save two dragons? I'm a princess, not a warrior."

Cannot you be both, Nora-human?

The dragon's voice, rich and deep, acted like a balm to Nora's grief. At last, she stopped weeping. *I don't know.*

I have never met a dragon speaker who was not fiercely strong.

Nora took his words in, savoring them like they were made of sweet, edible gold. *Fiercely strong.* She'd never thought of herself in such terms. Could it possibly be true? *I'd like to be strong,* she thought.

You are, Osmius echoed.

Nora looked across the room at the glowing lantern and nodded, embracing both the mission and her grief.

31

At first, survivors used a barter system. By the time I was a teenager, however, our town had a basic bank, run by my parents and three other trusted families. They issued handwritten bank notes, making trade even easier.

Our community's first bank-note counterfeiter was my youngest sister. The rest of us kids had to hold back laughter as our parents confiscated her smudged, messy BANK NOOT.

-The First Generation: A Memoir *by Liri Abrios*

When Krey and Ovrun stepped into the warehouse, Nora rushed up to them. She'd lit two more lanterns, and Krey squinted. The brightness didn't bode well when all he wanted was sleep. All the flying had sapped his strength.

"Come sit down." Nora beckoned them to follow her. "We need to talk about what's next."

Krey was too tired to argue. He sat on the floor, resting his elbow on his knee and propping his chin in his hand. Ovrun sat nearby, and Nora plopped down, facing both of them.

"I've been thinking," she said, "about how we can . . ."

That was all Krey heard until a sharp, "Krey, wake up!" jolted him out of his nap.

He lifted his head, blinked, and yawned. "What?" He figured he couldn't have dozed for more than a minute, but his voice was already low and groggy.

Ovrun said, "Nora thinks you should take her to talk to her aunt."

Krey's eyes, which had been threatening to fall closed again, snapped open wide. "Why the hell would I do that?" His voice reverberated through the big room.

Nora released a loud sigh. "You are the most predictable person I've ever met. I knew you'd get pissed off before I got a chance to explain."

"All I did was ask why!" He was still yelling. In his sleepy haze, he couldn't find any motivation to stop.

She rolled her eyes. "Oh yes, the way you asked it was so open and diplomatic. I can tell you're ready to have a calm, mature conversation about this."

Krey gritted his teeth, closed his eyes, and drew in a long breath through his nose. He dragged his eyelids back open and met Nora's gaze. "Sorry. I'm exhausted, but I really want to understand—by the stone, Nora, your aunt is probably in league with your father. Why would we go to her?"

Her dark-brown eyes flashed with anger, but her voice was level. "I know my trust in my father was misplaced, but I'm even closer to Aunt Dani than I am to him. I could be wrong about her, but I don't think I am. And it's not like we'll be stupid about it. We'll fly straight to the residential building at night. If she's not on his side, she could be a resource to us. She might even be able to tell us how my father got this mind-control faculty."

Now that was almost tempting. Krey was dying to know the

source of Ulmin's talent. He could only think of one thing that could give someone the ability to control minds: a talent he'd read about in an extremely rare book. It was a dark, dangerous magic that usually didn't work, had terrible side effects, and would never work on so many people at once. *That can't be it*, Krey told himself. *Ulmin must've discovered something new.*

"What are you thinking?" Nora asked.

He shook his head. No way was he going to be the group's conspiracy theorist, bringing up an old magic no one had even heard of. "I get why you want to talk to Dani, but if she's in on this and we confront her, she'll know we're getting close to the truth. It's too risky."

"We won't tell her we know about the militia unless we're sure it's safe!" Nora was talking quickly now. "We'll tell her we're still looking for Zeisha. She's got to be worried sick about me. If she's not on my dad's side, she'll give us any information she's got, just to get me to come home. If she does anything suspicious, we'll fly away. Nobody will be able to follow us."

Against his better judgment, Krey found himself considering the proposal. Dani was smart and capable; she might have information that could help them. Plus, learning that Ulmin was the general had changed everything. They'd never be able to stop the king unless they allied with someone inside the palace. He turned to Ovrun, who was already watching him. "What do you think?"

"I think it's worth the risk. I'm just trying to figure out if there's a way for all three of us to go. It seems safer."

Krey nodded slowly. "If we walk instead of flying, we can all go. Then I can fly you both inside the residence fence separately. It'll be tougher if we need to escape, but I think it's worth it to have us all there. Nora needs to talk to her aunt, and Ovrun can fight if anything goes wrong."

Nora's mouth broke into a small smile. "So you'll do it?"

"Yeah." He yawned again. "But if either of you wakes me up in the next ten hours, all bets are off. Can you please collect feathers while I sleep?"

Without waiting for a response, he grabbed a pillow, lay down, and tuned out the world.

Nora looked at the small stash of food Krey was putting in his pack. It was all they had, and they'd need more—sooner, rather than later. "How much money do we have left?" she asked Krey.

"About twenty quins."

Her eyes widened. She had underwear that cost more than twenty quins. "We're gonna need food," she murmured.

"We should also replace the bow Ovrun had to give to the trogs, but we can't afford to."

Ovrun slipped his pack on his shoulder. "If we really get desperate, I can pay my mom a visit. She'll help us out if she can." He shrugged, but his brows were furrowed.

Nora knew Ovrun had taken pride in using his guard wages to help support his family. The last thing he'd want to do was ask his mom for money. She thought about her favorite shoes in her closet back home. They'd probably cost at least 150 quins. Warmth entered her cheeks as she recalled how she'd complained when she'd gotten them, because they were a darker gray than she'd requested.

"Let's go," Krey said.

Outside, the early evening sky was still bright. It was a chilly day, but as they walked briskly, Nora still felt a layer of sweat collect under her arms, in her socks, and beneath her hat. She was so tired of having only two sets of clothes, neither of them ever really clean. *What will Dani think when she sees me?*

Darkness fell as they traveled. Krey had gotten to know the terrain well, due to his flights to and from the city. He led them through the wilderness, far from the road. As the sun set and stars emerged, they discussed the militia.

"Something's been bugging me," Krey said. "The king somehow shares his mind-control talent with this Overseer woman. But he was gone for over a month during the two-hundredth anniversary tour. Could he have shared his power over such a distance?"

Nora stepped around a tree as she mulled over the question. "I don't know. There's so much of this that doesn't make sense. I've never even heard of someone sharing their faculty."

"Yeah, neither have I," Krey said with a sigh. "Any ideas, Ovrun?"

"Hey, if the two of you don't know how this magic works, imagine how clueless I am."

They continued to chat as they walked, but with so little information available, it was hard to come up with any good theories. After hours of travel, they skirted Cellerin City, walking well north of its outskirts. They all got quiet, except for occasional bouts of contagious yawning.

The sight of the woods east of the palace perked Nora up. They navigated carefully through the thick, dark trees. As always, Nora watched for the unicorn that was said to live there. She didn't catch any glimpses.

Soon, the tall palace fence came into view. Nora fought off a silly urge to run and kiss it. *I guess I've actually missed this place.*

"Guard," Krey whispered. The three of them hid behind trees until the guard passed. "Nora, let's go," Krey murmured.

She got on his back and squeezed her eyes shut as he took to the air. When they got close to the residence, she murmured, "Hello, friends," knowing the caynins' sensitive ears would hear her. Krey soared over the residential fence, landed by the icehouse entrance, and set her down. Two caynins approached, wiggling with delight. One of them sniffed at her sleeve, then backed away. She stifled a giggle. *Even the caynins think I stink.*

Without a word, Nora pulled out her key. It was difficult to use it in the dark, and for a minute or two, she feared her father had changed the locks. But it slid into the keyhole, and when she rotated her wrist, she heard a satisfying *click*. After closing the door behind her and Krey, she turned on the light.

Thank the stone, one of the chests was full of ice. They both fueled up in case something went wrong. Then Krey whispered, "I'll get Ovrun."

"Okay." She turned off the light and walked out with him, waiting quietly as he flew off. Before long, Krey and Ovrun were in sight. Nora made a quiet clicking sound with her mouth, and two caynins came running. "It's okay," she whispered soothingly. When Krey and Ovrun landed, the caynins didn't make a sound. Nora scratched behind the animals' ears and led her two friends through the icehouse and into her rooms.

Nora drew in a deep breath, savoring a scent that was as familiar to her as her own skin. She loved everything about her rooms—the fireplace, her soft bed piled with warm linens, her closet full of gorgeous clothes. More than anywhere else in this big palace complex, these rooms were *home*. To her horror, a little yelp-sob exited her mouth.

A hand grabbed hers, and Ovrun's warm breath hit her ear. "You okay?"

"Mmm hmm." She forced herself to stop crying and whispered, "Let's go."

It must be past two in the morning. No one should be up. Still, Nora's heart threatened to burst from her chest. She led both her friends through her dark rooms and opened the door to the hallway. It squeaked, the sound echoing in the late-night hush. She gritted her teeth, but no one came to investigate. They took silent steps toward Dani's rooms, which were next to her niece's.

Nora released Ovrun's hand and opened her aunt's door. After leading her companions through the dark sitting room, she entered Dani's bedroom alone. As expected, her aunt was asleep, snoring softly. It was too dark to see much of anything, but Nora made her way to the bed, found her aunt's mouth, and held a hand over it. "Aunt Dani," she whispered, "it's me."

She had to repeat the message twice, accompanying it with a shoulder shake the second time. At last, Dani woke and gasped. Before her aunt could cry out, Nora's hand came down on her mouth. Dani tried to push Nora's hand off.

"Aunt Dani, it's me," Nora whispered. "Don't say anything, okay?"

When she felt Dani nod, she removed her hand. Dani's promise not to say anything lasted less than half a second, but to her credit, she kept her voice low. "Nora! Are you safe, sweetheart?"

Happy tears filled Nora's eyes. "Yes. Let me turn on the light." She flipped the switch. Squinting at the sudden brightness, she returned to the bed. "Krey and Ovrun are with me. Can we talk to you?"

Dani answered by pulling her niece into a tight hug. She spoke right into Nora's ear, in a bare whisper. "If those two boys abducted you, just say, 'Yes.'"

Nora pulled back, the question erasing her tears. "No, Aunt Dani, they didn't abduct me!" From the bedroom doorway, Krey snorted a laugh.

Dani stepped out of bed. Her wavy, brown hair, usually pinned up, hung down her back. She walked to the door. "If either of you hurt my niece, I will find you and make you wish you'd never met her." She only came up to Ovrun's chest, but she tilted her head to glare at him. "I don't care how big you are."

Ovrun cleared his throat. "I understand, ma'am."

"Very well. The two of you can have a seat on the couch. Nora, please fetch my robe."

Nora crossed to a hook on the wall to retrieve her aunt's robe. As soon as Krey and Ovrun had left the doorway, Dani turned and murmured, "Now, be honest. Are they holding you against your will? Blackmailing you?"

Nora tried not to laugh. "No, Aunt Dani. I'm with them because I want to be."

Dani let Nora help her with her robe. "Well then, we'd all better have a good chat."

They all sat, Krey and Ovrun on a couch, Nora and Dani across from them in two adjacent chairs. Light from Dani's bedroom spilled into the room.

Nora locked eyes with her aunt. "We're still looking for Krey's girlfriend, and I'm not moving back home until we find her. Can you help us?"

Dani's expression was unreadable. Nora held her breath. As the silence continued, she glanced at Krey and Ovrun. Krey was leaning forward, elbows propped on his knees, eyes burning into Dani. Ovrun's whole body looked tense, ready to leap up and fight if needed.

At last, Dani spoke, her voice quiet. "I've learned so much since you left. I've put things together I was trying to ignore before. But, Nora"—she finally met her niece's gaze again, her eyes shining with tears—"I don't want to tell you, honey. I don't want you to know."

Nora swallowed. She could trust her aunt; she knew it, like she knew her own name. "Aunt Dani," she whispered, "we know what my dad is doing."

Dani's mouth dropped open. "You do?"

"Some of it. But we need you to tell us what you know. Please."

Dani started to cry, which brought Nora's tears back to the surface. "I don't know what happened to him," Dani said. "He was always so good, so kind. He's still kind to me, but . . ." She trailed off, sobbing into both her hands.

At last, she got herself under control. "When you broke into Sharai's office and then ran away, I told your father you'd be with Krey or possibly with the apprentices in Sharai's secret program. Your father sent guards to Krey's new residence, but they said he wasn't there. Later, he sent a couple of guards to Ovrun's house in case he was helping you.

"But he didn't send guards to any sort of apprenticeship location. I asked why, and he said the address was never put into writing, so you couldn't have found it when you went through Sharai's papers. Later, his story changed. He said the apprentices were all traveling.

"Every time he talked to me, I believed him, but when I was alone, I doubted it all. He kept saying, 'Trust me, she didn't go there.' The more he said it, the less I trusted him. One day, he left the palace for a meeting. I looked through the papers in his desk." She paused, covering her mouth and drawing in a deep, shuddering breath.

"What did you find out?" Krey's voice was low and hard, and it drew Dani's attention away from Nora.

Her voice was choked as she responded, "I found references to a lyster militia. He's going to use them to fight New Therro."

Nora's brows rose, and she saw the same expression on both her companions' faces. The militia's purpose was a surprise, but it made sense. Her father was playing the role of the patient negotiator while he built a force strong enough to suppress the New Therroan resisters. *And it's not just any militia. It's a lyster militia, created to fight a mostly non-magical community.* Nora barely contained her tears. *Oh, Dad, they want to negotiate. What happened to you?*

Krey recovered first and spoke in a strained voice. "Zeisha would never purposefully become a soldier. How does he expect to convince them to fight for him?"

He was testing Dani; Nora knew that. Seeing what she knew. Seeing if she'd lie.

"I don't know," Dani said. "But in his papers, I saw references to trogs. Maybe he's somehow using them as guards? There wasn't enough information to make sense of it."

Nora sat up straighter. Dani didn't seem to know about the king's ability to control minds—but she had given them some new information. Were the trogs doing more than tolerating the militia? Maybe the trog who'd first shot at Krey was guarding the militia, rather than trying to keep people out of trog territory.

Krey stood and took a few steps, then sat on the low table, his knees almost touching Dani's. His jaw tightened twice before he finally spoke in a hushed voice. "The King of Anyari is controlling his militia through their minds. Do you have any idea how he's accomplishing that?"

Dani blinked several times. "You already knew about the militia?" When she saw Krey's curt nod, she said, "I don't . . . how is that possible? Their minds?"

Krey's eyes closed, and Nora wouldn't have been surprised to see his entire body light up in angry flames. But he kept his temper in check, folding his arms tight across his chest and dropping his head. The room was silent for at least a full minute before he looked up and sighed. "I didn't want to mention this, but I need to know. Has he been eating any . . . animal brain matter?"

Even in the dim light, Nora could see her aunt's face grow pale. Dani's breaths came faster, and a desperate "Ohh—" exited her mouth.

Nora looked back and forth between her newfound friend, whose gaze was intense enough to slice through metal, and her aunt, who was clearly on the verge of panic. "What's going on?" Nora blurted, then brought her volume down. "Eating brains? Krey, what the hell are you talking about?"

Krey's gaze remained on Dani. "Has he?"

"Of course he hasn't!" Nora shot back. "Everyone knows animal brains are poisonous."

At last, Krey shifted his gaze to Nora. "That's true. For everyone except a small percentage of magic eaters who can use them as fuel for their telepathic talents."

For the first time since they'd sat down, Ovrun spoke. "I've never heard of that!"

"Most people haven't," Krey said. "I found it in a handwritten book my aunts purchased. It may be the only copy of the book that exists. A group of magic eaters experimented with eating brain matter in the early postday years. A couple of them were able to use it as a fuel. It allowed them to influence minds. But the others all died— a huge tragedy when humanity was trying to rebuild its population. The word never spread, and among those who did know, it became taboo to even talk about brain eating. Plus, this is different than other talents. It's addictive. Once someone starts, they want to do it more and more. It can drive them mad."

Nora tried to process all that as she looked back at her aunt. "Aunt Dani, is my dad . . ." She took a deep breath and forced the words out. "Is he a . . . by the sky, what do you even call it? A brain lyster?"

Dani finally removed her hands from her mouth. She swallowed several times, then spoke in a hoarse voice. "Nora, when your mother died, your father was devastated for months. One night, I caught him in his room, holding a knife to his wrist. He brushed it off when I asked him about it, and he refused to talk to a doctor.

"Another time, he wouldn't eat for days. I don't think he was sleeping much either. I was worried enough to follow him when he left the residence. We used to have a hunter on staff, and your father walked to the man's cabin. I caught your father with a fork"—she stopped and shuddered, then pulled her hand away from Nora. She pressed both hands against her mouth.

"A fork?" Nora prompted in a whisper.

Dani pulled her hands off her mouth and folded them tightly. "The hunter used to clean animals behind his house. That's where your father went. By the time I arrived, he'd broken open the skull of a cervid. He had a fork inside it. I couldn't tell if he'd eaten anything, but I supposed he hadn't, since he would've gotten sick within seconds. I brought him back to the house, and I planned to keep a close eye on him, but . . ." She trailed off, her mouth dropping open in sudden recognition of the truth.

"But you felt like you shouldn't?" Krey asked.

Dani nodded. "Yes. Every time I tried to stay close to him, just to make sure he didn't do anything dangerous, he told me he was fine. Whenever he said that, I felt peaceful. I believed him. So I let him heal. In his own way."

"You also mentioned that lately, you haven't realized he's lying until you leave the room," Krey said.

"He's been controlling me too," Dani murmured.

"Did you ever see him eating brains after that first time?" Krey asked.

"No, but he's always been close to our family chef. In fact, the chef's salary is twice what it should be, compared to other members of the staff. He could be supplying the . . . well . . . the fuel to Ulmin."

Krey stood and walked back to the sofa, shaking his head. When he sat, he said, "I don't get it, though. What you talked about, Dani—him being able to nudge your mind in a certain direction for a short period of time—that's normal for brain eaters. What he's doing with the militia is different. He's somehow sharing his powers, enabling someone who works there to control a whole group of soldiers, all day long. Nora even said the woman controlling the militia does it from a different room. None of that should be possible; I don't care how many animal brains your father eats."

"Is that why you never mentioned this magic before?" Nora asked. "Because you didn't think it was possible?"

Krey shrugged. "Yeah. It doesn't fit. I didn't want you to think I was nuts."

Dani sat up straighter. "Do you think he can hear my thoughts? Will he know that I've talked to you?"

"If that were the case," Nora said, "he would've figured out our plans when we were still at the palace." Her aunt's shoulders fell in relief. *She's afraid of him.* Another knot of grief filled Nora's throat.

"A brain eater can influence others, not read minds," Krey said. He fixed Nora with an intense stare. "Can you think of any time your father might've controlled you?"

Nora thought about it, then shook her head. "No. Never. But . . . what if he does it next time I see him?"

"A brain eater establishes his power through touch. If your father has never touched you with the intent of controlling you, he has no power over you."

"So when I see him, I can't let him touch me." Nora swallowed. "But I can't . . . I can't imagine him trying to control me, even now.

He loves me. I'm sure of that." She looked at Dani. "Of course, I can't believe he'd do it to you either."

"He did it to me because he didn't want me to know his secrets," Dani said softly. "And while I agree he'd never want to control your mind, you're learning his secrets too."

Nora refused to let the truth of that statement sink into her heart. She'd consider it later.

After a pause, Dani said, "I wish I could tell you more. I wish I knew where the militia was."

Nora exchanged glances with Krey and Ovrun, then said, "We know where it is. I've been talking with one of the guards." Out of the corner of her eye, she saw Ovrun smirk. She tried not to smile. She wasn't about to tell Dani that the guard was a house-sized reptid.

"You know where the militia is?" Dani asked. "I suppose that means you're planning to rescue Zeisha?"

Nora nodded. "And the others too, if we can. But I was hoping . . ." She hadn't told her companions this part; she knew Krey in particular would think she was being ridiculous. She had to try, though. "I was hoping you could think of some way to convince my dad to stop what he's doing. If he could just see logic, then we wouldn't have to . . ." She trailed off as Dani slowly shook her head.

"Oh, sweetie, I've been thinking about that very thing. You don't know how many times I've nearly confronted him with what I know. Something has always stopped me, though. And I'm glad I've stayed quiet. If brain lysting is as addictive as Krey says it is, we can't convince your father to stop." Her breath came out in a long sigh. "Oh, by the stone, everything makes sense now. He's lying and manipulating, just as anyone suffering from addiction would do. If I thought talking to him would change anything, I'd do it. But the more I've seen how deep his lies go, the more I've realized I don't even know your father anymore."

Tears spilled out of Nora's eyes and down her cheeks. She forced words through her tight throat. "Then we'll have to do what we can do to stop him." She held her breath. She knew what was coming next. Dani would try to keep her niece home, through guilt, bribery, fear, or a combination of the three.

When Dani didn't say a word, hope sparked in Nora's chest. "I know you probably don't want us to go," Nora said, "but since we've made our decision, can you help us?"

"Help you?"

"We need money. For food and supplies. Maybe even for orsas; we're wearing ourselves out with all the walking. We've used all of Krey's money, and"—she looked at Ovrun—"Ovrun's family needs every quin they've got." Ovrun gave her a look that, once again, melted her.

"I can't encourage you in this venture." Dani's voice drew Nora's attention away from Ovrun. "What you want to do is too dangerous. There are others who can fight—"

"What others?" Nora demanded, then brought her volume down. "If we try to bring anyone else into this, my father will find out! He'll stop them, with weapons or with his mind." She took her aunt's hand again. "This is the only way, Aunt Dani!"

"But if I make it possible for you to go, and something happens to you—"

"You're not making it possible for us to go," Nora said. "We're going regardless. But you might make it possible for us to live through it." She locked her eyes on her aunt's. Dani didn't say a word. Determined to wait her out, Nora didn't either.

At last, Dani drew her hand away from Nora's and walked to her desk. Nora heard the clink of coins. A lot of coins. She wanted to cry —and then she wanted to laugh as she saw Ovrun's eyes grow nearly as round as the quins Dani was gathering.

When she returned, Dani was holding a large coin purse. "Who's the most responsible of the three of you?"

"Probably Ovrun," Krey and Nora said in unison.

Her face somber, Dani handed the purse to Ovrun before sitting down. "Nora, you'll want to visit your closet before you go," she said, looking pointedly at Nora's filthy outfit. "Krey and Ovrun, you need new clothes too, but be careful where you go shopping. People in the city are looking for you. Nora, there's one full chest in the icehouse. I wanted it to be there in case you returned. Fill up your large travel chest. You and Krey should stay fueled up. As for the orsas, I suggest you get them at some out-of-the-way stable."

"We may be gone for months," Ovrun said. "Renting three orsas will cost thousands of quins."

Nora's eyes widened. She'd had no idea it was that expensive.

"Yes," Dani said. "There's plenty in the coin purse for that. Bribes too, so you can get people to stay quiet." She briefly closed her eyes, then fixed her gaze on Nora. In a choked voice, she said, "Come back home, please. Safely."

Nora left her chair, leaned over, and gave her aunt a tight hug. When she rose, so did Dani.

Krey and Ovrun were already standing. Krey nodded his head at Dani, but his eyes were still wary.

"You two boys wait over there," Dani said. "Let me talk to my niece."

Ovrun and Krey stood across the room while Dani pulled Nora to the side. "Be careful," she said quietly.

Nora gave her aunt a confused smile. Why did this conversation need to be private? "We're being as careful as we can, I promise."

"I'm not talking about your efforts to rescue Zeisha. I'm talking about Ovrun. I've seen how he looks at you."

A wash of heat overtook Nora's face and neck. "What do you mean?"

"Oh dear," Dani smiled and placed a cool hand on Nora's warm cheek. "It's not just him, is it?" She didn't wait for an answer, instead hugging Nora and speaking in her ear. "Is he honorable?"

"He is." Silently, Nora added, *Way too honorable.*

"Don't do anything you'll regret," Dani whispered. "Sooner or later, you'll be queen. You'll need the right person ruling next to you."

"I know." Nora's chest tightened as, once again, the expectations of her family—and the nation—smothered her.

Dani pulled back and held Nora's shoulders firmly. "Be careful. I love you."

"I love you too, Aunt Dani. I'll see you soon. I promise."

32

I grew up around weapons, mostly bows and knives. Hunting, was, after all, a necessity.

My mom told me that when she was young, she'd known someone who owned a pistol. Such weapons were highly illegal, and most had been destroyed many years earlier. The gun's owner died on The Day.

"Guns are designed to instill fear," my mom said. "I could've taken his weapon when he died, but I couldn't bring myself to."

-The First Generation: A Memoir *by Liri Abrios*

KREY TAPPED his foot as he watched Nora whispering with her aunt. He half-expected Dani to scream for guards to arrest them.

At last, Dani walked Nora toward the door. Krey caught Ovrun's eye, trying to send him an unspoken question: *Are you willing to tackle this lady if she turns against us?* Ovrun gazed back at him cluelessly, and Krey stifled a frustrated groan.

"Be careful," Dani said when she got to the door. Yet again, she hugged Nora.

As they hurried to Nora's quarters, Krey kept an eye on Dani's open door. When they arrived in Nora's sitting room, he closed the door silently and picked up the lantern he'd left there. He lit it after making sure the shutter was mostly closed. No way would he risk catching someone's attention by using Nora's overhead light. "Ovrun," he whispered, "grab a chair and shove it under the doorknob."

Ovrun just stood there, and Nora shot Krey an incredulous look. "What?"

Krey grabbed a chair and did it himself. "Come on, let's go!"

"What are you doing?" Nora whispered. "I'm not leaving until I grab some clothes."

"Clothes? Your aunt is probably fetching guards right now."

Nora clenched her fists and stomped right up to him. Her voice was dangerously quiet. "Surely you're not talking about the same aunt who just gave us a significant portion of her savings."

"That's true. Ovrun, hide the money; that's the first thing the guards'll grab." He gave Nora a pleading look. "Please, we have to go! Now!"

"You are unbelievable!" Nora hissed.

"She was way too willing to talk to us, that's all I'm saying."

"No, that's not *all you're saying*. Dani just proved how trustworthy she is, and some day, when you're not so wrapped up in your bitterness, you'll see that too. Until then, keep your hateful paranoia to yourself." Despite Nora's hushed voice, she said the final sentence with enough vitriol to make Krey back up a step.

"Nora—"

"Shut up, Krey." Nora squeezed her eyes shut for two long seconds. When she opened them again, her anger seemed to have fled. "You have very good reasons not to trust my family. But Dani not only told us what she knows, she also gave us a huge gift. Let her help you, just like you're letting me help you. Please."

The gentleness in her words and eyes broke through any arguments he might've made, and his own ridiculousness struck him forcefully. He took a deep breath. "Okay."

She stared at him, one eyebrow raised.

"Also," he said, "I'm sorry." It was a pitiful apology, but he wasn't sure how to make it better.

"Like I said, I understand." She pointed to her closet. "My travel ice chest is in my closet. You and Ovrun can fill it up while I grab the things I need."

Ovrun retrieved the chest. He and Krey entered the icehouse. After they filled the chest, Krey fueled himself with feathers. He experimented with holding the chest and floating off the ground. When he incorporated the chest into his magic, the ice chips inside caused him to shiver, which made him laugh.

Nora entered with a full pack. "Krey, before we go, we should eat as much ice as we can manage. It'll go to waste here."

"Good idea." Krey knelt next to the large chest, which was still mostly full, and began to eat. Nora did the same.

When neither of them could consume any more fuel, they extinguished the lantern, and Ovrun put it in his pack. Krey and Ovrun picked up the travel chest, and they all walked out. Once again, the caynins loped up to them but didn't bother them.

Krey flew with the chest and left it under some closely spaced trees in the woods. He returned for Ovrun, dropped him off, and went back for Nora. "Ready?"

"Seriously, just don't ask." She sounded queasy but quickly hopped on his back.

"Hey," he murmured, "before we go? Thanks. For putting up with me."

"You're welcome," she whispered. "Now don't drop me."

He chuckled and took to the air.

They were barely past the residence, not even close to the

palace fence, when a noise reached Krey's ears. *Uh-uh-uh-uh!* It was a caynin, and it was close. Krey looked down and cursed. An angry animal and a lantern-toting guard were both looking straight at him.

As Krey accelerated, Nora hissed, "She's got a gun!"

Panic shot through Krey's gut and limbs. His focus broken, he lost his connection with Nora. They dropped at least five mets before he recovered, again enveloping her into his magic. The mistake had brought them dangerously close to the ground. Having heard Nora's voice with its sensitive ears, the caynin was silent. But Krey could almost feel the guard aiming at them. He pulled up, trying to regain his earlier altitude.

"Stop!" the guard called. "Come down, or I'll shoot!"

They couldn't outfly a bullet. Krey made a rapid turn to face the guard, eliciting a squealing gasp from Nora.

"Ice!" he shouted, catalyzing his own fuel and hoping Nora was doing the same.

The guard's handgun was pointed directly at them. Krey shot a compact ball of ice from his hand, his panic propelling it with more force than he'd ever used before. Just as it hit the guard in the chest, her pistol fired.

Krey froze, expecting an agonized cry from himself or his passenger. Instead, all he heard was Nora gasping in a teary voice, "Did she miss? I think it would've hit us by now, right?"

Krey laughed with relief. "Yes, she missed." He sped toward the palace fence, praying not to get shot. Nora was shaking, which made it harder for him to fly efficiently. He was about to ask her to be still, when he realized she was sobbing.

"I couldn't . . . get my magic to work," she said through tears. "Too . . . too scared."

Once they were over the fence, he squeezed one of her knees where it gripped his waist. "It's okay. We're safe."

When they landed by Ovrun, Nora was still crying. She slid off Krey's back, and Ovrun immediately pulled her into a tight hug that was more than a little friendly. "What happened?" Ovrun demanded.

For a brief moment, Krey pondered what Ovrun and Nora might've been up to on his solo trips into the city. He shook off the thought and gave Ovrun a quick update.

As soon as he finished, Nora pulled away from Ovrun. She was still sniffling but seemed to be herself again. "They'll send guards to search the forest," she said. "Let's go."

"Follow me," Krey said. He couldn't carry the heavy ice without incorporating it into his flight magic, so he catalyzed some feathers, picked up the ice chest, and flew low to the ground. He moved forward briskly as Ovrun and Nora ran behind him.

When they were nearly at the edge of the forest, Krey left Ovrun and Nora in the trees while he flew high into the dark air. He returned and reported, "There are two mounted guards on the road, and three guards are searching the forest on foot. If we stay off the road, we'll be fine."

"We need orsas," Ovrun said.

"We need sleep first," Nora said, still panting from their run. "I'm not trying to free a dragon when I'm exhausted."

They exited the forest. Nora and Ovrun alternated between walking and running while Krey hovered next to them. They decided to sleep in the abandoned house they'd stayed in before. They entered the city on a minor road and went straight to the house. Cuddled together on the stinking floor, they slept soundly.

When they woke, it was late morning. They'd brought water and dried food with them. When Nora had eaten her portion, she stifled her complaints of continued hunger. They'd get more food when they could.

For much of the day, they discussed their next steps. By dusk, they'd come up with the best plan they could, considering how little they knew about what was going on behind the walls of the militia warehouse.

Ovrun looked between the boards on the window. "It's getting dim out there." He put on his hooded jacket and exited through the back door to purchase food and rent orsas.

"Let's start eating ice now," Krey said. "I'm guessing we'll need magic to free that dragon. I'll eat feathers too."

Nora released a long sigh, shaking her head at the memory of her utter uselessness when the guard had fired at them. The ill-timed failure had stomped all over her confidence.

She approached Krey, who was kneeling at the open ice chest, and set a hand on his shoulder. "How did you stay focused when that guard shot at us? You were using both your faculties, and I couldn't even use one."

He turned to look at her. "You were already afraid when we started that flight. I wasn't."

"Didn't the gun scare you?"

He laughed. "You have no idea."

"So how'd you do it?"

He closed the chest and sat back, resting his elbow on one raised knee and running his fingers through his thick hair. It was several seconds before he answered, "I honestly don't know. But when you really need your magic, you'll be able to use it."

"How do you know that?"

He shrugged. "Because I trust you."

Nora blinked. "That's good to hear."

"It's good to say. And I meant it. Now, let's feast on some ice."

They started eating the ice, most of which had stayed frozen, thanks to the chest's insulation and the chilly weather. Krey ate bits of feathers too. When they couldn't consume any more, they lay on their backs, hands on their uncomfortably full bellies.

"We should eat more in a little while," Nora said.

Krey groaned. "I taught you too well." He turned on his side, propping his head in his hand. "So, how's Ovrun?"

Nora stared at the ceiling. "Why don't you ask him?"

"Maybe I should ask how the *two* of you are."

"We're fine." She tried to keep her voice casual. "It's nice to have friends."

Krey had the audacity to laugh loudly at that. "Yeah, friends are great. Zeisha and I are good friends too."

Despite her full belly, Nora flipped over, pushing herself up on her elbows. She tried to glare at Krey, though she could feel a smile threatening to break through. "Remind me, because I swear, I've forgotten—what exactly makes this your business?"

He returned her stare, adding a bold grin. "You just said it's nice to have friends. Well, I'm your friend. Friends talk about things." When she didn't say anything, he added, "Every time I fly with him on my back, I can sense his entire body. The guy's got so much muscle, I'm pretty sure it's illegal. I'd be surprised if you weren't attracted to him."

With a groan, Nora lowered her chest to the ground, resting her head on her arms. "I know, it's awful. He's way too hot for his own good. And for mine."

Krey raised his eyebrows, and his expression turned serious. "He's a great guy. You could do a lot worse."

"My dad would never let me be with Ovrun." She halted, taking a deep breath against the pain that those words caused. "Maybe it doesn't matter what he thinks anymore, but I have to hope someday he'll be himself again. If not, my Aunt Dani will be my guardian. Eventually, I'll marry a lyster with good leadership skills and plenty of education. My dad or Dani will have to approve of him. In fact, they'll probably hand-choose my spouse. Just like my grandmother did for my dad."

"Wait, did you say the king has to be a magic eater? I've never heard that before."

"You know the stats as well as I do, Krey. If I marry a lyster, each of our kids will have a fifty-percent chance of developing a magical faculty. If I marry someone without magic, the chance goes to one in twenty. Krey, my ancestors have ruled this area as mayors and monarchs. They were all lysters, starting with Liri. Cellerinians expect their leaders to be magical."

Krey examined her for a long moment, his forehead furrowed. At last, he said, "All the big decisions—your career, if you'll marry, who you'll marry—you don't get to make any of them, do you?"

She let out a cynical laugh. "I'm allowed to choose which one of my kids will be the next monarch. But my ministers will expect me to choose a lyster."

Krey groaned. "Better you than me."

"Thanks, Krey, that's very comforting." He started to apologize, but she cut him off. "It's fine, it's not like I can do anything about it. Come on, let's eat more fuel."

It was dark by the time Ovrun returned, carrying food and water and leading two orsas. He tied the animals behind the house, then left to get the third orsa.

Bundled in their warmest clothes, Nora and Krey stood outside, lest anyone from this sketchy neighborhood decide to run off with the orsas. "Another cold front," Krey said.

"Yeah." Nora wasn't thinking about the weather, though. She had her arms around the neck of the orsa she'd claimed as her own. Ovrun had said it was brown, but in the dark, she could swear it was black, just like Blue, her orsa back home. She rubbed her cheek against the fur under its chin.

"*OHH-AHH,*" the orsa said.

"I miss Blue," Nora murmured.

"I bet." Krey was standing next to the other orsa, one of his hands on the animal's neck. The pale light of a distant streetlamp outlined his stiff stance.

"Do you know how to ride?" Nora asked.

"Zeisha's family has an orsa, so I've ridden," he said.

"How many times?"

"A few."

He sounded embarrassed to admit he wasn't an expert at something. "Just bend over low if you start to lose your balance," Nora said. "You'll be fine."

When Ovrun arrived, he strapped the ice chest behind the saddle of the orsa Nora had chosen. They all mounted and set off.

Nora's heart and breaths seemed determined to keep pace with her animal's quick footsteps. She had plenty of fuel in her belly, but she didn't think anything would make her feel ready to rescue a dragon.

She wasn't sure if she was close enough to communicate with Osmius, but she gave it a shot. *Osmius, we're on our way to rescue your mate.*

His warm voice responded immediately, calming Nora's nerves. *Thank you, Nora-human.*

Nora led the way, using the map Osmius had engraved on her mind. She kept the dragon updated on their progress. Once they left the city and its street lamps, they navigated by the light of the stars. Before long, Nora's connection to Osmius flickered in and out, then faded to nothing.

Nora looked back at Krey. He seemed comfortable on his orsa, so she suggested they speed up. All three travelers patted their animals' backsides, and the orsas started trotting, their feet creating a satisfying rhythm on the packed-dirt road.

Krey let out a short, panicked cry. Nora turned to see him bouncing in the saddle. He was hunching so low over his animal, he was nearly hugging the thing. A loud guffaw burst from her chest before she could hold it back.

"Shut up, Ulminora," Krey muttered.

Nora tried to stop laughing, but a few more giggles broke through.

Once Krey again got comfortable on his orsa, the journey was smooth. Sooner than Nora had expected, they crossed the river on a well-kept bridge. Before long, they arrived at the mountain.

After a bit of searching in the light of a lantern, they found the footpath Osmius had shown Nora. It was too narrow for the orsas, so they tied the beasts to an out-of-the-way tree and started hiking.

An hour later, Nora was panting. "Good thing we left when we did," she said. "It didn't look this far from the viewpoint of a dragon."

Ovrun responded with a grunt. Even he was tired.

Another half hour passed before they reached the place Osmius had warned them about, where the path appeared to end. Before Nora had lost touch with him earlier that night, the dragon had warned her that they shouldn't use a lantern after this point. Ovrun extinguished it, and they all climbed over a tall stone. Sure enough, the path continued on.

They tried to travel quietly, though it seemed at least one of them jostled every loose rock and stepped on every twig. Eventually, they encountered the two trees, twisted together, that Nora had been looking for. "Slow down," Nora whispered. "Be absolutely silent."

Painstakingly, Nora crept along the path, testing every footstep before she put her weight down. She, Krey, and Ovrun were still louder than she wanted to be, but she hoped nature's noises would swallow the sounds of steps and breaths.

Light shone dimly ahead. Nora forced herself to walk even more slowly. They stopped where the path curved around a large rock outcropping. Nora peeked around it.

It looked like someone had carved a chunk out of the mountain, leaving an expanse of fairly flat ground, about ten mets square. Lanterns illuminated four men, all large compared to Krey and Nora. Two of them made Ovrun look almost small. Behind them, the mountain rose up again, but there was a large, dark expanse in the rock—the entrance to the cave they were guarding.

Nora sent a thought toward the cave: *My name is Nora. Osmius sent me to save you.*

There was no response. After a minute or so, Nora reached out again. *My name is—*

A voice—rich, stunning, and distinctively female—interrupted. *I heard you. If you speak truth, I shall be more grateful than you can imagine. If you lie, you shall not survive the night.*

IN THE DARK: 9

"I SAW A DRAGON IN MY DREAM," Isla whispered.

Zeisha moved the string to the second toe of her left foot. Seventeen weeks, two days. She took her friend's hand. "Sometimes it's nice to have dreams that have nothing to do with our real lives."

"It was a memory. The dragon was here."

"Here? In this room?"

"In another room, open to the sunlight. Near the place where we fight every day."

Zeisha thought about that for a minute, then said, "Do you remember the night we all woke up to a loud noise? We were only awake for, I don't know, less than a minute probably."

"Yeah. We both thought we'd dreamed it until we realized we both remembered it."

"Maybe it was the dragon," Zeisha said. "Roaring."

"Maybe."

Zeisha squeezed Isla's hand. "Tell me more about the dream, before you forget. I'm sure the dragon was scary."

"That's the thing. He wasn't scary at all. There are plenty of people around who want to hurt us . . . but the dragon, I think he wanted to help."

33

A young boy in our community discovered he could eat ashes to make fire. At first, I was envious. Surely fire magic was more fun than plant magic.

Then I heard how difficult it was for him to control his magic. In the first month, he started three fires in his family's house. He's lucky he didn't burn the place down.

His parents built him a small, stone hovel. For a whole year, that was the only place he was allowed to eat ashes and make fire. When he was done practicing, he'd sit in that cold room, with no clothes and no linens, until his parents were certain all his magic was spent.

-The First Generation: A Memoir *by Liri Abrios*

KREY FELT Ovrun's elbow nudge him. At the signal, he crept along the path, back the way they'd come. He gritted his teeth against his annoyance; moving this slowly was torturous.

Another nudge, and Krey halted. Ovrun drew him into a huddle with Nora, their three heads touching.

"Did you talk to the dragon?" Krey asked in a bare whisper.

"Yes. She said if we're really coming to rescue her, that's great. If we're lying, she'll kill us."

"Whoa," Ovrun said. "How many guards?"

"Four. Wearing the same uniform you used to wear."

He sighed. "I wonder if I know any of them."

"Hang on," Nora said. After about half a minute of silence, she spoke again. "The dragon says the guards' names are Zef, Kadish, Jushuen, and Thar."

"I know Jushuen," Ovrun said. "I thought he quit."

"Guess he just got reassigned," Krey said. "Do you trust him?"

"I'm not sure. He's a nice guy. I don't know how loyal he is to the king, though."

"The dragon just told me she's bound with chains, held by huge padlocks," Nora whispered.

"Does she know where the keys are?" Krey asked.

"In Jushuen's front pocket. He's the one in charge, but all four guards have pistols."

"They only give firearms to the most trusted guards," Ovrun said.

Krey shook off his dread and squared his shoulders. "Let's make a plan."

A quarter hour later, they were ready. In the dim moonlight, Krey saw Nora take Ovrun's shoulders and pull him close to breathe, "Be careful." Krey almost expected her to follow her words up with a kiss, but the two of them shared only a brief hug.

Krey clapped Ovrun's back. "You got this."

They returned to the rock outcropping that blocked their view of the dragon's prison lair. Ovrun peeked around the edge. He turned and whispered in Krey's ear, "Jushuen is the one with curly hair that hits his collar."

Ovrun walked past the barrier, and his loud, confident voice rang through the night air. "Don't shoot. I'm Ovrun, a royal guard." Hopefully Jushuen, who'd last worked at the palace months earlier, wouldn't know Ovrun had been fired.

Krey heard the guards scrambling around. Two voices shouted at Ovrun to stop.

"The king sent me with a message." Ovrun's voice remained calm. "Jushuen, you know me, let me get closer so you can identify me."

"Okay, come closer," a voice called.

A few seconds later, Krey peeked around the corner. Ovrun was standing off to the side, and he'd distracted all four guards so they were facing away from Krey and Nora's hiding spot.

Krey took to the air, flying behind the guards and into the cave. The lantern light from outside shone on a dragon who was even larger than her mate. Her glinting, faceted eyes appeared to be fixed on Krey. He tried unsuccessfully to hide a shudder. "Hello," he whispered softly.

The dragon answered with what sounded like a huff. Hot air from her nostrils blasted Krey. He forced his attention back to Ovrun, who was talking to the guards.

"The king sent me to tell you to release the dragon," Ovrun was saying. "A wealthy group in the capital found out we captured her, and they're threatening to go public."

"I don't believe a word you're saying," one of the guards shouted.

"That's enough!" another voice said. "I know Ovrun. He's trustworthy. And I don't know about you guys, but I'm ready to be done climbing this mountain every night. Ovrun, just tell us the visitor password, and we'll know you're supposed to be here."

Krey groaned inwardly as their plans fell apart with that simple request for a password. They'd hoped Jushuen would trust Ovrun enough to take him inside the cave. Krey would've waited in the shadows at the top of the cave, ready to dive down and put Jushuen in a headlock if he didn't willingly give up his keys. The dragon was even in on the scheme; she'd agreed to defend herself and her rescuers from the remaining guards.

Time for an alternate plan. Krey thrust himself back into the air and flew silently toward the four guards, whose backs were still to him.

"Why would they give me a password when Jushuen already knows me?" Ovrun was asking. It didn't sound convincing to Krey, and he knew the guards wouldn't buy it either. Hovering behind Jushuen, Krey blocked out the discussion and focused on the man's pants. All he needed to do was grab the keys.

The problem was, he couldn't tell which pocket the keys were in. *I could try both at once. But he'll feel it; I'm no pickpocket. Even if I get the keys, what am I gonna do with them? Ovrun and I will both get shot.*

Krey returned his attention to the conversation.

"We're not releasing the dragon!" The guard who spoke turned to gesture at the dark cave, then shouted, "Jushuen! Behind you!"

No! Krey turned vertical and propelled himself straight upward, as fast as his magic would take him. Beneath him, guards shouted, and for the second time in twenty-four hours, Krey heard gunshots. This time, there were too many to count. The chances of anyone hitting him were slim; he was high in the air, and they couldn't see him well in the dark. Ovrun, on the other hand—

Before Krey could create ice to take out the shooters like he'd done the night before, Ovrun roared with unmistakable pain.

Pure fury catalyzed the ice Krey had eaten hours before. He rained dense, freezing spheres on the guards below. He was too high to aim well, but one guard cried out. Krey grinned and formed another ball.

Before he could throw it, a stream of flames shot straight up into the sky, aimed at Krey. *Ash eater!* Krey sped through the air in an insane zigzag course. The ash eater didn't let up, carving the black sky with a blinding, continuous ribbon of orange heat.

Krey roared with panic as fire lit up his left jacket sleeve. He slapped at it with his right palm, dropping at least twenty mets in the process. When his clothing was no longer flaming, he flew as fast as he could, away from the guards.

In seconds, he was out of the ash eater's range. His arm seemed to be fine; the flames must not have burned through his shirt. His relief, however, was short-lived. All at once, agony flooded his right palm. He touched it gingerly and found that it was covered in huge blisters.

Krey stifled sobs as he soared through the sky. He needed medical care, but they had to finish their mission, one way or another. He pictured Zeisha's face and dug deep into his well of determination. *Forget the pain. Focus.* A minute or so later, he landed in a tree with a view of the cave area. Silent tears washed over his cheeks.

The scene below sent dread into his heart. Golden lantern light shone on Ovrun, who was prone on the ground, dark blood underneath him. He was moaning.

A moment later, it got worse. Nora exited her hiding place.

Krey wanted to shout at her to turn around and go back to the orsas. One of them, at least, could escape uninjured. It was too late for that, though.

The guards shouted at her, but she spoke in an authoritative voice he'd never heard her use. "I am Ulminora Abrios. Put your weapons down."

Krey pushed all the air out of his lungs, clenching his teeth as hard as he could. His hand was in so much pain, he wanted to gnaw it off. From the looks of Ovrun, he was in worse shape. And there was Nora, letting the royal guards know that she was involved in all this. So much for keeping her father in the dark.

"It's her!" Jushuen shouted. "Your Highness, what are you doing here?"

"She's been missing for weeks!" another guard said. "Grab her!"

"No!" Again, Nora's voice brooked no argument. "Drop your weapons. If you choose to touch me, I hope it's with a hand you don't mind losing."

Krey watched as all four men dropped their guns to their sides.

"Place your guns in your holsters," Nora commanded.

They obeyed.

Nora ran to Ovrun and knelt by him. "Where are you hit?"

Krey couldn't hear the quiet response. Nora lifted Ovrun's arm, then tore off her scarf and began wrapping it around his left bicep. An arm wound—he could survive that, as long as it hadn't hit a major artery.

The guards were focused only on Nora. This was Krey's chance to get close again. And this time, he wasn't going for the keys.

He returned to the sky, and the cold air felt both wonderful and torturous on his burned hand. He cursed; how was he supposed to do anything with a destroyed right hand? *Please, God, tell me that ash eater doesn't have any fuel left.*

The guards huddled together, whispering, and Krey found an angle of approach that would keep him out of sight of all four men for as long as possible. If they only kept their eyes on Nora, he could do this.

No time for caution. Krey flew directly at the nearest guard and, using his left hand, pulled the man's gun out of its holster.

"Hey!" The huge guard turned, but Krey was already out of reach, pointing the gun at the guards. "Get him!" the guard cried.

Nora screamed, "No!" as Jushuen reached for his gun.

"I'll shoot!" Krey threatened.

Jushuen froze. The ash eater, however, lifted his hand and once again shot flames toward Krey.

Krey cursed and flew evasively. The fire kept coming, paired with gunshots. Krey evaded both bullets and flames, but his fear and pain destroyed his customary magical efficiency. His feathery fuel ran out, and he plummeted at least three mets to the hard dirt, dropping the gun somewhere along the way. Frequent changes of direction had resulted in him staying close to the scene, and he landed between the guards and Ovrun.

The fall knocked the wind out of him, and before he could

recover and push himself up, two guards pinned him down, one on his back, the other on his legs. Krey groaned and tried to breathe.

"Stop!" Nora cried. "Let him go! I'm here on behalf of my father, and he's—"

"No, you're not!" a guard shouted. "He would've sent you with a note or the password or something!"

Even with the side of his face smashed into the ground by a heavy hand, Krey could sense the shift in the air. The guards didn't believe any of them, not even the princess.

The weight on Krey's legs lifted, and he heard Jushuen speak. "Shackle Ovrun and the other guy. I think we can get the princess down the mountain without restraining her, especially if she knows we'll kill her friends if she doesn't cooperate."

Krey's eyes found Nora. For a second, she looked panicked, but then her expression turned intense and focused.

From the cave, a massive *ROAR* erupted.

Krey felt the weight on his back shift, and he heard the other guards move, probably to look at the cave. *Nice distraction, Nora.*

The princess ran several steps away and bent down briefly. *What's she up to?* She sprinted to Ovrun. She knelt, then leaned over him, giving him a hug and whispering in his ear.

"What are you doing, Princess?" the biggest guard bellowed. Apparently the guy had gotten tired of trying to figure out why the dragon had roared.

"Nothing. Just helping my friend sit up." Nora leaned over Ovrun again. He draped his good arm over her shoulder, and she pulled him into a seated position.

"Appreciate the help, Your Highness," Jushuen said. "Now move, so I can get these shackles on him."

"Hang on," Ovrun said, his voice strained but surprisingly strong. He reached behind him, and when he lifted his hand, there was a pistol in it.

Krey smiled. *That must be the gun I dropped!* Nora, bless her, had picked it up when the guards were distracted. Thank the sky she'd gotten the weapon to Ovrun; he was the only one of them who actually knew how to use it.

"Ovrun," Jushuen said, "don't be stupid."

An ear-splitting *BANG* sounded, and the gun in Ovrun's hand kicked back. Jushuen screamed, and Krey heard him fall. "Hands up, all of you," Ovrun said. "A hand wound is bad enough. Next time, I'll aim for the chest."

"The gun's empty," the biggest guard said. "There were ten bullets to start out with. I shot at your flying friend nine times. You shot once."

Krey had to admire Ovrun, who remained calm and pulled the trigger. All that emerged from the gun was a soft *click*.

"Zef," Jushuen groaned, pain thick in his voice, "burn him."

Krey held his breath, prepared to see his friend turned into a torch.

Nothing happened. *Finally, a little bit of luck. The ash eater is out of fuel.*

Nora stood. "Guys, can't we just talk?" She held up both hands in a calming gesture, and Krey rolled his eyes. Talking wouldn't work right now.

Then a hard ball of ice shot out of each of Nora's hands. The guard on top of Krey toppled to the side. Krey leapt to his feet and took in the situation. The guard who'd been pinning him down was lying on the ground, a broken ball of ice by his head. The largest guard was clutching his throat. Jushuen was on the ground in agony, cradling a bleeding hand. And the one remaining guard, the ash eater with no fuel, was pulling his gun out of its holster.

Krey turned on his frost magic, but his pain made his magic sluggish. Even as he felt ice forming in his palm, he knew he didn't have time.

Unlike the ash eater and Krey, Nora's weapon was ready. One more ball of ice flew out of her raised hand. The ash eater's gun fell to the ground, accompanied by the ice that had smashed into it.

Krey dove to the ground and grabbed the gun. He leapt up and pointed it first at the ash eater, then at the other guards. Hoping he didn't look as inept with a weapon as he really was, he said, "My friend told you to put your hands up."

Two guards raised their hands high. The man who'd been on top of Krey was still on the ground, probably unconscious. Jushuen, sobbing and holding his bloody hand to his chest, lifted his uninjured hand.

"Nora," Krey said, "Ovrun doesn't look good."

She spun around. Ovrun was clearly woozy. She caught him by the shoulders and eased him to the ground.

Krey confiscated the remaining guns and locked the guards in their own shackles. He returned to Jushuen to find that he'd lost consciousness. Krey easily retrieved the keys from the guard's pocket.

Heart still pounding from all the action, Krey crossed to Nora and Ovrun. He knelt next to them. "I think the dragon speaker should free the captive. I'll take care of Ovrun."

Nora looked up, her eyes puffy from tears. "The bleeding's slowed down already." She lifted her hands, and in the dim lantern light, her palms looked black. She wiped them on her pants and walked toward the cave, muttering epithets at the guards as she passed.

Krey used his good hand to peel away the cloth Nora had wrapped around Ovrun's wound. "She's right; it's not bleeding much anymore," he said softly. "How are you doing?"

"I think it was just a graze," Ovrun said. "But"—he groaned in muted agony—"I've never hurt this much. I'm having trouble staying conscious."

"I think I should wrap it in clean cloth," Krey said. "Or at least something less bloody than what's on here now."

"What did Nora use?" Ovrun asked.

"Her scarf."

"She must be cold," were Ovrun's last words before he passed out.

Krey took his jacket off, stifling a scream as it passed over his blistered hand. The garment was too thick to wrap tightly around the wound. He removed his shirt and put his jacket back on.

When anything touched his hand, pain ripped through it. This wouldn't be an easy task with only one good hand. He was relieved Ovrun couldn't see him fumbling around.

Once his shirt was torn into a few rough strips, Krey examined Ovrun more carefully. The bullet had carved a furrow into Ovrun's tricep.

Krey did the bulk of the wrapping with his left hand, using his injured hand in smaller ways when he really needed it. He tucked in the end of the makeshift bandage just in time for Ovrun to wake with a moan.

"You're gonna be okay," Krey said. "We'll get you to a blood eater if we can. But even if we can't—it's disgusting, man, but it'll heal."

Ovrun let out a sound that Krey was pretty sure was a hybrid of a groan and a laugh.

"You okay if I get up?" Krey asked.

"Yeah."

Krey used another strip of his shirt to bandage Jushuen's injury. The hand was mutilated, and it would probably never work the same again. Even a skilled blood eater couldn't fully heal a wound like that.

They'd already found a shackle key on the same ring as the dragon's padlock key. Krey retrieved shackle keys from the other three guards' pockets too.

A noise emanated from the dark cave, and Nora exited, followed by the massive dragon. Lantern light shone off the beast's shiny, black, reptid skin. Krey could now see that her compound eyes were gold, just like her mate's. Her brutal beauty took his breath away.

Nora approached Krey, and they both walked to Ovrun. "Osmius's mate hasn't told me her name," she said, "but I think she trusts us a little bit. I told her about Ovrun's injury, and she offered to fly us out of here. Of course, she might just be offering because it's the fastest way for us to lead her to Osmius."

"What about the orsas?" Krey asked.

"We'll board them at a nearby stable. She said she can lead us to one a few clommets from here."

Krey looked over at the dragon, who'd unfurled her massive wings and was flapping them. It was probably the first time she'd gotten to do that since her imprisonment. Dread filled his gut at the thought of riding atop such a creature. "I can fly myself, at least for now," he said. "I just need to eat some more fuel."

"She said she can fly much faster than you, and if you want to stay with us, you'll go on her back."

His heart dropped. Bile rose in his throat. He swallowed. "Is this how you feel when you fly with me?"

Golden lantern light gleamed off Nora's teeth, which were bared in a bright grin. "Yep."

34

Even at a young age, our local healer loved using his gift. He did not, however, love collecting his own fuel. Someone devised a schedule. Every week, different families gave the boy blood from the animals they butchered.

One week, it was our family's turn. My mother handed me a clay jar full of yellow blood and told me to deliver it to the healer. I argued that it was too gross. She told me I was seventeen and needed to get over myself.

When I arrived, a line of patients waited in the yard. I went inside and gave the young healer the blood. "Oh good," he said. "I just ran out." He tipped the jar up and drank greedily.

I fainted from disgust and woke to find the boy sitting over me. He was making good use of the fuel I'd brought, using magic to heal a nasty gash on my forehead.

-The First Generation: A Memoir *by Liri Abrios*

CLIMBING onto the dragon's back was surprisingly easy. From afar, a dragon's skin looked sleek. Up close, however, Nora saw that the basket-weave texture provided perfect handholds and footholds. She used these natural grips to pull herself up. The dragon's back was too broad for her to straddle it like an orsa, so she sent out a mental message: *How should I position myself up here?*

Choose a posture that will prevent you from falling, came the response.

Nora rolled her eyes. *I'd like to hold onto your skin like I was doing when I climbed up. Did it hurt you?*

Peals of dragon laughter resonated through Nora's mind. *Do not think so highly of yourself, human.*

Nora missed Osmius's moniker for her, *Nora-human*. She'd introduced herself, but apparently this dragon wasn't ready to be on a first-name basis.

After some trial and error, Nora ended up lying on her belly, her legs and arms spread wide, knees bent. She gripped the dragon's skin with her fingers and the toes of her boots. "Come on up!" she called to Krey and Ovrun.

There was plenty of room on the dragon's long body for all of them to assume the same flying position, but Krey and Ovrun could each only hold on with one hand. Nobody knew if Ovrun would stay conscious. They decided that Nora should ride in the rear, with Ovrun in the middle and Krey in front. Krey positioned his legs over Ovrun's arms, and Nora pinned Ovrun's ankles with her arms. Hopefully, his friends could keep him from falling if he passed out again.

Once they were all situated and still, the dragon stood.

"Whoa!" Krey cried. "Some warning would've been nice!"

Nora tried not to laugh. Krey had eaten a few feathers before climbing on the dragon so he could save himself if he fell. He was the only one of them who shouldn't be scared. Like so many fears, this one was illogical.

The dragon's wings spread wide with a fantastic *snap*, and she took to the air, eliciting gasps from all three passengers and curses from the bound guards they left behind. Just as she'd promised, the dragon flew far faster than Krey. Nora, however, felt more secure than she did on her friend's back. The dragon's back was broad, and Nora's grip was tight.

Then the dragon started to dive, and Nora and Krey both screamed. Even Ovrun groaned. The dragon said nothing, but she did decrease her angle of descent, switching to a gradual spiral.

They landed near their orsas at the base of the mountain. When the three riders dismounted, the dragon gave Nora directions to a stable, using a mental map as Osmius had done. They set up a meeting place, and Nora, Ovrun, and Krey mounted their orsas.

Nora's father would figure out what she'd been up to, but they all hoped to delay that eventuality. Osmius's mate had agreed to destroy the mountain path in two places, making it more difficult for the next guard shift to discover their injured comrades and the missing dragon.

The dragon had been ready to kill the guards, but her passengers had insisted that would make things worse for all of them in the long run. Besides, Nora couldn't have lived with herself if she'd allowed such cold-blooded killings. She was concerned about the injured guards. Hopefully they'd be rescued soon—but not too soon.

The stable was only a few clommets away, but within five minutes, Ovrun started swaying in his saddle. And Nora could hear the pain in Krey's voice. She watched both her friends, her entire body tense. In their condition, they had no hope of taking down the militia.

They made it to the stable, which was attached to a small home. Nora stood back, not wanting to be recognized. The owner was none too happy when Krey woke him by banging on his door. Then he saw how much new business they were bringing him. His mood improved. Krey offered him a large tip not to talk about their visit, and he turned positively cheerful.

As the man took the orsas to empty stalls, Nora and Krey again ate as much ice as they could stomach. There was no good way to carry the heavy chest on the dragon's back, so Krey asked if they could store it in the stable. The man consented—for an extra fee, of course.

Nora and Krey carried the chest between them and set it in a storage room. Even using his good hand, Krey groaned as he moved. *That's it,* Nora thought. *We've got to get them some help.*

She had a quick chat with Krey, who readily agreed. He approached the stable owner. "Is there a blood lyster nearby?" he asked. "I've got this ingrown toenail, and walking really hurts."

The man looked down at Krey's boots, his lip curling in slight disgust. He gave Krey directions to the nearest blood lyster, adding, "She won't be happy to have visitors this time of night. Then again, if you're as reasonable with her as you were with me, she'll come around."

They left their orsas and headed for the blood lyster's house. When Krey knocked, a tiny, old woman with skin covered in loose wrinkles answered the door. Despite the stable owner's predictions, she didn't seem to mind being woken. She wouldn't accept extra pay for the late hour, and when Krey offered her a bribe to stay quiet, she responded with a curt, "I never speak of my clients to anyone. I don't need money to keep that promise." Nora liked this lady.

"You're in luck," the blood lyster said once they were all in her dark, little house. "The butcher brought me fuel a few hours ago." She beckoned her guests to follow her through to a little room in the back, where she lit several lanterns. Nora retreated through the doorway, still wary of being recognized.

She watched from the shadows as the woman took a towel off a metal pitcher, poured a little bit of thick, yellow blood into a cup, and began drinking it. Nora shuddered and looked toward her companions. Krey was watching with fascinated intensity, and Ovrun, who was already pale from his injury, had turned his face away.

The woman slurped the last of her fuel and licked her lips as she set the cup down. "Now, show me what you boys need," she said. When she saw Ovrun's arm, her wispy, white eyebrows rose. "I didn't consume enough fuel."

After drinking more, she worked on Ovrun first, washing the wound, then placing her hands on either side of it. Before their eyes, Ovrun's injury began to heal. It didn't completely close up, but it looked like it had skipped at least a couple of weeks of natural healing. The lyster squeezed Ovrun's hand. "Best I can do, dear."

Nora wanted to ask her to do more; there were healers in Cellerin City who could've made Ovrun's arm almost as good as new. Every lyster, however, had their limits, and Nora believed the woman had done her best. The partial healing might be enough. Ovrun was no longer pale. He lifted his arm in the air and smiled broadly for the first time since he'd been shot.

Krey's hand was easier to heal, and when the woman finished, the skin looked almost normal, though it was still quite pink. Krey's face relaxed as he flexed his hand.

They thanked the healer, paid her, and headed out. The dragon was waiting for them in a nearby field. Nora had to listen to a bit of grumbling from the impatient beast, who hadn't known about their detour to see the healer. Soon, however, they were back in the air.

I need mushu leaves, the dragon told Nora. *They give me fire. We will bring some to Osmius as well.*

They flew back to Cellerin Mountain at shocking speed. The dragon stopped at a large grove of mushu trees and let her passengers climb down, instructing them to gather the long, skinny leaves for Osmius. Then she flew above the trees to eat her fill.

Nora, Ovrun, and Krey pulled leaves from low-hanging boughs, stuffing their packs full. At one point, everything got suddenly brighter. When Nora looked in the sky, she saw the dragon expelling a great stream of fire from her huge mouth. The creature soon returned, carrying a bundle of mushu leaves in her front claws. She landed, still holding the leaves, and allowed her riders to climb up again.

They returned to the sky. Nora could see the lights of Cellerin City in the distance, approaching more rapidly than she would've dreamed possible. Despite her speed, the dragon's flight was smooth and stable. *This is actually pretty peaceful,* Nora thought.

At that moment, the dragon's massive wings beat the air furiously, and her speed increased dramatically. In front of Nora, Ovrun gasped, and Krey let out a cry. Nora's own heart raced as she shouted a silent message. *Whoa—any chance we could slow down?*

The dragon didn't seem to hear the request, continuing to fly impossibly fast through the dark sky. They entered a low cloud, and the sudden loss of starlight and wash of damp air scared Nora so much that she couldn't even scream. Krey and Ovrun didn't have that problem, releasing panicked shouts. When they exited the cloud, Nora held on even tighter to the dragon's now-slick skin and begged, *Please! We're gonna fall off your back!* They didn't slow.

Then the fiery voice of Osmius infiltrated Nora's terrified mind. *You found her!*

Nora's eyes widened. They'd reached the point where she'd lost communication with Osmius on their way to the mountain. She'd been on the verge of contacting him before his mate had turned into an insane racing dragon. *Has she been talking to you?* Nora asked.

Yes. The joy in that word was unmistakable.

Tell her to slow down! She's about to drop us all!

A few seconds later, the female dragon slowed her flight. Nora squeezed her eyes shut and released a sigh of relief. *Thank you.* She sent the thought to both dragons.

"What was that all about?" Krey demanded.

Nora explained. To her surprise, Krey laughed. "If I was flying and found out Zeisha had been rescued, I'd do the same thing."

What is your plan? Osmius asked.

Before Nora could send out a response, the dragon she was riding replied, *We will rescue you.*

I am not the only one who needs rescuing, Taima.

Hearing the name of the dragon she was riding, Nora stopped

breathing. All was quiet in her mind for several seconds until she heard that rich, female voice again.

You told her my name. Disbelief and accusation added heat to her words.

My love, Osmius said, his tone gentle and low, *forgive me. It was unintentional. She and her friends shall honor your name, as they have honored mine.*

We will, Nora promised.

From her prone position, Nora's entire body lowered as the great dragon sighed. *Tell me what we need to do,* Taima said.

The winter sky was still black when Taima and her three riders reached the ruins of Deroga. Krey gazed down into the vast ruins. "By the stone, I'm sore," he muttered. "I guess hanging on for dear life will do that to you." He was cold too, having used his shirt to bandage Ovrun's wound. His jacket wasn't designed for rapid flight through the winter air.

When they neared the warehouse, they suddenly dropped straight down. Krey barely prevented himself from throwing up as his torso lifted several simmets from the dragon's back. He tightened his grip.

"Archer!" Ovrun cried. "On our left!"

Krey looked. Sure enough, the moonlight barely illuminated someone on a nearby rooftop, aiming at them with a bow.

Taima blew a great stream of orange fire toward the trog, eliciting three gasps from her back. The fire nearly hit the archer.

"Bring us closer!" Krey said. "And no fire, please!" As soon as the archer was in earshot, Krey shouted, "Put the weapon down! We want to speak to your leaders!"

The man put his bow down. His voice was surprisingly calm, considering his near-incineration. "We have no leaders. Trogs are all equal."

Krey rolled his eyes. There were always leaders, whether or not they had official titles. "Fine. Bring out the people everyone seems to listen to."

"We will meet you in the street." The man picked up his bow, then walked to a hole in the roof and began climbing down a ladder. A few minutes later, he exited out the front door and jogged to a nearby building. After a wait that felt interminably long to Krey, the archer returned to the street, accompanied by a woman with a lantern.

"Will you instruct your archer to put his weapon down?" Krey shouted from above.

"No," the woman responded in a strong, low-pitched voice. "You ride a weapon."

Krey stifled a laugh. "We won't hurt you if you don't hurt us. Deal?"

"Yes."

"Taima," Krey said, "Can you let us off in the street, then circle above, just in case?"

Taima descended. The archer kept his arrow aimed at her until she landed. Then he lowered his weapon, and Krey, Nora, and Ovrun climbed down. As soon as his feet hit the street, Krey felt naked. What he wouldn't give for a bow right about now.

He examined the trogs in the lantern light. The archer he'd first spoken to was short and skinny, probably a few years older than Krey. His hair and beard were curly and wild.

Next to him was the woman, who was well past middle age. Her thick, white hair was woven into two braids that reached her waist. She, too, was rail-thin. And he saw something in her hand that he hadn't noticed from the air: a handgun. *Seriously? Another gun?* The Cellerinian government manufactured very few guns. Only select royal guards and some members of the small military used them. The trog's gun, however, was probably a preday relic.

Taima's guards' guns were in Ovrun's pack. Ovrun's eyes shifted to Krey, a question in them. Krey shook his head slightly. Escalating this confrontation wouldn't help their cause.

"Why do you come to our city?" the woman asked.

They'd agreed Krey would do most of the negotiating. "Please lay down your weapons. We aren't armed."

With a curt nod, the woman laid her gun in the street. Her companion did the same with his bow.

Krey got right to the point. "We know there's a militia a few blocks from here. We also know some of your people have been helping them."

The woman crossed her arms. "*Your people*, he says. New-city folk think all trogs are the same. Six clans live in Deroga. All different."

Six clans, huh? "I'm aware of that," Krey said. "I assume your clan is the one helping, since the warehouse is so close." He received no response except hostile stares. "I came here to ask why you're helping them. Do you really like new-city folk living here? You like their messengers and supply wagons traveling your streets? Why do you help them?"

"We owe you no answer," the woman said.

"Listen, tell me honestly that you love having them as neighbors, and we'll leave."

The trogs watched him wordlessly.

"That's what I thought," Krey said. "I know you don't want to disclose any secrets, so let's keep this theoretical. If trogs were to work with new-city folk who invaded their territory, why would they do it?"

There was a long pause before the woman said, "New-city folk could promise food. Supplies." Her chin rose, and even in the dim light, Krey could see the anger in her eyes. "Maybe they promise to use one small building. Maybe trogs take their deal. But new-city folk take a big building. They fill it with many people and a dragon. They tell trogs not to get close, or the dragon might hurt them. When trogs say deal is dead, maybe new-city folk say they have soldiers.

Maybe they give trogs a little food and many threats, and trogs let them stay."

Krey could see the effort she was putting into keeping her shoulders square and her jaw tight. She was determined not to appear defeated, but her words told a different truth. He responded gently. "Let's say all that was true. Would that little bit of food be enough to convince trogs to help? Would they give new-city folk safe passage and even guard the big building?" He could almost feel the arrows that had flown by him the first time he visited.

The woman continued to glare. Next to her, the archer blurted, "They make my cousin mind sick! I want none of their food!"

Krey blinked. "Is your cousin a brain eater?"

The archer's mouth remained closed, but the woman demanded, "How do you know about brain eaters? That is a trog secret!"

Krey's eyebrows rose. "The trogs aren't the only ones who've discovered it. But very few people know about it."

"You know," the woman said. "New-city people in that building know. Who else knows?"

"Good question," Krey muttered.

"I'd never heard of brain lysting until a couple of days ago," Nora said. "But we know there's a brain lyster at the warehouse. Is it your cousin?"

The archer didn't answer, and Krey's chest churned with anger. Zeisha was a few blocks away, and at this rate, their conversation would last until spring. He'd been patient, but damn it, he had his limits. "Let me get to the point," he snapped. "We're doing everything we can to stop the militia. If you help us, we're more likely to succeed. And if you're willing to help us, you have to be honest with us. No more of this *maybe* stuff. If you want these people out of your territory, start talking."

The silence dragged on even longer than before. Finally, Krey said, "Fine. We'll do it ourselves."

"Wait," the woman said, her voice commanding. When Krey returned his attention to her, she said, "Come inside. We will talk."

They entered the same building the woman had exited. She took them to sit at a large trestle table. The archer got cups of water for all of them.

When they were settled, Krey asked the archer, "Does your brain-eater cousin live at the warehouse?"

"No. He works there for a short time. Three moons ago, he stops."

"Why did he stop?" Nora asked.

The archer folded his arms. "First, I will tell you why he starts. One day, the new-city king comes here. Someone tells him we have a brain eater. The king says he needs my cousin to help him. He offers food and money. My cousin says yes. He goes to the big building. He is gone for more than one moon. Then he comes home."

Nora turned to Krey and Ovrun. "His cousin was there for over a month, and he came home three months ago. That lines up with the king's two-hundredth anniversary tour."

Krey nodded. The king must've needed to share his magic with both the trog and The Overseer for it to last long enough until he could visit again. But why had the trog magic eater gone home? Wouldn't it be better to have two mind controllers rather than one? He returned his attention to the archer. "Why did your cousin stop working there?"

The archer blinked rapidly, and a tear escaped one eye. "I tell you, he is mind sick. They say he is too sick to help them."

"What do you mean by *mind sick*?" Nora asked softly.

"My cousin is young when he finds his brain magic. He uses it one time. We trogs know this magic. It is dangerous. A terrible power. His mother never lets him use it again. But when the king asks for help, my cousin says yes. In that building, he eats brain every day. So much, it steals his mind. The king comes back. He sends my cousin home." The archer made a motion with his hands around his head, like his wiggling fingers were muddling up his brain. "His words are jumbled. He forgets his own name. He punches people. Every day, he gets worse."

Krey released a sigh. The poor guy. "Did he tell you what he did in the big building?"

The archer started crying harder, so the woman spoke for him. "When he first comes home, he can talk a little. He tells us he lives in the big building with a woman brain eater. She controls all the soldiers. She teaches him. He helps her." The woman pointed straight at Krey, eyes blazing. "And your king is the boss of it all! He gives his power to our trog and the other woman. With his power, they control the soldiers. How can we fight a king who is so strong? Strong enough to share his evil magic with others? We cannot. So we let the soldiers stay here. Some trogs even help them."

"Would you fight them if you could?" Krey asked.

The woman nodded firmly, and the archer replied, "Hell yes."

Compared to normal trog speech, the slang phrase seemed out of place. Krey cleared his throat, suppressing a chuckle. "Then help us," he said. "We will do everything we can to give your city back to you." He gave in and grinned. "We even have a dragon."

"So do they," the woman said.

Krey leaned across the table, locking the woman's gaze in his own. "Their dragon is only cooperating because they captured and threatened his mate. We freed her. She's the one flying above us right now. We'll free the dragon at the warehouse, and he'll help us."

"How do you know this?" the woman demanded.

Krey licked his lips, then pressed them together, unsure whether he should answer the question.

Nora made the decision for him. "We know because I can talk to dragons."

The woman's eyebrows shot up, but she quickly recovered. She stood and gazed at her three guests. "We will fight with you. When?"

Krey stood. "Today."

35

We used to play a game called How. We kids would think of a preday item and ask our parents as many questions about it as we could, until we came up with a question they couldn't answer.

"Beverage maker!" one of us would shout.

Then the questions began. How did it work? How was it made? How were those components made? How much did it cost? How did you buy one? How were they stored before they were sold? How were they disposed of?

Our parents' answers were filled with words that had little meaning in our world: circuits, warehouses, solar energy, digital currency, recycling. Eventually, we stumped them with our questions, but not before their answers thoroughly confused us.

It seems to me that preday convenience was impossibly complicated.

-The First Generation: A Memoir *by Liri Abrios*

THANK the stone for winter's late sunrises. The early-morning sky was still dark, hiding Krey and the dragon he was riding.

Krey held onto Taima's textured skin with fingers that were already sore from their previous flights—especially his right hand, which was still sensitive even after their visit to the healer. *So help me, if dragon riding becomes a regular thing, somebody's gotta come up with a good saddle.* He started imagining what a saddle for such a massive beast might look like. Then they took a sharp turn, and all rational thought escaped his mind.

"Please be careful," he gasped. "I almost fell just now."

The dragon's massive head turned, and moonlight reflected off one of her faceted eyes. At that moment, he was glad he couldn't hear her thoughts. She probably despised carrying this whiny human on her regal back.

Well, I'm not any more thrilled about it than you are, you over-grown reptid.

Krey, Nora, and Ovrun had agreed that someone should ride on Taima's back to survey the area. Taima could then pass on any pertinent information to both Osmius and Nora on the ground.

Krey had nominated Ovrun for the dragon ride. Ovrun had refused, saying that if something unexpected came up, he wanted to defend them all. Even with a sore arm, he was still the best fighter. Krey had taken the assignment with more than a few muttered curses. He'd have preferred to fly on his own, but he needed to conserve his fuel.

He looked down and squinted, trying to see Nora, Ovrun, and the trogs. They were supposed to be hiding in various spots near the militia warehouse. Between the elevation and the dark sky, he couldn't see anything. He had to trust they were all in their places, ready to proceed with the plan.

Any minute now, the female trog they'd negotiated with would approach the warehouse office and demand to speak with the people in charge. Hopefully, her distraction would delay any planned patrols so that Taima could rescue Osmius. Taima still had mushu leaves in her claws, and Krey's backpack contained all the leaves he'd gathered. The female dragon wouldn't just free her mate; she'd restore his fire.

If the trog leader occupied the militia leaders long enough, the dragons would use the opportunity to burn a hole in the metal building, creating an entrance for Krey and the others. Maybe, if everything went perfectly, they'd rescue the sleeping lysters and bring down The Overseer before any of the militia leaders even knew they were under attack.

A light caught Krey's eye. Someone had just stepped out of the office. The person walked into the massive bay where Osmius was imprisoned.

"That's probably Cage," Krey told Taima. "He's their dragon speaker. Tell Nora to tell the trog leader not to approach until Cage goes back inside." He continued to ramble, finding it distracted him from his panic. "Osmius might've told you this, but Cage kept him in line by threatening to hurt you. So, you know, he's a real great guy. He—" His words were cut off by Taima's huge wing, which had bent in a way he wouldn't have dreamed possible, curving up to slap him on the backside.

"What was that?" he asked, his voice an octave higher than usual. Taima repeated the gesture, and Krey took the hint and shut up. Likely, she was communicating with her mate and couldn't hear past the talkative teenager on her back. He continued to scan the street.

With no warning, Taima dove at such a steep angle, Krey's boots lost their grip on her skin, and his whole body lifted. He couldn't help it; he screamed. Sweat broke out on his palms and fingers. His grip slipped.

Just as he let go of the dragon's skin and felt the wind shove him into the open air, his addled brain remembered a glorious truth. *I can fly too.* Just half an hour ago, he'd fueled up with feathers and ice, all provided by the trogs. "God!" he gasped, a one-word plea, as he plummeted and tried to turn on his magic.

His talent responded, lifting him high into the sky. His first instinct was to fly far away from this insane, diving dragon and the havoc she seemed intent on wreaking, but he brought his focus back to who was waiting below. *Zeisha.* He had to convince Taima to stick to the plan. He went into a steep dive, just as the dragon had done. Taima had landed in the street, and he touched down next to her head.

"We have to get back in the air," Krey hissed. "If anyone sees you, you'll mess up our whole plan."

Taima didn't even look at him. Her face was pointed straight at her mate's prison cell. Krey continued to whisper to her, begging her to leave.

Cage exited the prison bay. When he saw Taima, he flinched, yelped, and dropped his lantern.

A thought flitted through Krey's mind: *Good thing the lantern oil didn't catch on fire.* Then the entire street lit up as Taima breathed pure-white fire on the man who'd manipulated her imprisoned mate.

"No!" Krey cried, but he could barely hear his own voice over Cage's screams. Taima's fire did not abate. The man fell to his knees. At last, his agonized cries ceased. Taima stepped forward and continued her fiery onslaught, consuming the dragon speaker's clothes, body, and broken lantern. When she stopped, Cage was nothing more than a pile of smoldering, black, unidentifiable matter.

Taima ran toward the bay where Osmius was being kept. Krey watched her, his mouth open. She shoved her mushu leaves into the space, then stepped forward as far as she could. Blinding, white light shone from the huge room. Taima was melting her mate's thick chains, a task that might take several minutes.

Suddenly, it struck Krey that he was standing all alone in the middle of the road. He shot up into the air, then realized he still had a backpack full of mushu leaves. He zoomed back down and threw the whole bag into the big bay, hoping it didn't get caught in the line of Taima's fire.

Everything was quiet. Krey circled over the street. As the minutes passed, he found himself wondering if somehow Cage's screams had gone unnoticed.

Then a loud, grating noise filled the air. Narrow bands of light appeared at the bottoms of the four massive bay doors to the left of the dragon prison chamber. The strips of light grew larger as the tall doors slowly rose.

Another movement caught Krey's eye. Taima was returning to the street, followed by Osmius. Shackles remained on his back legs, but the chains were broken.

The grinding noise of the doors opening was joined by the earsplitting *cracks* of two sets of dragon wings unfurling. Both dragons joined Krey in the air, just as the four bay doors stopped moving.

Lines of people, all carrying lanterns, exited the bays. They positioned themselves in the street, still as statues. They all wore tight shirts and pants made of gray fabric. Krey quickly counted them. *Thirty-five.*

In unison, all the militia members moved. Some began to jog, still carrying their lanterns. Others stayed in place and shot fire, ice, stones, and vines into the sky, all aimed at the dragons and the human hovering above them.

Krey and both dragons flew higher. The magic eaters below intensified their attacks. They were all young, but they were shockingly powerful. Their stones and ice were like bullets; their fire was unremitting; their vines just kept coming. *I guess that's what happens when you're forced to practice nonstop for months, and you have no fear.*

When Krey was out of the line of fire, he leveled off and hovered high in the air. His eyes followed a vine that was still rising. The person shooting it appeared to be male. Krey's gaze shifted to another vine, thick and strong, that was falling back to the ground. He tracked it to its source. He couldn't see the facial features of the person wielding such magic, but there was enough lantern light for him to make out one detail: a wild mass of shiny, black curls.

Zeisha.

Krey's entire body surged with energy. Desperate to reach Zeisha, he went into a steep dive. He'd pick her up and carry her far away, out of The Overseer's mental range.

He only made it a few mets before Osmius flew directly beneath him, catching Krey on his broad back. Krey screamed in frustration, but the shock of being picked up in such a way also forced his mind back to a logical track.

If he picked up Zeisha, she might kill him. He was willing to die for her, but if she was still imprisoned, it would be a meaningless sacrifice. He and his allies had to stick with the heart of their original plan: *Find The Overseer. Disable her or kill her so the magic eaters can escape.*

Osmius flapped his wings and made a gentle turn. He and Taima both landed on a tall roof. Krey dismounted. As he refueled with feathers, he took in the scene below.

The bay doors were closed. The militia members who'd started running had now taken positions around the entire warehouse. As Krey watched, a feather eater collected three comrades and carried them, one under each arm and one on his back, to the roof. He set them down, and all the soldiers went still.

Thirty-five skilled magic eaters surrounded the building Krey needed to enter. He had no doubt they would all protect their Overseer with their lives.

Nora didn't even want to speak to Taima. Now was no time to hold a grudge, of course, but it was hard not to. The trog leader was supposed to create a perfect distraction so they could carry out their entire plan undetected.

Too late for that, she thought. *What are we supposed to do now?*

Nora, Ovrun, and four trogs were hiding between two buildings, half a block from the warehouse. She peeked out from behind a corner, wishing she could see more from this distance.

Osmius spoke into Nora's mind. *Thirty-five magic eaters are guarding every side of the building, including four on the roof. They attacked us with magic, but we are safe, including Krey and Taima. We are on the tall roof you waited on earlier.* He paused, then added, *Nora-human, you freed my mate. Thank you.* It was at least the fifth time he'd thanked her.

We need to figure out what's next, Nora said.

The militia will attack if we approach.

Nora took a deep breath and turned to Ovrun. "There are four lysters on the roof. The others are around the building, waiting. What do we do next?"

"We have to get to The Overseer. The only way to do that is to fight."

Nora nodded. She didn't like the answer, but she'd known it was coming. Their newly allied force included seven lysters: her, Krey, and five trogs. That didn't sound great compared to three dozen members of a lyster militia. However, Nora's force also included forty non-magical trogs who were ready to fight, plus two dragons.

All they had to do was get inside the building and incapacitate The Overseer—a woman who could control them if she touched them. And as they fought their way in, they had to protect the very people they were fighting. The goal was to save the militia members, not kill them.

This would not be easy.

Her eyes took in the trogs, who all wore black shirts. Were they trustworthy? They wanted to protect their territory, but if things got bad, would they slink back to their hiding places? Or would they run to get their bows so they could kill everyone?

All the unknowns dug into her mind, shredding her confidence. This wasn't a game. Moments from now, she'd be risking her life. And despite the difficulties of the last few weeks—eating too much shimshim meat, sleeping on a hard warehouse floor, and learning the truth about her father—she treasured her life in a way she never had before.

She'd met Krey, a friend who made her laugh. Sure, he had a tendency to blow his top, and he'd probably never trust her family, but he trusted *her*. Did he have any idea how much that meant to her?

Then there was Ovrun, the guy who was sweeter than anyone she'd ever spent time with, whose ridiculous physique distracted her even at a time like this. Despite their hopeless future, he made her feel adored in a way no one ever had before.

She blinked against tears that wanted to fall, then took Ovrun's hand. When he looked at her, she beckoned him to bend down. He did, and she whispered in his ear, "I don't want to die."

Despite the four trogs with them, he used his good arm to pull her into a tight hug. She knew he meant it to comfort her, but all she could think was, *Oh, those muscles.* As ridiculous as the thought was at a time like this, desire provided its own brand of comfort.

"I will do absolutely anything I can to keep you alive," His breath was warm on her ear. "I'm scared too, Nora. But we're fighting for something worthwhile. We got this."

"We've got this," she whispered back, half-believing it. On a whim, she added, "A kiss before we go?"

He pulled away, grinning. "Not 'til we get out of this alive."

She shook her head, but she was smiling too. If he was trying to motivate her, it worked. She forced her smile to flee, took a deep breath, and addressed her little group with a voice that sounded more confident than she felt. "It's time to fight."

Ovrun held his fingers to his mouth and let out a loud whistle. That was the sign for everyone to come out of hiding. He ran into the street, followed by Nora and the others.

Ahead, the soldiers let out a shout, all at the same pitch, at precisely the same time. It was eerie, far more frightening than if they'd screamed out threats.

The mind-controlled militia set down their lanterns and waited for their attackers.

36

My parents always told me I should only use my magic for good. But I loved creeping up to the door of my brother's room with a branch in my hand and making it grow long enough to tickle his ear. It didn't matter how often I did it; he jumped every time.

-The First Generation: A Memoir *by Liri Abrios*

———

WHEN KREY HEARD Ovrun's whistle, he soared into the sky, determined to neutralize a couple of militia members before anyone spotted him. The dragons, too, flew off the roof. They had their own plan for assisting in the battle.

Krey halted above the warehouse roof and shot a ball of ice from each hand. One met its mark, hitting a young man in the head hard enough to send him to his knees. The other glanced off a female lyster's shoulder. She cried out and pointed at Krey.

So much for stealth. Militia members on the roof and the ground raised their eyes toward him. He flew evasively, continuing to shoot ice. But there was too much magic coming his way: ice, fire, and—*oh God, no!* Vines advanced toward him, formed by two hands he knew as well as his own.

He pushed himself higher, screaming, "Zeisha! It's me!"

Her eyes were blank as she accelerated her vine's growth. The end of it slapped Krey's ankle, then fell back to the ground. If he'd been a few simmets lower, the thing would've wrapped around him. He had no doubt it was strong enough to bring him down.

Shaking and breathless, he flew out of reach. Zeisha had always been talented—but now she was stunning. And terrifying.

On the ground, lanterns cast flickering light on a fierce battle. Krey watched as a vine shot out of Zeisha's hand. It wrapped around the neck of a black-clad trog. Zeisha pulled the vine taut, and a young woman next to her knelt to touch the ground. The dirt beneath the choking trog trembled and cracked. It rose up into a large, loose mound of cloudy, quivering dust. Zeisha's vine detached from her hand. The dirt swallowed the vine and the trog, then settled back to its smooth, hard-packed state. All that was left was a mound, like a freshly filled grave.

Krey blinked, trying to see through tears that had invaded his eyes. He'd found Zeisha, but she was still so very lost. He forced himself to pull his gaze away from her. If they were to win this battle, he had to play his part. That meant helping Osmius.

As if on cue, the great, gray dragon dove toward the battle. A frost eater sent spheres of ice toward him. Osmius vaporized the ice with one huff of white flame. Krey held his breath as the winged beast targeted an isolated militia member near the edge of the fighting. He grabbed the young woman and returned to the air.

Krey's breath escaped in a victorious laugh. *One less mind-controlled magic eater for us to worry about.* He spun around and followed the dragon to the rooftop.

Osmius held the struggling soldier in the claws of his massive back feet. Krey tied the woman's wrists and ankles with rope provided by the trogs. It wasn't an easy job with the way she was fighting back. "You'll thank me for this later," he muttered as he tightened the last knot.

Only when the militia member was fully restrained did Osmius release her. The young woman bared her teeth at Krey, revealing bits of brown in them. *A dirt eater.* She would've gladly created a chasm to swallow them all up, if only they were on the ground instead of the roof.

Osmius flew off, and Taima soon arrived, her claws gripping a young man's torso and arms. As soon as the new captive saw Krey, he started shooting balls of ice. Krey sighed. *Can't tie those hands if they're making ice.* He hooked his elbow around the magic eater's throat, cutting off his airflow.

The second the frost eater passed out, Krey let go. He bound the magic eater and used a strip of the young man's shirt as a gag. Frost eaters didn't usually exhale anything but snow, as it was painful to send ice through the throat's soft tissues. With a mind-controlled magic eater, however, Krey wasn't taking any chances.

Taima left. Krey put a few feathers in his mouth. Shivering and chewing, he considered what he'd seen below. The militia members were horrifyingly strong. And supposedly The Overseer was controlling every one of them.

She shouldn't be able to control more than one or two people at a time. Apparently her inconceivable power came from the king, but that didn't make sense. There was no precedent for the sheer quantity of magic The Overseer was using, nor for the king's ability to share his strength with her.

Krey massaged his temples, trying to rid himself of such fruitless confusion. He didn't have to understand Ulmin's dark magic to fight against it. He fixed his eyes on the sky, waiting for Osmius to return with another captive. *The militia is strong, but we'll take them out. One soldier at a time.*

Nora followed Ovrun into the fray. He was big but quick, and he successfully dodged a stream of fire before diving low and taking the militia member down.

Another lyster, a young man, sprinted toward Nora. The calm coldness in his gaze scared her more than his muscular body. He shot small rock pellets out of his palms, one after another. Nora had never seen a stone lyster catalyze his fuel at such a speed. In the time it took her to lift her hand, several rocks hit her neck and face. She shot a large ice sphere at him. It hit him in the chest, making him stumble. A trog took advantage of the stone lyster's distraction to tackle him.

Nora turned away, looking for someone else to attack. Their goal was to get into the building and find The Overseer, but the mind-controlled soldiers wouldn't let anyone get close to the warehouse.

Ahead, Nora saw Ovrun with his arm around a struggling lyster's neck. The young woman fought his chokehold with all her might, and when her fist connected with his left tricep, where he'd been shot, he roared in pain. Even through that, he remained light on his feet, spinning around to keep tabs on his surroundings. When the woman collapsed, Ovrun dropped her and ran ahead.

All trogs were taught to fight, and from what Nora could see in the flickering, yellow light, they were doing pretty well. Her own combat skills left much to be desired, so she stood back, looking for someone small that she might have a hope of taking down.

There. A thin, petite girl, about Nora's age, was shifting the dirt under two trogs, who struggled to stay on their feet. Nora rushed toward the girl from behind. The trogs had just started sinking into the ground when Nora tackled the girl, halting her magic.

Nora tried to get her arm around the girl's neck, like Ovrun had just done to the other soldier, but the girl bucked, her sharp elbows coming up to strike Nora repeatedly. A second later, the girl somehow flipped Nora over, pinning her down with two bony knees. The girl grabbed Nora's neck and squeezed.

Nora opened her mouth to scream, but nothing came out. She

tried to suck in air. It was impossible. *She's killing me she's killing me she's killing me!*

Suddenly, the wiry girl seemed to fly off Nora, who sat up, coughing and gasping, clutching at her bruised neck. She spied Ovrun tackling the militia member and grabbing her throat. The girl's eyes soon went blank, but Ovrun kept squeezing.

"Hey!" Nora tried to scream the word, but it came out as a hoarse croak. She grabbed Ovrun's arm.

He cried out—it was his bad arm. But it got his attention. He looked up at Nora, then let go of the girl, his eyes wide. "Thanks," he said, shaking his head as if to rid himself of his fury. His eyes flashed back and forth, taking in the battle. The trogs and soldiers in their immediate vicinity were engaged in their own fights. His attention returned to Nora, and his hand rested lightly on her throat. "You okay?"

She nodded and coughed again. "Yeah."

He surveyed the area and ran off to help a trog whose impressive speed and flexibility were barely keeping him away from a bombardment of magical fire.

Nora looked for someone else she could incapacitate. The unmistakable flap of dragon wings sounded overhead. Osmius was diving down.

Then something slammed into Nora from behind, so hard that it knocked the wind out of her before she even reached the ground. Pinned down, she felt her arms wrenched behind her. For a second, she panicked, and then her desire to live took over. The militia member had her arms, not her hands. She shot a ball of ice straight up. It connected with a *crack*. She shot another and another.

The weight on her back disappeared. She scrambled to her feet, expecting to see that Ovrun or a trog had rescued her. Instead, she was greeted with the sight of a big, male militia member, flying away.

Ovrun ran up to her. "Stay with me!" he shouted.

She gladly complied, but a few seconds later, Osmius spoke to her mind. Following his instructions, she fled from the fighting.

Krey gazed at the sky. Osmius was still circling above the warehouse. What was taking so long? Tapping his foot, Krey scanned the street below. Dawn was on its way, but it was still too dark to see much of the fight on the ground.

The *crack* of dragon wings caught Krey's attention, and he looked up to see Osmius and Taima both flying toward him. Neither of them were carrying militia members. *Why not?* What Krey wouldn't give to be a dragon speaker.

The creatures landed, and Taima used a wing to nudge Krey toward Osmius's back. "Again?" Krey groaned as he climbed up. He secured himself, and Osmius leapt into the air, leaving Krey's stomach back on the roof.

After a short flight, Osmius landed a few dozen meters from the edge of the battle. Nora was waiting there. Krey dismounted, and Osmius stood guard as the two humans spoke.

"What's going on?" Krey asked.

"The militia members know what the dragons are doing. Every time Osmius tried to dive, he got attacked. One of the fire lysters burned a hole in his wing. He and Taima can't keep picking people up."

Krey cursed, then narrowed his eyes. Nora sounded like someone had taken sandpaper to her throat. "Why are you talking like that?"

"I got choked."

"Choked?"

"I'm fine. Listen, you and I have to go back in. We need all the lysters we can get. The trogs are great, but it's hard to fight magic with muscle."

"Let's do it, then." As they ran off, he saw Taima approaching Osmius, who was still on the ground.

"She's bringing him rocks," Nora said.

"Rocks?"

But Nora was too focused on her mission to answer. Krey took her cue and sprinted ahead. As they entered the fight, he leapt over vines, melting ice, and churned-up dirt, the detritus of a magical battle. He also passed several trogs and militia members who were dead or unconscious. He'd hoped that by now, someone would be breaking into the building, but soldiers still guarded all the entrances and the roof. His heart sank.

He spotted a female trog and a male militia member circling each other. The man was an ash eater, but his flames were coming in short spurts. He must be nearly out of fuel. Krey blew thick snow directly at the man's hands, rendering his small amount of fire useless. The trog tackled the ash eater, and Krey held the man's hands down while the woman rendered him unconscious with a swift kick to the head. Krey grimaced. *That's gonna hurt.*

Krey had feared he would panic during the battle. Instead, a strange calm flooded into his mind and body. He heard, saw, even smelled militia members as they were about to attack. Magic at the ready, he used his talents with greater efficiency than ever.

He knocked out a male vine eater with a well-aimed ball of ice. A kick to the groin disabled a stone eater. Krey left the young man for a trog to take care of. When he saw a dirt eater with her hands to the ground, he flew in, grabbed the woman, and threw her at an ash eater. Both tumbled into the path of waiting trogs.

Krey pivoted and saw that a young woman in gray was in the process of charging him. He couldn't avoid her, but he did shift his weight. When she hit him, it was at an angle. He didn't fall. She grabbed his wrist, and he pulled away. She must've realized she couldn't win the fight, because she ran.

But something felt different. It took Krey half a second to realize what it was. The soldier had taken the pouch of feathers he kept inside his coat sleeve. She must've seen it sticking out. He started to pursue her, but a large, young militia member stepped into his path.

Krey didn't allow himself to dwell on the loss of his fuel. He continued to fight like he'd never known he could do. Many militia members were fighting with only their bodies now, their magic spent.

Even with his feathers gone, Krey still had plenty of magic in him. He hoarded it like a greedy tycoon, only shooting ice or taking to the air when it was absolutely necessary.

Frequently, rocks rained down from above, dropped by dragons who had excellent eyesight and aim. A few errant rocks hit trogs, but generally, the dragons' fly-by stonings seemed to help.

Krey fought through the battleground, ending up on the opposite side of the building from where he'd started. His eyes landed on a young woman. Like all the militia members, she wore plain, gray clothes. They were tight, highlighting her short, hourglass figure. Her hair was in a ponytail, a wild cascade of glossy, black curls.

Zeisha.

She was turning around, evaluating her surroundings, looking for someone to attack. In the orange-gray light of early dawn, she looked more achingly beautiful than ever. Krey's senses unhooked themselves from the world around him, honing in on her soft skin, shining with sweat and effort; her lips, parted to draw in breath; her—

Someone hit him from behind with the force of a bag of bricks, knocking him down. His face hit the dirt. Teeth cut the inside of his mouth, and metallic blood coated his tongue.

The taste of it brought Krey back to the battle. With a grunt of physical and magical effort, he pushed himself into the air, incorporating his attacker into his magic. As always, he felt an instant, shocking connection to the body now flying with him. It was a man, all corded muscles and well-trained limbs, smaller than Ovrun, but even stronger.

The man didn't panic or make noise as they rose into the air. He wrapped his legs around Krey's waist, locking his ankles together. Krey shouted in pain as the militia member squeezed his strong thighs around Krey's middle.

One bulky arm circled Krey's chest. A hand found Krey's neck and squeezed.

Unable to breathe, Krey halted his upward flight and flipped over, facing the sky. The quick movement jolted the man's hand free, but his legs and other arm were still tight.

Krey turned himself vertical. The man was trying to grasp his neck again, but Krey fought him off. The man's thighs tightened further. Groaning, Krey flipped upside down and performed a harrowing corkscrew dive. As the ground approached, he again turned horizontal with his belly to the sky. Moving in jerking motions to detach his stubborn passenger, he spread one of his arms wide, pointed his palm behind him, and threw a block of ice, its edges blunt.

The ice missed. He tried again. This time, he heard the *thud* of a hard solid meeting soft skin. The man's grip loosened. Krey shot another block of ice. Again, it connected hard. Like someone had turned the man's muscles into rolls of soft fabric, his arms and legs slipped off Krey.

Krey flipped to face downward again, horrified to see the man tumbling through the dawn air. Catalyzing feathers like his well was limitless, Krey pursued him, pushing his speed to its limits. He positioned himself below the unconscious man, caught him a dozen mets from the ground, drew him back into his magic, and flew him to the top of a building, well outside the battle zone. Krey returned to the air, and a terrible truth struck him: in two minutes of panic, he'd used most of his flying fuel.

He knew he should land and save his fuel, but now that he'd found Zeisha, rescuing her was all he could think of. If her magic was gone by now, he could overpower her. *Can I even bring myself to do such a thing?*

Then he saw her below him. A vine ran from her hand to the throat of a young, male trog. The man was on the ground, limp. Zeisha pulled the vine even tighter.

Don't! Krey silently begged. Determined not to get distracted like he had before, he scanned the fighters on the ground. His eyes met the cold gaze of a militia member he recognized from earlier in the fight. *Ash eater.* Half a second later, a stream of orange fire pursued Krey. "Damn it!" he shouted, evading the attack.

The ash eater turned his attention elsewhere, and Krey again found Zeisha. He flew back towards her, but his feather magic was fizzling out.

He dropped lower, flying a met or so above the heads of those fighting below, hoping to avoid the attention of the ash eater, who appeared to be one of the few militia members who still had magic.

Krey dipped low enough that his toe nudged someone's head. With effort, he brought himself back up, but it was no use. His magic would be completely gone in seconds. A curse exited his mouth as he made a quick landing.

Krey pushed past fighting trogs and mind-controlled soldiers, trying to reach Zeisha. She was several mets away, her vine still taut around her victim's neck. A young, male trog was charging toward her. Krey ran, determined to get to Zeisha first.

His toe tangled in a vine at his feet. He fell hard but felt no pain. Scrambling up, he watched with horror as the trog approached Zeisha.

"You kill my husband!" the trog screamed. Then he was on top of Zeisha, whose vine at last broke free from her hand, though its other end was still attached to the prone man. The trog attacking Zeisha wasn't big, but he was fueled by grief. He easily overcame the thrashing young vine eater beneath him. He grabbed her throat and squeezed.

Krey sprinted toward them, but two women, grappling viciously, entered his path. He clambered past the fighting women. Two balls of ice left Krey's hands, slamming into the head of Zeisha's attacker. The trog tumbled off her.

Zeisha leapt to her feet and turned toward Krey. Her eyes, so beautiful yet so lacking in vitality, met his. Before he reached her, her hand snapped up. A vine shot out, wrapping tight around his neck.

Once again, he couldn't breathe. Eyes bulging, he grasped the vine, but it was too thick to break. He sent balls of ice toward his beloved's legs, but she didn't even flinch when the cold weapons slammed into her knees. Then Krey couldn't even use his ice magic anymore. All his body could do was attempt to draw air into his starved lungs. Blackness crept into his vision. *No, it can't end like this!*

Suddenly, the vine loosened. It fell to the ground at the same time Krey did. His knees and one hand struck the dirt hard. His other hand grasped his neck. He gasped and coughed violently. When a bit of his reasoning returned, he looked up to see what had happened to Zeisha.

Someone was standing between him and the girl he loved. His eyes traveled past expensive boots; up long legs clad in tight, gray pants; to a long dagger in a sheath at her waist. At last, his gaze landed on her face. She had sharp, beautiful features; smooth, brown skin that spoke of an age no older than his; and long, straight hair.

"I've been watching this battle," she said. "Watching you. I have bigger plans for you than death by vine."

Krey coughed and tried to speak. Nothing came out of his bruised throat. He didn't even have the strength to stand. All he could hope was that someone from his team would rescue him.

Suddenly, it occurred to him that, while he could hear fighting in the distance, everyone around him was still. Trogs and militia members, all facing outward, surrounded him and the woman. It was like they were all part of the same team, guarding the woman and Krey.

Oh no.

The woman grinned, white teeth shining, and placed her right hand on Krey's head.

Pain gripped his brain, twisting and stabbing, like nothing he'd ever felt.

As quickly as it had begun, the pain disappeared. Every thought that had been racing through Krey's mind halted.

He stood, still gasping but no longer panicked, and looked into the young woman's pale-brown eyes, waiting for instructions.

37

A trader who visited our town said he could talk to dragons. Not with his mouth, but with his mind. He said some dragons were even his friends.

My parents didn't believe him, but I wanted his tales to be true. He told us about dragons who battled one another for lairs and mates. He described to us the beautiful lands the great creatures discovered on their long flights.

That was decades ago. Still, every time a dragon flies overhead, I send my thoughts to it. I've never gotten an answer.

-The First Generation: A Memoir *by Liri Abrios*

NORA RAN THROUGH THE BATTLE, dodging attacks. Nearby, a militia member was regaining consciousness. As she'd done several times to other gray-clad soldiers, Nora knelt, squeezed his neck with the inside of her elbow, and murmured a quiet apology when he passed out.

She stood and looked around. Many people from both sides were prone, but there were more trogs left than militia members. *We might actually win this thing.*

Above, Osmius and Taima were still dropping rocks on militia members. An idea came to Nora, and she sent a message to both dragons. *Most of the militia is out of magic. I think you should start picking them up again. If you can get me to Krey, I'll tell him you need him again so he can tie—*

Osmius interrupted her, his voice loud and urgent in her mind. *Nora! Run! I will pick you up!*

What?

Get away from the battle!

She obeyed, running down the street and looking over her shoulder to ensure no one was following. A shadow overtook her, and then Osmius landed next to her. *Get on!*

She scrambled onto his back. It wasn't as broad as Taima's, and Nora easily found a secure position. They took to the air. Below, trogs and soldiers still fought on two sides of the battleground, but a couple dozen people were standing in the street, utterly still, arranged in concentric circles. *What's going on down there?* she asked.

We'll talk when we stop. They soon landed on the tall building's roof. Two militia members were tied up there, squirming around. Taima stood on the edge of the roof, overlooking the battle.

Nora dismounted. *Tell me what's happening!*

I saw people with knife wounds, Taima said. *I did not know anyone was fighting with blades.*

Osmius took over the narrative. *The Overseer has arrived. She stabbed at least two of the trogs, but she is bringing most of them under her control by touching their heads.*

What about Krey and Ovrun? Nora asked.

Both controlled by her, Taima replied.

Nora's breath caught, but she didn't allow herself to cry. Under the dawn light of the orange sky, she saw more trogs and militia members turning to join the mind-controlled masses. Three black-clad trogs were fleeing toward the ancient buildings they called home. She couldn't blame them. Before long, the fight ended, everyone having joined the mind-controlled group in the street.

What are we going to do? she asked.

No! The word shot out of Osmius's mind, in a tone saturated with dread and pain. *He comes,* he said. *I feel his mind. I must go, or he will turn me against you.* He leapt off the building.

I shall come with you! Taima cried.

No! Stand back so he can't see you! Osmius commanded in a voice of harsh authority. *Save all the—* His thoughts suddenly ceased.

Please, stay! Nora begged Taima. *We'll free Osmius together!*

Taima puffed smoke from her nose, but she didn't argue. She flew across the roof and hovered just below the back of the building, out of sight of the battle on the other side. As she'd done on this roof before, Nora lay flat. She hadn't asked Osmius who was coming; she didn't need to. It was her father. Clearly he'd already grasped the dragon's mind with his own.

She squinted, trying to catch a glimpse of her father's carriage. Why was he coming? The trogs had said he came once a week. Had he somehow found out that his dragons were missing? Even if that were the case, would he have had time to travel all this way? The orsas that pulled his carriage were fast, but not that fast.

Movement in the sky caught her eye—something smaller than a dragon. A moment later, she identified the familiar sight: a person flying, carrying a passenger. *Orsas aren't that fast, but feather lysters are.* Osmius flew to meet the duo, escorting them toward the ground. As one, the circles of mind-controlled soldiers below took a dozen steps back, creating a large, open space. From her high perch, Nora saw someone with long, black hair in the center. The Overseer.

Osmius landed in the circle, followed by the feather lyster and his passenger.

Taima, we have to go, Nora said.

I will burn them all to save my mate. Taima's beautiful voice held a frightening hardness.

And then the monarchy will hunt you down and kill every dragon they can find, Nora shot back. *Including Osmius! The man that just landed is my father. Let me talk to him. If anyone can stop this, I can.*

Long seconds passed. *Very well,* Taima said at last.

Her heart threatening to sprint out of her chest, Nora scampered to the back of the roof. Taima positioned herself so her back was level with the roof, and Nora mounted her. For the first time, she realized Taima's skin was not pure black. The morning light revealed an amber tinge to it. It was stunning next to her golden wings. *I'm ready,* Nora said.

They took off at a reckless speed and quickly arrived above the battleground. Below, Nora saw her father's gray-streaked, dark-brown hair. He looked up and pointed, and Osmius shot into the air, aimed at Taima, sunlight glinting off his outstretched front claws.

Osmius! Nora cried.

The beast she'd grown to love didn't answer. He flew straight at Taima, who twisted one way, then the other, trying to evade her mate's attack.

Get me closer! Nora cried. *My father will stop this if he knows I'm here!*

Taima attempted to descend, but she had to pull up again to avoid her mate. There was a terrible, ripping sound as a claw tore into Taima's wing. She breathed out a great stream of fire. It hit Osmius, but it didn't harm him. Dragons must be immune to their own fire. Taima continued her frantic flying, trying to evade Osmius's sharp teeth and claws.

Nora screamed. One of her hands slipped. As soon as she got it back into place, the other came loose. But they were descending. Nora regained her grip, the hard, reptid skin digging into the soft flesh of her fingers. She embraced the pain. "Dad!" she screamed, her voice still hoarse. "I'm up here!"

She was close enough now to see his eyes, which widened. She locked her gaze on him alone, searching for compassion in his expression.

"Nora!" King Ulmin called. Half a second later, Osmius halted his attack and glided back to his position on the ground.

"It's me, Dad. Make room. Let her drop me off."

The group once again stepped back in unison, making enough space for the huge female dragon to land.

"Come down, Darling!" Nora's father called. "You don't know what dragons are capable of. They're beasts!"

A single sob burst from Nora's chest. She knew very well what dragons were capable of: fierce pride and loyalty. Yes, there was a beast here. But he was human, not reptid.

She was convinced, however, that her dad had never faked his love for her. He cared for her, but he was addicted—to the disgusting practice of eating the brains of animals, to his power over minds and over his kingdom. If anyone could reach through that addiction to touch the gentle heart within, it was her.

"Wait!" her father cried. "Come back!"

It wasn't until she heard him that she realized Taima had risen higher. *What are you doing?* Nora asked.

I cannot let your father touch me and control me. I shall land outside the circle.

Seconds later, Nora was on the ground, just beyond the standing, silent bodies of trogs and soldiers. Taima returned to the air and circled above. All at once, the people in front of Nora shifted a step, creating an open corridor that led straight to her waiting father.

Her pulse was so frantic, she could feel it in her fingertips. If she walked in between these people, would they attack her? Would they swallow her up and deliver her to her dad so he could control her too?

No. He loves me. He wouldn't control me. She took a deep breath and stepped in the passage. Within seconds, she glimpsed Krey's mop of unruly hair. When she'd nearly reached the center, she found Ovrun. His jaw was squared, his eyes fixed straight ahead. Nora wiped tears off her cheeks and kept walking. Again, she fixed her gaze on her father, ignoring everyone else. What could she say to stop him?

"Sweetheart." Her father held out his hands as she approached.

She halted. "Dad, please don't touch me."

His shoulders fell, and he dropped his hands. "Very well." He stepped back, giving her plenty of space to enter the wide, open area. "I'm so glad to see you. I'm so glad you're safe."

Nora stepped into the circle. Behind her, men and women stepped in unison. She didn't have to look to know that her pathway was now closed.

Her father's expression was full of tenderness and hope. It broke Nora's heart more than cruelty would have. To avoid crying, she pulled her gaze away and sought Osmius. The sight of him—his body fairly bursting with strength, his domed, faceted eyes exuding danger—brought her no comfort. Nora looked away. Next to Osmius sat a middle-aged woman, munching on diced feathers. *Dad's transportation.*

Nora's eyes fell on the only other person in the center of the circle: The Overseer. As soon as her gaze fell on the young woman, Nora stopped breathing.

Like every member of her militia, The Overseer wore tight, gray clothes. Her black hair was long and glossy, framing a lovely face. She was even taller than Nora. For years, the princess had envied that height.

"Faylie," Nora whispered.

As soon as the word left her mouth, she started weeping. Her instincts had been right; her friend was part of the militia. The most important part. Faylie had been sitting inside that building, telling the militia to attack Nora, Krey, Ovrun, and a host of innocent trogs. *How could she?*

Faylie met Nora's gaze, and in her cold eyes, Nora saw the truth: The Overseer was just as controlled as her soldiers were.

At last, Nora returned her attention to her father. "Dad," she whispered. She had so many questions, and she didn't know where to start. How was Faylie controlling so many soldiers? The trogs said her strength came from the king. But surely an occasional meal of brain matter couldn't give him such power. None of this made sense. Magic wasn't supposed to work this way.

As much as she wanted to understand her father's dark magic, another question hammered in Nora's heart. It was the oldest of questions, the one she'd seen written over and over on the suburban chapel. She had to ask it. "Why?"

"Oh, sweetie." Her father sighed deeply and started to reach out for her but pulled his hand back. "I wish you could have a couple more years to enjoy childhood before you face the harsh reality of ruling."

"I'm seventeen. I'm not a child." But her voice was soft, and at that moment, she felt very much like a child.

"You can't fault me for wanting you to stay young."

She forced another question out: "Why Faylie?"

"She's so talented, Nora. And so strong, nearly as strong as I am. She is finally living up to her potential. In return, I'm taking care of her mother; I've given her luxury she's never dreamed of."

A sob burst from Nora's mouth. Her real father, the man he'd been before his wife was murdered, would never think money could make up for stealing someone's child. Nora brought herself under control by a force of pure will. "This is not the way to make peace with New Therro."

His eyebrows twitched, and she knew her knowledge had surprised him. He recovered almost immediately. "New Therro isn't interested in peace."

"How do you know that if you won't negotiate with them?"

"Nora, protection officers have prevented six New Therroan terrorist attacks in the past two years."

Now she was the one caught by surprise. Six? For a moment, she was horrified. Then a worm of doubt wriggled through her mind. The Office of Kingdom Protection was competent, but they weren't perfect. If they'd prevented six attacks, wouldn't they have missed one or two? Yet Nora had never heard of any New Therroan terrorist attacks. Sure, there had been mild violence at some protests, but nothing that seemed premeditated.

She kept her thoughts to herself. Time to try another tack. "Dad, no matter how just the cause, this is wrong. You know it is." She gestured at the silent men and women all around them. "Every person here deserves to own their own mind. Even the dragon deserves to be free!"

"Nora, what is our purpose as lysters?" His voice was gentle.

Again feeling like a little girl, she repeated words she'd learned over a decade ago, back when she used to go to chapel services with her parents. "To serve God and others with our magical faculties."

"What are these people doing, if not serving?"

"Slavery isn't service!"

Her father shook his head. "Please, try to understand."

He continued talking, but Taima's voice penetrated Nora's mind. *Conversation is not the answer. I will free Osmius, if I must burn every person here to do it. Tell him to release my mate's mind, or fire will rain on you all.*

"Dad!" Nora's hoarse shout brought his calm speech to a halt. "The dragon above us will kill us if you don't release her mate!"

One of his eyebrows lifted in an aristocratic arch. "And you know that how, dear?"

Nora thrust a pointing hand into the sky. "Because she just told me!"

He blinked, and something ugly crossed his face. Jealousy, perhaps, or greed. "You're a dragon speaker," he whispered.

Tell him my fire will hit him first! Taima bellowed in Nora's mind. *Once he is gone, they will all be free!*

"No!" Nora screamed. Without thought, she ran to her father and threw her arms around him. "Daddy, she says she'll kill you first! Please, let the dragon go!"

"Down!" the king shouted. At once, the serene scene exploded into action. Ulmin threw himself into a crouch, pulling Nora down with him. Bodies piled on top of her and her father. Panicked in a crush of sweaty humans, Nora screamed.

"Shh," her father said. "They're protecting us."

Of course—they weren't attacking her. They were a human shield. "Dad, no!" she shouted. "Just let the dragon go! Please, let them all go!"

The weight atop her lifted as the crowd shifted just enough to partially uncover her and her father. "Look in the sky, Nora," her father said softly.

Above, tiny prisms reflected off both dragons as they fought with horrifying ferocity. Taima attempted to defend herself, but she clearly didn't want to hurt Osmius. Nora sobbed as she watched Osmius's teeth and claws tear into his mate's side, her stubby tail, her wings.

"I can't stay here with that dragon so near," Nora's father whispered in her ear.

The crowd shifted again, creating a small circle around the king. "Up!" he barked at his feather lyster. The woman leapt to her feet. King Ulmin, however, didn't immediately get on her back. He hurried to Faylie and whispered in her ear. They both looked at Nora. Their expressions couldn't have been more different: a cruel smile on The Overseer, naked sorrow on the king.

"Goodbye, sweetheart," Nora's father murmured. He leapt on the feather lyster's back. They took to the air and were out of sight in seconds, flying low between the city's tightly spaced buildings.

Nora returned her attention to the air. Taima was, at the moment, evading her mate. How long would it be before Osmius regained his own mind?

"Princess Ulminora." Sarcasm saturated Faylie's greeting.

Nora turned. "Faylie, I know you remember me. Let these people go. Please. My father's gone now. I'll protect you."

A laugh, free of any true humor, burst from Faylie's mouth. "I don't need protection."

"This can't be the life you want. You had dreams, Faylie. You wanted to be a teacher. Don't you remember?"

Her old friend's gaze swept over her soldiers. "If you don't understand the appeal of this, Princess, you don't deserve to rule." Her eyes flicked upward, and her lips pressed together in a frown.

The mind-controlled crowd again moved as one, tightening the circle around their leader and Nora. A few seconds later, two people grabbed Nora's arms with hands as strong as steel. Nora turned to see a large, male trog holding her on the right. She shifted her gaze to the other side and let out a mournful yelp. Ovrun was the one holding her left arm with an inescapable grip. His eyes were blank, his jaw tight.

Nora felt herself lifted until her toes hung above the dirt. Her captors moved her forward and set her down in front of Faylie, so close that her former friend's warm breath ruffled Nora's hair. Ovrun and the trog retained their grips on Nora's arms. The rest of the mind-controlled crowd stepped forward yet again, pressing in on all sides.

Nora tried unsuccessfully to control her breathing. "What are you doing?"

Faylie lifted her chin, looking into the sky. "Your dragon friends are circling above, both in their right minds. Despite the female's threats, I don't think they'll attack when you're right next to me and we're surrounded by innocents."

What can we do, Nora-human? Osmius asked.

Nothing, she replied. Aloud, she said, "Please, Faylie. I know you don't want to hurt me."

Faylie's face broke into an amused grin. "I'm not going to hurt you. I'm going to induct you into the militia. Just like your father told me to do before he left." Seeing the horror on Nora's face, she chuckled. "It's not like he can let you escape to tell the world our secret. And he really doesn't want to kill you. This is literally the only safe place in the world for you right now."

Disbelief and fury swirled in Nora's mind. She kicked her right foot hard, connecting with The Overseer's shin.

Faylie gasped, and her skin flushed with pain. Hands grabbed Nora's legs, holding them in place. "When I take your will," Faylie hissed, "it will only hurt for a moment. But after what you just did, I want you to hurt more than that. So, you get to remain free for a little longer. Lucky you." She drew a sharp dagger. Its razor edge was coated in drying blood.

Hands—how many, Nora didn't know, but it felt like at least eight—grabbed her hair, head, ears, and neck. They yanked her head back as far as it would go. "Ovrun, please!" she screamed.

Laughing, Faylie leaned over Nora, meeting her gaze. She rested the tip of the dagger on Nora's right cheek, under her eye and next to her nose. "I remember Ovrun. You always did like him. I was watching the battle from the windows; I saw him protecting you. He couldn't care less about you now."

Nora sobbed uncontrollably as Faylie pressed the dagger point against her skin. "No! Please! This isn't you!"

The blade entered her skin, and Faylie drew it slowly across Nora's cheek. The pain was unlike anything she'd ever felt, far surpassing the ankle she'd broken when she'd fallen off Blue, or the terrible headaches she got when she was sick. Her mouth dropped open, and she screamed. The dagger continued its leisurely journey across her face, releasing rivers of thick blood onto her cheek.

Ice.

The word, spoken in a deep, fiery voice, entered Nora's mind. She realized Osmius had been talking to her, perhaps since the dagger first penetrated her skin, but she'd blocked out everything except her pain.

Now, as the blade passed under the center of her eye, the dragon's voice broke through again. *Ice, Nora-human.*

Hands! The single thought was all she could manage. She couldn't shoot ice; her hands were pressed against her legs. She couldn't budge them a simmet.

Mouth! Osmius replied.

Nora's mouth was still open, her desperate screams the only sounds in the still street. Confusion joined her agony. Did Osmius want her to be quiet? Then it hit her. She could send ice out of her mouth. A cold weapon, directed at the cold lyster in front of her.

Nora-human, Osmius said, *you must kill The Overseer in order to release the prisoners.*

No! She's my friend!

You must!

Emptied of empathy, Faylie continued to carve. Nora could no longer handle the pain. All that was left was to block it out. Her mind entered another plane, and suddenly, she could reason again. Thoughts darted through her brain at incredible speed, yet despite the pace, everything was sharp and clear.

She couldn't kill her friend. She only needed to render her unconscious. Surely Faylie's magic didn't work while she was sleeping. If Nora's hands were free, she'd knock out Faylie with a massive ball of ice.

But ice shot from the mouth always originated in the throat. The only thing that would fit through Nora's throat and stop her friend was a spike. But did that spike have to be lethal? Nora could shoot it into Faylie's cheek. That would stop her, right?

No, it wouldn't. Even with an impaled cheek, Faylie would still be conscious, controlling her militia.

Truth, sharp as Faylie's dagger, embedded itself in Nora's mind.

Osmius is right. Faylie has to die.

Yet as certain as Nora was of this fact, she was just as sure of another: she could not bring herself to do such a thing.

It had taken perhaps three seconds to reach those conclusions. At the end of her brief foray into logic, Nora's mind reawakened to her torment. She roared, then started sobbing. Salty tears entered the gash on her cheek, ratcheting up the torture. "Stop!" she screamed. "Faylie! Stop!"

Something in those words broke through Faylie's coldness. Her hand halted, but the knife tip remained embedded in Nora's cheek. Panic filled Faylie's eyes. Tiny lines formed between her brows. Her mouth was still sneering, but her lips quivered. They barely moved as she spoke three words in a strained voice. "I . . . can't . . . stop."

Faylie's hand shook, the dagger's tip digging even deeper into Nora's muscle, creating another wave of agony. "Please," Nora groaned. "Faylie." She locked eyes with her friend, saw the struggle there. With everything in her, Faylie was striving to regain control of her will.

Then, in an instant, Faylie stopped shaking. Cold darkness swallowed the desperation in her gaze. The battle was over. She had lost. Her dagger resumed its sadistic task.

Pain exploded in Nora's face yet again. Nausea slashed at her gut.

You must do it, Osmius told Nora, grief saturating his words.

No! Nora shouted back. But this time, it was a protest, not a refusal. Perhaps Osmius's voice, filled with the stone's power, had finally convinced her. Perhaps she was desperate to save the people around her. Or perhaps she simply wanted—needed—to end her own torture. Whatever the reason, she felt the shift in herself. She hated it. And she accepted it.

She was nearly out of fuel, but she tightened her pathways to gain efficiency. She gathered her agony, as if it were itself a magical catalyst. Nora stopped breathing as the icy spike filled her airway. Was ice even strong enough to do what she wanted it to do?

Maybe normal ice wasn't. But this was magical ice, filled with the power of a stone that had slaughtered billions of people. This, Nora promised herself, would be the densest, strongest ice she'd ever formed. Strong enough to free the people around her. Stronger than hesitation. Stronger than betrayal.

The dagger's cruel tip reached Nora's ear.

A sick smile distorted Faylie's mouth. "Too much pain to scream?" Her face was still directly above Nora's, her eyes focused on her brutal task.

A scene from the past filled Nora's imagination. *Her and Faylie. On the lawn, next to the pond. Nora's mouth opened. Snow puffed out. Faylie smiled—a silly, beautiful smile. Flames streamed from her mouth. Fire and snow collided, sizzling. Obliterating each other. The two girls laughed and laughed, clutching their bellies.*

Wrapping her heart around the memory, Nora opened her mouth as wide as it would go. A spike of razor-sharp, magical ice shot up, slicing the tender tissues of her throat. She felt no pain. The weapon exited her gaping mouth and entered Faylie's eye, not stopping until its entire length was lodged in her brain.

The dagger dropped.

Faylie fell.

Around Nora, scores of eyes widened in awareness. Soldiers and trogs alike began to move. The man on her left released his steely grip on her arm and pulled her close.

"Ovrun—" she said, before her vision went black.

38

My father once cried as he told me about the young children he encountered in those first weeks after The Day. They would ask, over and over, when they could go home.

"I was practically a kid myself," my dad said. "How was I supposed to tell these children that everyone they'd ever known was gone, and they could never go home?"

-The First Generation: A Memoir *by Liri Abrios*

WAKING in the middle of a crowded street was . . . disconcerting.

Krey's awareness rushed in, and he cried out, taking in the chaotic masses around him. Trogs in black and soldiers in gray stood everywhere, but nobody seemed to be doing anything.

Acting on instinct, Krey rushed at the nearest militia member and tackled him, knocking over three additional people. Before he could get his arm around his enemy's neck, the young man shouted, "Stop! Help!"

Krey halted. Mind-controlled soldiers didn't panic. He looked around and realized the mouths of most of the militia members were agape, their eyes filled with confusion. *They're free.* Krey got off the man's back and helped him up, shouting in a hoarse voice, "The battle is over!"

He didn't know if anyone could hear him in the pandemonium, but the trogs seemed to be coming to the same conclusion. Somehow, they'd won.

The last thing he remembered was meeting the mind lyster. She'd said something, but he'd only half-listened, because he'd been trying to get Zeisha back in his sights.

Zeisha—she's free too! "Zeisha!" he screamed, bringing his hand up to his aching throat, where her vines had choked him. "Zeisha!"

He pushed through the crowd, frantically searching for glossy, black curls. He didn't see her, but as he ran, he saw the tall building in the distance and remembered there were still two bound militia members on the roof. They had to be panicked. But Krey didn't have the fuel to fly up there, and it would take too long for him to climb the stairs.

Cursing, he ran toward Osmius and Taima. Yellow blood seeped from multiple gashes in Taima's dark skin. When had that happened? Krey pushed the thought aside and told Osmius what he needed. Osmius nodded, and Krey climbed on the dragon's back. *Last dragon ride ever, mark my word.*

As they flew, Krey looked for Zeisha. However, Osmius flew too quickly for Krey to see much, and in seconds, they were on the roof. Two crying lysters awaited them, one of them gagged.

Krey untied the young woman's gag and began working on her ropes, all the while trying to explain what was going on. The woman hardly seemed to hear him over her cries. Finally, Krey pointed at the street. "See all the people in gray? They're in the same predicament as you. Once we bring you to them, we'll explain everything."

He moved on to the male magic eater and started untying his bonds. "The dragon is trustworthy," he said. "We'll all ride him down to the ground."

"There are no stairs?" the young man asked.

"There are, but it's dark, and this is a really tall building. Riding a dragon isn't that bad." Krey hated lying to these poor people, but he had to calm them down.

Several minutes later, they were all on the dragon's back, which the magic eaters took in stride. Did no one else realize how terrifying it was to ride on a massive, flying beast?

They made it safely down. Krey pointed the magic eaters toward their fellow former soldiers. Then he entered the crowd and again shouted, "Zeisha!"

"Krey?"

He spun around, and there she was, her eyes wide, tears rushing down her smooth cheeks. She was standing with another young woman in gray. Krey pulled Zeisha into his arms, then lifted her from the ground and spun her around. People skittered out of their path.

"Krey, what's happening?" Zeisha's voice in his ear was breathless. "Your neck—you're hurt!"

He put her down and realized he was crying as hard as she was. He had to get a grip on himself. His mind probably hadn't been stolen for long, yet he'd been utterly confused when he regained his faculties. What must it be like for Zeisha? She'd left Tirra over three months ago; had The Overseer controlled her since then? Based on Zeisha's wide, desperate eyes, he feared the answer was yes.

His heart cracked with grief. He took her face in his hands. "Are you okay?"

"There was a big knot on my head, and it hurt. A lot. But someone healed me. I'm okay, I'm just—I don't know what's going on."

He hadn't realized she'd gotten hurt. She'd probably been knocked out by a trog, then regained consciousness for the end of the fight. "I'll explain. You're safe now. I promise. Come sit."

Zeisha's eyes calmed, her panic seeping out along with her continued tears. "Krey." The word was soft, almost reverent. She followed it with a smile that made his heart ache even more. "Explain later. Kiss me now."

"Oh, by the sky, I love you." He brought his mouth to hers. For months, he'd dreamed of her lips, but he'd forgotten just how soft, warm, and impossibly wonderful they were.

Her hands snaked up his chest and shoulders. Her fingers tangled into his hair. He held her even closer, his lips moving across her cheek, to her ears and neck. She was salty with sweat, covered in dust, and absolutely perfect.

"Krey?" she whispered. "We're not alone."

"Hmm?" He'd never been one to display a lot of affection in public, but as his mouth explored her collarbone, he didn't care who was watching.

Zeisha laughed softly. "Seriously, I need to introduce you to someone."

"Right now?" he murmured against her neck.

"Yes, she's important. We kept each other alive out here."

From behind Krey, a female voice added, "When we weren't trying to kill each other."

That got Krey's attention. He lifted his head and shifted his gaze to the girl Zeisha had been standing with.

She looked about their age. Her straight, brown hair was in a messy braid, and she wore an embarrassed smile. "I'm Isla."

Krey stepped closer and shook her hand. "I'm Krey. Zeisha's boyfriend."

Her smile grew. "I guessed that. Good to meet you, Krey." She tilted her head to the side. "Where are we?"

Krey let out a long breath. "Let's all sit, and I'll explain."

"Thank you," Isla said. "And after that, I'll give you two some time alone. I promise."

Nora's eyes fluttered open, meeting the gaze of a rough-looking trog. He was kneeling over her, one hand on her cheek and the other on her neck.

"What the hell?" She swiped his hands away and pushed herself to a seated position. "Who are you?"

"Nora."

She swiveled her head and found Ovrun next to her.

"He's a healer," Ovrun said. "Do you remember the cut on your cheek? And the bruises on your neck?"

"Oh." Nora brought her hands up to her face and neck. The strangulation bruises were gone. She could feel a narrow cut under her right eye, and it was sore. Crusty, dried blood covered her cheek and neck. She looked down and found red all over her shirt too. "What happened?" she asked.

"I was hoping you'd tell me."

In a moment, it all came back. Faylie. The dagger. The ice spike. *I killed my friend.* Nora squeezed her eyes shut, and the broken skin on her cheek pulled painfully as her face screwed up with unshed tears. "I remember," she whispered.

"Almost done," the trog said in a soft voice that belied his heavy brows and thick neck. "I already heal your throat. Inside and out. May I finish your face?"

Unable to speak, she nodded.

He brought calloused fingers back up to her cheek, and a few seconds later, he removed them. "The scar stays," he said.

She reached up and touched the thin, hard band of skin. "Thank you," she managed to whisper.

He nodded and got up without another word. As if his exit had given her permission, Nora started sobbing. Ovrun pulled her into his arms. She grasped his dirty shirt and cried into his chest for what felt like forever. When her tears abated, she didn't pull away. She couldn't bear to meet Ovrun's gaze. He deserved to know what happened, but she couldn't form the words.

"When I came to," Ovrun said softly, "I saw a woman on the

ground in a pool of blood. I'm guessing that was The Overseer? And you stopped her?"

Nora's tears returned. "Yes."

"You're amazing."

The words were so quiet, she wasn't sure she'd heard them correctly. She pulled away from Ovrun's grasp and looked up. His awed expression confirmed that yes, her ears were working. *I have to ask.* "Did you see who it was?"

"No, she was facedown."

"Then you don't—you don't understand. The Overseer . . . oh, Ovrun. It was Faylie." She started sobbing again. "I killed Faylie."

He pulled her to him and held her even tighter. After a time, she calmed, tears replaced by exhaustion. "I'll never forgive myself," she murmured.

He took her shoulders and gently pried her off him, locking eyes with her. "Did you save everyone here?"

Nora nodded.

"If you could've saved us without killing her, would you have?"

She nodded again.

"Like I said, you're amazing."

"I don't believe you," she whispered.

"I'll keep telling you until you do."

Her face started to crumple again, but she held her breath until the urge to cry passed. Someday soon, she'd have to come to terms with what she'd done to Faylie. Doubtless she'd be dealing with it for years. But right now, she had to put it aside and figure out what came next.

She looked past Ovrun. Some trogs and militia members were sitting or lying down. She knew others, like her, had injuries. There were plenty of people chatting softly. It all looked very calm. Farther out, bodies lay at the edges of the street. Hopefully some of them were merely unconscious. "I wonder how many died."

Ovrun's shoulders fell. "I don't know yet."

"Were there any other leaders in the warehouse?"

"No. We think they got out the back door as soon as they realized things were going south. Probably when Taima showed up."

Nora allowed herself a small smirk. "Maybe they'll get caught by trogs."

Ovrun's hand came up to her cheek, and despite the dried blood there, he rested his warm palm on her skin. "When my mind came back, I saw all the blood on your face, and . . ." He shuddered. "I'm glad you're okay."

"I wouldn't say I'm okay, Ovrun." Nora sighed. "What do we do now?"

"What I want to do is drag you away from here and do whatever I can to make you forget any of this ever happened."

Now, that was the best idea she'd ever heard.

Unfortunately, Ovrun kept talking. "But nobody here knows what happened. You're the only one who can tell them. Then we've got to figure out how to get everyone to safety. The workers who escaped will probably go back to the city to get word to your father."

My father. Nora sat up straighter, her head clearer than it had been since she'd regained consciousness. "Ovrun, my father was here. A feather lyster brought him. They're on their way back to the city."

Ovrun cursed. "We have less time than we thought." He caressed her cheek. "When do you think you'll be ready to talk to everyone?"

She stood. "It doesn't matter if I'm ready. Go on, use that big voice of yours. Gather everyone in front of the bay where they kept Osmius."

Ovrun ran off, and Nora walked toward Osmius and Taima, who were huddled together away from the survivors. As she walked, two people, seated apart from everyone else, caught her eye. One was in gray, but the other wore a dirty, blue coat. She smiled, relieved to see that Krey was safe. *And that must be Zeisha.* Nora adjusted her course so she could meet the girl they'd all fought for.

She stopped when Zeisha leaned toward Krey and kissed him. It wasn't a quick kiss; neither of them looked like they had any intention of stopping. *Okay, not the best time for an introduction.* Nora knew she should keep moving, but she couldn't help watching. There was unmistakable passion between them, enough to bring warmth to Nora's cheeks.

This kiss, though—it was somehow special. Nora had experienced passion with Ovrun, and, to a lesser extent, with other boys. She stood, head cocked to one side, trying to figure out what was different about Krey and Zeisha's kiss.

They truly know each other. The truth hit her like a soft stone, nearly taking her breath away. There was a confidence in the way those two touched each other, a selflessness. Krey and Zeisha, she was certain, weren't just kissing because they wanted each other. They were kissing because they loved each other.

An ache filled Nora's chest, catching her off guard. Was she really jealous of an annoying, small-town boy and a girl who'd lost months of her life in captivity?

Yes. I am. The couple kissing in the dirt had something Nora hadn't witnessed in years. Not, she realized with another pang, since her mother died. Her parents had truly loved each other. She saw the same genuine devotion in Krey and Zeisha. The scene elicited a craving in Nora, one she'd never felt before.

She pulled her gaze away and resumed her walk toward the two dragons.

With Osmius and Taima on either side of her and Krey and Ovrun behind her, Princess Ulminora Abrios addressed the crowd.

She'd given plenty of speeches, usually before people who could only be called *adoring fans*. She remembered blowing cold snow over the laughing crowd in Tirra, the day she met Krey. The day that changed everything.

This speech felt nothing like that one. The trogs didn't care who she was. She wasn't *their* princess. Many of them greeted her with hostile glares. Yes, they had their territory back. However, ten trogs had died fighting a battle they could've stayed out of. Time would tell if they felt the sacrifice had been worth it.

The militia members, who'd lost two of their comrades, responded to Nora better than the trogs. When she introduced herself, most of the soldiers gaped at her. Some even looked impressed. Their expressions, however, quickly shifted again. Eyes narrowed and foreheads wrinkled as they waited to learn more about the months they'd lost.

Nora didn't mince words. "Those of you in gray shirts were forced into mental slavery by my father." She ignored the pain that accompanied that statement. "He used you to create a lyster militia."

Few of the soldiers reacted with surprise. Word had started spreading as soon as everyone had come back to their right minds.

"What happened here today?" someone in gray shouted.

Nora told them about the battle. She explained how she, Krey, and Ovrun had joined with the trogs, trying to disable militia members and get to The Overseer.

She gestured to the dragons on either side of her. Tears filled her eyes as she gazed at Taima. Yellow blood still seeped from the majestic beast's injuries. "We allied ourselves with two noble creatures." As she described the dragons' roles in the battle, she never mentioned their names. Osmius and Taima sent her a gentle, unison *thank you.*

A trog's loud voice rang out through the still street. "A woman touch my head. Then I wake, standing in the street. What happen in between?"

Nora's right hand fluttered up to her cheek, and when she felt the dried blood there, she gritted her teeth against a flood of remembered agony. She dropped her hand and, trying to keep her voice clear and calm, told everyone about the arrival of The Overseer and the king. The only detail she excluded was Faylie's name. She couldn't say it without weeping. When she finished describing how her spike of ice had killed The Overseer, the crowd was silent.

At last, a voice rang out. "How did the king and this Overseer control our minds?"

Nora briefly closed her eyes. Whatever she told them, it wouldn't be enough. They'd want answers to the same questions that were tormenting her.

She met the gaze of the young woman who'd asked the question. "We don't know how his magic works. But I vow to you that we will learn the truth and stop the king." Murmurs swelled in the crowd, and Nora sensed their dissatisfaction with her response. Well, she wasn't satisfied with it either. In time, she'd find answers.

A former militia member raised her hand. She looked terribly young. Then again, everyone in the militia was young. "Can we go home now?" she asked.

Nora squeezed her eyes shut, and the tragedy of the entire situation rushed at her like a runaway wagon. Her father had stolen so much from these people. They just wanted to return to their lives and families. How could she tell them that if they went home, the king would certainly recapture them?

Krey must've sensed her difficulty, because he stepped forward and spoke to the crowd in a hoarse voice. "Right now, the king is on his way back to Cellerin City. He doesn't know that we won, but he does know that we've joined with trogs and dragons to fight him. He will send people to secure this warehouse. When he sees that his militia has been freed, he'll look for all of you. All of *us*. I'm sorry, but we can't go home."

Nora looked up at him, seeing the grief in his tight jaw and wet eyes. She knew he missed his family as much as everyone else did.

As Krey's words sank in, the crowd grew unsettled. Shouts erupted: "Where are we going to go?" "What do you mean, we can't go home?" Trogs joined in the verbal fray, and one loud voice rose above the others: "You must leave our city!"

Nora raised her hands to quiet the crowd, but no one was watching her. The shouting grew so loud, she feared a fight would break out. Just as she turned to Ovrun to suggest he speak up, Osmius spoke to her. *We will calm them.*

Both dragons lifted their mouths toward the sky, and great jets of orange flame emerged. There were gasps and screams, and then everyone went silent.

"We will not fight each other again!" Nora said, not trying to keep the anger from her voice. "That would just make the king's job easier! Those of you who were in the militia, I want you to gather over there." She pointed. "Figure out which three of you were captive the longest, and send those people here to meet with us. Trogs, send up two or three people who can represent you. Healers and anyone waiting for healing, go over there." She pointed again. "We'll figure out what comes next, and we'll do it quickly, because we don't have time to do it any other way!"

Miracle of miracles, everyone started moving. Two healers—one trog, one soldier, gathered with about a dozen injured people. Taima walked that way too.

Where are you going? Nora asked the dragon.

They are using my blood to heal.

That brought a sad smile to Nora's mouth. *Thank you.* She turned to Krey and pointed at his throat, which was still covered in bruises. "You'd better get that healed before we start our talks."

Krey nodded and jogged toward the healers. Before long, the trog and militia leaders approached Nora. She greeted them politely, but she didn't dare hope they'd get through this next part without arguing.

"New-city folk do not belong with trogs."

It took quite a bit of effort for Krey not to roll his eyes at the gray-haired, male trog who'd said the same thing at least four times now. *He was the oldest person in the fight today,* Krey chided himself. *He's infuriating, but he deserves respect.*

"They don't have anywhere else to go," Krey said firmly. "If they leave the city, the king will capture and kill them. You may not care about that, but you should care about this: the king may also come after you because you fought with us. Every member of that militia trained for months to fight with magic. Don't you think it would help to have some people like that on your side?"

The female trog who'd originally met with Krey, Nora, and Ovrun spoke up. "When we agree to join your fight, you tell us we will be free from the king. Now you tell us the king will attack?"

"None of us were thinking that far ahead." Maybe he was being too honest, but Krey couldn't take it back now. "I bet you thought ahead, though. You considered the risks, and you decided it was worth it to defend your city."

The woman folded her arms, but she didn't argue the point.

Krey shifted his attention to the two women and one man who represented the militia. Each one of them looked to be around his age. They hadn't contributed much to this meeting. They were probably still in shock.

The female trog spoke again. "We will let them stay."

Krey's eyebrows shot up. "Really?"

"One condition," the woman said. Her mouth curved in a small smile. "Well . . . five conditions."

"Five?" Nora asked.

The woman pointed at Nora. "One." Her wrinkled finger shifted to Ovrun. "Two." She pointed at Krey, Osmius, and Taima. "Three. Four. Five."

"What do you want from us?" Nora asked.

"You will stay. You will fight with us."

Krey caught Nora's gaze, then Ovrun's, receiving tiny nods from each of them. It wasn't like they had anywhere else to go.

"I'll ask the dragons," Nora said. She looked between Osmius and Taima. Seconds passed, then a minute, then two. At last, she said, "The city is no place for dragons. They'll find a lair in the mountain range southeast of Deroga. It's close enough for me to communicate with them. When we need their help, they will come."

Krey nodded. "Do we have a deal?"

The female trog slapped her hand hard on the table. "Your hand on mine," she said to Krey. "The trog way."

He placed his hand on hers.

The woman turned to the former soldiers. "One of you."

A woman with sad eyes and short, black hair added her hand to the pile.

"Welcome to the Star Clan of Deroga," the female trog said.

39

During hungry times, my parents organized community music nights. We had no food, just instruments, singing, and dancing. The physical activity made us even hungrier, I suppose. But everything's bearable when you're dancing.

-The First Generation: A Memoir *by Liri Abrios*

"Trogs know how to party." Nora looked up at Ovrun and found him grinning and bopping up and down to the music. He looked ridiculous. She kind of loved it.

They were on the ground floor of a tall building, in what had once been a lobby. The trogs had turned it into a community space, with tables and benches along the edges. The center of the room was open and currently occupied by dancers. It was just past dusk, and countless candles lit up the space.

Three trogs stood along one edge of the dance floor, playing a fast-paced tune. Two of them strummed stringed instruments Nora had never seen before, and the other beat a set of four hand drums.

Nora hadn't known what to expect when the trogs had agreed to let thirty-five outsiders move in, but they'd caught her off guard when they'd suggested a celebration.

The white-haired, female trog, who'd finally introduced herself as Eira, had explained, "The coming time will be difficult. We must start strong."

"We don't expect a party," Ovrun had said. "You lost ten people today. We know you're mourning."

Eira had lifted her chin. "When trogs die, we dance. It honors them. They are with us still."

Nora couldn't argue with that. Eira had then explained that soon, they'd all get assignments: cleaning, cooking, hunting for shimshims, and more. Nora had stifled a groan when she'd realized shimshim meat would still make up a major part of her diet.

Plenty of trogs were dancing. About a dozen former militia members had joined in, while others sat on the sidelines, alone or in small groups. Some of them ate simple food the trogs had put out on community tables. Others stood, eyes glazed, struggling to adjust to their new reality. Nora waved at Zeisha's friend Isla, who was chatting with another former soldier.

Ovrun extended his hand. "Want to dance?"

Her mouth widened into a broad smile. "Sure."

Nora's usual dance moves didn't work for the trog music, so she moved however it felt right. Ovrun did the same. Despite the fact that they were in Deroga, dancing with trogs they'd feared would kill them a day earlier, the party felt fabulously normal. All day, Nora had fought off flashbacks of getting her face carved up and killing Faylie. The music helped banish such thoughts.

She scanned the crowd, looking for Krey and Zeisha. Eventually, she spotted them sitting alone at a table, faces close together as they talked. Again, that strange surge of envy slid into Nora's mind. She turned her attention back to Ovrun.

"They're disgustingly cute," he said, nodding toward the reunited couple.

Nora laughed. "That they are." She, Ovrun, Krey, and Zeisha had spent most of the day together. Nora had immediately liked Zeisha, who exuded sweetness. "I can see why he loves her. On the other hand . . ." She trailed off.

"Yeah, I don't know what she sees in him either," Ovrun said.

That had already become a running joke between the four of them. Once again, Nora laughed at it. But when her gaze found Ovrun, he wasn't laughing. He was watching her, his lips parted and his eyes dark with desire. Nora swore her heart was melting into her ribs, even as it beat furiously.

The musicians transitioned into a slow, sweet tune. Ovrun took both Nora's hands and twined his fingers in hers. Then he twirled her so her back was to his chest, his arms crossed over hers. They swayed together, and despite their slow movements, Nora's breaths came faster. Ovrun spun her to face him again.

She let go of him and reached up, resting her hands on his shoulders. He brought his hands to her waist. Her gaze roamed across his broad shoulders and his muscular arms.

"Hey, eyes up here," Ovrun murmured.

She looked up and found him watching her, smirking. "You've got great eyes," Nora said, "but the rest of you—it's very distracting."

Ovrun let out a low, growly laugh that rearranged Nora's insides.

"Ovrun," she ventured, "I'm sure you realize this by now, but . . . it doesn't matter what my dad thinks of you."

He closed his eyes briefly and released a short sigh. "I know. But you're still in line to be queen."

"I don't think I want to be."

"You might not be able to avoid it." He shook his head. "And that's not my world. I don't even want it to be."

Nora swallowed. "What *do* you want?"

He looked off to one side, then met her gaze again. "A simple life.

A wife and a few kids. Work that I enjoy. A house and maybe a little bit of land."

"I gotta say"—Nora pressed closer to Ovrun—"that future sounds pretty perfect."

His eyes narrowed. "Somehow I doubt you'll end up living a simple life."

"I might! Everything's up in the air now. Are we really basing our decisions on something that might never happen?"

"I don't know," he said, his voice low. "What decisions are you talking about?"

She let her gaze meander down to his lips, then back to his eyes, her mouth quirking in a hopeful smile. "You promised to give me something when we made it out of the battle alive."

He licked his lips, and she could see him trying not to smile. "It's probably a bad idea."

"Maybe," she whispered.

He pulled her off the dance floor, sat on the edge of a table, and pulled her close. Then he stole her breath with a kiss that burned away every worry about her future. If a crowd hadn't surrounded them, she didn't think even Ovrun, with all his logic and honor, would've stopped.

But they were surrounded, and Ovrun did stop, pulling his lips off hers and pressing his forehead against hers. "Like I said," he murmured between rapid breaths, "probably a bad idea."

"Best bad idea I've ever had."

It must've been past midnight when Eira approached the table where Nora, Ovrun, Krey, Zeisha, and Isla were all sitting. For at least an hour, they'd been talking quietly and snacking on some sort of delicious, dried vegetable. Eira sat, and the table quieted.

"Ten people in uniforms go to the warehouse," she said without preamble.

Krey sat up straight, as did his companions. "They go there—you mean they're on their way? Or are they there right now?"

"They go. They walk through the building. Then they leave. On orsas."

"What should we do?" Krey asked.

"We watch. As always. If anyone threatens us, we kill them." Her tone was bland, like she was talking about tomorrow's breakfast menu.

"Do you have any feather eaters?" Krey asked.

"Not in Star Clan."

Krey nodded; it was an uncommon talent. "Then I'm the only one," he said. During the battle, a trog ash eater had, in a moment of panic, killed the militia's feather eater. Krey leaned across the table toward Eira. "Make me one of your scouts. Put me on a tall roof, the best vantage point in the city. If the king sends more people, I'll fly back to tell you. All I need is feathers."

She nodded once. "I will provide feathers. You must sleep now. Tomorrow, you watch."

Krey smiled and slapped his hand on the table. "It's a deal."

She covered his hand with hers.

Next to Eira, Nora spoke. "My father will be furious when he finds out his militia is gone. Are you willing to tell the other clans in the city to be on alert?"

Eira's rheumy gaze turned to Nora. "I already send messengers. Before I come here."

"I thought the clans didn't get along!" Krey blurted.

"We do not." Eira stood. "But we are not savages." She walked away.

EPILOGUE

IT HAD TAKEN every bit of Krey's self control not to ask Zeisha to come with him to this cold rooftop. He'd been up here most of the previous day, and he'd quickly realized just how boring it was to watch a horizon for hours on end. Chatting with Zeisha would've made today's shift positively delightful. They could've distracted themselves in other ways too. That thought made him grin.

He pulled his blanket tighter around his shoulders. He hadn't asked Zeisha to come, because she would've said yes—and it wasn't safe for her to be here.

Krey and the others were now members of the Star Clan. This building was in the territory of the Tree Clan. Representatives from all six clans had met the previous morning, agreeing to be on alert for intruders and to work together if invaded. Eira had gotten permission for Krey to keep watch atop this building. She'd even procured a note to that effect. The Tree Clan, however, was apparently notorious for its overly enthusiastic archers. A note in Krey's pocket wouldn't protect him from an arrow.

He'd been as careful as he could, flying very high most of the way, then dropping quickly onto the roof. He didn't think anyone would find him—unless someone had seen him land and was, even now, walking up the building's stairs. Or, he supposed, a flyer might spot him. Eira didn't know if the Tree Clan had any feather eaters.

Considering the unknowns, Krey was glad he hadn't brought Zeisha. After being separated from her for so long, however, he'd hated leaving her.

He removed a water bottle from his pack and took a sip. As he screwed the lid back on, he saw movement in the distance. He squinted. His perch, a very tall building near the edge of trog territory, gave him a good view of the expansive suburbs and the land beyond.

There it was, the thing that had caught his eye. It was like a dark shadow in the distance. Krey looked into the orange sky. The morning sun was behind him, and there were no clouds to cast shadows. He brought his attention back to the ground, hoping he was imagining things.

Minutes went by, and the shadow continued to approach. Sick dread twisted Krey's stomach as suspicion morphed into certainty.

He threw his bottle and blanket into his pack and slung the bag onto his back, wishing he'd eaten more feathers while he was watching. He'd have to fuel on the go, as he'd done so often lately. And he'd have to fly faster than ever. The trogs needed to know that the approaching shadow wasn't a shadow at all. It was a horde of men and women, hundreds of them. Most marched. Some rode orsas.

The Cellerinian Army was invading Deroga.

A NOTE FROM BETH

Thank you for reading *The Frost Eater*! Reviews make a *huge* difference to authors and readers. Will you write a short review on Amazon? I can't tell you how much I'd appreciate it. (While you're there, click on my author page and Follow me!)

Want to know what happens next ? Keep reading for a sneak peek of Book 2, *The Vine Eater*. Visit Amazon to order it today!

Dive into my first series, the Sun-Blessed Trilogy, by downloading the prequel novella, *Birth of Magic,* absolutely free! Snag it at bit.ly/BirthOfMagic.

THE VINE EATER: BOOK 2 OF THE MAGIC EATERS TRILOGY

SNEAK PEEK

Below is an early version of Chapter 1 of The Vine Eater. *While the content may change by the time the book is published, I hope you enjoy this little taste of what's in store for Nora, Krey, Ovrun, and Zeisha!*

-Carol Beth Anderson

Zeisha Dennivan held out her hand. A vine burst from her palm, shooting straight into the air. Just when she thought it would halt, the growth accelerated, like the plant wanted to pierce the orange sky above. At last, it stopped growing and dropped to the dirt street, collapsing into a tangled mess of strong, green coils.

The warmth of creative magic continued to saturate Zeisha's hand. She savored the sensation, examining the vine where it merged with her palm. Her skin rose up, like an inverted funnel, forming the plant's cylindrical base. Over the course of a couple of simmets, the vine transitioned from smooth, tan skin into tough, flexible, green plant matter.

Zeisha let go of her magic. The plant's base separated from her palm and slid to the ground. Her skin retained a bulge for a moment before flattening. Zeisha lifted the coiled vine into her lap, her eyes widening at its weight. She shook her head. *So much magic.*

A female voice behind Zeisha asked, "How much fuel did you have to eat to create that vine?"

Zeisha turned to see a tall figure approaching. The young woman's sleek, dark hair, cut in an angled bob, shone in the sun. Like Zeisha, Princess Ulminora Abrios—who insisted on being called *Nora*—was seventeen. Yet somehow, she managed to look like an elegant, sophisticated adult, even on this dusty street. "I ate a few pieces of bark," Zeisha said with a smile.

Nora walked around to face Zeisha. Her navy-blue pants were expertly tailored and looked terribly expensive, but she didn't seem to care about that as she sat cross-legged in the dirt street. She reached out and touched the vine. "Incredible. Could you do things like this before . . . well . . . you know, before?"

Yes, Zeisha knew what Nora meant by *before.* Before a man claiming to be recruiting magical apprentices had lured her away from her hometown, then taken her on a trip to the capital. Before she and several other magic eaters had ridden in a dark, enclosed wagon, which had at last released them inside a large building in an unknown location. Before a tall, young woman had touched Zeisha, mentally enslaving her and forcing her into a magical militia.

Zeisha shoved a black curl behind her ear. Like it had a mind of its own, the hair popped out and settled again in front of her left eye. "Back home, I could make vines," Zeisha said, "but they were very short."

Nora reached out and lifted one of the vine's coils. "This is impressive."

"Apparently I'm a fantastic learner when my mind isn't my own," Zeisha murmured. Realizing how ungrateful she sounded, she smiled at the princess. "Thank you, Nora. For everything."

Two days before, Nora had killed The Overseer, the woman

who'd controlled the minds of every militia member. Zeisha and the others had at last woken from their mental captivity. "Krey was the one behind the rescue plan," Nora said. "From the beginning, he was convinced you'd been kidnapped. He would've done anything to save you. You've got a good boyfriend, Zeisha."

"I do." Zeisha looked down and ran her fingers along the vine in her lap. Krey was stuck on a tall roof clommets away, keeping an eye out for danger. Everyone expected the king, who'd been the militia's general, to retaliate for the loss of his soldiers. Krey's ability to fly made him the perfect lookout. Zeisha was proud of him—but she also wished he were here with her, right now. She bit her lip, then returned her attention to Nora. "Did you see Krey's neck after the battle?"

"Yes."

"I did that to him." Zeisha swallowed, trying not to cry as she remembered the bruises and red welts on Krey's neck. Marks from the vine that had strangled him.

"You can't be sure it was you," Nora said. "There were other plant lysters in the militia. One of them might've attacked him. And whoever did it, the healer took care of him. He's good as new."

"It was me." Zeisha lifted her gaze to meet Nora's. "He would've told me if it were someone else. Instead, he avoided my questions."

Nora placed her cool hand on top of Zeisha's. "Even if that's the case, it wasn't really you. It was The Overseer." She swallowed. "And my father. They're the ones that controlled you and the others."

Zeisha nodded, but the words didn't comfort her. Again, she dropped her eyes to the strong vine in her lap. A terrible question came to her. *Did I kill anyone during the battle?*

"Zeisha?" Nora's voice was quiet, gentle. "Are you okay?"

Zeisha almost asked the question that was swirling in her mind, but she couldn't convince her mouth to form the words. Instead, she forced a smile. "I'm fine. Did, uh, did you need something?"

Nora returned the smile. "Eira said if we're all staying here, we have to earn our keep. We had one day to rest. Now it's time to go to a meeting and get our assignments."

Zeisha stood, lifting the heavy, green coils. She imagined herself shooting a similar vine at Krey. Wrapping it around his neck. Tightening it until he couldn't breathe.

Shaking her head to rid herself of the thought, she walked to the side of the street and tossed the vine against a deserted building. She jogged to Nora. "Thanks for finding me. Let's get to work."

As they walked, Nora examined her surroundings. The street was full of empty buildings. Old Skytrain tracks, some of them crumbling, crisscrossed the sky. She turned her attention to Zeisha, who was looking at the city, her eyes wide. Zeisha was beautiful, with her short, hourglass figure and that amazing mass of glossy, black curls. She was also one of the sweetest people Nora had ever met.

"What do you think of Deroga?" Nora asked.

Zeisha's eyes met Nora's. "I don't know what to think. I grew up hearing about preday cities, but I never dreamed I'd see one in person, much less live in one."

Nora laughed. "I know what you mean."

All of the buildings on this street were ancient and abandoned. Deroga had once been a busy metropolis. Then came the apocalypse, an event known as *The Day*. Radiation from a mysterious stone killed nearly everyone on the planet of Anyari. The half-million remaining humans gathered into small groups around the globe, rebuilding civilization from the ground up. Few people had stayed in cities like Deroga, which were full of useless technology and rotting bodies.

Now, two centuries after The Day, six trog clans inhabited Deroga. Trogs were eccentric, to say the least. They lived in Deroga's preday buildings, shunning mainstream, postday communities. Months ago, the Star Clan had had made a deal with the king, allowing the militia to use one of their buildings.

By the time Nora, Krey, and their friend Ovrun had arrived in Deroga to rescue Zeisha, the Star Clan had grown resentful of the militia's presence. The trogs had agreed to join the fight to free the militia, and the city, from the king's influence.

Now the king would be looking for his formerly mind-controlled soldiers—and for Nora and her friends. Nora's stomach cramped as she thought about him hunting her. It was bad enough for a country's king to steal the minds of his people. It was infinitely worse when that king was your father.

"I can't believe Eira is letting us stay here," Zeisha said.

Nora pulled her thoughts away from her father. "Neither can I." Eira was the unofficial leader of the Star Clan. Nora had to admit she was a little afraid of the elderly woman. "She knows her people are in danger now that they've made a stand against the king. The trogs need you and the other militia members to fight on their side. You're all so strong."

Normally, Zeisha had a ready smile. Now, her full lips pressed together in a tight line. "What is it?" Nora asked.

Voice quavering, Zeisha said, "I didn't want to hurt anyone. I never wanted to fight at all."

Nora put an arm around the shorter girl's shoulders. "At least now you'll have control over your gifts. You don't have to do anything you don't want to do."

"I hope that's true," Zeisha said softly.

Nora gave Zeisha's shoulders a squeeze as they turned the corner onto the busiest street in Star Clan territory. They walked to the high-rise building where, two nights before, the trogs had thrown a party.

Ovrun was waiting outside for them. Nora couldn't hold back a grin. "Where were you at breakfast?" she asked.

"They asked me to hunt for shimshims. There are only a few hundred people in the Star Clan, and they ration food carefully. With three dozen extra residents, we'll need more protein." He turned to Zeisha. "I think they're going to ask you and the other vine eaters to help with their rooftop farms."

Zeisha's customary smile returned. "I'd love to do that!"

"They're almost ready to start." Ovrun gestured for them to enter.

Nora walked in, purposefully brushing her shoulder against Ovrun's broad chest as she passed. All three of them walked through the building's former lobby, which the trogs now used as a community space.

During the party, the whole place had appeared magical, thanks to countless candles. Now, with daylight entering through glassless windows, the room looked like entirely different—especially the walls. At night, they'd been swathed in shadows. Today, Nora's jaw dropped as she took in the murals painted on them.

The style was unlike any art Nora had seen before. The bold strokes, geometric shapes, and bright colors certainly wouldn't fit in the elegant palace she'd grown up in. But the art was stunning.

The shapes themselves were abstract, but they came together into pictures that grabbed Nora's attention and wouldn't let go. Three of the scenes were of a bustling city, full of technology. *Preday Deroga.*

However, Nora was most drawn to the wall that depicted a woman, wearing a multicolored gown, kneeling over a dead child. The child's skin was stark white. Red circles, clearly representing blood, streamed out of its eyes, nose, and mouth. The woman's mouth was a gaping, black crescent. Nora could almost hear her wailing cry. Other dead bodies lay in the background. Green grass and trees and a bright-orange sky gave the macabre scene an ironic beauty. It was the most incredible depiction of The Day that Nora had ever seen.

"I guess we better sit," Ovrun said.

Nora pulled her eyes away from the murals and tried to anchor herself in the present. She walked toward the center of the room, where most of the militia and quite a few trogs were seated on benches at long tables. She, Ovrun, and Zeisha joined them.

Eira began the meeting. "We meet now with the new-city folk

who are staying with us. You will tell us what you can do. We will give you work."

They started at the front of the room. As each militia member disclosed their skills, the trogs assigned them jobs. When it was Nora's turn to stand, she was at a loss. Her ice lysting wasn't much use here, since she didn't have the fuel she needed to use her magical faculty. The trogs didn't have any spare ice, and there wasn't any snow on the ground. Her cheeks grew warm. "I'm afraid my practical skills are . . . limited.

Next to her, Ovrun stood. "She's been learning archery. She could come with me."

"We need no unskilled hunters," a rough-voiced man said.

Nora wasn't about to let the idea go that quickly. "I'll get better the more I try. I also know how to clean shimshims. I'm sure I could learn to clean other animals too."

The man looked at her thoughtfully, then nodded. "Ovrun will teach you to shoot. You will clean the game."

Nora repressed a grin and sat down. She hated skinning and cleaning dead shimshims, but she'd do it all day if it meant roaming the streets with Ovrun instead of holing up inside some damp, old building. She caught Ovrun's eye, and he winked at her.

"Eira!" a voice shouted from behind the seated crowd.

That sounded like Krey, Nora thought as she turned. Sure enough, Krey was flying through the room, above the heads of the crowd. He stopped when he reached Eira.

The elderly woman listened carefully as Krey spoke in her ear. Then she nodded once and spoke, her voice ringing through the open space. "The army is coming to Deroga! Star Clan, we go underground!"

Order *The Vine Eater* on Amazon today!

ACKNOWLEDGMENTS

When I'm writing a book, I work with a small, brave group of alpha readers. They read the book in chunks, in all its early-draft messiness. Then they tell me how I can make it better. Heartfelt thanks to these alpha readers: Eli Anderson, Becky Brickman, Kim Decker, Brooke Hunger, Stephanie Lynn, Kristin Newton, Becki Norris, and DeDe Pollnow. You are all jewels, as delightful to me as bollagrape juice!

I also have an absolutely fantastic beta reader team. They read a revised, but still not final, version of the novel. Their feedback makes the final version deeper and more polished. I can't thank these people enough: Author Danielle Ancona; Rebecca Ann; Becky Brickman; Denise Campbell; Kim Decker; Brenda Elliott; Caroline Hannam; Lisa Henson, Capital Editing Services; C.M. Irving; R. Mark Jones; Katie Lee; Stephanie Lynn; Tracy Magouirk; Madysun Meschino; Becki Norris; robin; Sarah Dooley Rothman; Marjorie S.; Michelle Sundholm; and Nikki Tuggy. If I could invite you all to eat wonderful food and dance to bad music at an Anyari Day celebration, I would!

There are all sorts of unique names in fantasy novels, and I've asked newsletter readers and social media followers to contribute their name ideas for my books. Many of the character and location names in *The Frost Eater* came from their suggestions! Here are the contributors, with the names they suggested in parentheses: Abigail Swire (Cage), Ana Anderson (Zeisha, Kamina, Lerenor, & Cerinus), Beth Harris (Cruine), Cheryl (Onna), Jamie Brown (Isle, changed spelling to Isla), Julie Simmons (Fayla, changed to Faylie), Kristina Adams (Zef, Eira, and Taima), Marie-Eve Mailhot (Evie), Melissa (Wallace, changed spelling to Wallis), Patrice Einsel (Jushua, changed to Jushuen), Peter W. Bailey (Thar), Ruth Barnett (Ruli), and Shelia Kieser (Kadish). The name Sharai comes from Ezra, a book of the Bible. And if you can figure out where the name Osmius comes from, kudos to you!

Andrew Hall is a talented photographer and designer, and a photo in his post-apocalyptic series inspired the scene with the "Why?" graffiti on an old chapel. Follow Andrew on Twitter at @andhphoto.

My sister, Becki Norris, gave me a seed of an idea that turned into Faylie's subplot. Thank you, Becki!

Thank you, Victoria Hearne, for your last-minute hunt for errors!

Mariah Sinclair (mariahsinclair.com and thecovervault.com), people *love* this cover. Thank you!

Thank you to BMR Williams creating the map of the Kingdom of Cellerin!

Twitter is the primary way I stay connected to other writers. Thank you to the incredible #WritingCommunity, especially my friends in the Hugs4Pups/Inappropriate Acres group and my #Syn7 crew! You've given me countless laughs and so much encouragement.

Thank you to God, who is with me every moment.

And readers, thank you for picking up this book! I love writing, and you make it all worthwhile.

-Carol Beth Anderson
Leander, Texas
2020

ABOUT THE AUTHOR

Carol Beth Anderson is a native of Arizona and now lives in Leander, TX, outside Austin. She has a husband, two kids, a miniature schnauzer, and more fish than anyone knows what to do with. Besides writing, she loves baking sourdough bread, knitting, and eating cookies-and-cream ice cream.

facebook.com/carolbethanderson

twitter.com/CBethAnderson

instagram.com/CBethAnderson

bookbub.com/profile/carol-beth-anderson

CPSIA information can be obtained
at www.ICGtesting.com
Printed in the USA
FSHW020755150120
66089FS

9 781949 384055